Spies and Deserters

A Novel of the American Revolution

To David
Thanks for
all your support
and your
friendship
Marty

Martin R. Ganzglass

PCW
A Peace Corps Writers Book

ALSO BY MARTIN R. GANZGLASS

Fiction

The Orange Tree

Somalia: Short Fiction

In the American Revolutionary War Series

Cannons for the Cause

Tories and Patriots

Blood Upon The Snow

Non-Fiction

The Penal Code of the Somali Democratic Republic (Cases, Commentary and Examples)

The Restoration of the Somali Justice System, Learning From Somalia, The Lessons of Armed Humanitarian Intervention, Clarke & Herbst, Editors

The Forty-Eight Hour Rule, One Hand Does Not Catch a Buffalo, A. Barlow, Editor

Cover: *The Taking of Major Andre by the Incorruptible Paulding, Williams and Vanvert*
Published by T.W. Freeman, 1812
Image Courtesy of The Anne S.K. Brown Military Collection, Brown University

In Memory of My Grandparents and Parents
Immigrants All

Spies and Deserters
A Peace Corps Writers Book.
An Imprint of Peace Corps Worldwide

Printed in the United States of America
by Peace Corps Writers of Oakland, California.

For more information, contact www.peacecorpsworldwide.com
Peace Corps Writers and the Peace Corps Writers colophon are trademarks of PeaceCorpsWorldwide.org

This novel is a work of fiction. The historical figures and actual events described are used fictitiously. All other names, characters, places and incidents are products of the author's imagination. Any resemblance to living persons is purely coincidental.

ISBN 978-1-935925-87-3
Library of Congress Control Number
2017938254

First Peace Corps Writers Edition, April 2017.

"We saw a number of the graves of those who fell in that battle. Some of the bodies had been so slightly buried that the dogs or hogs, or both, had dug them out of the ground. Here were Hessian skulls as thick as a bombshell. Poor fellows! But they should have kept at home . . . But, the reader will say, they were forced to come and be killed here, forced by their rulers who have absolute power of life and death over their subjects. Well then, reader, bless a kind Providence that has made such a distinction between your condition and theirs. And be careful, too, that you do not allow yourself ever to be brought to such an abject, servile and debased condition."

Private Joseph Martin, White Plains, NY 1780

Part One
The Winter of Despair and Merriment

Chapter 1 - Starving Together at Valley Forge

Captain Chatsworth led the detachment of dragoons down the narrow road, their horses' hooves clattering on the frozen ground. Patches of ice glinted in the moonlight. Twenty paces ahead, at a slight bend in the way, their local Tory guide stopped and raised his hand, listening and looking off to his left into the dark gloom of the woods. The twenty-eight troopers waited, their horses snuffling and emitting puffs of warm breath.

It could be an ambush, Chatsworth thought. Perhaps the militia had been forewarned. Or their guide, who knew the back roads and was supposedly the Colonel's neighbor, was playing a double game and betraying the 16th Dragoons instead. His Quaker-like outer coat with no pockets had initially aroused Chatsworth's suspicion. He unstrapped his fuzee, the short-barreled musket the troopers carried, and held it loosely across his saddle. Nothing for it but to wait, he thought.

Suddenly, there was a crashing noise in the dense bushes. The guide let out a yelp and fled, his plow horse clumsily clearing a low stonewall as he disappeared into the darkness. "I hope he breaks his neck," Chatsworth muttered. He signaled with his hand for his men to remain where they were, then waved four of them forward. The scouting party vanished around the bend in the road followed by silence as the steady clop of their horses' hooves was swallowed up by the enveloping blackness. Clouds passed across the three quarter moon. Chatsworth sat motionless in the saddle, sweating under his brass helmet despite the cold and felt a chill on the back of his neck. They were almost thirty miles west of Philadelphia seeking to kidnap the Colonel of the Chester County Militia from his home near Downingtown.

After several minutes the scouts reappeared.

"We saw some stray cattle. Nothing more," the Sergeant said, shrugging as if he had suspected all along there were no Rebel militia hiding in the forest.

Chatsworth led the troopers forward until he could perceive a widening in the road where it was joined by another. According to their guide, the Colonel's house was the closest of the two after the Downingtown crossroads. He could make out a few buildings. If the terrified Tory had not run off, Chatsworth would have asked if there was a way to avoid going through town and approaching the Colonel's house from behind. He weighed the risk of arousing the town by riding on against leaving the horses tethered and proceeding stealthily on foot. Better to remain mounted, he concluded. They could fight their way out on horseback if necessary.

At his signal, they formed into lines of three across and galloped through the crossroads, past several low wooden buildings and the tavern that served as the center of town, and surrounded a large two story stone house just off the road. A horse from the barn whinnied in alarm, but Chatsworth had already leaped down and was pounding on the door with the butt of his fuzee.

"Open up in the name of the Crown. Resist and you will be shot," he shouted. A light appeared in an upper window, the shutters were thrown open and a grey haired woman in her nightcap peered out.

"Who are you to disturb our sleep?" she screeched in outrage at the black shadows of the riders below.

"We are the Queen's 16th Dragoons and have come to arrest Colonel Hannum," Chatsworth replied. "Open this door immediately."

The woman held the lantern out the window, the light reflecting on the troopers' helmets with their red dyed horse hair crests. "He is not here," she responded, her voice betraying fear as she quickly withdrew leaving the shutters ajar. Chatsworth stood back and motioned for the troopers to break the door down. As it splintered, there was a scream of surprise from outside.

"We have bagged him, Captain," came a triumphant cry from the rear of the house. The Rebel Colonel, shivering and hatless and looking undignified in his nightshirt and boots, was brought around to the porch by two troopers firmly holding his arms.

"He attempted to escape through a back window."

Chatsworth looked at the man, his hair unkempt, his thin naked legs sticking out the bottom of his white night shirt like a plucked chicken.

"Take him inside, let him get dressed but watch him closely," he ordered. "Seize all of the horses in the barn and a wagon if there is one. The rest of you, anything you can easily carry is fair to take from this Rebel scum." Chatsworth wiped his muddy boots on the rug in the center of the parlor, while his troopers ransacked the house with Mrs. Hannum following and haranguing them as godless heathens. Her venom increased as her husband's hands were tied behind his back, despite his promise as a gentleman not to try and escape.

"You mean not to try again," Chatsworth said with a dismissive wave of his hand. "Your word is of no worth to me." The Colonel was led outside and helped onto one of his own horses with a trooper pushing him hard against the pommel and sitting comfortably in the saddle behind him.

"Captain," one of the troopers called. "Behind the barn. Look at this."

Chatsworth followed him. The light from his lantern shone on a shrouded, bare footed corpse, stiff and frozen, laid out on a rough plank. The Captain bent down and pulled the rigid cloth away from the body's face. In the candlelight, Chatsworth saw evidence of a slashing wound on the side of the neck. The eye nearest to the gash was closed as if the man knew it was fatal and had no need to see it. His other eye was open, as was his mouth that formed a grimace, revealing several missing teeth. The remaining ones were stained black by gunpowder. Probably one of the Colonel's militia, he thought, dead for some time, and awaiting a proper burial when the ground was no longer frozen hard as stone.

"Load him in the wagon. He may be useful to us," Chatsworth ordered.

They left the Colonel's home to the shrieks of his wife that they were no better than savages. Whether it was because one of his men had taken her gold watch or the corpse in the wagon, Chatsworth had no idea and did not care. [1] None of the homes showed any lights. Good, he thought. They had time to leave a calling card.

Their local guide had mentioned the house on the far side of the tavern was occupied by a Rebel sympathizer, a loud mouth he said, who bullied his Tory neighbors. They deposited the corpse of the Rebel militiaman, standing propped up against the bully's front door, facing in. When the sympathizer opened it, he would be greeted by a one-eyed dead man, who would fall into his arms - a warning to be careful which side he chose.

Chatsworth sent two scouts ahead of the column. This county swarmed with Pennsylvania Militia and patrols of Continental Dragoons who sallied forth from their army's base at Valley Forge. He would breathe easier when they reached the burned out homes surrounding Philadelphia. On orders from General Howe, the British dragoons had torched several mansions, used as observation posts by the Rebels or staging areas for attacks on British sentries manning the Philadelphia redoubts.

John Stoner, who had ridden with the dragoons and now was Superintendent Galloway's aide, had told Chatsworth in confidence of the resentment at what some Philadelphians called the shocking massive conflagration. Chatsworth had dismissed the good citizens' disapproval. Shock was what these people needed to keep them in line. [2] His dragoons could live with the bitter looks and the whispered words as long as people remained docile and obedient.

Obsequious "Ramrod John," Chatsworth thought. The only man in the entire British Army to have killed a Rebel with his fuzee's ramrod. Speared him like a wild Indian, having forgotten to reset it before firing. The man was a contemptible coward and obnoxious as a fawning hanger-on. Always reminding Chatsworth that he had saved his life as if it was a debt to be collected. It was difficult to tolerate the man. Trying so hard to be the gentleman he was not. Not surprising,

Chatsworth thought. After all, he was only a farmer's son.

Still, he recognized John could be useful to the dragoons in his position as aide to Superintendent Galloway. His network of spies and sympathizers knew where the Rebel leaders were hiding. There was talk of even venturing forth into New Jersey to capture them. Chatsworth wanted those long distance forays for the 16th. They might bag a few members of Congress. Or a Rebel General like Charles Lee, who had been captured the previous year at White's Tavern in a daring action led by Tarleton. [3] There was glory to be gained in such raids.

Adam Cooper let the slack rope slip from his hands and stepped back from the A frame hoist as the twelve-pounder settled into the wagon. He turned away from the strong wind, his tri-corn held snugly on his head by a linen strip knotted under his chin over a neck stock Will Stoner had given him. He had two, Will said, both given him by Elisabeth. A worn nut-brown scarf covered the neck stock and wound around Adam's collar to keep the blowing snow from going down the back of his dark blue short jacket. The stout canvas breeches were better than wool, but his toes were frozen in his thin black shoes. He wiggled them, feeling the rags inside his stockings and hoped the blisters caused by frostbite would not break.

A few of the men in the work party were barefoot, constantly shifting from one cracked bloody foot to the other, leaving dark crimson spots in the snow. Others, wore a patchwork of threadbare coats, woolen blankets and jackets, their calves covered by thin stockings with more holes than fabric, arms wrapped around their shoulders for warmth. Unwashed, infested with lice, constantly scratching and ill-kempt with scraggly hair and unshaven faces, Adam thought this work crew more resembled the destitute denizens of the wharves of Boston than soldiers.

Now it was the turn of the carpenters to repair the splintered oak supports of the gun carriage and its axle. Adam looked up at the grey sky and the light snow obscuring Mount Joy. Most inappropriately named, he thought, almost snorting to himself. He stared off to the left at the more aptly named Mount Misery. Nothing more than a steep hill, barely visible through the falling snow, the smoke rising on the plateau below from the rows of the cramped fetid oak log huts housing the army.

Will had been right. Adam, Captain Holmes and Titus had arrived just in time to starve together at Valley Forge. Fire cakes and water was all they had eaten for the past four days. Barely enough to keep body and soul alive, Adam thought gloomily. An inauspicious beginning to the first week of the new year.

The three of them were assigned to Colonel Sargent's company of the Massachusetts Artillery Regiment. Captain Holmes moved in with two other officers. The huts of the rest of the Company were filled with their complement of twelve men and there was no room to spare inside. When Adam and Titus had found a hut among the Continentals with several empty bunks, the men unanimously objected to sharing quarters with Negroes. On their first night at Valley Forge, the two black Marblehead Mariners slept in a tent. Adam was incensed and vowed not to spend one more day under canvas. Captain Holmes intervened and they were placed in a cabin with only five other men, all from a New Jersey regiment. Of the rest of that hut's twelve man complement, two had died a week ago in their sleep, three others with camp fever and the chills of ague were in a barn that served as their Regiment's wretched hospital, and the remaining two were so covered with sores from "the itch" that they were confined to the scabies isolation huts. [4]

The first day in the hut, Adam and Titus scoured the bed frames with boiling water and took the dirty straw bedding outside and covered them with snow to kill any remaining lice and fleas. Their attention to cleanliness won the grudging approval of the five white Privates although Adam sensed their unease at sharing quarters and cooking pots with Negroes.

Not that there was anything to cook. There were daily rumors of large supplies coming from New England, the soldiers imagining the provisions the wagons were carrying - beef, good flour for baking bread, whiskey, soap to scrub and get rid of the infernal lice, vinegar to prevent dysentery, blankets, breeches, shirts and warm coats, and most importantly for those who were now barefoot, calfskins to make boots and shoes. Yet nothing arrived and their only meal of the day was the fire cakes and water from the valley creek, and a mug of bark coffee.

At night, the huts were freezing. Despite the fireplace and clay caulking of the walls, the roof made of branches and sod leaked prodigious amounts of cold air. It rained one night and by morning the water on the dirt floor was ankle deep. One advantage to there being only seven men in the hut was they could all sleep at one end near the fireplace and cluster near the hearth to keep warm during the day.

Because so many horses had died of starvation and disease, the men yoked themselves to sleds and carts and hauled the firewood from the surrounding forest to the encampment. Adam thought his feet would freeze solid to the ground. The regimental doctor had issued instructions for the men not to walk on frostbitten toes, to heat them gradually with warm water, and remove blisters containing clear or milky fluid and coat the skin with lard. It was good advice but impractical because there was no lard and he had to trudge out in the cold to get firewood to keep the rest of his body warm and heat the water.

Adam found Valley Forge a far cry from the easy acceptance and camaraderie of the Marblehead Mariners' barracks. He remembered when Will and Big Red first joined them at Cambridge in the spring of 1776. Big Red, now standing patiently in his traces, was not the same horse he had first seen in Massachusetts or in the long retreat through New Jersey. Or even at Trenton, dragging a cannon through the storm to attack the Hessians. His shaggy coat barely concealed his ribs. The horse's large hip bones protruded from his flanks like door knobs. Yellow mucus oozed from his nostrils as his head drooped toward the ground.

Adam walked over to where Will stood, gently rubbing his horse's lower jaw.

"He is not right. His stomach feels tight."

"So does mine," Adam answered. "And it is the same cause. Lack of food."

Will shook his head. "No. It is more than that." He bent down and put his ear next to Big Red's stomach. "There are no noises. Nothing is moving through." He straightened up with a worried expression on his face.

Adam shrugged. He knew little about horses, rode them poorly and cared about them even less. He watched as Will undid the traces and walked Big Red a few steps away from the wagon. The horse lowered his head and stood with his lank haunches against the wind. Slowly, he nuzzled a small pine tree and began nibbling at the bark.

"Soon that bark will look like strips of beef to us and taste as good," Adam said, putting his arm around Will's shoulders. Will looked at the remaining artillery, placed at the triangle formed where the lane from the outer line of defenses joined Gulph Road leading back to camp. The carpenters had dismantled the broken gun carriages and were loading them on to the wagon.

"Sergeant. Get that horse hitched back before we freeze to death," one of the men shouted. Will led Big Red back to the wagon. Adam heard one of the men curse as the wind changed direction and blew toward them. It always seemed the case. No matter which direction they went, the wind blew in their faces.

Adam trudged with Titus and the rest of the work crew along the ice-rutted road. Will and Captain Holmes, bent forward into the strong wind, walked slowly besides Big Red. As they came to the rows of snow covered huts of the regiments encamped closest to Gulph Road they heard shouting in unison- "No Meat! No Meat!" followed by hoots of soldiers imitating owls and the high raucous cawing of crows. The shouting and bird sounds seemed to have started at the huts nearest to them and seemed spread throughout the encampment. [5]

"I do not see a single officer emerging from their quarters to quiet this outbreak," Holmes said. Adam focused on the huts at the beginning of each line, the ones set aside for the two ranking officers of every company. The doors remained closed, the long icicles hanging from the roughly hewn corner beams. Other soldiers walking along the road to the Grand Parade ground stopped to listen. Some of them joined in, breaking ranks to stand on the lower slats of a split rail fence, cupping their hands and hooting loudly.

"Look at that horse," someone shouted.

Adam turned to see Big Red lying on his side in the road. Will knelt beside him and undid the traces, now taut to the wagon fork. The starving horse lay there, breathing heavily and then struggled to his feet. It staggered over toward the fence and lay down again on his side.

"When that one dies, if we get to him soon enough, we can skin him for moccasins to cover my poor bloody frozen feet," one soldier said, staring down at his blackened naked toes. "Not as good as calfskin," another grumbled, before being wracked by a wheezing deep cough. "But better than rags and wood," he added in a hoarse voice, after hacking up a thick wad of yellow phlegm.

Adam moved closer toward Will, thinking the soldiers might hasten Big Red's end. The horse writhed around on the ground, rolling from one side to the other, pawing the frozen earth with his hooves. Will stood back watching and then knelt at his horse's head. "Come on big boy. Get the knot out. Roll some more."

"What is he doing?" Adam asked. "What is the matter with him?"

"I believe he has a twist in his intestine. It comes from not eating forage. It will kill him if he does not undo it," Will said anxiously.

Adam watched the horse thrashing violently from side to side, mashing down the snow on the side of the road, kicking his legs out and arching his back.

"Looks like he is in his death throes now boys," a soldier said gleefully. Adam motioned to Titus and the two of them took their muskets from the wagon and rejoined Nat and Will. The cries of "No Meat! No Meat!" coming from the men in the huts, oblivious to the drama playing out on the road nearby, sounded to Adam like a satanic prayer for the death of his friend's horse. Their bird cries were the calls of turkey vultures arriving for the feast. What bestiality and sins will men commit when they are starving? What are their limits? And what are mine? he thought to himself. Why had he followed Captain Holmes and come to this place? No answer came to mind other a vague sense he wanted to fight but not at sea where, if captured he would be hung as a pirate. He gripped his musket tighter, glad that the bayonet was affixed and not in its sheath.

Big Red had stopped thrashing and lay with his belly against the ground, his legs bunched beneath him. He heaved himself up, shook his head, sending snot flying in every direction and then, in a sudden gesture of sheer exuberance, kicked his two rear feet in the air, rose up on his hind legs pawing the air and stood quietly, emitting loud gaseous horse farts. Adam waved his hand in front of his nose to dissipate the odor.

Will led Big Red slowly back to the wagon and redid the worn, leather straps.

"If I do not get him some forage soon, it will happen again and this time, it will most likely kill him." Adam shook his head in commiseration. Another week like the last one and they would all starve to death or succumb to disease, man and beast alike, he thought. He felt the strength ebbing from him each day.

They unloaded the gun carriage at the big shed that served as a repair depot, and blacksmith shop. It was near General Washington's stone house, his headquarters since late December.[6] Will took one of the metal buckets the blacksmiths were using for immersing the hot iron, carried it outside and returned with it full of snow. Wrapping a cloth around the handle, he held it near the forge until the snow had melted and carried it outside to Big Red. The horse drank greedily. Will repeated the process three more times before Big Red was sated.

Reluctantly, they left the carpenters to work in relative comfort near the two flaming forges. Adam walked with Will who was leading Big Red toward the Massachusetts Artillery's rows of huts between the star redoubt and another inner defensive line off Nutt's Road.

"He needs plenty of water to flush through him," he said by way of explanation. "It may prevent another seizing up until I can get him proper forage."

Adam nodded. All he wanted was the rations he was due that had not been issued for several days. One pound of beef or pork, and one pound of flour, not the sour kind. He had no need for the gill of rum or whiskey, although he would appreciate the weekly allotment of soap and vinegar.

Two women, both Negroes, were walking toward them on the road, their cloaks billowing around them from the wind at their backs. They carried covered baskets looped around their arms, their hands hidden by a cloth muff. Their feet were bare except for the thinnest, low-sided shoes, that served only to keep the soles of their feet from contact with the ice and snow. One, older than the other, kept her eyes downcast as they approached. The other, much younger and appearing to be more slight, despite her bulky cloak, eyed the four of them and Big Red with curiosity. Will and Nat moved the horse to the side of the road.

As the two women passed, Adam impulsively untied his tri-corn, removed it from his head and bowed. As he did so, he caught sight of a well-turned ankle. The younger woman laughed and acknowledged him with a nod of her head. She had high cheek bones, her skin was the color of polished oak and her eyes were an unusual green grey. The older woman, tsk-tsked and hurried along her companion, who looked back once more.

"Do you know who they are?" Adam asked Will as he held his tri-corn tight to his head with one hand.

"Not by name," Will answered. "They are part of General Washington's household help. One is a cook. The other I have seen her come and go from the General's house but I know not what she does."

"Are they indentured servants," Adam hesitated, "or slaves," he asked, spitting out the word.

"I do not know," he responded, looking at his friend. "Does it make a difference?"

Adam shook his head, not wishing to continue the discussion with Will. How could he even begin to understand? Of course it mattered. An indentured servant was a person, free to engage in conversation and use her own time as she pleased. A slave had no time that was her own and was considered the property of her master. He knew what his father told him when he had tried to court his mother before he purchased her freedom. Adam vowed to find out who the younger woman was. Then, he would know what was permitted and what was not. Maybe he would not care.

The following day, with no burdensome assigned duties, Adam stayed in the vicinity of the General's headquarters when he surmised the younger woman might be sent out on errands. He warmed himself at the sentry fires and made himself useful by hauling and stacking additional firewood. On the second day of his seemingly casual hanging around, shortly after noon, she came out alone and hurried easterly along the road that paralleled the river. He left the axe leaning against a tree trunk and trotted after her.

"Excuse me ma'm," he said tipping his tri-corn in greeting. She turned but without slowing her pace, rewarded him with a smile. "Permit me to introduce myself? Private Adam Cooper, formerly of the Marblehead Mariners and now attached to the Massachusetts Artillery. I am a free man from that Commonwealth."

"I could guess from your accent you are a New Englander," she said. "I have heard many such officers speak at the General's Headquarters and their words are strange to my ears."

"Your accent," Adam said slowing his pace to walk with her, "is like the sound of gentle waves washing on a shore. 'Tis soft and sweet. But you have not told me your name?" He looked at her, admiring her high cheek bones and noticed her skin was blemished here and there with marks of the pox.

"My name is Sarah Penrose." She had looked at him directly and he caught a glimpse of her green grey eyes, before she turned away. "I have been lent to General Washington by Reverend Penrose of New Jersey. Before," she hesitated, "that is before I was sold to him by my master in Virginia." [7]

Adam felt a hollowness inside. She was a slave with her master's last name. He feigned cheerfulness. "And where Miss Sarah are you off to now?"

"I have been tasked by the General's cook, Isaac Till, to purchase several items for the General's dinner. He is entertaining five members of Congress today and we have need of whatever vegetables I may purchase. There is a place where local farmers bring produce. I have sterling to pay. They will sell to me. They have in the past."

"Permit me to accompany you there and back. With so many men on short rations, the contents of your basket may be too much of a temptation."

"I am of the General's household," she said proudly. "That is protection enough. However, I do accept your offer for companionship. May I inquire how you came to be a freedman, Private Adam Cooper? There are many such in this winter camp but you are the first I have spoken to directly." [8]

"I was born free," Adam said and related how his father purchased his mother's freedom from her master almost two decades ago for twenty-six pounds sterling.

"Reverend Penrose has allowed that after, he has been paid fifty-three pounds, I shall be set free. I keep forty shillings each month for clothing and my necessities. The remainder is paid directly to my master. I am not able to save much."

"I will put aside all of my wages to help you gain your freedom," Adam blurted out.

"I do not intend to trade one owner for another," she replied haughtily.

Adam bowed. "And I did not intend to cause offense. I hope to earn your admiration and love and one day ask you to marry me. Please note Miss Sarah, I did not say make you my wife. For no one should make another human being do anything against his or her will."

"Are you always so forward with the young ladies Private Cooper? We have met only once and already you are talking of marriage."

"No," he replied rather meekly. "I am normally shy around women. I cannot explain it other than to say my feelings for you are true and well-intentioned. I believe in time you will feel the same way of your own free will."

"My life has been nothing but being forced to do things against my will," she replied. "Deep in my heart I do believe your words about free will. I have read books that say the same thing."

"How did you come by your education?" Adam asked, afraid he might offend her by the question.

"The Reverend's wife undertook to teach me to read when I first came to their house five years ago. Their daughters were learning French when Reverend Penrose sent me to be part of General Washington's household. It sounds like a pretty language," she said wistfully.

"Your accent is pretty enough for me."

"I'se bin edjucated," she replied, teasing him with a plantation dialect. He liked her playfulness but inwardly winced at the sound.

Adam left her as they approached the General's Life Guards, wishing they could talk for much longer. As he walked away, he was more certain than ever he would marry her, although she had given no such inclination. How many years would it take for the two of them to accumulate fifty-three pounds? If Sarah would accept, he had almost a third of that amount from his share of privateering. As a Private, he made six and two-thirds dollars a month. At the rate of one pound to two and two-thirds dollars, in a full year the total would be close to forty pounds. How much of that could he save? The numbers tumbled around in his head. His stomach growled to remind him first he had to survive starvation and this disease-ridden camp before he could think ahead a year and of buying Sarah's freedom.

John looked up as his orderly entered the office and placed a sheaf of reports on his desk.

"Yes, Corporal?" Stoner asked. "Why are you standing there?"

"There is a Mrs. Bates waiting outside, sir. She says you were expecting her though not who sent her."

"It matters not to me who referred her," John said with a dismissive wave of his hand. He opened one of the folders before him. "Tell her I am engaged and she must wait. Ask the serving maid for another pot of coffee. This one has grown cold and is unfit to drink."

He caught a look of disapproval on the Corporal's face that quickly disappeared. The impertinence of the man, Stoner thought. Maybe a transfer to the redoubts and a few frozen nights of sentry duty would improve his attitude.

He knew all about Ann Bates, having first made inquiries in a general way with Superintendent Galloway. He had asked about Loyalist spies who regularly passed between the lines, not revealing that he was particularly interested in females. Galloway was livid with anger that day and John had taken advantage of his mood. The Superintendent's wife had arrived from the countryside the day before and John had expected him to be in a merry frame of mind.

"Can you imagine John, the effrontery of these Rebels," he shouted, his long, narrow face convulsed with rage. "Safe passage for Grace, my dear wife through the lines while they confiscate her belongings in the carriage trunks. And the furniture in our country house," he said his voice rising almost to a screech. "All declared forfeited by decree of those rascals who pretend to be the Pennsylvania Assembly." [9]

He praised John for his initiative, thinking his aide was intent on helping in the hunt to kidnap Patriot leaders. "First, let us strike terror amongst those in Pennsylvania and then turn the dragoons loose in New Jersey as well. No Rebel leader shall sleep easily at night. Let them fear to hear horses' hooves and to feel the cold night air as they are taken back to Philadelphia in their nightshirts. We will bring them to trial and hang the most prominent ones for treason to the Crown. The others can rot in jail." John let Galloway rant on, nodding in agreement. Let the fool think what he wanted.

His real intention was to ensnare Elisabeth van Hooten. She had been too clever in hiding her actions. The men he assigned to follow her as she went to the market on Fridays, usually in the company of her Quaker landlady, Mrs. Lewis, and then her social calls, teas and parties, reported nothing untoward. Now, he would find someone to befriend her instead.

Several names had been given to him as reliable but Mrs. Bates was one of only two women. She was a seamstress, who made dresses and garments for those in Philadelphia who were not among the most wealthy, but aspired to be invited into those social circles. She lived with her husband, a repairer of guns, in a small one-story house off Elfreth's Alley. His shop was near the Hessian Barracks, close to the waterfront.

Ann Bates frequently disguised herself as a peddler and entered the American lines, to sell thread and needles, scissors, small knives and bars of soap, lice combs and the like to the female camp followers of the American Army. As she went from one group of women to another, she listened to their complaints about short rations for their men, lack of medicines and the fear of inoculation against the "speckled monster." All the while she counted the numbers of men on the Grand Parade ground, observed the drilling, noted the artillery emplacements, and picked up gossip about Generals' wives and the comings and goings of foreign officers. Passing back through the British lines, she would report to an Adjutant of Major Andre's, accept her pay in sterling and resume her identity as a seamstress. [10] Now John thought it was time to put her to talents to use in Philadelphia. He closed the folder on his desk and called loudly to his orderly. When he showed Mrs. Bates in, John studied her standing in front of the door before offering her a seat. She was of hefty size, large boned with a washerwoman's figure, and ruddy complexion to match. She stared back at him with a mixture of curiosity and caution, neither fearful nor defiant, but watchful, waiting to see where this encounter would lead. Her lips were thin and tight, serving as the guardhouse to her thoughts. "May I," she said breaking the silence as she undid the clasp to her dark brown cloak and slipped it from her shoulders. John pointed to the clothes tree in the corner and waited for her to turn around before motioning to the chair in front of his desk. She was dressed appropriately for the winter weather and presentably, as one would expect from a seamstress. She smoothed her dress before sitting and placed her hands in her lap, her intense grey eyes studying him.

"You have come recommended to me by an officer whom I shall not name. He has extolled your keen sense of observation behind the American lines. He has also praised your quickness of thought and ability to seize opportunities when they arise." He expected her to acknowledge this praise with some sort of false modesty. Instead, she inclined her head slightly in acceptance.

"How may these talents be of service to you, Lieutenant?" she asked. John disliked her challenge and the directness of her response. It was time to make her understand she was not an equal in this conversation.

"Have you ever carried letters or packages for someone to the American camp?" he snapped. "Something that our sentries would seize unless it was borne by a trusted person, someone with an authorized pass or known to them."

"I bear a pass signed by Major Andre himself," she said somewhat defensively. "I am permitted to bring sundries and items to the American camps for purposes of performing my duties."

John waved his hand. "I have no concern about such trifles. I am interested in illicit goods or correspondence, not sanctioned by your masters."

Mrs. Bates shifted in her chair uneasily. He guessed she was struggling to determine what would be the correct answer, or rather the response to satisfy him. Her face remained fixed, her brow unfurrowed, her lips set. Her grey eyes revealed nothing.

"I confess I have on occasion carried love letters from one or two of my clientele to their beaus, young men they knew before the King's troops drove the Rebels from Philadelphia."

John put his elbows on his desk and rested his chin on his clasped hands, covering his mouth. He stared at her, waiting to see if she would offer any further information. She remained silent. He liked that.

"Well, Mrs. Bates," he said lowering his hands and smiling. "I believe you are just the person I want for an extremely difficult task. Everything I now tell you is strictly in confidence. No need for others to know. At the appropriate time, when we apprehend this spy, your role will be recognized and you will be well rewarded."

John explained the basis of his suspicions about Elisabeth, exaggerating his role with the dragoons on Long Island and the encounter with her father. He described the unsuccessful efforts of his men who had followed her.

"I wish to employ you Mrs. Bates to befriend her, gain her confidence and in so doing, subtly let her know you do a trade behind the American lines. I believe this will induce her to take advantage of the opportunity presented and pass to you letters or packages for you in turn to transmit to her spy handlers among the Rebels. The trap will then be sprung and she will be caught and exposed."

He noticed her appraising him and for a moment thought she knew of the gossip about his embarrassing accusation of Elisabeth at Major Andre's ball the prior month. He almost sighed with relief when she mentioned money. "I will need to be compensated for such activities. After all, spending time with Miss Elisabeth will necessarily decrease my business as a seamstress."

John nodded. "Tis a fair request. I trust five pounds sterling a week will suffice." She nodded her assent. "I will send a man for you when I desire your report. Avoid suspicion," he said, and as an afterthought, "but do not keep me waiting too long." Best she be reminded who paid the piper.

When the door had closed behind her, John was satisfied with their meeting. It had gone well, he thought. Mrs. Bates was just the person to encourage Elisabeth's trust, a plain sensible woman, an experienced seamstress with no airs or frills . Once he had Elisabeth's compromising messages in hand, he would decide whether to turn her in or make her beg for his silence.

Chapter 2 - Setting a Trap

Elisabeth was giddy. Not from the wine served at the early supper at three. She had imbibed in moderation. It was the excitement, the pleasurable anticipation of attending her first theater performance. She honestly acknowledged that it was more than just keeping up appearances while spying for General Knox. She was eager, nay thrilled to attend a play at the Southwark Theater, escorted by Captain Montresor. She was titillated by the garish red two-story building with its ornate cupola and the promised licentiousness of women performing the female roles on a public stage. After arriving by carriage, Elisabeth and Montresor proceeded on a temporary boardwalk that had been erected to protect the ladies' slippers and the Officers' immaculate white stockings from being spattered by melting snow and mud.

The inside was brightly lit with candles set in sconces and chandeliers. A low iron spiked fence separated the green curtained stage from the gallery. Oil footlamps illuminated the apron. The interior was vast, with seating for more than six hundred patrons. The noise of so many voices shouting greetings and the gay laughter of women rebounded off the wooden ceiling.

Mary Lewis had sternly warned Elisabeth not to accept the Captain's invitation. In a scolding manner, she reminded Elisabeth she must adhere to some degree of moral rectitude. There was no harm, Elisabeth told herself. All the young Philadelphia ladies from the best families of high society were in attendance. She and the Captain were seated in the second row of an upper level box, along with Lieutenant Colonel Richard Fitzpatrick, whose father, Montresor whispered, was an Earl in the House of Lords. Colonel Harcourt, Colonel Mawhood and his wife occupied the cushioned seats in the box's first row.

On the other side of the gallery, in the spacious lower level box adorned with a large British flag, Elisabeth recognized Joseph and Mrs. Galloway, seated next to General Howe and Mrs. Loring, an attractive blond, known to be his mistress. Major Andre and Peggy Shippen shared another box with her parents, two of her sisters and their beaus. Below, the gallery itself was so crowded with officers in uniform, it looked like a field of red poppies. The dresses of their female companions were like orphan flowers scattered as if by chance amidst the rows of red.

In the midst of all this gaiety and excess, she thought guiltily of the half naked, shoeless deserters from Valley Forge who had escaped through the lines and straggled into Philadelphia with their pitiful tales of starvation, disease and the relentless cold. She was ashamed that Will and the men she knew were suffering so, while she enjoyed a brick house warmed by plentiful firewood and was well fed, now that the two forts comprising the Americans blockade of the Delaware had been captured.

Elisabeth leaned forward to scan the boxes on their side of the gallery and as she did so, she noticed Lieutenant John Stoner, twisting around in his seat in the pit. He spied her and stared arrogantly upward. Elisabeth nodded her head slightly with what she hoped was the correct amount of condescension. Her gesture hit home as John Stoner turned red in the face and looked away. Pleased that she had retained her composure she inclined her head toward Montresor. He had forgone a wig and instead simply powdered his hair for the event. She had to admit he looked elegantly masculine tonight. With all the excited voices in the theater, she brought her mouth closer to his ear to be heard. The memory of Will telling her how much it pleased him when she did that almost made her hesitate.

"The Playbill promises the characters are portrayed by the Officers of the Army and Navy," she said in a playful tone. "Yet you told me there are some women's parts to be performed by members of our fairer sex. Surely, neither the British Army nor Navy have women officers?"

Montresor threw back his head and laughed. "My dear. I adore your company," he said. "You always find mirth, sometimes unwittingly in the most unlikely places. While the male performers, known as Howe's Strolling Players, with the permission of His Excellency, are all officers, the women you will see on stage do belong to the Army and Navy in one sense." He chuckled waiting for her to guess his meaning. When she continued to look puzzled he added, "They are the mistresses of some of the Officers." Elisabeth blushed deeply and Montresor chuckled again. "Dear Elisabeth. General Howe, our respected Commander-in-Chief sits in plain view with his mistress, a married woman, in yonder box. What is displayed in public should be no cause for embarrassment."

"Perhaps Mrs. Loring is the reason our Army remains master only of this city and some parts of the banks of the Delaware and Schuylkill," Lt. Colonel Fitzpatrick said bitterly.

Colonel Harcourt turned around in his chair. "It is my considered opinion that no thought should have been given to Philadelphia until our army had joined forces with General Burgoyne and captured Albany. The Rebel General Washington would not have risked a battle to prevent our march northward or we would have annihilated his pitiful forces in the process and put an end to their miserable rebellion." [1]

Elisabeth imagined British troops marching into Albany and entering her parents' home and taking up quarters. Some of the same British officers who were present in this theater would occupy the Van Hooten household, taking what they wanted at will, eating all of the stored provisions and confining the family to a few small rooms in the back of their own home. She had seen it happen in Philadelphia. So far, she and Mary Lewis had not been compelled to quarter any officers, probably due to the influence of Captain Montresor. She was not certain of this but thankful for the overall protection his rank and position provided her, especially against that despicable John Stoner.

She knew the British had lost a battle near Saratoga in mid-October, about a month after the American defeat at Brandywine.

Their army of more than five thousand men, commanded by General Burgoyne, had surrendered. The rumors of the Rebel victory had reached Philadelphia by early November. It was a common topic of conversation among the officers at the teas and dinners she had attended. She had written in invisible ink in her letters to Will to report the deep dismay among the British Officer corps, the impact on their morale and their dissatisfaction with their Generals, particularly Sir William Howe.

In early February, British newspapers detailing the exact terms of the surrender arrived in Philadelphia. Montresor provided Elisabeth with The London Chronicle of December 11, 1777 that contained the very Articles of Convention signed by the American Major General Horatio Gates and British Lieutenant General J. Burgoyne. Judging by Colonel Harcourt's harsh words, the arrival of these newspapers had reignited the criticism of General Howe for his ill-considered strategy.

"Our own army also suffers from General Howe's improper practices of promotion," Fitzpatrick added, glancing at Harcourt. It was well known the 16th Dragoons blamed Howe for the failure of London to promote their Lieutenant Colonel. "Every day I grow more disgusted with the folly and inequity we are condemned to endure while a parcel of mere boys with inferior claims are promoted based on the volume of their flattery of our General. It is enough for me to consider selling my commission." [2]

Colonel Harcourt shrugged. "My promotion is more important to my dragoons than me. Rather it is my wish for a more aggressive campaign instead of comfortable winter quarters and a delay until spring to resume the offensive. We should sally forth now from Philadelphia and move to crush the remnants of the Rebels." A drum roll sounded, drowning out his words and Elisabeth turned her attention to the stage, while committing to memory the Colonel's comments. It would make for interesting reading at Valley Forge.

The actors, save for the women, had assembled on stage, some in costume, others in uniform with small props to indicate their roles. One officer stepped forward and the drummers ended with a flourish.

"Sir William, assembled guests and ladies," he said in a loud, clear voice. "With the permission and support of His Excellency, we are Howe's Strolling Players." There were cheers and applause. Several officers in the gallery stood and faced the General's box clapping ostentatiously. Howe offered a slight wave in acknowledgement.

"The proceeds from our mirthful performance," the officer on stage continued, "will benefit the widows and children of our brave soldiers who have shed their blood in our noble endeavor to end this treason against our most gracious King." He was interrupted by men shouting "God Save the King," and "Hear! Hear!" accompanied by the stomping of feet in unison from the officers in the gallery.

The officer held up his hands for quiet. "This evening, we present a comedy called 'The Liar,' for your amusement. But first," he signaled for a drum roll, "a prologue written by one of our prominent local poets." The actors stepped forward on the apron and recited a long poem over the general hubbub of the audience. Elisabeth half listened to the first several verses, while she studied the upswept hair styles and gowns of some of the ladies in attendance. Many were more revealing than she would have been comfortable wearing.

Once more ambitious of theatric glory
Howe's strolling company appear before ye
O'er hill and dale and bogs and wind and weather
With many a hairbreadth 'scape we've scrambled hither
Now beats the Yankee busom at our drum
Hark Jonathan, zounds here the strollers come.

At the last two lines, the actors had dropped their clipped English accents and attempted a broad New England manner of speech that Elisabeth recognized as mocking of uncouth Americans.

Spruced up with top-knots & their Sunday dress
With eager looks the maidens round express
"Jemma see—a'nt this a charming sight?
Look Tabitha—Oh Lord, I wish 'twas night." [3]

The audience broke out into hoots of derision, laughing at the Colonial bumpkins, their peculiar manner of speech and their obliviousness to their own ignorance.

The green curtain was drawn back to reveal painted scenery of a garden with two benches and a chair in the foreground. Elisabeth listened intently, laughing at the broad humor and blushing at some of the more bawdy lines, often directed toward the ladies in the cast. The sound of thunder echoed across the theater, followed by the patter of a heavy rain. The flat of the garden scene seemed to miraculously glide off stage revealing another painted setting of the interior of a snug cabin. [4] The audience clapped in appreciation. Elisabeth was embarrassed by the lewd advances of one of the characters toward a buxom young serving maid and hid her flushed face behind the printed playbill. Some in the audience cheered the young male performer on with shouts of "deflower her now," and "give her a flourish." One officer in the gallery offered to come on stage and do it himself if the actor was not up to it. His comment drew a raucous response from his comrades. Montresor grinned and leaned over.

"My dear. Your natural innocence enhances your beauty and creates a glow by which the candles in these sconces pale in comparison."

"Why Captain Montresor," she replied coyly. "This play has inspired your poetic side. That pleases me greatly. But tell me," she said, wishing to deflect the conversation to a safer subject, "how do they create the sounds of the impending thunder storm? I thought to cover my head it was so convincing."

He laughed, casually putting his arm around the back of her chair and leaned over to whisper in her ear. "It is a military secret." He paused dramatically. "I will reveal it willingly, because your beauty compels me to tell you. Rolling cannon balls for the thunder and musket shot in a tube for the downpour. I believe they use birdshot for a lighter rain." She smelled the claret and felt the warmth of his breath on her cheek. If he were Will, she would have leaned her head on his shoulder despite being in public. Instead, she straightened her back and focused anew on the stage.

The play ended to loud applause. During the intermission, while the scenery was changed for a brief farce called "A Trip to Scotland," servants brought wine and cheese to the occupants of the boxes. Vendors selling fruit and a variety of other food stuffs circulated in the gallery, loudly touting their wares. When the villain of the next performance appeared on stage, he was greeted by apple cores and nuts, as well as boos and cries of displeasure from the rowdy crowd.

It was past eleven when Captain Montresor helped her alight from the carriage and escorted her to the door of the Lewis home. Ever the gentleman, he effected a deep bow and lightly kissed her extended hand, letting his lips rest on her skin a trifle too long, she thought.

"Remember. It is my innocence that pleases you," she said with a slight smile.

"It is the promise of the loss of your innocence that intrigues me," he replied, bowing again before re-entering the carriage.

Troubled by his words, Elisabeth unlocked the door and let herself in. It is a difficult line to draw between leading him on and maintaining her virtue, she thought. It was a danger to spying she and Will had never anticipated. Elisabeth fell asleep thinking of Will in a crisp, clean blue uniform sitting next to her in the theater, whispering in her ear and laughing along with her. Across the gallery, John Stoner stood in a box with a pistol aimed at his brother. He fired and she awoke with a start. The shutter banged against the window and blew back to reveal snow falling on the street below.

Early Friday morning, she and Mary Lewis left the house and hurried to Market Street. The flimsy wooden flaps of the stalls were already propped open with knobby, notched sticks. The plain slatted tables were covered with winter vegetables, parsnips and potatoes, carrots, cucumbers and cabbage, pickled in the fall, apples from the slate racks of farmers' cold rooms, jugs of cider, mushrooms and herbs gathered from the forest, sacks of flour, fish freshly caught that morning and carted up from the river and slabs of beef, veal, lamb, some local wild game, venison, rabbit and squirrel and, imported from the Caribbean, cinnamon, cloves, pepper, bay leaves and other spices.

Elisabeth took Mary's arm as they went over slippery cobblestones from stall to stall, weaving their way through the crowd of women, some looking hungrily at food they could not afford, others competing for the best there was to offer. Prices were set by Superintendent Galloway to prevent inflation. These meant nothing when the item was in great demand. Mary purchased two fish that were cheap and reasonable and passed by a meat seller offering veal and lamb for exorbitant amounts. Elisabeth found Mary to be a frugal and shrewd purchaser even though she had more than enough money. Her one extravagance, now that the blockade had been lifted was tea – her favorite hysop tea brought by ship from England every few months.

Elisabeth was dependent upon Mary for all her necessities, having no source of income of her own. Mary Lewis maintained her husbands' wagons and hired them out to sutlers and the British Army Quartermaster's Corps at six pounds sterling per day. In addition, promptly on the first of the month, she received rental from different ship owners and merchants for the space they rented in the three warehouses Edward Lewis owned down by the river.

Although Elisabeth benefitted from the abundant and varied supply of foodstuffs brought to the city, inwardly she seethed at the farmers' refusal to provision the starving soldiers at Valley Forge. She knew it was their greed, not loyalty to the Crown, that drove them to the Philadelphia markets where they received payment in sterling or pieces of eight, instead of the almost worthless Continental dollars offered at the American camp.

Elisabeth stood behind Mary's short stout figure as she bargained with a farmer selling live chickens and arranged for delivery of the bird to her cook. Further up the street, they stopped at a stall where a small group of women were purchasing flour, running the powder through their fingers, assessing the color, texture and fineness.

"Nothing but the best quality here ladies," the man behind the counter shouted, pointing to sacks of flour arrayed on either side of him. "Forty shillings for a pound of the finest wheat, thirty for rye and twenty five for barley malt. 'Tis all cut and stored well - no moisture or weevils in this lot," he said sifting his thick fingers through the brown colored wheat meal. "Buy the best wheat and I will drink the barley malt with you," he said, winking at one of the younger women.

Mary ordered four pounds of wheat flour. As she drew her pouch full of coins from under her apron, the woman next to her said quietly, "Make him weigh it again. His thumb was on the scale." Mary looked up in surprise. "Elisabeth. Did you watch him for the weighing?" Elisabeth shook her head.

"Weigh it again, please," Mary asked in a loud voice.

"You do not trust me Madam?," he said angrily, appraising Mary's short stature and Quaker cloak and cap. "I run an honest shop and my scales are fair and balanced."

Mary insisted and the stall owner became abusive. "You Quakers are all alike. You take no side but your own while accepting the Crown's protection. I have no need for your money. If you do not trust me then take your business elsewhere." He waved his hand in dismissal.

"If you do not weigh that four pounds of wheat again, no one else here will trust you," the woman standing next to Mary said loudly. The other women began chanting "Weigh the wheat. Weigh the wheat." The man became red-faced. He anxiously glanced up the street, concerned the commotion would attract a city patrol.

"Perhaps you were distracted. If it comes up short, I will consider it an honest mistake," Mary said pleasantly. The man grumbled and, making a big show of the uselessness of his doing so, put four polished brass cylindrical weights on the pan on the right. The scale tipped down while the pan on the left containing the wheat rose up. He scooped more flour from the barrel and poured it until both pans balanced. "Must have been fuzzy minded when I weighed it out," he said, as he poured the wheat from the scale into Mary's used flour sack.

"Mistakes can happen to the most honest among us. Intentional misdeeds are the devil's work," Mary said agreeably, handing the man one pound sixty shillings and tucking her coin purse securely under her apron. They moved away from the stall. Elisabeth placed the purchased flour in her basket and covered it with a cloth. She noticed the woman who had warned them had paused before a cider stand ahead of them.

"Thank you, sister, for your alertness," Mary said, touching the woman's shoulder. "It was short by almost one quarter of a pound."

"Closer to a third if you ask me," the woman replied, still fuming from the encounter. "However there is no need to thank me. We women must look out for each other in these times. There is no dearth of cheats and rascals eager to take advantage of us."

Mary introduced herself. "And this is my friend, Elisabeth Van Hooten."

"It is a pleasure to make your acquaintances," the woman replied. "My name is Ann Bates," she said, repositioning her basket on her arm and closing her cloak against the cold wind. She looked the women over. "I see both of you are well dressed. I am a seamstress and even ladies such as you may be in need to modify some dresses or even repair a worn garment, coverlet, quilt or cloth."

"I am perfectly competent in sewing my own garments and do not engage in the licentious behavior common now in Philadelphia after the arrival of the British," Mary said rather brusquely. Then, realizing she was being impolite to the woman who had saved her from being cheated, she added, "Elisabeth, however, does on occasion attend a dinner or tea."

Ann appraised Elisabeth's willowy figure. "I have also been of service to many young ladies who need to look their best at certain times."

Elisabeth smiled brightly, thinking she would prefer not to rely so much on Peggy Shippen's dressmaker. She disliked being the recipient of Peggy's charity. Her friend always managed to make Elisabeth feel not only beholden but inferior as well.

"If I wished to avail myself of such services, where would I find you?" Elisabeth asked.

"My shop is off Elfreth's Alley. Not far from here. I think you will find my rates reasonable, and," she gestured with her head back toward the flour merchant's stall, "I do not cheat my customers."

Mrs. Bates left them at the cider stand and Mary and Elisabeth hurried back toward the Lewis home.

"While I disapprove of your attending all manner of teas, dinners and now even theater, where scandalous behavior takes place in public, both on and off the stage," Mary lectured as they walked quickly on, "Mrs. Bates appears to be a sensible woman. At least she would ensure you would wear modest dress, befitting a proper lady."

"You are a dear friend Mary and I truly appreciate your understanding of what I must do. Please, for the sake of our friendship speak no more of my social activities. I will visit Mrs. Bates soon for Captain Montresor will be escorting me to the usual weekly ball at the City Tavern."

Mary snorted. "The City Tavern. That cesspool of vice. The only saving grace for you is your attendance with me at the New Jail to help those poor unfortunate soldiers held in that dreadful place, freezing and starving to death inside. And we are already late. The guards will not let us pass after three in the afternoon."

After depositing their own purchases at home, they scurried up Walnut Street, stepping in the now grey, dirty slush that made the pavement more slippery. The forbidding stone jail was within the shadow of the former Pennsylvania State House, now a prison for Rebel Officers. According to the rules signed by Provost William Cunningham, posted in public houses around the city and displayed on the jail's gates, the more than five hundred enlisted men were allowed to receive food and sundries between the hours of one and three on Tuesdays and Fridays. Only certain items were permitted - bread, cooked or cold vegetables and soap. No drink of any kind, especially rum or other alcoholic beverages were allowed. Nor were any containers, either sealed or unsealed, such as jars, jugs or crocks. All baskets were subject to being searched and anyone carrying contraband goods would be arrested immediately. Items of clothing and blankets were also permitted.

Today, in addition to food, they were bringing a few of Mr. Lewis's old linen shirts and two worn blankets, although Mary feared they would be confiscated by the guards and either given to their camp followers or sold at the open market near the wharves. The rumors were dozens were freezing to death each day so she felt obligated to try.

The guards were British soldiers declared invalided for regular duty but deemed fit for prison service. There were only a few women lined up for inspection of their baskets.

"It is a pity there are not more of us," Mary said, shaking her head in disgust. "Our good Quaker women, brought up in our faith of compassion for the poor, sick and suffering souls amongst us, have been frightened away by the rigidity and untruths of our Church's leaders." [5] Elisabeth was surprised by the ferocity of her comment and was about to inquire as to her meaning, when it was their turn at the sentry table.

Mary pulled back the cloth covering her basket and removed a few loaves of stale bread, some parsnips and a head of cabbage. She showed the guard the shirts and he made her unfold them, felt the cloth and grunted, whether in approval of the quality or that they were not hiding any contraband, she was not clear.

Elisabeth threw back her hood, revealing her blond hair and smiled at the guard. "I have a few old blankets for the poor souls inside," she said, "bread and the few vegetables we can afford to spare."

"I'd wager you'd keep me warm beneath these blankets on these accursedly cold February nights," he said leering at her.

"Oh sir. I am sure someone as handsome as you has no trouble attracting the ladies for that purpose. Besides, I am already spoken for by a Captain on General Howe's staff," she said sweetly, leaving unsaid the consequences to this Private if he continued to make lustful remarks to her. She knew he would assume she was the Officer's mistress.

"And why would sech a lady as you who warms the bed of a King's officer, bring food to sech scum as we have imprisoned here?" he asked, picking at a sore on his cheek.

"My Captain knows I do this mission of mercy. He regards it as proof of my innocence which he says makes me more desirable to him," Elisabeth replied, echoing something of Captain Montresor's expression of admiration.

The guard smirked, undressing Elisabeth with his eyes. "Tis our lot that the Officers git the fine ladies and we poor soldiers ar stuck with the poxy whores and weathered camp followers who lift their skirts for a piece of soap, a dented spoon or a glass of rum." He salaciously looked her up and down one more time. "You may pass through to the entry hall," he said waving the two of them on.

Inside, it was much colder, as if the very walls retained the icy temperatures and rebuffed any warmth from the air outside. Elisabeth pulled her cloak closer around her shoulders and throat. The air was dank, bone-chilling, with a whiff of the stench from the living held inside.

They approached the long table in the entry hall and placed the contents of their baskets on the bare wood. Elisabeth thought how little there was to share among all those prisoners, even if the guards permitted the foodstuffs, clothing and blankets to be distributed. Yet for some, it would mean life or death. She knew of the reports of the prisoners not receiving even a morsel of food for five days at a time. All they could do is come on the days allotted, leave what they had brought and hope for the best.

She was relieved once they were outside the gates in the waning afternoon sun and away from the forbidding stone building. "A proper lady does not engage in lewd banter with men like that," Mary said disapprovingly.

"Harmless flirting for a good cause cannot be immoral," Elisabeth replied, wondering whether Will would agree. They passed the State House where more than sixty captured Rebel officers were imprisoned. Rumors were the conditions here were only slightly more tolerable than for the prisoners held in the City Jail. Wives and relatives were forbidden to visit, and after a recent escape, the guard had been doubled and not even the charity of the women of Philadelphia was accepted.

Elisabeth would include something about the miserable condition of the prisoners in her next letter to Will. She would couch it as idle gossip. Perhaps, some arrangement with respect to the treatment of British prisoners could lessen the harsh conditions at the City Jail and State House. As they passed near Elfreth's Alley, she remembered she needed to visit Mrs. Bates soon, well before the weekly ball. She had a notion of how she wanted one of her dresses altered so it would look more fashionable.

John Stoner walked down Broad Street into the teeth of the wind. He should have been at home before a warm fire or perhaps, after dinner, visiting Mrs. McCoy's establishment for a taste of one of her delectable young ladies. Instead, he braved the bitter winter afternoon cold, searching for Captain Chatsworth. He had sent his man to the Captain's quarters. The stupid sod had returned without even having inquired where Chatsworth might be this afternoon. The man was useless. He regretted hiring him but the prestige of having his own "batman" gave him pleasure. Maybe threatening to cut his wages would improve his performance.

He pushed open the door of the City Tavern located on the south side of Market Street. It was a relief to come in from the cold. Even if Chatsworth was not within, he would drink a beer and mingle with other officers. To his delight, he saw the Captain seated at a table surrounded by several dragoons. It was obvious they had all been drinking for quite some time.

"Ah, John." Chatsworth called out in greeting. "You have torn yourself away from all those reports to go out on the town? Here fellows. Make room round the table." Three of the dragoons shifted on the bench, one commenting loudly that there was no need for a chair back for 'Ramrod John.'

John realized he would have to spend time in faking merriment and serving as the butt of their jokes until he could speak to Chatsworth in confidence. He amused them with a few tales of gossip his spies had brought him, including one of two officers whom he discreetly declined to identify, both of whom had the same mistress but did not know it.

"You must reveal her name," several of them urged. "Perhaps, we could add a third or fourth to complicate the situation." John half listened to the ribald comments as the dragoons discussed the possibilities of the poor maid forgetting with whom and when she had made the assignation and rushing from bed to bed to fulfill each lover's desires.

He was tired and bored by these drunken troopers. He wanted to get Chatsworth alone and dangle before him the plan for a foray to New Jersey. He was sure he would have the Captain champing at the bit. And when John arranged for Elisabeth to learn of the imminent raid it would require her to act quickly and without her usual caution, turning to Mrs. Bates as a trustworthy messenger immediately at hand. He leaned over to Chatsworth, cupped his palm over his mouth and suggested they ask the tavern's owner for a private room to talk.

Once inside the owner's office, a small garret on the second floor, overlooking the snow covered race track, Chatsworth immediately lost the haze of alcohol.

"Well, John. What do you have for me?" he asked in his clipped British accent.

Stoner smiled. "This is a grand opportunity for glory and promotion and I trust you will remember who it was who made this possible." May as well plant the hook of indebtedness early, he thought.

"Do you recall that fine home in Princeton General Cornwallis occupied as his headquarters?" Chatsworth nodded in assent.

"It belongs to John Witherspoon, a rabble-rousing Presbyter Reverend. He is one of the signers of the document the Rebels have misnamed their Declaration of Independence, a pack of lies and insults against the Crown. Witherspoon is a member of their Congress and until recently was in York where they have been holding forth." John leaned forward as if the next piece of information was the best. "His son was killed at Germantown. The grief-stricken Reverend is taking his son's body back to Princeton to be buried in the family plot at the Presbyterian Church."

Chatsworth, excited by the information, stood and began pacing the small room. "We could cross the Delaware north of Darby and proceed on the Jersey side. A hard ride would bring us to the outskirts of Princeton within a few hours, camp in the surrounding woods overnight," he said thinking out loud. "Then seize the good Reverend in the early dawn, and be back in Philadelphia in time for a late dinner."

"It may take you longer than that. There is another prize to be plucked."

Chatsworth stopped pacing and sat down opposite Stoner.

"Go on."

"Dr. Benjamin Rush. Another signer of their treasonous document. He is in charge of a hospital at Princeton. You could capture both and bring them back to Philadelphia trussed up like pigs for market."

"Two would be a fine prize," Chatsworth said, gloating as if he envisioned already bringing them before Colonel Harcourt. "I do not want to seem greedy but are there any wounded worthy of snatching as well?" he asked.

"I have no specific information but I would doubt it. They keep their wounded senior officers in homes of Rebel sympathizers. My network will soon locate such places."

"Well then. We will simply torch the hospital and bring back the good Reverend and Doctor Rush," Chatsworth said. "Thank you John for this information. I am certain Colonel Harcourt will approve. He has been eager for any kind of action for his dragoons." [6]

John left the City Tavern well pleased with himself. Chatsworth was like a hound on a fox. Once he knew the dragoons were ready to leave, John would call on Mrs. Bates and instruct her to contact Elisabeth. He reveled in the thought of confronting her with her own traitorous letter in his hand.

Chapter 3 - For the Love of a Slave

The early February blizzard delayed Will's departure. He was anxious to leave Valley Forge. He fretted about Elisabeth and was frustrated by his helplessness to protect her from his older brother. None of his friends offered any solace. Nat was worried there had been no letter from his wife about her health nor the well-being of their infant son. Adam was never around and when he was, he was morose and truculent.

Big Red seemed to have recovered but without forage soon, his intestines would knot again and this time could prove fatal. Every day brought the death of more men from disease, exposure or starvation. Burial crews built fires and hacked at the frozen ground with pick axes and shovels. Dead horses lay all about the camp. Over two hundred had died since the beginning of January. The starving troops lacked the energy to bury their large carcasses.

Not even his promotion to Lieutenant at the beginning of February had raised Will's spirits. Doubling his pay to thirteen and one third dollars per month, the equivalent of almost ninety-five shillings, meant nothing if you were never paid. He might as well be earning a Colonel's wages of fifty dollars per month for all it mattered. [1]

Despite General Knox's words about Will's bravery at the battles of Brandywine and Germantown, he was certain he did not deserve the promotion. He was only elevated in rank because so many officers were resigning their commissions and returning to their homes and farms. Most explained their families were starving and they needed to provide for them. Others simply left to be with their loved ones. [2] If he did not merit being promoted, then General Knox had lied to him about the reasons for it. That distressed him even more.

The rumors in camp about the hired wagoneers' abandonment of the wounded in Reading had been true. After a three-day journey over ice-rutted roads, crowded into wagons with little in the way of food or blankets, the wounded had been left in the streets of Reading to fare for themselves. Some froze to death, unable even to crawl to a home and seek shelter. New General Orders had been issued. Henceforth, all incapacitated soldiers at Valley Forge would be moved only by wagons driven by military personnel. [3]

Two new hospitals had been established, one in Yellow Spring, a little more than ten miles from Valley Forge. Will was one of the drivers in a sixteen wagon train transporting soldiers to the other hospital at Princeton. Most of them suffered from typhus, fevers and fluxes which left them barely living skeletons, too weak to sit up but not quite dead yet. The hope was that by moving them from the makeshift, overcrowded converted barns at Valley Forge, they would recuperate with some modicum of medical care.

They left Valley Forge two days after the blizzard. The snow on the road leading toward the ferry above Trenton was reasonably packed down which made for steady progress. Adam sat on the far side of the seat, his musket across his lap pointing outward. Two women plodded alongside the wagon, grabbing on to the slats when they slipped on the icy stretches. They said their husbands were among the poor souls lying on the rough planks of Will's wagon. Many of the soldiers were shoeless, with hardly a shirt or blanket amongst them for warmth to protect against the wind. After a half mile, once they were out of sight of Valley Forge, Will had motioned to the women. They clambered up on the coarse wooden seat and huddled against each other for warmth, sandwiched between Will and Adam.

"We would have walked to Princeton if necessary," one said. "I would not abandon my man, knowing how the helpless soldiers were mistreated at Reading."

"That will not happen at Princeton. There is a hospital there," Will said gruffly. He had no desire to engage in conversation and Adam's sullen countenance indicated he was even less inclined to do so.

When they reached the Delaware, the Captain in charge of their wagon train noticed the two women and listened to Will's explanation.

"These wives, if they truly are and not poxy camp followers, will have to justify their share of the rations. Tell them they are to take care of any of the sick in need, and not just their men," he said to Will before tramping down the line of stopped wagons. The two women, who were bent in the back tending to their husbands, peered over the sideboards and nodded they had heard the Captain's words.

"And what are we to do with this one who has died?" one asked. "He is past being taken care of," she said with some bitterness. Will looked at the ferry and the wagons ahead. They were fourth in line to cross and he did not want to give up his place.

"We will place him in the back of the wagon," Will said removing the L- shaped bolts that held the tailgate. He thought he would need Adam to help lift the body but the man was so wasted, he could do it himself. "Give this to one of the living," he said to the woman, handing over a blanket that was so thin, he could see through it. He leaped down from the wagon and plunged his hands in the snow up to his wrists to wash the feeling of death from his fingers. No time to bury him now. They would find a place in New Jersey, or at worst, he would be interred in the hospital's graveyard. In this frigid weather, his body would not rot.

Once across the river, Will and Adam paced back and forth, flexing their stiff legs, while waiting for the remaining wagons. Adam patted the fat pockets of his short jacket. The red facing, which had looked so bright when they had first met at the Marblehead Mariner barracks in Cambridge, was worn and faded.

"I am not hungry," Will said, waving his hand.

"Maybe Big Red is," Adam replied lifting the flap to reveal yellow hay. "I wandered into the ferryman's barn to warm myself," he said answering Will's questioning look. "He had plenty and what I have taken he will not miss." He grinned at Will who put his arm around his friend's shoulder and walked with him back to the wagon. Will pulled some of the hay from Adam's pocket and held it in his palms. He felt Big Red's rough upper lip nuzzle his hands and the slight touch of his teeth against his skin as the horse took the dry stalks into his mouth. After Adam's offering had been eaten, Will remained stroking Big Red's muzzle and scratching him under the chin.

"Why did you volunteer to come, Adam?"

His friend did not answer directly but looked back in the direction they had come. "Sarah was born a slave. Like my mother and father." He gazed at the grey cold sky, averting Will's stare. "Sarah's father was probably her master, the owner of the Tidewater plantation where she was raised. He sold her at age twelve. She has not seen her mother since." Adam's voice choked with anger. "She does not even know if her mother is alive. Or worse."

"What could be worse?" Will asked.

"Worse is being sold like a cow or brood mare. To a new master who abuses her and subjects her to his filthy lusts and breeds her to give birth to more slaves," he shouted. Some of the other soldiers turned and looked at Adam. "Worse is losing your daughter and never hearing from her again. Slaves do not write to each other, Will, as you and Elisabeth." He saw the hurt in his friend's eyes and realized Will was ignorant of the basic conditions of slavery.

"I am sorry, Will. Sarah's situation steals my reason."

Adam reached out to pat Big Red cautiously. "It is true that Reverend Penrose and his wife have been kind to her," he said more calmly. "However, he is still her master, this religious man, this Presbyterian Minister," he said snarling at Penrose's title. "He demands fifty-three pounds sterling for her freedom. Do you know how many years it will take to raise that sum? And all the while, this Reverend could sell, yes, sell my precious Sarah to another." He turned suddenly toward Will.

"You ask me why I volunteered to come to Princeton. I was becoming unmoored." His eyes had a wild desperate look. "As if I were on some storm- tossed sea. Nay, that would have been better because I have survived nor'easters on the St. George's Banks. I was afraid I would take Sarah and flee and kill the first man who tried to prevent me from doing so. Even General Washington himself."

Will looked at the nearby soldiers. "Adam. Keep your voice down. You do not want others to hear."

"You are right. I do not. But back at camp, I cared not. I needed to get away. I am not sure what I will do when we return. I am hoping my reason will return and prudence govern my actions. I fear, however, my impulses will prevail." He wiped his hand over his eyes as if trying to clear the desperate thoughts from his mind.

"I am your friend, Adam. You saved my life in Cambridge. I am here for you." Will said. "And always will be." He took Adam's callused hand and clasped his two over it, as if by warming his friend's he could transfer some comfort and hope.

The wagons made poor time on the frozen, rutted roads and it took another two days to reach Princeton. Will lost track of how many more invalids died. All he knew was they lost another one on their wagon. The hospital was in Nassau Hall, set back on the west side of the Princeton Trenton highway, the very same massive four story building that the Americans had assaulted with cannons and forced the British to surrender a year ago. Many of the windows were still broken. Will saw that the wooden fence surrounding the expansive lot, as well as the shrubs, had long since disappeared, burned as fuel to heat the building. Even absent the tall posted gate, the Captain led the wagons through where it had stood and directed the drivers to form a line two abreast along the length of the building.

A tall man emerged from the central entrance and strode down the stone steps. He was hatless and coatless with long wispy white hair that covered his unusually large head. He angrily confronted the Captain as he dismounted from his horse.

"I am Doctor Benjamin Rush. Why was I not informed by courier in advance of the arrival of this cargo of misery. I count sixteen wagons with Lord knows how many sick and diseased. Where am I to put them, Captain? Tell me that," he demanded.

"My orders are to deliver these men to this hospital," the Captain replied testily. "If you were not informed, you may write General Washington himself."

"Oh, I will do more than that Captain. I will write to the Congress, complaining about this gross failure of procedure, which pales, I say pales compared to the negligence concerning procurement of food, firewood and adequate supplies."

The Captain looked at the formation of wagons lined up in the hospital yard. "There are no supplies at Valley Forge. While 'tis unfortunate some of the sick died on the way, the remaining one hundred and seventy or so would certainly have died in camp."

"Is that so, Captain? You are a medical practitioner I assume. No, of course you are not. I have more than five hundred here already. They are dying at the rate of four or five a day, from fevers, ague, jaundice and the bloody flux. Some freeze to death at night and we find their emaciated corpses in the morning." The doctor, waved his arms like a giant gawky bird, and continued venting his anger at the deplorable state of the hospital. [4]

"Leave the medicine to me and those competent to practice it," he snorted. "You can be of service by helping to bring discipline to this building. Establish guards, let no patient out without a written order. Those sick but able to walk sell their meager possessions for rum and food in the town. There are drunken fights every night within this building that is a hospital in name only." [5] He motioned to the drivers waiting in place.

"Order your men to carry these miserable wretches inside. We will try and find room for them. And then, form work patrols and send them out to cut firewood. Perhaps, for once, no patient will freeze to death tonight."

There were few stretchers available. Although it brought them into contact with the foul-smelling, sick men's blistering skin and pus, and their shit stained pants, Will and Adam found it faster to carry them on their backs.

The rooms on the first floor were bitter cold. Men lay shivering on beds of dirty straw, filling every available space in the small rooms with their wasted figures. The stench of human excrement and sickness was overwhelming. The cold only added to the sense of foreboding that this was a place from which one did not emerge alive. Will followed Adam up the central staircase two flights and as gently as possible, eased the sick soldier from his back and laid him down on the cold wooden floor. The room, barely large enough for eight, now had almost twenty lying side by side. It was slightly warmer on the third floor with the late afternoon sun providing rays of light through the drafty windows.

"It seems hardly worth the journey for these unfortunate souls," Adam grumbled as he carried another soldier up the central staircase. Will grunted in agreement. The man felt light as a feather and even by the third floor landing, Will was not winded. As he lowered the man to the floor, the soldier grabbed Will's collar. His grip was surprisingly strong for one no more than skin and bones.

"Promise me a decent burial, Lieutenant," he said, the spittle on his lips forming little bubbles at the ends of his mouth. "No common grave for me. A separate plot, please and a marker. My wife will need a marker to find my body."

Will pried the soldier's fingers loose. "I promise," Will assured him, although unsure whether he would even be in Princeton when the man died.

"Your word as an Officer. Give me that comfort."

"You have my word," Will said. The man beckoned Will to bend closer. "My name is Gillet. Henry Gillet," he wheezed, partially raising himself up. "Private in Colonel Israel Angell's Rhode Islanders. My wife's name is Judith, after her grandmother," he said as if that fact were important to him. "Judith Gray Gillet," he whispered, as his head fell back on the floor.

The Private's lips were still forming his wife's name as Will backed out of the room and scrambled down the steps, pursued by groans, coughs and piteous cries at every landing. In these cramped quarters, every man was alone with his fears and memories, Will thought, gratefully sucking in deep breathes of the fresh, cold air.

Many of the drivers were reluctant to remain in the cold woods cutting trees. They drifted off and ensconced themselves before a warm fire in one of Princeton's several taverns. By the time the sun had set, Will and Adam were only one of two details still at work. They loaded the wagon in the dark and drove the familiar spur of the Princeton Trenton highway to Nassau Hall. The pile of newly felled and trimmed trees on the hospital grounds was modest, perhaps enough to last one or two days if used sparingly. They added their logs to the stack.

Will's immediate concern was to find fodder and water for Big Red. Candles shone through the first floor windows of a two story stone house on the road past the hospital. Some of the shutters hung askew. Other windows were broken and many of the rooms were dark. The British probably had looted it after they withdrew from Princeton.

Behind it, in the early evening darkness, he could make out the shape of a large barn and heard the whinnying of horses within. He was tempted to simply unhitch Big Red, lead him inside and take oats and fodder without permission. Instead, he decided to knock at the door and ask first. The Captain would requisition what was needed if the owner refused.

With Adam standing beside him, Will lifted the large brass knocker and waited as the sound reverberated through the door. He was about to raise it again when he heard the bolt being pulled back and the door opened. And there stood Captain Samuel Hadley of the Massachusetts Artillery. It was Hadley who reacted first, flinging the door open so hard it banged loudly against the doorstop. He strode out into the cold to grasp Will tightly by both shoulders, his fingers kneading Wills muscles beneath his uniform, before embracing him and banging him on the back.

"Will. It is you. What a surprise. And Private Cooper also," he said reaching down the top step to grab Adam's arm. "Come, come inside and out of this winter chill."

"What are you doing here?" Will asked recovering from his surprise. "We knocked only to ask to use the barn and obtain oats, fodder and water for Big Red."

"Although it is to you I owe my life, it was your horse that bore me from the battlefield. Certainly, to the barn first, place him in any empty stall. You will find a few sheaves of hay that are not too moldy and oats in a barrel toward the rear," he said. "But Adam. I recall you preferred to ride the waves rather than horses. Come inside and warm yourself near the fire while Will attends to Big Red."

Will grinned as he pumped water and filled the third bucket for Big Red. He thought Hadley seemed well recovered from the wound he had received at Brandywine. The grip of his arm, the one Will had prevented the surgeons from amputating, seemed strong and firm. He hurried back to the house, eager to hear Hadley's account since he had last seen him at the field hospital near Darby.

A servant led him to the kitchen where there was warm water in a basin for washing. Will scrubbed his hands and face, slicked back his hair and found his way into the main sitting room. The Captain and Adam stood off in a corner of the room engaged in quiet conversation. Dr. Rush loomed somberly by the low fire, his arm leaning on the mantle, his gaze on a heavy- set elderly man hunched down in a wide armchair, staring into the flames. Some of the spindles on the back were broken and strips of a torn floral red fabric hung down below the seat. He turned his head slowly and studied Will. He had small dark eyes beneath thick black eyebrows, that contrasted with his thinning white hair. A fleshy double chin was partially covered by a white broadcloth scarf that enveloped his thick neck.

"You are welcome to my home, Lieutenant, such as it is after the minions of the Crown have seen fit to ravage it and destroy all of my books and papers." He spoke in a deep raspy voice with a thick Scottish burr. "That unfortunately is not my greatest loss," he said. "My eldest son died for our cause." He cleared his throat. "James, even though a young man, was esteemed by others, respected already for his constant practice of Divine worship and was truly of unblemished character." He sat as if transfixed by some image of the young man and then lifted himself wearily from his worn chair. "You must excuse me. There is some correspondence from Congress that demands my attention." He waved his hand as if in benediction and lumbered from the room.

"Reverend Witherspoon's son was killed at the battle of Germantown," Dr. Rush said. "He was interred yesterday in the churchyard after the ground was sufficiently thawed by fire to bury him. Two of my doctors who succumbed to typhus, despite my best efforts to save them, are buried there as well." He slammed his hand down on the mantle. "This hospital and the others in my department are a disgrace. We labor under intolerable conditions for doctors and patients. I have begun a letter to General Washington and the loss of two of my doctors to typhus, impels me to complete it and dispatch it at once." [6] Rush patted his waistcoat pocket to assure himself his spectacles were there and without a good night, left. His heavy footsteps echoed on the stairwell as his shadow ascended the wall, lit by one stub of a candle until all was dark as they heard the door to his room close.

No one spoke for sometime. Hadley and Will's initial exuberance were dampened, not just by the gloom of the wrecked interior. It was the knowledge that Witherspoon's son who had been born and raised in this home was now buried nearby. The same cemetery contained the graves of the doctors who had perished aiding the soldiers, many of whom were themselves were close to death, lying in misery in the hospital.

The sounds of a servant's words from the kitchen and a woman's voice ended the feeling of despair and sadness. Hadley's face broke into a broad smile as Mercy Van Buskirk came in, wiping her hands on her apron.

"I have just come from the hospital," she said stopping in mid-sentence. [7] "Why Will Stoner. Indeed, it is you. What a pleasant surprise."

Will bowed slightly. "It is my pleasure to see you Miss Mercy."

"You may call her what you wish, but I call her my wife," Hadley said with a big grin. "We were married in Morristown a fortnight ago and she will return with me to Valley Forge. I am fit for service again, according to my beloved wife." He put his arm around her shoulder affectionately and escorted her toward the fire.

"Will. I never thanked you for saving Samuel's life," she said looking over her shoulder. "Rescuing him from the oncoming Grenadiers and bringing him to safety." She offered Will her hand. "I should have penned my thoughts of gratitude and sent you a letter."

"I only did my duty," Will said.

"Nonsense," Hadley shushed his wife who was about to reply. He launched into a detailed description, for Adam's benefit, of the desperate battle to halt the British advancing on the right flank of the American lines at Brandywine, his being wounded and regaining consciousness outside a field hospital in the cold darkness of the battle's aftermath.

"While I was recuperating in Morristown," he continued, "I wrote to General Knox of your bravery under fire on the hilltop, and your loyalty to me in preventing the surgeons from amputating my arm." Hadley lifted his arm high above his head to demonstrate it had healed. "I recommended you for promotion to Lieutenant. It pleases me greatly to see you are now an officer."

General Knox had not lied to him about the reasons for his promotion, Will thought. He never should have doubted the General's intentions. He vowed he never would again.

"And your Elisabeth?" Mercy asked. "Is she well?"

Will did not know how to answer. He blurted something about her remaining behind in Philadelphia and then changed his explanation, saying she had been unable to escape in time before the British occupied the city. He saw the confused looks on Hadley's face and the quick look Mercy gave her husband. Will's voice broke as he said he had not heard from her in a few weeks. Helplessly, he let his hands fall to his sides, upset he could not tell them the truth, and afraid for Elisabeth knowing that his brother suspected she was a Rebel spy.

John Stoner controlled his excitement and strolled nonchalantly down Second Street, headed toward Elfreth's Alley. He would have preferred summoning Mrs. Bates to his quarters. However, there was an urgency that he speak with her and he did not trust his man to convey that she should come immediately to his office.

The entrance to the Alley was a middle green high wooden door adjacent to the imposing columned entrances to two townhouses on either side. One would not know the Alley existed, assuming instead the door opened on to a narrow courtyard between the brick buildings, a private space to be enjoyed by the townhouses' residents. He planned to impart to her the intelligence that the 16th Dragoons would be leaving in two days to raid Princeton and capture two prominent persons there.

Colonel Harcourt expanded the plan, according to Chatsworth. More than one hundred Dragoons would leave for New Jersey to support the Loyalist Militias fighting the Rebel bands. [8] They would remain in Monmouth County for a two week campaign, while Chatsworth would immediately lead a flying squadron north to Princeton to capture the traitors and bring them to Philadelphia.

John latched the green door to the Alley behind him and ambled down the cobblestones in the shadows of the three story red brick homes on either side. Mrs. Bates's shop was at the end abutting a stone wall, a modest building with her store's bay windows on the first floor and rooms above where she and her husband lived.

As he opened the door, a small brass bell attached to the inside rang gently. Mrs. Bates emerged expectantly from the back room with a scissors in her hands. Her face registered her surprise to see him.

"I decided to come in person this time. The information I have for you is most important." He walked around the long table lined with fabrics, his hand idly caressing the cloth. "I trust we are alone."

"Yes, but I fear not for long," Mrs. Bates said, casting an anxious glance through the bay window. "Your young lady has made an appointment to visit my shop this afternoon. In fact I thought it was she when you entered."

Elisabeth must not see him in the company of Mrs. Bates. He had been foolish not to formally arrange a meeting. His craving to expose Elisabeth as a spy had led him to be hasty and incautious in his actions.

He looked at the curtains leading to the back room. "May we go in there and talk." Mrs. Bates nodded and led the way. Quickly, John related the plan by the Dragoons to raid Princeton, capture Reverend Witherspoon and Doctor Rush and bring them to Philadelphia. "Today is Wednesday. They will leave on Friday morning and could be in Princeton by this Saturday. Be sure and emphasize this urgency to Ms. Van Hooten."

"I will do so," she replied. The bell on the door jangled. "Leave through the back." Mrs. Bates put a finger to her lips and pointed to a low doorway leading into the kitchen. She left him and walked into the front room to greet Elisabeth.

John looked around the room. Instead of stepping into the kitchen, he squeezed behind two tall shelves closely packed with rolls of cloth. Hidden there, he could see through the vertical crack where the two wooden frames did not quite meet. He breathed quietly and waited.

Elisabeth entered the back room first, followed by Mrs. Bates. She wore a simple plain gown of brown that consisted of a bodice and skirt joined together. The skirt opened in the front to reveal a cream colored petticoat as part of the dress.

"The dress you asked me to modify for the City Tavern ball is here," Mrs. Bates said, reaching to the right beyond John's view. He heard a cabinet door creak open. "The silk fabric is very rich and was difficult to sew without revealing the alterations. I hope you find my work satisfactory." John heard a rustling of cloth, Mrs. Bates saying "Here let me take that," and then, he caught a glimpse of Elisabeth's stocking covered calves beneath her short linen under-petticoat. She had her back to him, her blond hair curling down her neck. Her shoulders were covered by her shift. Nothing but her firm white flesh beneath those undergarments, he thought. She moved out of his narrow field of view and grunted as Mrs. Bates laced up the stays. Another rustle of cloth and Mrs. Bates said, "There you are. That green becomes you. You look lovely," she chirped pleased with the outcome. "Here see for yourself in that mirror."

John caught a fleeting look of Elisabeth as she glided by in stocking feet.

"You do not think the bodice is too low? Perhaps too revealing?" he heard Elisabeth ask.

"My dear. I assure you it is quite a few inches higher than what most young ladies will be wearing that night. I do not approve of the flaunting of bosoms. You have nought to be ashamed of in this dress."

John leaned forward and turned his head so the right side of his face was against the rough backing of the shelves trying to see more of Elisabeth. With one eye he glimpsed the green of the gown from the rear and watched as Elisabeth bent down to put on her shoes. He imagined her firm buttocks pressing against the under-petticoat, now concealed by the outer petticoat and gown. She twirled around in front of the mirror, testing the length. Her movements created a gentle swishing noise.

"I hope that your young man is not in the Dragoons. Otherwise, he will not be in Philadelphia for any parties this weekend."

"This dress is for the ball next week," Elisabeth said. She held the side of her gown in one hand and pirouetted about the room, looking down at her stocking feet. He saw where the fabric of the bodice came to the top of her breasts, thrust up by the stays. A pity Mrs. Bates had not left it lower for his viewing pleasure. "But why might that be if my escort were a Dragoon?" Elisabeth asked. John heard the tightness in her voice and recognized her effort to suppress any eagerness.

"My husband has been repairing the fuzees for the 16th Dragoons. You know how men chatter boastfully about exploits yet to be accomplished," she said dismissively. Another rustle of silk. "They are going on a raid to Princeton to capture some doctor and another member of Congress. It is like a fox hunt for them." John heard Elisabeth exhale as Mrs. Bates undid her stays. "A chance for a dashing ride, derring-do and glory and to wreak havoc on a Rebel town." Mrs. Bates moved into his field of view, Elisabeth's street dress in her arms.

Elisabeth followed on stocking feet. He saw her standing in her shift and petticoat facing him, her chin thrust upward, the milk white skin of her neck directed his gaze downward to her high rounded bosom, as Mrs. Bates helped her into her street clothing. Through the linen he could see the swelling of her breasts. He licked his lips slowly, watching as Mrs. Bates stood behind her and buttoned Elisabeth's plain brown dress.

"Well, my escort is Captain Montresor. He is the Chief Engineer to General Howe and would be unaffected by any such business," Elisabeth said calmly. John waited for her to ask another question. Instead, Mrs. Bates also paused, just long enough and after a few moments provided what Elisabeth wanted to know.

"Good for you then having captivated your Engineer Captain. These Dragoons will miss any merriment this Friday. They leave for Jersey and expect to return with their captured Rebels by Sunday morning the latest." John heard Elisabeth moving about the room and Mrs. Bates wrapping the altered gown in old linen.

"Take this home and try it on again. Ask your friend Mrs. Lewis for her opinion. If you want any further minor modifications, I cannot do so until Friday the earliest." She paused for the obvious question from Elisabeth. What a wily woman, John thought.

"I may have some changes," Elisabeth said slowly. "Mrs. Lewis is very critical of bodices that are too revealing. May I not come by tomorrow?"

"No. I am sorry my dear. Thursdays are the days I pass through the lines and sell needles, thread, scissors and other sundries to the poor women unfortunate enough to be part of the Rebel camp at Valley Forge." She sighed. "In this cold weather the trip is a burden but they pay in coins and the money is useful."

"Very well," Elisabeth said. "I had some other errands to run this afternoon but perhaps I will hurry home and see if Mary approves. If she does not, I will be back this very day."

I am sure you will, John thought, smirking to himself. Going home to write a letter to warn of the impending raid. I will have trapped her before this night falls. He heard the bell tinkle as Elisabeth left the shop and stepped out from his hiding place, surprising Mrs. Bates.

"I thought you had left through the kitchen door," she said reprimanding him. "Lieutenant Stoner. I run a decent business. I strongly protest your watching proper young ladies in their undergarments." Her anger and indignation was genuine. John was in too good a mood to remind her of her place.

"I compliment you on your performance, Mrs. Bates. You are a very clever woman," he said inclining his head as a small gesture of respect. "It was most wise of me to select you. I also admire your sense of propriety but remember, she is a Rebel spy and not deserving of any courtesies. I wager she will be back this afternoon. I could hear it in her voice. I am so certain of it," he reached inside his waistcoat pocket, "that I am willing to pay you a little bonus now for your work." He placed a five pound note on her cutting table. "To offset any discomfort you may experience passing through the lines tomorrow," he said with a smirk. "Bring me immediately whatever message she delivers to you today." He adjusted his hat against the cold and let himself out. It had been a most successful afternoon.

He thought of the image of Elisabeth in her undergarments. He definitely would have his way with her first before turning her over to the authorities.

Elisabeth sat at the small writing table in her room, with a sheet of paper before her on which she had marked the pigpen cipher - two horizontal and two vertical lines, creating a grid of nine square boxes, three across and three down. She wrote the letters in the boxes, beginning with the letter "B", as Will had taught her, three letters per compartment with the last box in the lower right having only two - 'Z' and 'A'. Slowly, constantly referring to the grid before her, she methodically drew the appropriate box on thin strips of paper she had torn, each narrow enough to fit within fabric sewed over buttons. Dipping her quill in the glass ink container, she placed a dot, representing the desired letter in the same position as that letter in the box, consulting the grid as a guide.

Angrily she crumpled two strips she had completed and started over. She had forgotten that the absence of a dot is the first letter, one dot for the second and two dots for the third letter. It was taking so long to commit the message to paper. There was not much time left in the day. She would bring it to Mrs. Bates in the evening if necessary. She thought of what to say to her - the buttons were just a small present for a gentleman she knew - would that sound contrived? How would she explain the need for Mrs. Bates to take them this Thursday? Her haste would arouse suspicion. After all, why not ask her to take them next week? Surely there was no hurry to simply deliver some buttons. She concentrated on writing the cipher correctly, but the questions nagged at her.

She needed Mary home to sew the messages into the cloth coverings of the buttons. But how could she be sure the warning would be delivered in time for someone to get the word to Princeton? She could not ask Mrs. Bates to deliver her package before selling her sundries to the camp women. And even if she turned it over to some officer, what assurance was there that he would act promptly? After all, Mrs. Bates would say, they were only buttons. She put down the quill and touched the grid and the strips of paper with the ciphers to the candle flame. The ashes floated slowly to the table. No, she concluded. The only way to ensure the warning reached its destination in time was for her to pass between the lines. Tomorrow.

She heard the front door close and Mary calling to see if she were home. Gratefully, Elisabeth raced downstairs and found her in the kitchen. "I have just come from the Meeting House," she said. "Why my dear, you look distraught. Is all not well with you?"

Elisabeth told about her visit with Mrs. Bates, the imminent raid on Princeton to capture some doctor and a Reverend who was a member of Congress and bring them back to Philadelphia.

"I suspect it is our own Doctor Rush," Mary replied. "Although why he would be in Princeton instead of at Valley Forge where soldiers by the hundreds suffer from disease and illness seems strange. His duty would be to remain there, I would think."

"Mary. Strange or not, I have resolved to cross the lines tomorrow morning and convey this information to Will. I have thought it through and it is the only way."

Mary shook the pot to assure herself there was enough water and there was no need to go outside to the pump. "I am in need of some tea and will brew enough for both of us," Mary said. "I had expected news of my husband at the Meeting Hall but there was none. Our Minister believes John and the others are still at Winchester." She hung the pot on a hook over the fireplace, stoked the logs with an iron poker and held her hands toward the flames. Elisabeth dragged the short bench toward the hearth and the two women sat in silence side by side.

"No, Elisabeth. It will not do for you to go."

"I must and you shall not stop me."

"Perhaps I can prevail upon your reason," Mary said as she wrapped her hand in a thick rag and lifted the pot off the hook. She poured two cups at the small kitchen table. Elisabeth sat rigidly straight in her chair, like a skittish colt eager to bolt and be on its way.

"First and foremost, what if Mrs. Bates sees you, whether before or after you pass the lines. That will arouse her suspicions. Have you thought what you would tell her is your reason for being there?" Elisabeth remained silent but Mary's question was troubling.

"In addition," Mary continued, "you are too pretty and refined not to arouse the interest of sentries and Loyalist Militias who guard the roads from the city. They will question you closely and since you obviously are not a market woman, they will be most suspicious." Mary gently lowered her cup. "Your warning will do no good, my dear, unless you are able to deliver it." Elisabeth was beginning to regret having impetuously destroyed the ciphers she had written so laboriously.

"I could wear old clothes and a worn cloak. Disguise my appearance. Carry a basket of some goods we could contrive together," Elisabeth said, effecting confidence that she could deceive the posted guards or militiamen.

Mary wagged her finger. "It will not serve, my dear. And I must say," she continued, "I am chary of the information you have obtained. We have never heard of such a hospital in Princeton. The very journey from Valley Forge to there would kill the poor wretches, exposed to the harsh elements of winter as they would be." She took another sip of tea, savoring the taste, before continuing. "Mrs. Bates may be unknowingly passing along false rumors she has heard though I do not doubt the good woman's integrity."

"We must assume the information is correct," Elisabeth responded. "Otherwise, if it turns out to be true and I did not communicate the warning, I would be responsible for their capture. And if the Dragoons set homes and even the hospital on fire, the deaths of those poor wretches would . . ." She turned toward the fire, seeing the flickers of the flaming logs consuming a building in a snowy field.

She felt Mary's hand on hers. "Yes, my dear. We must convey the warning despite my reservations. But I will cross the lines tomorrow. I will be as Mrs. Bates will be, carrying scissors, needles and half used spools of thread to sell to women from the camp at Valley Forge."

"No, Mary. You must not. I cannot ask you to. . ."

"You did not. I told you I will go. Think about it Elisabeth. Who has a better possibility of not arousing anyone's suspicions? Mary Lewis, a plain Quaker market woman, whose husband has been unjustly imprisoned by these Rebels and needs to sell sundries to make ends meet. Or you, a pretty young lady who some may recognize as having been escorted around town by a well-known Captain on General Howe's staff."

Elisabeth knew Mary was correct. She imagined her friend's rotund figure blending together with a group of other women, passing by the sentries and trundling down the road toward Valley Forge.

"But who will you meet with and whom will you tell?"

"I shall ask for your Will and if he cannot be found, I shall seek out William Knox, who you told me is the General's brother."

Elisabeth squeezed Mary's hand. "You are compromising your faith's neutrality by undertaking such a mission."

Mary shook her head in disagreement. "It is not my faith which has declared neutrality but our Leaders. The precepts of my faith require me to save lives and you consider this information will do so." She wagged her finger at Elisabeth. "I still believe these are false rumors. Imagine, a hospital in Princeton while those in need of the care of skilled practitioners such as Doctor Rush are at Valley Forge." She tut-tutted and shook her head. "The very idea is nonsense."

Chapter 4 - The Hospital at Princeton

In the pre-dawn mist, Captain Chatsworth led the troop of thirty-four dragoons out of the dankness of Frog Hollow and up the sawmill road. A frozen brook lay on their right, shrouded in winter fog. It was the same route the Rebels had taken more than a year ago when they launched their surprise attack on the British in Princeton. Now it was the dragoons' turn.

They rode past the apple orchards where much of the battle had taken place. The twisted dead branches of the fruit trees, fatally maimed by heavy musket and cannon fire, appeared as gnarled, grasping fingers in the mist. They left the road and trotted up the sloping open fields toward Witherspoon's house, hidden above the hill on the south side of the Princeton Trenton Highway. A quick snatch of the two traitors in their nightshirts, a fast gallop down the highway, skirting Trenton in the early morning hours before most people were about, and then crossing the Delaware at Bristol where the ferry would be held by Loyalists and another troop of the 16th Dragoons. They would be back in their quarters in Philadelphia by evening.

At the top of the rise, Chatsworth paused and motioned with his hand for the troopers to form a line. At this early hour, a few candles flickered from the hospital windows on the far side of the road. The Reverend's home, closest to them was dark, save for a lantern burning outside the front door.

An owl hooted from somewhere in the gloom to his right.

Otherwise, all was silence. No barking dogs, no geese in a yard, honking to give the alarm.

Satisfied, Chatsworth drew his fuzee from the scabbard, held it aloft and waved the men forward. Once on the highway, by pre-arranged plan, they formed into three groups. Chatsworth led fourteen troopers at a gallop to Witherspoon's house while six others raced past to block the road leading into Princeton. The last contingent of fourteen rode into the darkened yard of Nassau Hall to deal with any armed soldiers he assumed would be within or in makeshift barracks in adjoining buildings.

Chatsworth pulled back on the reins and swung one foot over the saddle. Suddenly, the nine shuttered windows on the front of the house were thrown open. He heard the shouted command "Give Fire," and a blast of muskets pierced the darkness. The trooper next to him cried out as he was blown from the saddle. A second volley followed immediately. Chatsworth, with one foot on the ground and the other still in the stirrup was shielded by his mount. He fired his fuzee under his horse's neck at an open window. "Ambush," Chatsworth yelled as loudly as he could. He turned his horse away from the house, leaped back in the saddle and galloped back toward the highway. A swarm of horsemen swept around the rear of Nassau Hall with shouts of "Have at them! Cut them down!"

Chatsworth with his remaining troopers rode into Nassau Hall's open yard as the dragoons there fired a volley at the oncoming Rebel cavalry. Chatsworth yanked the reins to turn his horse to face the Rebel cavalry, presenting a smaller target. He drew one of the brace of pistols he carried in his saddlebag, kneed his mount forward and charged. He fired his pistol at point blank into the face of an oncoming trooper. The flash of the powder in the firing pan momentarily blinded him but he saw the man flop backwards. He was not certain in the confusion and darkness whether the shot from his second pistol had brought down another Rebel. Dropping the pistol back into the bag he unsheathed his saber and felt the cold metal of the hilt in his hand. He slashed at one man, the force of his sabre blow severing the Rebel's up thrust arm just below the elbow. The bloody forearm with the fingers still gripping the Rebel's sword hit Chatsworth's horse on the nose before it fell to the ground. He sensed rather than saw the Rebel cavalry hesitate as they lost the momentum of their initial surprise attack.

Damn the decision to forgo a trumpeter to accompany his troop on the raid, he thought. "To the highway. Back to the highway," Chatsworth yelled.

In the tumult and confusion that followed, the dragoons dashed down the road toward Trenton. Chatsworth led a rearguard action against a squad of overeager but inexperienced Rebel cavalry, attacking them as they slowed to cross a narrow wooden bridge. He fought with a wrath and anger brought on by the failure of the raid, taking savage satisfaction at cutting down those who had thwarted the kidnapping. Satisfied that they were free from further pursuit, they caught up with the rest of the dragoons and halted at a farm on the outskirts of Trenton. Only twenty-two of them remained.

Chatsworth posted four pickets on the road toward Princeton. The subdued troopers sat around the kitchen table and hearth, grimly wiping blood from their sabers, while the farmer and his wife nervously brought them cider and bread.

"I swear I will discover the spy who betrayed us and personally hang him from the highest gallows in Philadelphia," Chatsworth said, resetting the ramrod in one of his pistols. He glared at the woman and then her husband who were almost faint with fear of the cavalrymen in their home. Some Rebel sympathizer, Chatsworth thought, a farmer or traveler in the area, had spied them camping the night before. Rebel cavalry must have been summoned from nearby and arrived in time to fortify the Witherspoon house. Sooner or later, the Rebels would boast about this skirmish. Someone's name would be given out as having sounded the alarm. As he fingered the solid wood stock of one pistol with the silver oval on the handle, now engraved with his initials, he thought of John Stoner. He had given Chatsworth these two fine weapons as a gift after the fire in New York City. John was too obsequious at times but he did have his uses. Once they returned to Philadelphia, Chatsworth would ask Stoner to unleash his network of spies, paid informers and other lowlifes he relied upon to get him the names of those who had given the dragoons away. Then he would extract vengeance for the loss of a dozen of his men.

—∞—

The bright crisp sunlight of the mid-morning revealed the dark stains of blood in Reverend Witherspoon's yard, marking where the dragoons had fallen. Ten troopers in all had been killed, their bodies loaded in wheelbarrows and carted off to the graveyard. The wounded had been taken to a barn, to await their turn for the surgeon's saw or needle. Will walked across the yard, a trooper's jacket and breeches tucked under his arm. A long streak of crimson near the collar marked where the man's blood had spilled from the musket ball that had shattered his jaw. The red jacket was of good quality wool. He shuddered at the memory of feeling the dead soldier's still warm flesh when he stripped him of his clothes. He would give them to Private Gillet. It would at least keep the upper part of the sick man warmer than his threadbare and torn linen uniform.

When he reached the room on the third floor, Gillet was not on his straw pallet. Confused, Will retraced his steps from the landing, to be sure he was in the right room. He peered into their faces, asking each one where Gillet was. Most were too sick to answer and the response from those who could was "most likely died and carted away," or "died in his sleep which is all the more better for him."

He saw a townswoman in one of the nearby rooms feeding a soldier with a ladle from a soup pot.

"Do you know what has happened to the Private in that other room?" Will said pointing in a futile gesture down the hall.

She looked up at him with pity. "Lieutenant. I do not know any of these poor men's names or rank. You should ask Mrs. Hadley. She is about on this floor or the one below." Will ran from one room to the next until he found her distributing linen compresses to other women.

"Mercy," he said. "I am looking for a Private and he is no longer where he was yesterday. Private Gillet of a Rhode Island Regiment," he blurted out, as if that description would identify him to her. "He was in that room two from the landing," he said with desperation.

"Will," she said quietly. "Many of these poor men die during the night. The burial crews remove them to the Churchyard where graves have been prepared."

He did not wait for any further explanation but dashed down the stairs still carrying the jacket and breeches and ran through the snow toward the Church. A line of corpses, face up, lay in the shadow of the church wall awaiting burial. Will squatted down next to each man, staring at their faces, their sightless eyes, their gaping mouths with stained and broken teeth. None were Gillet.

"Sergeant," he called out to the man in charge of the burial crew. "Are there any other of our dead?"

"No, sir. Only the bloody dragoons," and he uttered a series of curses, as if the corpses of the cavalry could hear his damning their souls.

Back to the hospital, in the main hall, Will recognized one of the wives who had ridden in his wagon from Valley Forge. "Excuse me Miss. I need help in finding an invalid soldier." He described Private Gillet's room on the third floor.

"This morning we moved some of the sick men about. Dr. Rush ordered it, I was told. Those with the ague and bloody flux together in several rooms, those with whatever diseases the learned doctor calls them, I know not what, in others." She eyed the jacket and breeches Will held. "My husband suffers from cold and chills at night. If you do not find this soldier please think of my man."

Will mumbled he would and ran up the steps. Methodically, he went from room to room, stepping carefully around the emaciated men lying in their own filth, moaning or shivering on the straw-covered wooden planked floor. The stench of excrement and unwashed bodies filled his nostrils. He found Gillet in a room that for the moment was bathed in sunlight. Despite the warmth of the rays, Gillet was shivering under his thin jacket, reversed to cover his chest like a short blanket. Will helped him to sit up, put his arms through the sleeves and then lay the trooper's red coat over him.

"I am very pleased to see you alive," Will said, rolling up the breeches and placing them behind the Private's head as a pillow. Gillet's teeth chattered. "This fever weakens me. Earlier this very morning, after I was moved, a good doctor came and bled me, saying it would improve my health." He shivered under the red jacket. "I should have stayed in barracks, cold as they were, and not come here to die. They will take all of my blood and when I am drained dry, claim they have cured me though I be a lifeless corpse.

Damn them, the bloodsucking asses."

"You should not question the wisdom of the doctors. I have seen many men bled and rid of their fever and ready for service in a matter of days," Will said confidently. Gillet stared at him, wanting to grasp at his hopeful words but suspicious they were lies to ease his mind.

"I am to leave tomorrow morning." Gillet tried to sit up in protest. Will put his hand gently on his chest. "A good friend of mine, Private Adam Cooper, will remain here another few days until the wagons are to return to Valley Forge." He took Gillet's hand in his and squeezed his cold bony fingers. "Adam will look in on you each day."

"I thank him for his attention but he must abide by your promise for a separate marked grave. I depend upon you to tell him."

"I already have. Adam will honor my promise which I strongly believe will not be necessary to be fulfilled." Somewhere in the room, a soldier coughed steadily between gasps for breath, the sound in his throat like a rattling of coffee beans shaken in a dry pot. Will had heard that cough before. Death for that one was not too distant, he thought, willing himself not to look around. He patted Gillet's hand. "Warmth and nourishment will help you regain strength. I will see you in Valley Forge before the spring campaign against the British."

"I wish it to be true," he croaked, "but in a few days I will be no more and never see you, nor my beloved Judith, nor any other person that walks this earth." His eyes filled with tears and he turned his face away.

Will was about to utter some additional words of encouragement, but thought they would sound hollow with Gillet waking every morning to the sight of those who had died during the night.

Instead he knelt closer to the Private and began, in a calm low voice to talk about his love for Elisabeth, the anxiety he felt when they were separated, and his fear he would never see her again. He spoke of how his love sustained and carried him through his darkest moments. He told Gillet the story of Captain Hadley and Miss Mercy, their first meeting at the makeshift hospital in Morristown, of Samuel being wounded and her search and care for him and his recovery.

"I will ask Mercy, who is now married to my friend the Captain, to visit you. She attends at this hospital. Let her presence remind you of the love for your wife Judith that you have expressed to me. Think of that love as being unbreakable, as is mine for my Elisabeth, and let that be the strength that leads you to return to health."

Will stood up, arching his back to relieve the stiffness from kneeling. "I expect to see you at Valley Forge, Private Gillet," he said, as confidently as possible. He crossed the narrowing shaft of sunlight that pointed like an arrow to the door and quickly departed without looking back.

Early Sunday morning, with the frost still on the fields and a three quarter moon to guide him, Will saddled Big Red, made sure the bags with dispatches and correspondence were secured and rode south. Even in the early morning, there were people about on the Princeton Trenton highway - farmers and woodsmen in their ox-drawn sleds lumbering toward whichever town was the nearest, a few lone riders, perhaps tradesmen or mechanics and men on foot who had the look of deserters and the need to travel as far as possible in darkness.

Will reached Trenton shortly after dawn. An ugly grey sky loomed ahead. From the heights above the town, the scars of the battle of Trenton and destruction wrought by Hessian and British troops during the occupation more than a year ago were clearly evident. Will took the upper Pennington road that led around the town to the ferry. He was relieved to see the ice floes in the Delaware were few and far between. Across the river a group of blue uniformed soldiers clustered around a bonfire.

"Tis seven dollars for you and the horse," the ferryman said, emerging from his wooden shack with brown moldy boughs for a roof. He held his coat around his throat and scratched his ass.

"I am a courier on official business to Valley Forge," Will said turning Big Red to face the man.

"That is a big horse," the man observed. "I should charge you more for poling both of you across." A young boy, around fourteen with a jacket too big and breeches too short, came from around the cabin and stood next to him. At his age Will thought, I was hauling cannons from Fort Ticonderoga to Cambridge, and eager to be free of my father's yoke.

Two herdsmen, driving several bony cattle before them, came down the slope toward the ferry. Big Red snorted and pawed the brown snow. Will patted his neck, knowing of his horse's dislike of the cattle's smell.

"Now that you have other passengers," Will said, "you will take me across with them, and I will help pole." The ferryman hesitated, calculating how much he could charge the herders per head and make up the loss of a fee for Will.

"Done," said the man, counting the cattle coming towards the river. Will hefted the pole in his hand as the boy and his father pushed off from the shore. The flat-bottomed raft moved smoothly into the current. He was on the upriver side and, as Nat and Adam had taught him, he poled rhythmically with an eye to warding off ice floes.

"We are heading to Valley Forge with our beeves," one of the herders said to Will.

"When I last left, there was great need for meat for the soldiers," Will replied, glancing up at the cattle and thinking, they would not provide much sustenance for very many.

"Good. Then they will fetch a fine price even though it will be in Continentals."

"Why not sell them to the Crown for sterling?" Will asked, testing the man.

"He has a son with the Army," he replied, gesturing with his head toward the other herder. "Besides, 'tis our dooty to the cause." The way he said it made Will suspicious. Perhaps there was nothing to it but maybe the men intended to cross the Delaware as patriots and then with their greed as their guide, find a British foraging party and sell to them.

The ferry bumped against the frozen shore and the boy waded through ankle deep water to make it fast. Will mounted Big Red who jumped the short distance. The cattle bellowed in panic as the ferry rocked from the loss of the horse's weight.

A Corporal held up his hand and Will produced a note from Dr.

Rush, countersigned by Captain Hadley, for unimpeded passage. Will leaned down and took the note, tucking it in his waistcoat pocket and buttoning his outer jacket up again.

"I would question those herders closely. They say they are driving the beeves to Valley Forge. That is a long way to go on foot and they may prefer to sell to the Crown."

"Oh, do they now," the Corporal responded. "We have dealt with their like before. We will ease their travels by escorting them to the next crossroads." He grinned. "There is a Continental paymaster there and a large enclosure for cattle. They will be back across the river in no time but surely not the happier for it."

It took Will the better part of the day of hard riding to cover the forty-six miles to Valley Forge. He was stopped twice by roving militias and once by cavalry on patrol. It was almost dark when he found the Gulph Road leading to camp and the side road to the solid stone house that served as General Washington's headquarters. Tired from being in the saddle since dawn, he dismounted stiffly and tied Big Red's reins to the post. He was starving for he had nothing to eat but some hard bread and a bit of cheese Mercy had given him from Reverend Witherspoon's kitchen. Candles burned in every window, illuminating four of the General's personal guards, the flames reflected in the polished bayonets on their muskets. He unbuckled the saddlebags, slung them over his shoulder and, after stating his purpose was admitted.

An orderly sat at a small table in the narrow center hallway, barely leaving enough room for officers to pass into the adjoining rooms or ascend the stairway.

"Letters and dispatches for General Washington," Will said, feeling the rush of warm air from the fireplace ablaze in the room to his right. A group of officers sat on benches close to the fire, their backs to the hallway, listening to one reading from a sheet of paper.

"Name and rank," the orderly asked. He noted them down in the log, as Will flexed his fingers, stiff and frozen from hours of gripping the reins. They throbbed from being warmed too quickly.

"There are also letters addressed to the President of the Congress,"

Will said, pointing to a packet, bound with string that Dr. Rush had given him. The orderly placed them aside and handed Will the quill. It felt awkward in his hand and for a moment, he thought he would not be able to grasp it properly, the circulation not having fully returned to his fingers. He initialed the entry, leaving a smudge of dirt and blood from his split fingers on the page.

After unsaddling Big Red and leaving him in an empty stall in the barn, Will walked through the tamped down snow to his Regiment's line of huts. He was puzzled that there were only a few horses in the barn. Not that many could have died since he left for Princeton, he thought. He would have to see about oats and forage in the morning. He had already searched the barn and found nothing. Like so many other nights at Valley Forge, he and Big Red would go to sleep without.

His hut was deserted, cold and dank. He discovered a few mid-sized branches and logs and was able to start a flicker of fire using his flint to ignite the kindling. As the flames licked at the branches and then the bark of the logs caught fire, he warmed his hands, took off his boots and squatting on a roughly hewn stool, wriggled his stocking toes close to the fireplace. In the firelight, he noted the two pallets looked as unused as his was. He hoped the two others had not been taken sick and carried to one of the sheds that served as hospitals in Valley Forge. He would inquire tomorrow. He curled up in a ball close to the fire, with his wool scarf wrapped around his ears and his jacket collar high on his neck and exhausted fell asleep.

"Will. Will Stoner. Are you there?" The pounding of a fist on the wooden door awoke him. Stiffly, he arose, thinking the voice sounded familiar but, still groggy from his deep sleep, was unable to recognize it. He threw the wooden plank that barred the door from the inside and saw Billy Knox framed against the bright morning sky.

"Ah. It is so good to see you," Billy said, slightly out of breath. "This morning, at the Officers council, my brother heard you had delivered dispatches and sent me immediately to find you." He took Will by the arm. "Come with me to our quarters. You can wash there and have a better breakfast than fire cakes."

As they walked up the Valley Road, Billy told him General Knox had been extremely troubled by information warning of an enemy cavalry raid on the hospital at Princeton to capture two prominent patriots. He had feared for Will's safety. Captain Lee had dispatched a squadron, on General Washington's orders, and the account of the skirmish, in one of the letters Will had brought, was the first news they had. "Still, it did not answer whether you were safe or not and my brother sent me on the run to fetch you."

Will told him of the little of the action he had seen, waiting at a window defending the hospital but not firing a shot as Lee's troopers engaged the British Dragoons and chased them down the highway. He mentioned the burial detail the following morning but omitted telling of the British dead being stripped and their clothing given to the patients in the hospital, lying on their filthy straw, shivering under threadbare blankets. Some particulars were best left unsaid.

"There is not much for me to add other than Captain Hadley will be arriving in Valley Forge, along with his new bride."

"She will have much distinguished company," Billy responded. "General Greene's wife has been here since late January, and Mrs. Washington arrived by carriage the day after you left, sore and tired from her journey. However, our Commander is all the more in better spirits for her presence. And my brother received a letter from Mrs. Knox that she is leaving Boston and is on her way together with little Lucy to join us here." [1]

The building that Knox had chosen for his quarters, just across the junction with Yellow Springs Road, seemed to Will larger than General Washington's and solidly built. Billy directed him to their right, through the dining room and into the service quarters. Despite his hunger, Will stripped down to his breeches in the kitchen and washed his face and arms in warm water heated in pots in the wide fireplace, combed his hair, and did his best to make himself presentable. Billy joined him in the kitchen for a meager breakfast of bread and hot corn mush. Will wolfed it down and gratefully acknowledged another bowl placed before him by the female cook. He was thinking of Adam's professed love for Sarah and half heard Billy talking about food, a subject he always found unpleasant to dwell on. It only increased one's awareness of the lack of it.

"You will be joining the others from the Regiment west of York. I am told there is a surfeit of good beef, bread and even cheeses," Billy said.

"Why is the Regiment there?" Will asked, thinking this explained the emptiness in the barn and the officers gone from his hut.

"My brother petitioned General Washington for permission to move most of the artillery from Valley Forge. We are losing so many horses to starvation, there will be none left to haul cannons for the spring campaign." [2] Will finished mopping his bowl with the last crust of bread. "We cannot take to the field with untrained plow horses pulling six, nine and twelve- pounders. They may be good enough plodding down roads but not for maneuvering in battle." Will nodded his assent. He wanted to ask Billy what he knew about Elisabeth. There were others about in the kitchen. He restrained himself and would wait until he met the General.

It was not until mid-afternoon when Knox announced his arrival by a deep booming greeting to the two sentries posted at the entry to the yard. Will jumped up and was in the hall standing behind Billy when the General strode through the front door. Will could see he had lost some weight. His waistcoat was loose around his middle and turkey-like wattles hung beneath his neck. He broke into a broad smile upon seeing Will.

"Ah, brother. You found him. This brightens my day and lightens my heart to see you standing here whole and hearty. My lad, how goes it?" He unclasped his cloak and handed it to Billy, and wrapped Will in a bearlike embrace. "Come into the dining room and join me for my meal. We are on short rations, like everyone else, but we will share and make do." He put a meaty hand on Will's shoulder. "Billy. Tell the cook there is another for dinner and then join us. We have much to discuss."

The three of them finished a tureen of cabbage soup and a large pot of stew, with more onions and potatoes than chicken. Will thought in better times the General would have by himself devoured the one chicken, which was tough enough to be a rooster. Will appreciated sharing this meal that was far better than the normal fare he was accustomed to at Valley Forge. After the servant girl cleared the table and left them with mugs of watered mulled cider, Knox leaned forward and patted Will's hand.

"Your Elisabeth provided us with such vital information as to prevent the kidnapping of two of our most prominent leaders, Dr. Rush and Reverend Witherspoon. You know the Quaker woman, Mary Lewis." Will nodded, recalling her pleasant smiling face. He, Elisabeth, Captain Hadley and Miss Mercy had sat in her parlor, on Independence Day in Philadelphia after he and the Captain had protected the Lewis home from being attacked by a gang of thuggish patriots.

He warmed his fingers around the mug and listened as Knox told of Mary trudging down the Germantown Road, having passed through the lines, accosting a cavalry officer at one of the taverns and demanding to be brought to meet Will or Brother Billy. The officer had the good judgment to immediately ride, with her sitting side-saddle behind him, to the camp and not waste time looking for Will but to bring her instantly to this house, where fortunately Billy was present. Billy received her message, came forthwith to General Washington's headquarters, repeated the warning to General Knox and within the hour, orders were issued for Captain Lee to dispatch a squadron for the fast, hard ride to Princeton.

"I knew you had taken the wounded to Princeton and worried for your safety. It is a wonder that although your Elisabeth did not know, she through inadvertence or Divine intercession obtained information and conveyed it to prevent any harm coming to you." Knox leaned back in his chair, his hands clasped behind his thick neck. "It is an indication that Providence favors the two of you being together for life on this earth." He chuckled. "I too have interceded on your behalf with Elisabeth's father for his permission for her to marry you but have not yet been favored with a reply."

"And what word of Elisabeth since?" Will asked, the anxiety clear in his voice.

"Mary Lewis says she is well, and unknowingly protected by this Captain Montresor from any of your brother's mischief. Write her lad. Date your letter from Valley Forge. Tell her nothing about your excursion to Princeton or your going to York. No secret messages in invisible ink. There is no need. Tomorrow you will carry dispatches and letters from General Washington and others to the Congress."

"But that will be farther from Philadelphia. How will her letters reach me?"

"There is more than enough correspondence back and forth between York and Valley Forge to keep teams of couriers riding every day of the week. If the good members of Congress devoted more of their energies to the survival of our Army by providing the necessities of food, clothing, blankets and shoes as they devote to their scribbling, we could retake Philadelphia in a day." He paused as if thinking of some particular miscreant deserving of more of his anger but decided against it.

"You are to report to Colonel Sargent in York. He has established himself and most of our Regiment west of the city where there is ample forage and fields for practice. You will partake of the training of artillery horses and gun crews. If you can teach the men and horses to be as calm under fire as you and your big horse, by spring the artillery will be ready for the campaign." Knox stood up, his chair scraping on the hard wood floor.

"I will see you in a few months, Lieutenant Stoner. By then, with the help of Providence, we will drive the British from Philadelphia and you and Elisabeth shall be reunited." The General clapped Will on the shoulder. "Truly lad, there are better times ahead for us and our cause."

Will followed Billy to the kitchen, sat down at a corner of the table and spread the sheet of paper before him. He felt a warm glow and sense of tranquility he had not felt in weeks. The General's words of praise and his real concern for Will's well-being were better than any promotion. His optimism was infectious. Better to be infected with that than camp fever, he thought, as he put quill to paper and began his letter to Elisabeth.

Chapter 5 - The Madness of Anger

Georg slid the tin foot-warmer with glowing charcoal under Mrs. Kierney's feet. "Is goot?" he asked, adjusting the long blanket over her shoes.

"Thank you, Georg. It feels good," she said emphasizing the "d."

James Kierney flicked the reins lightly on Daniel's flanks. The horse responded and the sleigh, with Sarah sitting proudly besides James up front and his mother and younger sister seated in the back, glided down the road and across the newly completed bridge over the creek.

The family was off to church and on to visit friends overnight before returning on Tuesday. James had suggested Georg should be included on the trip, but his father explained not every one welcomed Hessian prisoners into their homes. Thomas thought it better for Georg to remain on the farm while he rode to the carpenter for a replacement horizontal gear for the mill wheel. Besides, there was much work to be done.

There always was, Georg thought, not that he minded. He enjoyed it all, working with his hands, whether hewing logs with a broad axe or carrying stones to make a wall. He had been happiest building the new grist mill and he knew Mr. Kierney had been well pleased with his work. Soon it would be spring again. Then Georg would grip the plow and walk behind the family's plodding ox, making furrows in the fields, his nostrils filled with the fresh smell of the newly turned earth.

He chided himself for daydreaming. The winter chores awaited. With the family gone, and a low, dying fire in the hearth, Georg set a ladder against the chimney searching for cracks in the mortar or spaces where the stones had come apart. Mr. Kierney was reputed to be the best stone fitter in the county. Georg admired his work, each stone fitting seamlessly into the next. He looked for tendrils of smoke and felt for escaping heat and found none. Satisfied, he climbed on to the roof and inspected the shingles adjoining the chimney. Then he scuttled along the peak to the other end and sat with his legs hanging over, enjoying the clear winter air and the view of a stand of uncut timber beyond the barn. When he had been brought to the Kierney farm, more than a year ago, that forest bordered the barn. Now, there were two cleared fields on either side, white snow-covered rectangles thrusting up to the new tree line.

A raven, cawing loudly, rose from within the woods, followed by two others, and circled before settling on the branches of a large oak about twenty yards from the barn. Abigail the cow mooed softly. The geese honked noisily and remained inside. Georg scanned the forest. It could be nothing or a bear, or worse, wolves. It had been a harsh winter and the smell of the farm animals could attract a hungry predator. The rifle was in the house, hanging on iron hooks, together with the powder horn. He waited, watching from his vantage point for any movement before climbing down the ladder and entering the house. He took the long rifle with him, walked to the barn and loaded it inside. The animals in their stalls seemed placid enough. He laid the rifle against a thick vertical pillar, raked the urine-soaked straw from the cow's stall and replaced it with a fresh sheave. Still wary, he carried the rifle in one hand to the half frozen mill pond, filled a bucket and returned to the barn. Inside, he sensed rather than saw something in the shadows. A ragged figure hobbled toward him, arms outstretched.

"Georg. Du must mir helfen."

"Christoph? Ist das du?" he asked not believing that this thin husk of a man with the long unkempt hair and beard was his companion from the von Seckendorf Company.

"Ja." Georg caught him as his friend collapsed in his arms. "Help me, please I have run away. I can take it no longer."

Georg, alarmed by Christoph's emaciated condition, supported him from the barn to the forge hut where he hurriedly restoked the fire. Christoph sat bent over, rocking back and forth, with his hands under his armpits. His tattered jacket, the original uniform issued when they had set sail for America, was threadbare and encrusted with dirt. The elbows were worn through as were the knees on his breeches. His chest was bare except for shreds of linen, he had no stockings and his feet were partly covered by two pieces of cracked leather. Christoph's foul body odor filled the warm confines of the little room.

"You stink like a pig," Georg said.

"That is where Mr. Langley made me sleep. In the pig pen. Ever since his son ran away to join the Rebels."

"Stay here," Georg said. As he sprinted up to the house he thought, that was an idiotic thing to say. Christoph was not going anywhere. It must have taken every bit of his waning strength to struggle to the Kierney farm, through the snow in this bitter cold. He grabbed some bread, cheese and a pitcher of cider. He left Christoph hungrily wolfing down the food and trudged back to the house. He returned with the large copper basin the family used for bathing. Filling it with snow, Georg positioned it next to the forge, placed a pot of water on the hearth and when it was hot, poured it into the rectangular basin, filling it until steamy tendrils wafted toward the low rough-hewn shingles.

"Christoph. Take off all your clothes and scrub yourself," he commanded, handing his friend a small piece of lye soap. "I will give you some of my clothes to wear." Georg wished he had a spare pair of shoes or boots but ever since he had arrived at the Kierney's he had worn wooden clogs. Not very good for traveling long distances but more than adequate for farm work. He opened the trunk the Kierneys had given him, took out a linen shirt, his only extra pair of breeches that he wore to church when he accompanied the family, and a patched wool jacket that was too small for him anyway. As Christoph dressed, Georg saw he had lost considerable weight. The two of them had both been more than six feet tall and robust when they were conscripted. Now, the sleeves of Georg's spare jacket hung on his thin frame and reached below Christoph's wrists. The breeches sagged from Christoph's bony hips and came down below the knee. Well and good, Georg thought. He had no stockings to give him anyway.

"Does Mr. Langley know you have fled?"

"They went to church," Christoph replied. "They will know I am gone when they return in the late afternoon."

"After he searches the woods near his farm, he will come here next. Shave yourself with my razor," Georg said, motioning to his knapsack hanging on a wooden peg. "I will go outside and cover your tracks."

Georg pulled the two-runner oak sledgebarrow from the barn. Dragging it behind him, he retraced Christoph's path from the woods to the barn, loaded it with logs and hauled it up the hill to the house. There he unloaded the firewood. He glanced at the hearth, noted the empty place over the mantel and remembered he had left the rifle in the barn. He brought the rifle with him into the forge. Christoph had finished shaving. Georg took the razor from him and, as best he could, he cut his straggly hair, leaving him with a stubby and rough haircut, but one that would not necessarily attract attention. He swept the cut hair onto a shovel and threw it into the fire, followed by the rags Christoph had worn.

"You cannot stay here," Georg said.

"I know. I want to rejoin our Regiment. In Philadelphia."

"Why? Why go back to fighting a war when the British have treated us so badly?" Georg took his friend by the shoulders, feeling his scarecrow frame beneath the shirt. "No. I meant you cannot stay in the forge room. I can hide you until Mr. Kierney returns. There is a root cellar. He is a kindly man. He will protect you."

Christoph shook his head. "For me it was not like it was for you. My farmer abused me from the first day in the saw pit. He housed me like an animal, treated me as a beast of burden and made it plain he cared not if I lived or starved to death." He pushed Georg away. "You saw yourself when we visited to help build the bridge. You heard him talk to your Kierney about me."

He sat on the warm bricks of the forge, his hands under his thighs, his bare feet just off the floor. "It was bad after the son ran away. It became terrible after his son was killed. I was his prisoner on his own farm." He looked up at the ceiling. Georg saw he was crying. "He blamed me, cursed me, beat me, whipped me. Once he hit me across the knees with a shovel. To him, I am a Hessian bastard. No more. No more," he shuddered.

Georg looked out the door. It was getting dark. The Langley family would be returning from church about now. Would he come looking for Christoph tonight? Or would he wait until light to scour his farmland and then head straight for the Kierney place? Georg decided to chance it and wait. Christoph could leave before dawn. He would give him his own knapsack, some food and a blanket. Christoph would have to make do with the shoes he had on his feet. He didn't dare steal the pair of Mr. Kierney's church shoes and besides they were too thin for walking the more than eighty miles to Philadelphia.

He made them a venison stew, filled with potatoes, beets and turnips and forced Christoph to eat slowly, afraid that too much rich food for his shrunken stomach would make him sick. They talked late into the night, at first about home, but then their conversation turned toward Christoph's leaving.

"You do not speak enough English to understand and be understood," Georg said, stating the obvious while stoking the fire.

Christoph nodded. "I will manage," he replied, reluctant to say anymore.

It seemed to Georg his friend's thoughts were already elsewhere. He feared he was so desperate to avoid being returned to Langley, he would deliberately seek to be killed by a Rebel patrol.

"Christoph. Take my scarf. Wrap it around your throat and pretend you have something wrong with your voice. Grunt and point. Do not talk. You will give yourself away."

His friend took the frayed brown length of wool and draped it over his shoulders. "Thank you, Georg. Thank you for everything."

When they parted before sunup, Georg walked Christoph to the road and watched him disappear into the dark, cold mist. He returned to the forge, careful to scuff over Christoph's set of footprints and made himself a bowl of porridge. As he milked Abigail, he dipped his fingers in the warm creamy froth and licked them clean. He debated keeping the rifle with him but decided he would not use it in any event. He removed his clogs at the door frame before stepping barefoot into the house, rehung the long-barreled weapon on the hooks over the mantel and returned to the barn.

He delayed going out into the cold, cleaning the three stalls, feeding the geese and laying down fresh straw. I am being foolish, he thought. Langley will come or not whether I am inside or out. He hitched Zak the ox to a flat sled and with some foreboding drove him down to the field newly cleared of trees to pry stones from the frozen ground. It was not a task that demanded his immediate attention. But from there he could see anyone approaching the farm from the direction of the road, or more importantly, from the Langley property. He did not want to be surprised while inside the small forge room.

The temperature had not warmed by noon and sleet was beginning to fall, driven by a bitter wind. Georg's fingers cramped as he gripped the iron pry rod. Maybe he would work inside in the afternoon. The passage of time was a good sign. Perhaps, Langley was still searching his own farm. Or maybe he was glad to be rid of Christoph and hoped he would simply starve or freeze to death in the woods. Zak let out a low rumble of a bellow and turned his head in the direction of the road. A man, hunched over against the wind and the sleet at his back, was driving up the Kierney farm road. His broad black hat obscured his face but Georg was certain it was Langley. As the wagon approached, he stood tall, one hand on the pry bar, the other shielding his eyes from the sleet.

When he was closer, the man noticed the ox first and then Georg. He dropped the reins, stepped down from the wagon and stomped angrily through the ankle-deep snow toward Georg.

"Where is he?" he shouted. "Where is that worthless Hessian bastard?"

Georg thought it best to pretend he spoke little English and understood less. He shook his head and repeated "nein, nein" a few times.

"Stop grunting your foul language at me. I know he is here. You are hiding him." He advanced on Georg with a short whip in his hand. Georg pulled the pry bar from the ground and backed away, holding the iron horizontally in front of him. Langley hesitated, seeing Georg had the advantage of him.

"Very well, you filthy mercenary. I will take this up with Thomas." He retreated to the wagon and hit the horse viciously on its flanks. Georg watched him as he headed toward the house. He thought it would be better not to be in the field and he led Zak to the barn and unhitched the sled. Unsure what to do, he started to walk the twenty yards or so to the forge. Maybe Langley was waiting inside, keeping warm until Mr. Kierney returned. He glanced nervously at the house as Langley emerged, the long rifle in his hands.

Georg dropped the pry bar and sprinted for the safety of the forge barn, running over the frozen rows of earth in the cornfield. He saw Langley kneel to fire. He threw himself forward, skinning his palms on the hard ground hoping the low stonewall bordering the field would shield him if Langley was aiming low. He heard the boom of the rifle shatter the winter silence of the farm. He thought the ball struck a tree trunk behind him. Langley wanted to kill him but had to reload. Georg ran the remaining distance to the forge, slammed the door and dropped the wooden bar to latch it closed. Never was he more thankful that his little hut was windowless. Still, he crouched as far away from the door as possible, squatting down behind the brick hearth.

Langley pounded on the door with the rifle butt. "Open up, you Hessian killer. Open up. I want Christoph. I know he is in there." The pounding continued until Langley tired of the effort. The door was well made. Now, in the silence, Georg was more afraid. What was he up to? Would he try and smoke him out by climbing on the roof, dropping green branches down the chimney and covering it? Would he set fire to the hut?

After several minutes, he heard footsteps approaching. "It will not be long now," Langley sang out. "I will have the two of you and then you shall see how I treat Hessian scum."

Georg heard a scraping sound where the door joined the frame. The wood plank of the door moved slightly. Again the scraping sound. Georg could see the edge of the pry bar inserted in the slit and heard

Langley grunt as he leaned against it. In time, he would tear the door off the frame.

Georg looked around the forge. His best weapon would be the log hook. When Langley got the door ajar, he would still have the pry bar in his hands. If he was quick enough, Georg could attack him before he had a chance to pick up the rifle. Cautiously, Georg picked up the iron rod with the hook at one end and crept up toward the door. Langley was on the other side, breathing heavily, leaning on to the pry bar and trying to wedge it further into the space where he had splintered one of the door planks. Georg thought it would give way in a few more tries. He gripped the rod and waited.

"Robert. What are you doing here?" Georg recognized Thomas Kierney's voice. "Why are you breaking into my forge barn?" For a moment, Georg feared Langley would shoot Mr. Kierney. The man was crazed. He held his breath, dreading to hear a gun shot. "Give me my rifle," Kierney commanded. "Now, Robert. What is this all about? Where is Georg?"

"In here," Georg shouted. "In here."

"Open the door," Mr. Kierney ordered.

"Yes, he is in there all right, with my Hessian, the two of them conspiring to murder us all, as his mercenary friends have killed my son."

Georg lay down the fire hook and unbarred the door. Langley rushed into the room looking wildly about. Georg moved closer to Mr. Kierney.

"You can see he is not here," Kierney said calmly. "It is a small room."

"Then he is hiding him somewhere."

"Georg. Is Christoph somewhere else on the farm?"

Georg shook his head. "Nein. Nein. Not here."

Kierney stared at Georg who held his gaze.

"Thank you, Georg. Come, John, up to the house. We can talk better there."

"You are just going to take his word? He is a lying Hessian. They are all killers, damned murderers for hire. You think he would not lie to protect his friend?"

"Come now, John," Kierney said taking his neighbor by the elbow and leading him to the door.

"Georg. See to my horse, unstrap the new wooden gear and feed the other animals as well. I will talk to you later."

Georg understood he was not to come up to the house until Mr. Kierney came for him. He was sitting in the forge, reattaching an iron hoe blade to its handle, when Mr. Kierney knocked and entered. He was carrying two mugs of hot mulled cider. They sat companionably on the forge's hearth.

"He is bereft of himself. The loss of his oldest son has taken away his reason. He blames all Hessians for John's death. The empty chair at his table every day serves to further increase his grief and fuel his anger. I gather he took it out on Christoph." Kierney's black eyes looked quizzically at Georg, waiting for his answer. Georg held his gaze, thinking this man had treated him decently

Georg nodded, knowing that by doing so he would be acknowledging that he had seen his friend.

"Christoph was here was he not?"

"Ja. He was," Georg replied. "Beaten, dirty, no food. Like me when I came here. But more bad."

"I suspected as much. You gave him food and he is gone?"

"I gave him. Food, clothes, blanket. He is gone" Georg gestured vaguely with his head toward the outside, not wanting to reveal Christoph was trying to rejoin their regiment. "We friends," he said simply, unable to convey in English the depth of their relationship, built upon all they had been through. Two farm boys from Hesse, conscripted and stoic together as obedience was beaten into them by brutal Sergeants. Then, the perilous sea voyage, standing in ankle-deep water in the hold, wide eyed with fear, praying for God to save them from the raging storms, followed by the bloody battles in New York and New Jersey, the terrible winter with constant patrols and ambushes and finally being captured together at Trenton.

Kierney grunted in understanding. "Robert had my rifle. Did he try and shoot you?"

Georg nodded. "One shot, from house. Bad aim," he said with a grin.

Kierney's thin lips formed a grimace, his dark eyes showed anger and then softened. "I am glad Robert missed. Let us go up to the house. You and I will share our dinner together. When Hannah and the children return, I will ask her to see about replacing your blanket and clothes. Perhaps others at our church will contribute."

One week after the ambush of the Dragoons at Princeton, Adam arrived at Valley Forge with the wagons, most of which contained nothing save for a few sacks of cabbages, turnips and potatoes they had seized from farms near Trenton. Will was already gone.

"He has left for York or beyond," Nat Holmes related. "Many of the artillery horses have been sent away." Adam half listened to the rest of Nat's explanation. With Will's departure, he had no one to confide in. The horses having been sent west, and the remaining ones too starved or sick to be of much use, Adam, Titus and the gun crews yoked themselves to the sleds and hauled the cannons and broken gun carriages to the carpentry shops and forges. It was strenuous work and difficult on short rations.

For once the icy, frozen roads were helpful. Adam and Titus, used to rowing for hours in stormy seas, with their broad backs and strong shoulder muscles, usually were at the head of two lines of men. To keep the gun crews' spirits up, and their thoughts away from their empty, knotted stomachs, Adam taught them a few sea shanties so they strained in unison, holding on to the leather straps of the traces with their cracked, bloody hands. Titus, who rarely spoke, sang in his deep low voice, as if the familiarity of the chants recalled better times, before he had lost his left eye at the race riot in Cambridge. The more the men sang, the more Titus's disposition improved.

To the contrary, Adam's mood darkened with each passing day and no sight of Sarah. Surreptitiously, as they approached the vicinity of General Washington's headquarters, he would slow the hauling of their sled, or encourage the men to take what he characterized as a hard-earned break along Gulph Road, hoping for a glimpse of Sarah leaving or returning from an errand.

In desperation, he asked Captain Holmes if he would make inquiries. They were standing, their backs to the wind, outside one of the forges waiting to load the newly iron-rimmed gun carriage wheels on the sled.

"Do you have a romantic interest in the young woman?" Nat asked.

"Yes sir, I do," Adam confessed.

"I recall the difficulties I encountered in persuading my dear Anna's father to favor my suit. It was only through the intervention of our good Colonel Glover that he gave his consent." He turned the worn collar of his short Marblehead Mariner's jacket up and stomped his feet. "Her father was right. He said I would be away for long periods of time and unable to properly support his daughter. Now she is with her parents in Salem, heavy with our second child and I know not her health or that of our infant boy."

Adam listened unsympathetically. How could Nat compare his difficulties to the obstacles he faced in courting Sarah? He wanted to shout, "She is a slave. She has no father. She must be bought, not wooed." He could barely control his anger. If Nat made inquiries, that would be helpful. At least he would know if she was still in camp and not sent back to her master in New Jersey.

Two days later, Nat brought news to still his anxieties and give him hope. Sarah had been serving as a cook for the French General, Marquis de Lafayette, and with that officer no longer in camp, had returned to General Washington's quarters. [1] Adam guessed the most likely time to meet her would be a few hours before the late afternoon dinner, when she might be about on some errand or another. For the next few days, he either feigned sickness or simply wandered off from the work detail and waited by the sentry fires near the General's house.

When he finally saw her, she seemed more graceful than he remembered. She seemed to float naturally over the rutted path like a leaf borne on the wind. He caught up with her on the road toward Valley Creek and was pleased she not only recognized him but seemed delighted to see him.

"Why Private Cooper," she said, her voice vivacious and cheerful.

"I heard that you had left camp. I had no idea when to expect your return."

"I am flattered, Miss Sarah, that you even noticed my absence. I will do my best to remain here until we resume the campaign in the spring. I hope the same is true for you," he added and instantly regretted saying it.

"I expect when your army takes to the field my services will no longer be needed and Reverend Penrose will require my return," she said, confirming his fears.

"We could run away," Adam blurted out. He saw them traveling north through New Jersey, with its many slave-holding families, and then what? The Reverend would certainly post a runaway advertisement in the newspapers of Massachusetts. Even her marriage to him as a freeman would not protect her from being seized and sent to her master. She would be alone while he was in his dory fishing for days at a time.

"You would desert your post and friends, abandon the cause you have volunteered to fight for?" she asked incredulously. "I am touched by the apparent depth of your affection but deeply troubled by your lack of character." She continued walking faster now, as if to escape his words. "Not to mention your judgment. I assume, Private Cooper," she said haughtily, "you would propose marriage or do you think of me as a kept woman of a deserter?'

"No. No, Sarah. I did not mean it so." He lightly touched her elbow and she slackened her pace. "I want to marry you and I want you to desire to marry me. Our relationship is thwarted by your status as a slave. We have only two choices: to purchase your freedom or to flee." He looked at her directly, his eyes pleading. "Your being a slave is a constant humiliation for me."

"For you?" she replied incredulously. "For you! Are you so blind as to forget who is the slave and who is free?" she hissed at him.

"Sarah, no" he stammered. "I meant I cannot properly court you. I am unable to appear in your home so we can become acquainted. There is nothing I can do and I have bitter, desperate and angry feelings because of it."

The road ahead, sloping down to the creek, was covered with a wide patch of clear ice. She reached out for his muscled forearm to steady herself and let her hand remain on his jacket.

"Why am I, are we," he corrected himself quickly, "deprived of the simple pleasure of sitting by a warm fire, chatting amiably with no concern for time? Where is the justice in being denied that? Sarah. When I think such thoughts, I want to batter down the General's door with my bare fists for the mere opportunity to visit with you."

"It is well that you not act upon that anger," she cautioned. "It will accomplish nothing other than your imprisonment or worse." She squeezed his forearm, whether from affection or to emphasize her words, he did not know.

"Have you ever been afraid in battle, Adam?"

He noted her use of his given name. "On land and on sea," he replied, "but not at the moment of combat. There is no time to mull over what may happen - only to fire your musket, charge the enemy, fire a cannon, reef a sail or . . ." His voice trailed off, as he recalled a cannon ball from a pursuing British frigate, crashing into their privateer and the screams of agony of his shipmates, crushed under the weight of a falling spar. If he had been one step forward, he would have been dead, or a legless sailor on the Marblehead pier. He shivered from the memory. "Why do you ask?" he said softly.

"I have experienced a most terrible fear, numbing and swallowing my mind. I was thirteen years old when I was sold to Reverend Penrose. The screams of my mother when we were separated remain in my ears to this day. I knew not where I was going. I did not know if my new master would abuse me or how he would use me. I knew nothing," she said angrily expelling the words like buckshot. "Knowing nothing creates the most overwhelming, horrifying fear."

They were almost to the small market near the creek. "Adam. What I treasure most now is certainty. It enables me to cope with the loss of my mother and the awful memories I have of her life on that plantation. Our master, who is my father, used her again and again in that manner. I have two sisters and one little brother. That I know of," she added vehemently. Tears streamed down her cheeks. "How many times must my poor mother give birth to children who are torn from her and sold like animals." She wiped her nose on the linen cloth. "To return to Reverend Penrose and his house, and the kindness I experienced there, is something I know. I do not have the courage or strength Adam, to overcome the fear of existing as a runaway."

"Sarah. Please let me. . ."

"I would not respect you if you deserted," she continued hurriedly. "Many slaves are being freed upon joining your army. You must continue to support the cause."

"Slaves may be freed for the expediency of replenishing our depleted ranks," Adam replied angrily. "Remember the General whose meals you cook is a slaveholder and a Virginia planter."

She removed her hand from his arm. "Yes, and the same General who signed the order authorizing the recruitment of slaves who will become freed men. As you are, Adam." [2]

"I was born a freeman," Adam reminded her sternly, "and, as such, voluntarily joined my regiment. It is an important difference." He became uncomfortable as the silence between them lengthened. "I will not desert and I will continue to make the most of being able to meet you on your errands. That is," he bowed, "if the lady will permit it."

She was smiling when he raised his head. "This lady would find that most acceptable."

Part Two
The Army Awakens

Chapter 6- Drills and Dinner

At the end of March, Private Henry Gillet, thinner and still feeling poorly, returned from the hospital at Princeton to Valley Forge. Once his fever had broken he had no tolerance for being bled further. When he had thought his days at the hospital would be his last on this earth, he wished himself back at camp among his fellow Rhode Islanders who at least would comfort him and see to a proper burial.

During his feverish haze, it seemed the only one who cared whether he lived or died was the Negro Private, the friend of Lieutenant Stoner. No, he recalled. That was not true. There was a woman, felicitously named Mercy, who came by frequently to make sure he was warm. At times, when his chills and fever were at their worst, he thought she was his wife Judith and called out to her not to leave him and wondered why she did. She said there were others to attend to. She was his wife. Why should she take care of others?

It was the colored Private who fed him when he was too weak to lift spoon to mouth and ensured no one stole his redcoat cavalry jacket given him by the Lieutenant. Gillet suspected Adam Cooper fed him some of his own rations to increase his complement of food. Pieces of bread for the soup, once a morsel of meat, a small portion of rum added to the tepid tea. And then his black, gruff countenance was gone. With no one to guarantee a marked grave for his wife Judith to find, Gillet decided to live.

The rows of the wooden huts for the Second Rhode Islanders still stood but some seemed woefully in need of repairs. Several had gaps in their roofs where a strong wind had shorn off the evergreen boughs or snow had caved in the rough shingles. Wisps of smoke blew toward the southeast from only half of the rock chimneys. The others pointed like rough grey fingers toward the clear blue sky, some still straight, others off kilter, accusing their makers of shoddy work. Gillet paused and pushed his shoulder against the plank door of the hut he had suffered and starved in for much of December and January. He smiled at the sight of his friend, Private Oliver Whipple, huddled at the rear against the glow of a smouldering fire. Whipple was reading a letter and did not look up until Henry called his name.

"We had given you up for dead," Oliver said, stuffing the letter into his shirt before grabbing Gillet by the arm and standing back to look at him.

"You are barely skin and bones but seem fit enough."

"Where are the others?" Henry asked.

"Out gathering firewood or digging new latrines," he said shrugging. "I was engaged at the barn this morning," he offered by way of explaining his absence from the work detail.

Henry looked around the hut. Only five of the twelve beds seemed occupied. Oliver followed his gaze.

"If you mean them, they are dead," he said wearily. "Phillips, Luther, Bright, Noice and Foster. All succumbed to typhus or the bloody flux. Batten and Vicker died of deep racking coughs. Cole froze to death one night, passing out from a gill and more of whiskey, not twenty yards from this hut."

His hands dropped helplessly to his side. "If they died in the morning, we buried them in the afternoon. When they died at night, we buried them in the morning. That is, if it did not snow or blizzard or sleet or hail or the devil himself blow a nor'easter to this God-forsaken camp."

Oliver gestured to somewhere outside where the burial grounds were.

"Are their graves marked?" Henry asked anxiously, worried his sickness could come upon him again and he would join those already gone.

"Do you think we have become heathens, Henry? They all were buried quite proper-like, with the Regimental Chaplain reading the appropriate Psalm, and the men all standing with tri-corns off, respectful and somber as the dirt was thrown on the coffin."

"I had best report to Lieutenant Tew," Henry said.

Oliver cackled, his arms flapping like a chicken. "You will have to fly to Providence to find him." Whipple's eyes raced around the room taking in the low ceiling beams, the chinks in the logs, leaping from bed to bed, back to the door and finally returning to Henry without fixing on his face. "The Major, Captains Olney and Hughes, and Lieutenants Tew and Curtis, all were given leave to return home to raise a Negro regiment. The General himself authorized it." [1]

"I would like to believe they will return," he said, more to himself. "Yes. They should return." He patted his shirt. "I wish I could see my dear wife and my little ones before the spring campaign is upon us." He lowered himself to a stool and removed the sheets of paper from beneath his shirt. "This is all I have. One letter in three months. She wrote it in early December. One of my daughters had a bad cough. There was little money and my brother is out privateering and has his own wife and young ones to feed. That is if he is not captured or killed."

Oliver's worries were interrupted by the door swinging open. Henry recognized the three privates from his company, although they had not shared a hut before he left for the hospital. They greeted him nonchalantly and then shambled close to the fire for warmth.

"You could have put more logs in the hearth, Oliver," snarled the one Henry recalled as Abraham Fish. He tossed his tri-corn on a bed and unknotted his frayed brown scarf. "I guess fixing the ladies' carriages is hard work. Not like digging in frozen soil to fill in latrines overflowing with shit."

Oliver stood up from his bunk bed. "My trade is carriage maker. The Colonel asked for volunteers to repair the carriage of General Greene's wife. [2] If I can be of some use I will. It does not take an apprenticeship to learn to throw dirt on shit."

"And what is that supposed to mean?" Fish said, turning to confront Whipple.

Henry stepped between them. "After Fort Mercer this past October, we have been through hell together. Both of you let this pass." [3]

The soldier finished untying his scarf and threw it carelessly on a bunk bed. "Will you be staying in this hut?" he asked Henry.

Gillet nodded. "I was here before being sent to the hospital at Princeton," he said by way of explanation.

"You will see, much has changed."

"Wait until we begin drilling," one of the others said. "From morning until night." Gillet looked puzzled. "Sergeant Billings says our company is next. We are to learn a new marching step," the third man added, sitting himself wearily down on a bunk bed. "To get us to the battlefield sooner so we can get ourselves killed faster. We are to be the first of our regiment to be trained. I have seen with my own eyes the others marching to and fro, this way and that. It seems to me a waste of time and strength." He bent over and rubbed one dirt encrusted ankle. "Not to mention wearing my already thin soled shoes down to my skin."

"You mean you want more time to play cards and gamble," Fish said, turning his back to the fire.

In his first two days since his return, Henry did sense a difference. Mount Misery actually looked pleasant with its beginning tinge of green. The ground was no longer frozen solid. His toes did not freeze within the hour of being outside. The warming temperatures brought with them a vile stench, a combined noxious stew of decaying dead horses and human waste. Many of the soldiers had used their huts for latrines instead of struggling through the frigid snows to relieve themselves in the pits. Now their living quarters smelled like cesspools.[4]

The rations were better too. Real bread and beef, cabbages and potatoes. Nothing like the fire cakes in the camp or the watery soup they had fed him at the hospital.

On the third day, in the early darkness of dawn, Sergeant Billings rousted the men from their huts and by 6:15 the company was assembled on the Grand Parade Ground. Colonel Angell waited on his horse facing the men with Captain Ward mounted next to him

When they were lined up, the Colonel urged his horse slowly forward. "Soldiers of Rhode Island," he said in a loud strong voice, surveying the irregular lines of ragged clothed men in front of him. "Captain Ward's company has been selected to be the first from our Regiment to train in the new drilling and marching. You will be competing with companies from Massachusetts, Connecticut and Virginia." His horse snorted as if to emphasize it too was concerned about the honor of the Regiment. "Others have been at it longer. But we are stalwart sons of Rhode Island. If you apply yourselves with diligence I am certain you will be cited first among all others. Captain Ward! Take command." [5]

There were seventy-eight men, standing loosely in seven files of ten and one shorter line of eight at the front. Instead of marching as they had before in straggling lines, they were told to keep the files close together. Sergeant Billings and another, accompanied by the beat from a drummer boy, shouted out the four-step cadence. Starting out on the left foot, they trudged back and forth on a small segment of the parade ground, ignoring as best they could the bellowed commands, drum beats and orders for other units. It was a natural pace and they grasped it quickly.

Turning as a company was another matter. Their files became mixed up, the men bumped into each other and became more frustrated the harder they tried. As tempers flared, Captain Ward intervened and halted their clumsy attempts to wheel as an entire unit. They broke the maneuver down by twenty man platoons, two files each, practicing right and left face and oblique steps and then upon the command, "Form Company," reuniting again. By the end of the morning, while they could not yet wheel as an entire company, they could perform as smaller parts with some precision.

"When did Sergeant Billings become such a drill master?" Henry inquired as his platoon rested at the edge of the parade ground. He remembered the sergeant, a tanner from Providence, as a gruff sort of fellow but quick to forgive and overlook slackness as long as a work detail accomplished its tasks.

"Shortly after the old Prussian arrived in late February," Whipple said, offering Gillet his canteen. "Our Sergeant was one of those selected to be drilled by von Steuben himself. That was hard service, drilling in the snow and rain from dawn to dusk."

"It put an edge on Billings," one of the others added.

"You should have been here," Fish said.

"I did not leave by choice," Henry reminded him peevishly.

"We loitered on the edge of the parade ground, warming ourselves by the fire, watching, while he drilled a selected group from morning until night," Fish continued.

"Do not forget about the hound," someone prompted.

"I was getting to that part," Fish replied, unhappy with the interruption. "He has a dog, long thick coated, tall with thin legs and face- just the hound for us here- no fat on him," he continued, caught up by his own account. "And then his master, this big trunk of a man, gold buttons on the calves of his boots, a long wool cape, a riding crop in his hand. He strode up and down the lines, shouting all the time like an enraged Hessian."

"He was able to count to four in English, I will give him that," another chimed in.

"Yes," Whipple said. "And he would curse the men in different languages. Sergeant Billings, one of the original soldiers the Prussian trained, returned to the our Company like a man who had been taught the gospel from on high and was on a mission to convert us heathens to the true faith without a moment to lose." [6]

"So what were the changes this Prussian brought about?" Gillet asked.

"There is no more questioning orders. All is discipline and precision. That a senior officer would drill the men, day in and day out, instead of sitting in some warm parlor planning maneuvers, writing dispatches or whatever else those generals do, is enough for me," Whipple explained. "Although, I concede Sergeant Billings could do well to afford us more time to rest."

"There will be no more for us now," a soldier called. "Here he comes."

In the afternoon, they practiced the new and simpler set of commands for loading and firing their muskets. Due to the shortage of powder, they dry- fired their weapons. At the end of the drill, the sound of their individual flints scraping metal was virtually simultaneous in each rank as they pretended to discharge their volleys. They ended the day, standing in ranks, the first rank mock-firing, the second rank moving smartly upon command about half a foot to the right so they were between the soldiers of the first rank, and then dry-firing.

The next morning, they practiced the same drills as before and then began instructions with the bayonet. They milled around, exchanging small talk as those with bayonets lent them to those preparing for the drill. Forming up in the front rank, Gillet held his piece horizontally and awaited further orders. The second rank held their muskets on an angle to clear the heads of those in the front. On command, "Charge Bayonet!" they advanced, with some behind stepping on the heels of those ahead. "Order in the ranks," a sergeant shouted, as the left of the second line began arguing with each other.

Free from work detail, they drilled incessantly for the better part of two weeks. They learned to stand at attention instead of milling around waiting for orders, although there was much grumbling and questioning of why one had to stand still when there was nothing to do. They trained until they were loading, dry-firing and returning to shoulder firelock in twenty seconds, almost in unison. Although they still thought it silly, they went through the motions of right and left dress on command and could change from the regular marching step to the quick step, then the oblique step. They knew wheeling, countermarching and breaking off and reforming by platoon and company and they learned to respond to drum signals for commands as well as shouted orders, which had sounded strange to them when they first began their drills. [7]

On the first Wednesday in April, it rained. It began as a steady drizzle which by mid-morning reduced itself to a fine mist. The Grand Parade Ground had long since been churned to mud by the drilling, marching feet of the various companies of soldiers. Gillet and Whipple stood at rest in the first file, waiting for the next drill to commence. Water dripped from Henry's tri-corn down his back. He longed to take off his hat and shake it out with his free hand, but resisted the temptation.

With Lieutenant Lodge in command, they went through the entire drilling sequences again, wheeling in formation, breaking up into platoons and then reforming as a company, breaking again and ending with a mock bayonet charge. It was only when they were drawn up and given the command to rest, that the company was aware they were being observed by a group of officers. Henry assumed the large caped figure with the long-coated dog lying quietly alongside his master's horse was von Steuben. The General conversed with another officer who nodded and rode forward to speak to Colonel Angell. The Colonel smiled and trotted his horse slowly toward them, followed by Captain Ward.

"General von Steuben has asked me to convey his congratulations to Captain Ward's Company. He has predicted if the Regiment performs as well as this company, we are capable of driving any British unit from the field. Well done, men. Well done, indeed." [8] In a break with discipline, the men cheered the Prussian General and then their Colonel. Von Steuben doffed his hat in response.

That night, extra rations of rum and meat were issued. For the first time since learning how to employ their bayonets as weapons, the men were permitted to again use them as spits for the beef. Gillet and Whipple shared one of the skewers, carving slices off the roast with their knives into a pan and chewing slowly with pleasure, letting the grease drip down their chins. The misty rain had stopped earlier, the sky was now clear and the stars above the army's cooking fires winked like beacons of heavenly approval.

"I do believe the General," Henry said. "I am much more the soldier now for all that drilling than I was before."

"We did well enough before," Whipple replied. "We beat back the Hessians at Fort Mercer."

"We were in a fort in defensive earthen works where no maneuvers were needed. Now, we are able to fight on a battlefield. Though we may be hard pressed I feel we will prevail in the coming campaign."

Henry's good feelings were enhanced by the return of some of the officers from Providence. Lieutenant Tew brought with him a letter from Gillet's wife, two pairs of new stockings, a piece of lye and a small strip of pale blue linen. She had made a dress for their six-year old daughter from the same material. She wrote that she wished him to imagine their little Sally wearing it now that spring was approaching. He brought the narrow blue band to his lips, seeing Judith seated by the small square table near the kitchen hearth, sewing by candle light, and imagining the delight in Sally's eyes as she whirled around their dining room in her new dress.

The thought of his fear of dying in the wretched hospital and being buried where Judith would never find him seemed so long ago. If he died in battle, true, he would never see Judith again. His soldier brothers would know where he had fallen and she would find him. Her love expressed in the letter assured him of that. He fingered the fabric again before placing it between the folds of Judith's letter and storing it in his haversack.

The news was almost all good for Oliver as well. Whipple's daughter had recovered from the cough, his family was managing, although money was scarce, and his brother had not yet returned from privateering. There was no information as to his ship being captured or wrecked so all were hoping for the best. It was dated March 4th, so perhaps his brother had already returned. "He is a good seaman and no news of a battle or capture is in his favor," Henry told him to assuage his friend's anxiety. Still, he knew from his own experience, the agony of awaiting news from home and the fear that some misfortune had already befallen a loved one; and all that remained was to receive the dreaded news weeks after the event had occurred.

Mary Lewis sat on the crimson cushioned seat of the Drinker family's carriage, squeezed between Elizabeth Drinker and Susanna Jones. Opposite her were Phebe Pemberton and Mary Pleasants, the five of them being driven to Valley Forge to meet with General Washington. They had a pass issued by Lord Cornwallis to cross the lines and plead for the release of their husbands and others, imprisoned because they, as Quakers, had refused to sign an oath of allegiance to the patriotic cause. Only Mary of the group had been to Valley Forge, but she said nothing about her prior dangerous journey. The stark barren landscape she had traveled through the past winter, to warn of the cavalry raid on the hospital at Princeton, was blushing green with grass and blossoming dogwoods. [9]

The women had labored for weeks drafting a paper arguing for the release of their husbands and other prominent Philadelphia Quakers. The twenty men had been detained since the past September, through the winter under harsh conditions in Winchester, Virginia. Although it was penned by Elizabeth Drinker, all five women had a part in its formulation. The paper began with the argument that the men had not been formally charged, only accused and such accusations were baseless. They were no threat to the Whig cause but instead remained steadfastly neutral in the ongoing brutal struggle, as required by their beliefs. The letter was addressed to the Congress then sitting in Lancaster. The women decided to make their case to General Washington at Valley Forge and hoped, with his support, the Congress would respond favorably.

At the last picket post, as at the preceding ones, they had once again explained the purpose of their visit and received a pass from the Colonel in charge to proceed. The five women collectively breathed a sigh of relief as they now approached General Washington's headquarters at Valley Forge, with their escort of six cavalry.

"It is past noon and it has been almost twenty-four hours since we left Philadelphia," Susanna observed. "Although the distance is short, the numerous delays were inevitable, but at last we are here."

Mary was nervous. She wished she could meet separately with General Knox, or at least his brother Billy, and seek the General's assistance in pleading their case to General Washington. They were the only two who knew of her secret role in preventing Dr. Rush and Reverend Witherspoon from being captured by British dragoons. Yet, she could not leave as soon as they arrived without arousing the suspicions of the other ladies.

The coachman and the two Negroes who had ridden postilion helped them down from the carriage. As they passed the uniformed headquarters guards, they were met in the hallway by a Colonel who informed them that General Washington was unable to see them immediately. However, Mrs. Washington had invited the ladies to join her in the sitting room. Upstairs, waiting to be announced, Phebe whispered "We should presume upon the good lady to intercede with her husband for the welfare of ours. Her influence may be substantial."

Susanna nodded in agreement. "She must be extremely devoted to him to have wintered at Valley Forge."

Once introductions had been made and courtesies exchanged, Elizabeth Drinker, being from the most prominent and affluent Philadelphia Quaker family, assumed the role of leader of the group. She described her long marriage to her husband, the hardship she and her young children suffered in his absence and her anxiety for his wellbeing. Shrewdly, she asked each of them in turn to relate their own trying circumstances. Following her lead, Mary Pleasants, Phebe, and Susanna emphasized the love they had for their missing men, and the difficulties of hiding from their children the overwhelming insecurity they felt for their dear little ones who may never see their fathers again.

While the four women sipped tea and urged the release of their husbands, Mary Lewis observed Martha Washington. She seemed a gracious and sympathetic woman. But there was an air of practicality to her and Mary sensed the General's wife thought more broadly than the situation of twenty Quaker prisoners. She decided to try a different approach. She would advocate that those in power should display a modicum of justice that in turn would persuade Quakers they would fare better under the Patriots than the Loyalists. They would be inclined to be less neutral and more supportive. That could cause her trouble when they returned to Philadelphia and when Elizabeth Drinker reported to the Assembly on their meetings.

Before it was her turn to speak, there was a polite knock on the door and General Washington joined them. He bowed slightly when introduced to each of them, apologized for having kept them waiting, and seated himself next to Martha on a brocaded settee. He listened politely to Elizabeth Drinker's summary of what four of the five of them had stated to his wife. The General, while extremely courteous, almost immediately responded that this was a civilian matter. He could do no more than grant them a pass to travel to Lancaster. There they would have to plead for their husbands' release, not with the Congress but before the Council. [10]

A sharp knock on the door brought the disappointing one-sided meeting to an end. An orderly entered and announced dinner was ready. Mary wondered, although it was the customary mid-afternoon time, whether the announcement was fortuitous or pre-arranged. At Martha's suggestion, the five Quaker ladies joined the General and his wife. They were escorted to a newly constructed single room wooden building behind the stone house kitchen, with its smell of freshly cut pine of the walls, wide planked floor and rafters. After some initial confusion the ladies were seated at a long Damask-covered table. Mary counted seventeen officers present. Elizabeth Drinker was close to the General and Mrs. Washington near the head of the table. To her delight, Mary found herself at the middle across from Captain Samuel Hadley.

"Mary Lewis. I state with all sincerity how delightful it is to see you at our Commander's table." At the mention of her name, a heavyset General closer to the end, turned and smiled warmly at her. He was a large man, well over six feet, she guessed, and more than two hundred and sixty pounds, judging by what she could see of him. From Elisabeth's description, she knew it was General Knox. Hadley introduced her to the younger officers seated nearby.

The officers peppered her with questions about the British in Philadelphia. In between the main courses of marinated roast chicken, a veal pie with savory, and planked shad surrounded by parsnips, Mary related her visits to the hospitals and the general condition of the troops about town. [11] She noted the fluctuations in the numbers of sick and incapacitated Hessians, the recent arrival of newly recruited Loyalist militias and the departure of some troops by ship. She realized she had acquired Elizabeth van Hooten's eye for detail and acute memory and was able to designate Hessian regiments and name individual officers.

The second course of crusted baked apples, potato pie and carrot pudding arrived as she lowered her voice and spoke of the abysmal conditions she had seen at the State House, where American officers were held prisoner. There was a general grumbling around her part of the long table at such shameful treatment, amidst suggestions to either hasten prisoner exchanges or threaten to treat the British prisoners in the same manner, if conditions did not improve.

Although she was not accustomed to dining with military officers, Mary was impressed by their good manners and amused that they first deferred to her and Susanna nearby, before helping themselves from the common platters. Clearly, she thought, the hard times of starvation when she had been at Valley Forge in January were past, although this was General Washington's table.

After dinner, Martha Washington again invited the ladies to her sitting room. Mary politely declined, stating that Captain Hadley, an old acquaintance from the first Independence Day celebration in Philadelphia, wished to pay her a courtesy call. As the other guests drifted into the main house, Hadley escorted Mary to a wagon waiting outside and helped her up on to the seat. Taking the reins from the stable hand, he urged the horse up the Valley Road, away from Washington's headquarters.

"We are going to General Knox's house. He will meet us there. Until he does my new bride, Mercy, who I am sure you remember, will be your hostess."

"I knew you were married and I am very pleased for the two of you."

Hadley seemed surprised. "Will wrote of your betrothal and wedding in his last letter to Elisabeth," she explained. "You know she is living with me?" Hadley shook his head. "I must see Will before I leave. Elisabeth asked me to personally reassure him of her safety. Could you arrange for him to meet with me?"

"That will not be possible. He is somewhere west of Lancaster with the rest of the artillery regiment."

"Oh dear," Mary sighed. "Elisabeth will be greatly disappointed that we have not met. She is anxious for me to return to Philadelphia with an exact account of his health and well-being."

They turned off the Valley Road and up a short tree-lined way. Two sentries flanked the steps to the narrow porch, and inside an orderly directed them to a small private sitting room off the central hall. Hadley beamed as his wife entered and embraced Mary warmly.

"How is our mutual friend Elisabeth? " Mercy asked. "When I last saw Will at Princeton, he could speak of nothing but her."

"Will was at Princeton? Not ill with any fever, I pray."

Hadley explained how Will had been one of the soldiers transporting the sick from Valley Forge to the newly established hospital and had been there when the British dragoons had attacked. "I was there, too. Indeed, we were staying with Reverend Witherspoon." He glanced at Mercy who nodded in agreement.

Mary clasped her hands to her mouth. "Gracious me," she said. "I had no idea until now, the information Elisabeth learned about the imminent raid . . ." she let her words trail off.

Hadley recounted the arrival of their cavalry and the successful ambush and rout of the dragoons. "It was all over shortly after dawn and the survivors fled down the Princeton Trenton turnpike. It seems that unwittingly, in addition to saving Reverend Witherspoon and Dr. Rush, Elisabeth also protected Will from harm. General Knox himself told me of your arrival and marveled at the coincidence. He attributed it as a sign that Providence had intervened. But why," he asked "did Elisabeth not send a message or come herself?"

Mary took a moment, still surprised at the information that Will had been at the hospital. Then, gathering her thoughts, she described the frantic meeting after Elisabeth had returned from Mrs. Bates's shop and their decision the information must be delivered in person.

"As for her coming herself, that was her strong desire. It was fortunate that I prevailed upon her that I should come in her stead. We surmised correctly as it turned out, having seen the numerous local Tory patrols on the roads, it was unlikely she would pass through the lines without arousing suspicion."

"I, too, am indebted to you for my husband's safety," Mercy said. "But what is the reason for this visit to Valley Forge in such an open manner?"

"None of my companions know of my prior traveling to this camp. And they must not. I would be condemned for violating the neutrality edict of the Assembly." Mary explained the purpose of the Quaker ladies' mission. "I intend to ask General Knox to intercede with General Washington and urge a favorable response to our plea. I have not seen my own husband for more than seven months and fear for his health and mental state."

Mary's obvious distress put a pall on the conversation, which did not dissipate with the arrival of tea. The heavy footfall of General Knox in the central hallway broke the mood. Mary jumped to her feet in anticipation.

"My dear courageous lady," he boomed, closing the door behind him, as if the wood would preserve the secrets his words were revealing. "I am honored by your presence in my house. My beloved Lucy would join us," he said pointing at the ceiling and the upstairs rooms, "but is indisposed at the moment." Seeing the alarm in Mary's eyes, he waved his hand to extinguish any thought of a serious illness. "Indisposed in a blessed way. We are expecting our second child and Lucy is experiencing some discomfort. Nothing more."

He collapsed with a grateful groan into a large wooden wing backed chair and unbuttoned his vest. "Captain Hadley and his bride have been let into our confidence about Elisabeth and your role in conveying the vital information she had gleaned about the perfidious mission of the dragoons." He bowed his head toward Mary in acknowledgment. "Which thankfully was unsuccessful due to your daring efforts in January."

Emboldened by the knowledge she had proven her worth to the patriotic cause, Mary began before the General could resume. "Now, it is I who must ask for your assistance in fulfilling the purpose of this visit by myself and the others, all Quaker ladies whose husbands have been unjustly imprisoned these long winter months." She made the case for why these prominent men were no threat and how, by acting toward them with decency and justice, it could enhance support for the cause among the Quaker community.

"Madam," General Knox acknowledged when she had finished. "If it were in my power to do so, they would be freed immediately. However, they were arrested by a civilian authority and I doubt whether General Washington will usurp that authority." He saw the look of disappointment on her face and leaned forward and grasped her two hands. "I acknowledge, we and many brave men at Princeton owe you a deep debt of gratitude. I will bring to General Washington's attention your role. I am certain he will write a letter to the appropriate civilian authorities, in as strong terms as possible, urging they act as you so fervently desire."

When they left the next morning, the other ladies were despondent.

"All we have achieved for our efforts is a pass from General Washington to journey the next fifty miles to Lancaster with no favorable word from him to the Supreme Executive Council," Elizabeth Drinker said.

"I am fearful," Phebe Pemberton added, "any words of kindness and sympathy we may receive from the members of the Council will be from their teeth outwards and all our travels will be for nought."

Mary could not reveal the encouragement she had received from General Knox, nor the obligation she felt General Washington would recognize. "I advise us to remain of good cheer. There is no telling what correspondence General Washington has forwarded to the Council on our behalf."

The women fell into easy conversation about their impressions of Martha Washington and the bearing and composure of the General himself. Every now and then, one of them would digress and discuss the struggle in managing their husband's business affairs, the recalcitrance of a warehouse tenant in timely paying the rent, or maintaining the household, and the atmosphere would become somber with the thought of facing these continuing difficulties without their spouses.

Their resolve was sorely tested after the second day. Their four-horse coach became mired in mud. The ladies had to disembark and climb fences in their skirts to circumvent a particularly bad stretch. The delay caused them to spend the night in less than favorable circumstances at the home of a farm family. The coachman and two Negroes slept in the barn with the horses.

They arrived in Lancaster the following morning, not in the best of spirits. In the late afternoon they met with Timothy Matlock, who claimed to have the ear of the Council and was sympathetic to their request for a meeting. The following day, they met with one of the Councillors, and the day after with another. Both men uttered supportive words and expressed concern. They held out the possibility of an appearance before the entire Supreme Council.

Two more days passed and the women despaired. "I do believe

the Council will not give us a hearing," Elizabeth declared. "We must consider journeying on to York where the Congress sits and plead our case to them."

"Those gentlemen may be engaged in more important matters and reluctant as well to interfere in a trouble within the jurisdiction of the Pennsylvania Council," Phebe observed. "We should wait one more day at least, before embarking on such a venture."

"Well, I for one, do not intend to sit idly in Lancaster where members of the Council are about. I will proceed to town after breakfast and scour the meeting places for them, in hope a chance encounter will prove fruitful."

"I will go with you, Elizabeth," Phebe said.

"And I, too," Susanna chimed in.

"We two Marys will remain here, in case someone from the Council comes to this address to advise us they have scheduled an audience," Mary said, nodding to Mary Pleasants.

Indeed, it was Mr. Matlock who called that evening when they were all together again.

"I bring you news to gladden your hearts. The Council has magnanimously determined to release your husbands and the others being held in Winchester. A courier has been dispatched and you may expect the entire body of men to arrive in Lancaster within the next few weeks."

Mary uttered a shriek of delight and clapped her hands. Elizabeth's face broke into a smile as the other women turned toward her as their leader and congratulated her and themselves on the news.

After Matlock had left the women talked excitedly about the expected arrival and wondered what had moved the Council to release the Quakers.

"We did not obtain a hearing but I suspect General Washington's letter was persuasive," Mary said. [12]

The idleness of the next several days was difficult to bear. Mary, using the good names of General Knox and Captain Hadley, learned that the artillery was closer to York than Lancaster. With the advent of spring, and the availability of fodder for the horses, they could be moving east toward Valley Forge at this very moment. She hoped that Will would arrive before her husband and the others so that she could see him and carry her impressions and a verbal message back to Elisabeth.

In the early morning of the tenth day after Mr. Matlock had imparted his good news, the first wagon of Quaker men arrived in Lancaster. Edward was among them, looking lean and worn but in good spirits. The second arrived before dark, with the sad news that two of their number had died during their imprisonment. The Quakers made plans to depart the next morning for Philadelphia. Although Elizabeth Drinker did not ask, it was clear she preferred her husband Henry to ride in the coach. That suited Mary for, after having been separated from Edward for so many months, she had no intention of prolonging it. Willingly, she gave up her place and rode seated between Edward and the teamster on the journey by wagon to Philadelphia. He permitted her to entwine her arm in his as she related the state of his businesses, although in his absence she had thought of them more as theirs or even hers - the tenants who were late in their rent; the repairs necessary to the roof of one of the warehouses; which employees had quit and which ones had performed admirably; what the latest storage rates were in the city; and the steady increase in river traffic.

The Drinker carriage with its team of four, arrived first and the knowledge of the men's release spread quickly amongst the Quaker community. By the time Mary and her husband reached the city along with the others, a service of thanksgiving and community dinner had been arranged. It was dusk when Mary and Edward returned to their home. Elisabeth was waiting for them and her delight at seeing them reunited was tempered by Mary's disappointing news that Will had not been at Valley Forge nor Lancaster.

"General Knox is optimistic about the coming spring campaign. When it resumes, the British may be driven from Philadelphia and you and Will be together again," Mary said, taking Elisabeth's hands in hers. Tomorrow, she thought, she would tell her of Will's presence at Princeton and the General's belief that it was Providence's hand that had led Elisabeth to discover the information and save not only two prominent patriots but her true love as well. Better to talk to Elisabeth confidentially until she ascertained whether her husband's belief in strict neutrality remained steadfast. There was no reason to think his imprisonment had made him more sympathetic to the Patriot cause. She would have to be careful. He may not approve of Elisabeth staying under his roof and being escorted about town by Captain Montresor. She thanked God for Edward's release, but recognized her husband's return could lead to complications, not just with Elisabeth but in what had become Mary's own commitment to the patriots.

—⁂—

The first week of May, the entire army was ordered to assemble on the parade grounds. The rumors rife throughout the camp were the spring campaign was about to begin. Instead, when the Second Rhode Island Continental Regiment assembled, Captain Ward read the special orders of the day - France had entered the war on their side.

Private Henry Gillet stood at parade rest, listening to Colonel Angell read the text of the treaty. The flowery words flowed above him like winged insects wafted on the morning breeze. What did all this mean, the soldier next to him asked. Henry shrugged. "I guess it signifies we are no longer alone in our fight with the British Crown." He thought of Judith and Sally and the blue ribbon in his haversack. "It means the war may end sooner and we may then all return home," he said and smiled.

When the Colonel concluded the reading and called for a cheer, the men dutifully shouted "Long Live the King of France" and tossed their tri-corns in the air. Then followed a thirteen gun salute, and the orders for the ranks to load their muskets and await the command for a feu de joie. They fired their guns in rolling sequence with nary a misfire and were soon enveloped in a white cloud of smoke from the powder. [13] At mid-day when they were dismissed to prepare for a what promised to be a bountiful outdoor feast to celebrate the new alliance, Henry caught a glimpse of Lieutenant Stoner, riding his big red horse and pulling an eighteen-pounder to the artillery cantonment. He would have to find him later and thank him for his words and compassion and show that he had indeed survived.

Some of the regiment went into the woods and emerged with dogwood blossoms festooning their tri-corns. Henry thought of attaching the blue ribbon to his hat. Better to keep it clean and safe. He accepted a blossom instead. He would put the ribbon from his daughter's dress in his cartridge box, to remind him of his loved ones before battle.

Chapter 7- In Licentious Philadelphia

John Stoner was consumed by two fears. One gnawed at him constantly - that Mrs. Bates would inadvertently reveal it was he who had told her of the dragoons' pending raid on Princeton. Or worse, she would learn how driven Captain Chatsworth was for revenge and blackmail Stoner for her silence. In his mind, he vacillated between paying or murdering her.

His other fear was losing at gambling. He could not quit, being intoxicated by the atmosphere of the gaming houses, the lure of high stakes being waged and the chance he could win a fortune. But he also could not afford to lose. His precaution against that event was to cheat, giving rise to another worse fear, of being found out.

Throughout the warm evenings of late April he had made the rounds of the gaming taverns - the "copper" halls in the less desirable parts of Philadelphia, populated by tradesmen, merchants, storeowners and warehousemen. Dressed in civilian clothes, neither too shabby nor ostentatious, he won steadily. He played cautiously so as not to draw attention to himself, honing his card counting skills. He knew from his spy network which places were fair and those where, if the decks were not rigged, the dealing boxes were. He played hazard liking the feel of the dice in the palm of his hand and dabbled at loo and piquet. However, he much preferred vingt-et-un and faro because they were fast-moving and winning depended more on skill than chance.

Once, he observed a player cheating at faro, by moving the bet to the adjacent card on the layout before the banker noticed. Another time, he was certain the man next to him had placed a bet on a losing card but astonishingly, his tokens appeared on the winning one. The stack had moved almost by a wave of the man's hand. John watched closely and discerned a single hair, barely visible in the dim candlelight, attached to the bottom of the stack. He said nothing but remembered the trick, trying and perfecting it in his quarters using a silk black thread.

In May, confident of his abilities, he moved on to the higher stakes games at the "golden" halls - Whites, Almacks and Crockfords, all bearing the names of the more elegant clubs in London. Chatsworth assured him they were nothing like the "real thing." John was tired of the endless comparisons by upper class officers, their condescending manner of speech, their inside knowledge of great men who had bet this estate or that fortune at one of the London locations, and lost huge sums of money without any emotion. Someday, he thought, he too could lose one thousand guineas at the turn of a card and not care a shit. Right now, he thirsted to win.

Tonight, as he eagerly proceeded down Walnut Street he would try the City Tavern. It was his first time at this club, noted for its faro bank, where many of the senior officers gambled and bets of fifty pounds a round were not unknown. He heard the street watchman call seven as the lamplighter ascended his tapered ladder and a bright yellow glow illuminated the cobblestones. He smiled to himself. Superintendent Galloway had accepted John's recommendation to restore the street lights. It gave the citizens a sense of normalcy Galloway thought would promote people's confidence in the Loyalist administration.

John smoothed his uniform jacket and felt the pouch of coins heavy in his inner waistcoat pocket. He straightened his back and pushed his way through the boisterous crowd of officers drinking and carousing in the large main hall and walked up the stairway to the second floor. He sauntered into one of the rooms and feigned interest at several games of cribbage underway at a row of tables. In another room, he watched seven officers seated around a table playing vingt-et-un against the dealer. John waited until a new deck had been shuffled and mentally began counting the cards, just to practice he told himself. A Major in the chair before him hesitated and doubled down, creating a stir around the table. The two stacks of tokens stood like lonely watchtowers protecting their owner from an assault launched from the dealing box. The first card drawn was a three on top of a nine. The second was a six on top of the other nine. Not good, John thought, for either hand, quickly recalling the number of low cards in the hands already played. The Major took a deep swallow from his tankard and indicated he wanted one more card on top of the three. The dealer put down a Queen and swept the stack into the bank, as the Major groaned. Nervously, he held his hand over the six and the dealer drew a Jack and turned over his down card - a seven. The other tower of tokens disappeared into the bank.

John smirked confidently, having correctly assessed the Major's misfortune and moved down the hall and into the first faro room. He saw Chatsworth standing behind one of the players and before John could turn away to leave, the Captain waved him over.

"Charles here is having a good run at the table," he said, placing his arm around John's shoulder. "He is up more than two hundred pounds after five rounds," indicating the Lieutenant sitting at the table with a large stack of tokens in front of him. John licked his lips enviously. When the round was over, Stoner, despite an earlier intention to keep twenty or so pounds in reserve, converted all fifty pounds in his pouch into tokens and ordered an ale. [1] These were the highest stakes he had ever played for. He took a chair at the table and tried to appear nonchalant and unperturbed. The first draw was pure guesswork simply because there were no cards to count. John placed small bets on the five and Jack on the faro board and watched where the four other players put their bets. The Lieutenant, perhaps now overconfident, put down a large stack of tokens equal to at least thirty pounds on the ten. The dealer drew the first card, the six of diamonds and discarded it, as required. He then pulled two more from the dealing box, the first a ten, eliciting a deep groan from Charles and a sympathetic one from Chatsworth. A bet on a card of the same denomination as the banker's card lost. Luck was with John for the player's winning card drawn was also a five and his Jack was higher than the banker's ten. John collected his winnings and before the next two cards were drawn, decided to go high and pushed a stack on to an eight and another on to the Jack again. The banker drew a seven as his card and a nine for the winning player's card. John collected on his high card bets.

As the game progressed, John filtered out the shouts of joy of the winners and their supporters and curses for their hard luck by the other players and the crowd behind them. He concentrated on the card count, coolly making his bets based on the knowledge that certain numbers had already been played. After several rounds, the stack of tokens in front of him was the largest among those at the table, and the group of officers was thickest behind him. He knew he had consumed at least three tankards and the heat in the room, despite the two windows being open, was making him groggy. The cautious voice inside him, urging him to leave after this round, was overwhelmed by the pleasure he felt from all the attention and the cheers of Chatsworth and others.

He now was gambling huge sums for him, twenty, thirty and even forty pounds on each two-card draw. Except for the fat Colonel two seats over, who was losing steadily, John was the biggest better at the table. By an incredible stroke of luck, which John attributed to his superior card counting, when the dealer called the turn for the final three cards, he predicted the exact order - the banker's card a three, the winning card a King, and the Hock, a nine. Several hands reached out and clapped him on his shoulders, another tankard appeared at his right hand and there were calls of "Bravo" and "well played." How could he leave the table now? His face flushed, whether from the accolades or alcohol he knew not. He loosened his waistcoat, rearranged his tokens and played on.

Gradually, over the course of the next few hours, he lost his touch and more significantly, his winnings and eventually his stake. When he left the faro room, just before dawn, holding on to the bannister to steady himself, he was down not only his initial fifty pounds but also four hundred plus pounds in winnings. He dragged himself to his quarters, blaming himself for letting a fortune slip through his fingers.

He came back to the City Tavern two nights later, drawn like a moth to a candle flame, vowing this time to stay sober and quit while ahead. He saw himself in his room, his strong box open, overflowing with his winnings of pound notes, guineas, Spanish dollars and pieces of eight. It never happened. He was seduced by the praise of those he knew were from aristocratic families, the ones who attended theater and belonged to gentlemen's clubs in London and visited each other's country estates, rode to the hounds and had coats of arms. He played on into the early morning hours, watching his stack of tokens diminish with each round. He was not even clear-headed enough to quit when he was gambling away his initial stake of another fifty pounds. He returned to his room, drunk and poorer, and fell asleep thinking of the privileges he would buy when he was rich enough. And so he returned to the faro tables over and over and lost much of the money he had carefully accumulated through theft and corruption since the beginning of the war.

John's official salary was not enough even to cover one long evening of betting at the faro tables. His current stream of income, from merchants who paid him to look the other way when they purchased food from smugglers which they sold for exorbitant prices on the black market, was not enough to offset his losses. He knew this was undermining Galloway's own efforts to control prices but John merely saw it as another opportunity to enrich himself. And besides, he reasoned, the Superintendent himself had promised John some extra benefits and he was only fulfilling that assurance.

In desperation, he decided to cheat. He would lose no longer. He had pocketed a token from his last miserable outing when his luck had changed for the worse. Carefully, in the privacy of his quarters, he attached a green silken thread that matched the color of the playing table to the bottom of the wooden marker. As he entered the Tavern, and went upstairs, he thought he would play in a different room, away from Chatsworth and the dragoons. Maybe the change would be for the better. In any event, there would be fewer distractions. He joined a table of five, glancing quickly at the other players, two Majors from the Light Infantry and a Lieutenant and Captain from the Grenadiers. He did reasonably well the first two rounds, carefully sipping on the claret and betting conservatively.

"My God, man," the Grenadier Captain said with disgust from the end of the table. "You play like a timid old woman." Several officers behind him snickered.

"It is a game of skill, not of bluster," John replied, regretting drawing more attention to himself.

"Are you implying I do not have the brains for faro," the Captain roared, his face flushed from the heat of the room and alcohol.

John sought to defuse the situation. "No, no," he stammered. "I only meant to explain my cautiousness."

"Well, you can count all you want but bet with the conviction of your numbers, man" the Captain ordered.

Intimidated, John increased the amount of tokens he placed on the faro board and was rewarded with four consecutive wins before the round ended. The next two rounds also went well for him. The chair next to him vacated and the Captain moved into the seat.

"We are both favored by luck at this table," he said, clasping John's arm. "Let us take turns standing drinks for the others." John could not decline and he and the Captain stood four rounds before John lost count, by which time, he recognized he was not remembering which cards had been played and which ones were still available. The Captain seemed unaffected by the alcohol he consumed and continued to win more often than not. John noticed his own pile diminishing and fingered the token with the thread in his pocket. Surreptitiously, he added it to the bottom of the pile of the large stack he pushed forward and placed on the ten. Two other players had also bet on that number. The dealer turned the first of two cards over. It was a ten. John had lost. He willed his hand to grasp the invisible thread and move the pile to the adjacent Jack, giving him a high card bet. The dealer was looking down at the second card drawn, a seven. John's hand moved toward the faro board and then stopped. Sitting next to the large mustached Grenadier Captain, he lost his nerve. The fear of being called out and exposed as a card cheat overcame his greed for winning. He let the dealer sweep the piles of tokens, including his marked one, into the bank and realized he had lost more than two hundred pounds in the course of the evening, all of his winnings and his stake. If he had only kept his winnings and left the table all of those nights, he would have achieved his dream, with more than enough money to purchase land, or a fine home, or both.

Back in his room, he opened his strong box and almost cried as he counted what remained. Forty three pounds. His fingers brushed against a velvet sack, tied with a silk ribbon. Clumsily, he undid it and poured the contents into his hand. He stared down at the pearl necklace and ring with the stone he thought was a ruby. Pillaged from that fine stone house in Brunswick. He slipped the jewelry back into the sack, closed his strong box and fitted the lock to his camp trunk. First, he would offer to sell them to his housemates. Some of them had money. If not, he could solicit the officers at one of the taverns where he dined, and with a new stake, return to the faro tables and win back what he had lost and more. Next time, if he had to cheat to win, he would act boldly. Confident of his new-found resolve, he pulled off his boots and collapsed on his bed.

Elisabeth van Hooten peered out the window of the Shippen's grand sitting room. There were more than a dozen carriages lined up below, each with a pair of cavalrymen, swords drawn, flanking the uniformed coachmen. Inside, the room buzzed with the excited chatter of more than twenty young ladies, including the fourteen selected by their British Officer escorts to be either the ladies of the Knights of the Blended Rose or the Knights of the Burning Mountain. They were dressed in exotic Turkish costumes, fashioned to be those of harem ladies, with bejeweled turbans and low cut bodices, said to be designed by Major Andre himself. Foremost among them was Peggy Chew, the one favored by Andre and daughter of former Pennsylvania Chief Justice Chew. Peggy Shippen and her sister had both been chosen for their beauty by the Captains of the frigates H.M.S. Rose and Phoenix. The three of them, anticipating the festivities at which they would preside, sat laughing and holding court on the plush crimson upholstered center banque. They wore elegant, expensive Lynn shoes, made of silk and satin with golden colored buckles set in long straps adorning their dainty feet. They had arrived from Boston less than a week ago and were rumored to have cost twenty pounds per pair. Only the Chew and Shippen families could afford such luxuries, Elisabeth thought.

The spectacle, created by Major Andre and called "The Misquianza," was to honor General Howe who had been recalled to London. The festival had the flavor of a medieval show, with a mock joust and tournament. Captain Montresor had assured Elisabeth this was all the rage in London. She was thankful she was not one of the Knights' ladies for she thought their costumes scandalous. The entire affair in her opinion was in bad taste, from the elaborate invitation bearing Howe's coat of arms proclaiming him victor, to the more than 3,000 pounds sterling each of the twenty-two senior officers had contributed to finance this elaborate display of the army's love for their Commander.

When Montresor had told her the cost to impress her, Elisabeth had almost blurted out that such extravagance was obscene given the rising prices for salt, sugar and food in general. The merchants from New York and the Caribbean who flooded the Philadelphia market and opened new shops stocked with both necessities and luxuries accepted only gold or silver in payment. She knew of families who were selling off furniture, cloth, dresses and other items to so-called "auction houses" to acquire hard currency to purchase food. Still, she had accepted Montresor's invitation to be his lady guest at the festivities, reasoning it was her role to attend and gather what information she could, and that her refusal would reflect poorly on the Captain, whom she thought of with a modicum of fondness.

Montresor met her as she alighted from the carriage at the wharf and offered his arm to steady her as they, along with several other couples, boarded a flat boat for the journey down the Schuylkill. The brightly colored pennants at the fore and aft fluttered in the slight breeze as the uniformed sailors rowed the boat out into the current. The vibrant yellow awning provided welcome shade from the mid-afternoon sun. Once all the boats were midstream, the flat-bottomed fleet proceeded down river to the accompaniment of music from military bands on anchored war ships. Crowds lined the Philadelphia waterfront to view the spectacle, cheering the guests on the flotilla and waving handkerchiefs and scarves. Elisabeth restrained an impulse to wave back.

"And where may I ask, will this grand fleet disembark?" she asked a bit too sarcastically.

"I could let our destination be a surprise, but I have another one for you instead which I believe will please you more." He smiled at her and pointed to a broad sloping lawn ahead with a large brick mansion at the summit. "The Wharton Mansion. Unfortunately, the family chose to support the Rebels and thus forfeited Walnut Grove and other properties." Elisabeth maintained a pleasant expression on her face while images of the families thrown out into the street with barely the clothes on their backs filled her mind. She had seen enough confiscations of property in Philadelphia following the British occupation to readily recall the wailing of distraught women and the young children's cries of fear.

"The Whartons are wealthy merchants and I am told they exiled themselves to their country estate northwest of Germantown," Montresor added, as if he had read her mind. Elisabeth inclined her head in acknowledgment, an unspoken thanks for the reassurance this particular family had not suffered.

"You have a sweet soul, my dear. And today you look especially fresh and attractive. It is as if your inner beauty has sought and succeeded in piercing your outward presence."

"Why Captain Montresor," she responded. "It must be this grand occasion which leads you to utter such amorous phrases."

"No, my dear. I assure you it is only your exquisiteness that so inspires me."

He withdrew a silken pouch from his uniform jacket. "I promised you a surprise. I am pleased you have refrained from wearing jewelry." He untied the crimson ribbon and extracted a pearl necklace. "These pearls pale in comparison to your beauty" he said holding it out to her.

Their fingers touched as Elisabeth took the long single strand necklace in her hand. She held it up to the sunlight and marveled at each sphere's purity. "It is lovely," she said softly. Montresor took it back and stepping behind her, lowered it around her neck and attached the clasp. She felt his warm breath on her nape and although they were in broad daylight in public, to her it was as intimate if they were alone in a candlelit bedroom.

The rest of the afternoon was a blur of activities and confused emotions. She thought the challenge by the Knights of the Blended Rose that their ladies were the fairest, and the contention by the other Knights that their ladies were more so, farcical and contrived. The mock combat afterwards, accompanied by trumpet blasts and drums, was simply boys playing at being chivalrous warriors from medieval times. It was downright silly. So was the outcome when some pompous officers serving as "Judges of the Field of Combat" ruled both sets of ladies of both sets of knights were the fairest of the land. Elisabeth stifled a laugh, observing Peggy Chew and the two Shippen sisters and the other eleven women, all of whom she knew, decked out like Turkish concubines, which had nothing to do with medieval England. But then she fingered the pearl necklace around her neck, felt Montresor's presence next to her, and recognized with dismay he was chivalrously courting her and, worse, she was pleased he was doing so.

She felt as if she were already betrothed to him as they, along with the other guest couples, proceeded through an arch bearing the Howes coat of arms and up the broad lawn to the mansion, between two long lines of soldiers standing stiffly at attention. Once inside the reception hall, the intimate magic was broken and Elisabeth slipped swiftly into the familiar role of being escorted to a ball. An orchestra played the well-known minuets and Elisabeth danced with Montresor for the first three dances. Then she stood to the side, observing the glittering crowd and drinking first cool tea and then claret. She noted the clusters of smartly dressed officers around the ladies of the Knights, ogling their figures that she thought were barely concealed by their gauzy costumes.

The dance was followed by a massive fireworks display, viewed through the open windows of the ballroom. Crowded together overlooking the lawn and river, Elisabeth felt Montresor behind her, not pressing against her but more protecting her from being pressed against. When the fireworks ended with a glittering crescendo of rockets exploding in bright whites and reds, Montresor hooked his arm in hers. [2]

"Instead of dancing, would you prefer to watch a high stakes faro game in the next room? Some of my friends are engaged." She nodded. "I have never been to any gambling club or room and know nothing of the rules," she said as he steered her toward the door. Mrs. Knox had taught her how to play poker but she could hardly tell Montresor that.

The large room with several faro tables was garish with painted panels adorned with gold ribbons and flowers. There were mirrors almost from floor to ceiling on the walls that made the room seem crowded, more colorful and vibrant. They ambled slowly from table to table, until Montresor recognized a Colonel he knew, seated before a large pile of tokens. Elisabeth watched uncomprehendingly and quickly became bored. She glanced nonchalantly around the room and in a mirror saw John Stoner at another table, deeply involved in the game, his eyes darting from one player's cards to another. When his round ended, he looked behind the dealer and saw her image in the mirror. His jaw dropped and he gaped at her. Her hand went to her flesh just above her breasts and gripped the pearl necklace resting there. She saw in Stoner's eyes a look of animal desire and furious hatred that scared her. She averted her eyes and when she sensed it was safe to look again, John's head was bent and he seemed fiercely intent on the cards being dealt.

She tapped Montresor's arm. "I am returning to the ball room to be with the ladies and enjoy some of the sweetmeats," she said and left him consoling the Colonel over his losses.

It was after two in the morning when Montresor and Elisabeth left the Walnut Grove mansion by carriage for Philadelphia. She sat next to him and the rough road jostled her into his shoulder. He moved closer and put his arm around her.

"Just to steady you, my dear. You realize I am quite fond of you." He waited for her to answer and she murmured something that she hoped could be interpreted as neutral and not a commitment. He put his hand under her chin and lifted her face to his. "There is something I must tell you, in strictest confidence." Elisabeth forced herself to smile curiously, every fiber of her alert to his words.

"With Sir William Howe departing, General Clinton will be the commander of the army. There is talk of our leaving Philadelphia, regrouping in New York and beginning a new campaign in the late spring."

"What does it mean leaving Philadelphia?" she replied not understanding. "Are you to join General Clinton's staff in New York?"

"No, no, my dear. Not just me. The entire Army will leave. There will be no British troops left behind to protect the Loyalists from the Americans." He patted her hand. "I do not care about them. My concern is for you. I am offering you safe passage with me to New York and my protection in that city."

"Oh," she gasped. "But what of all those citizens who have supported the Crown? And their families? Surely they are not to be abandoned."

He waved his hand dismissively. "Those that wish will be transported to New York. Do not have a care for them. You must think of your safety. And future," he added, squeezing her hand.

"I cannot at the moment," she stammered. "All the excitement of this night has confused me. I need time to consider. When will you leave?" she asked innocently averting his gaze. She was afraid her eyes would betray her joyous thought that if the British abandoned Philadelphia, it meant the Americans and her beloved Will would enter the city.

"Sir William departs in a week's time. The preliminary plans are for the army's withdrawal to be completed by mid-June the latest. I expect to leave by ship before then."

The carriage had arrived at the Lewis home where not a candle was showing. Mary had promised to leave the door unbolted. Montresor alighted and offered his arm to help her down. Elisabeth held his hand and. with her other, brushed the pearl necklace.

"Your gift has touched me deeply, as does your concern for my safety. I need time to sort my thoughts out. Please be patient with me."

He bowed and kissed her hand. "Of course, my dear. But do not dally too long. The army and this war will not wait."

She nodded and pressed against the door which creaked open. Once inside, she threw the bolt and leaned against the door seeking steadiness in its sturdy frame. The Americans would be in Philadelphia in less than a month's time. And Will would be here with her. She resolved that not one day would pass after his arrival before they would be married, with or without her father's approval. Hurriedly, she went into the kitchen and lit the candle in the holder. She must pen a letter to him, writing as usual about nothing. The lines in invisible ink would reveal the British intent to abandon the city. Tomorrow, she would talk to Mary as to how to respond to Captain Montresor's invitation to leave with him. Perhaps she could tell him the Quaker community would protect her.

Into the waning hours of the night, John Stoner played on with a precise, energetic fury. How did that strumpet come by his pearl necklace? He had sold it to a Major in Colonel Mawhood's 17th Foot who had said it was just the perfect parting gift for his American mistress. Obviously, he was not fucking Elisabeth so the Major must have resold it. The sight of her wearing that necklace infuriated him and for some strange reason cleared his mind. After ten hands of the current round, he remembered the cards played as if they appeared before him. Twenty cards played, thirty-one left. He placed his tokens decisively on the layout board, confident in the knowledge that none or only one of that denomination had been played. He won more often than not on the winning card, guessing the card the dealer would turn over as the player's card, and almost as often on the high card over the value of the banker's card. Oblivious to the congratulations and shouts of "well played" swirling around him, he raked in his tokens with practiced regularity, unsmiling and full of rage.

That Dutch bitch, he thought. Make a fool of him before Mrs. Bates, would she. Elude his watchers in the streets and pass secrets to the Rebels. He would catch her yet and then he would make her pay. Oh, how she would pay. Another eight drawn as the player's card. That made four out. The other numbers with all four cards played were threes, sixes, Jacks and Queens. It was so much easier at the end of the round, if one remembered the cards. And remember he did, consumed by a cold rage that progressively degraded Elisabeth until the point where she became, in his mind, one of the trulls at Mrs. McCoy's subject to his every whim and desire. He permitted himself a smirk of satisfaction that others around him interpreted as related to his success at the faro table.

John's night of gambling ended at four in the morning. He turned in his tokens at the bank and rode back to Philadelphia with more than eight hundred pounds in notes and coin in his saddle bags. The fury he still felt at seeing Elisabeth in the mirror wearing his pearl necklace was barely offset by his satisfaction at having replenished his strong box and then some.

He passed a few carriages returning from General Howe's farewell extravaganza to the city. Enjoy it while you may, he thought. When General Clinton announces the army will abandon Philadelphia, panic will ensue among the Loyalists who had hosted the British Officers at their lavish dinners, those who had joined the provincial regiments at Superintendent Galloway's urging or participated in his city administration. There would be ample opportunity, John thought, to make them pay dearly for early passage on merchant sloops, schooners and anything that floated, and to demand a bribe from the ships' captains and owners for the permission necessary to leave port, with contraband goods hidden in their holds. The chaos that would ensue was simply another money-making opportunity for him.

And he thought, there was another prospect, more dear to him than money, from the confusion and turmoil as the army prepared to leave. With Captain Montresor otherwise occupied and an end to all those elegant dinners, plays and chamber music concerts, he would pay Elisabeth van Hooten a call at her Quaker lodgings, beat her to confess her spying and show the Captain to have been played the fool. And then, he would do with her as he wanted.

Chapter 8 - The Campaign Resumes

The long, harsh winter at Valley Forge had been trying for Bant. Not because of the starvation rations, the bitter cold and rampant disease. For him, those were bearable. The enforced idleness and confinement to the cramped log huts, day after day, kept him in a perpetual state of nervousness and depression. His head was a seething pot of terror that boiled over and caused him to irrationally lash out at all around him. His fellow soldiers, even McNeil, avoided him, increasing his isolation.

He felt doomed. The others had not seen what he had witnessed nor caused the death of innocent men. His "demons" as the others called them, would come upon him unpredictably. The face of some soldier who looked like one of the militia hung by the dragoons could cause him to cry out in fear. A bare branch, jutting horse height from a gnarled trunk, would make him run away. Even the sound of horses' hooves, approaching from around a bend in the middle of the camp, would terrify him.

Bant frequently wandered alone away from Valley Forge, passing through the picket lines without challenge, hearing the words "lunatick" and "possessed by the devil," as he came and went at will. If he were asked where he had been, he could no more have told anyone than describe the surface of the moon.

The drills initiated by the Prussian General were a turning point. Bant found that concentrating on orders, marching, wheeling and maneuvering, occupied his mind. The discipline was a safe haven to turn to when his thoughts began to travel down darker paths. Often, he mentally ran through the drills. To the annoyance of his bunkmates when they were in the middle of eating, conversing or gambling with dice or cards, Bant sometimes would bark the commands out loud. He did not excel but he was better than most of the riflemen in his company who maintained their reputation for disdain of military discipline and order. They all had rebelled against loading and firing on command. They were not infantry with muskets, required to lay down a concentrated volley to hit anything. They were riflemen who could consistently put a ball through a paper target at three hundred yards.

Reluctantly, they had followed Colonel Hand's orders and practiced the fifteen-step drill from priming, loading, ramming the charge home, returning the rammer, aiming and firing. Except they refused to waste any powder as an act of defiance. Their Colonel accepted this in good grace, knowing that Colonel Morgan's rifle regiment, to the man, had initially refused even to drill. Only after a few of the insubordinate leaders had been court-martialed did Morgan's men appear sullenly on the parade grounds to learn the marching and maneuvers.

And now, Bant, McNeil and several other volunteers from their company, filling the gaps in Colonel Daniel Morgan's Rifles due to desertions, disease and death, were marching in step toward Philadelphia with a force of around two thousand men, commanded by the young French General. [1]

"What do you think of our savages," McNeil said, gesturing to a file of Indians loping alongside the road beside the marching troops. Bant kept the cadence of their quick step and studied the Redmen as they trotted silently by in their moccasin-clad feet. Most carried muskets, a few had rifles and some had bows and quivers strapped to their backs. They wore shirts decorated with colorful beads, over breechcloths and leggings that were decorated with dyed tufts of animal fur. He stared at their heads, shaved except for a crest of hair down the middle, topped by a tuft with three feathers, two standing straight up and one drooping down the back of their necks. [2]

"They move quickly enough," Bant replied after a while, as the last of the Indians disappeared around a bend in the road.

"They make me uneasy," McNeil said. "I do not trust them. Never did back home either. I intend to sleep with one eye open tonight. You will be well advised to do so, too."

Bant glanced at his friend to see if he was serious. There were no Indians in Morristown and its environs. "These the same kind of Indians you have at home?"

"Indians are Indians," McNeil replied quickly. "They are treacherous savages. You never know what they are thinking and they covet everything you own." [3] Bant kept his thoughts to himself. He was more afraid of his recurring nightmares than one of these Indians creeping up on him as he slept.

"And this French General," McNeil continued. "Rumors in the camp are he is spoiling for a fight. That is music to your ears, right Bant? You need to play a tune with that rifle of yours. Much time has passed since you brought down a Redcoat."

Bant grunted in reply and shifted his rifle on his shoulder. He preferred to carry it in his hand, with the barrel pointing forward. That had changed with the new close marching in formation. It still did not make sense to him as a rifleman. Better to move quickly in single file as the Indians did. Yet, he admitted, he was eager to be going into battle again. It did not matter how they arrived as long as he was there with his rifle to greet the British.

The entire force camped on a hilltop from where they could see the lights of Philadelphia, less than ten miles away. The men of Morgan's rifles were sent further forward as pickets and scouts, along with the Indians. They settled in on both sides of a road that led straight to Philadelphia, a partial moon above and the intermittent flicker of fireflies amidst the dark shadows of the bushes. Bant ignored McNeil's warning when he came off sentry duty and slept soundly enough for him.

He awoke, to find a low-lying fog enveloping the road, the woods and the meadows he knew were off to his right. Bant realized he had been awakened by the sounds of tramping feet and horses' hooves. As he sat up and grabbed his rifle, he heard several short whoops and then rifle fire. He heard the orders shouted for his platoon to form up, immediately followed by an order to quick march to the front.

Around him, several riflemen ignored the drills, discipline and the first order and simply ran forward toward the sound of gunfire. Bant dashed headlong with them through the woods and positioned himself with a line of riflemen and Indians firing down the road toward an approaching wall of British infantry. Calmly, he sighted on a Redcoat and brought him down with a ball to his throat. The British troops hesitated. The remainder of the two platoons arrived and let loose a concerted volley that decimated the Redcoats' ranks. Bant could clearly hear the drums and shouted orders to form battle lines as if they were approaching the entire Rebel Army. He reloaded and fired three more times, certain he had killed with each shot. Musket balls whizzed through the tree branches, showering the Americans with twigs and new grown leaves.

There was a brief respite in the musket fire from the British and a troop of dragoons galloped through their lines and charged. Bant aimed at one of the lead troopers, his sabre raised high, his mouth open in an unheard shout. Out of the corner of his eye he saw the Indians, about fifty of them, stand up and in defiant unison, issue the most blood curdling sound Bant had ever heard, before unleashing a hail of musket fire and arrows. The dragoons' horses reared up and bolted. The trooper Bant had targeted was thrown from his horse and turned to retreat on foot. Bant sighted at the rear of his head just below where his death's head helmet met the hairline, fired and saw the dragoon fall forward and lie still on the ground. [4]

The riflemen and Indians slowly retreated, keeping up a steady fire at the advancing infantry marching with fixed bayonets up the road and through the adjacent brush. Bant took in the view from the top of the hill where they had camped the night before. To their rear, the main American column was retreating in close order down the road heading to the ford across the Schuykill. To their front, a mass of Redcoats was advancing in quick march toward the hill.

The one hundred or so riflemen and Indians formed a long skirmishing line and methodically picked off the pursuing Redcoats. Then, with the shouted command coinciding with their instinct, they fell back a distance, and well hidden in the dense brush and woods, laid down their accurate fire to slow the British advance. In this way, they retreated until they reached the last ridge before the bank sloped down toward the river. The ford was no more than thirty feet wide at this point, with clear water running swiftly over a stony bottom. [5]

Bant sighted on a tall Sergeant carrying the colors of his Regiment. He fired, pausing long enough to see the man fall, struggling to keep the flag from the ground and, then without reloading, hastily slid down the embankment and sprinted into the water. At midstream, being short, the water rose above his waist. He heard the shouted familiar orders from the drills at Valley Forge - "Fire by Division! Division Make Ready!" coming from the south side of the river. His right foot, in his well-worn moccasin, slipped on a large rounded stone and he felt himself falling. McNeil grabbed him under his arm and pulled him forward until Bant regained his balance. They scrambled up the bank and through their lines as the command was given, "Take Aim! Fire!" The wind blew the smoke back over the Americans and Bant clearly saw several British infantry fall before they loosed their own volley. He rested behind the lines, facing away from the river, his back against a tree trunk, his rear on the ground, protected by the narrow hollow formed by the roots of a tree. The Redcoats fired once more and then, in response to drum signals, reformed their units, pivoted and left the field. Bant heard cannon fire from the direction of Valley Forge and looked quizzically at McNeil, kneeling nearby.

"Signal fire," his friend said. "I guess the rest of the army will be joining us soon."

The Lieutenant who commanded the two platoons of Morgan's Rifles ordered them to form up. "Cross the river, spread out and harass their rear guard as far as their pickets outside Philadelphia." He pointed at the Oneida who were already wading rapidly across the Schuylkill. "Hurry men. We do not want to be outdone by savages."

Bant cautiously placed his feet on the stony bottom, holding his rifle and cartridge box above his head. He had to run to catch up with McNeil and the others. He licked his dry lips and realized he had left his canteen on the far side of the river. No matter. He would appropriate a canteen from one of the Redcoats he brought down.

Eagerly he ran forward through the trees following the retreating red line of troops.

—∞—

For the second time in the same week, Will rode Big Red to General Knox's house past the junction with Yellow Springs Road. Behind him spirals of smoke rose from the base of Mount Joy where the offal pits were located. Better to have skulls and hooves, guts and bones to burn, he thought, than no meat to eat at all. The twice-weekly incinerations, ordered for sanitary reasons, were a smokey signal that the period of starvation and deprivation were long over.

He dismounted and walked his horse to the adjacent field, now green with the new grass of late May, loosened the saddle cinch and dropped the reins. Big Red would graze and be here when Will returned. Excited and anticipating the good news that he would soon be in Philadelphia with Elisabeth, he took the salute of the sentries and bounded up the porch.

The last time he had been at the General's headquarters was together with the other officers of Knox's Regiment, to sign the oath of loyalty to the United States of America. There was talk that by renouncing allegiance to George the Third, the officers were entitled, following the end of the war, to one half their pay for seven years. And there was a pay increase as well. As a Lieutenant, Will would now receive twenty-six and two thirds dollars per month. [6] It mattered not to him. He was in the war of independence for the duration and needed no monetary inducements or oath to ensure his commitment to the cause.

Following the solemn oath signing in the presence of Captain Hadley, and Nat Holmes, recently assigned to Knox's staff, the General himself told Will privately that information provided by various agents, including Elisabeth, gave every indication the British would soon be abandoning Philadelphia. Will had read her letter, prattling on about some extravagant festival and the crucial message in invisible ink - the army, under the new command of General H. Clinton, would be retiring to New York City.

This morning, Billy, in his capacity as his brother's secretary, had sent a message asking Will to attend the General at ten. It could only be to inform him when he would ride in the vanguard of American troops triumphantly into Philadelphia and be reunited with Elisabeth. He paced the small room off the alcove, ignoring the looks of other officers waiting for their meetings, and glanced frequently at the uniformed clerk manning the desk. An hour passed and Will was beside himself. One moment he thought he would be mounting Big Red and dashing down the road to Philadelphia to catch the American contingent already under way. The next, he thought the British had decided to force a fight for the city and Elisabeth would be in danger during the ensuing battle. He was lost in these competing visions of the future when Billy called his name from the open door to the General's office.

Knox was hunched over his writing desk, his copybook off to one side and a stack of letters and papers strewn about. A candlestick with a few burnt stubs of wax lying nearby was evidence he had labored long into the night.

"Ah, Will," he said greeting him with a smile. "Sit down. Sit down." Will murmured his thanks and thought the General looked tired and worn.

"How is Mrs. Knox?" he asked.

"My dearest Lucy is well enough. Although heavy with our second child, she has maintained her social schedule with Mrs. Washington and the other wives. She is fond of parties and dinners and will not let her delicate condition inhibit her enjoyment in any way."

Billy produced a letter from the pile and Knox waved it at Will. "This is good news for you and Elisabeth. The recent dispatches from General Schuyler in Albany included a letter from Mr. Van Hooten - a response to my beseeching his approval for your suit of his youngest daughter." He flourished the paper dramatically over his short grey flecked hair, his eyes twinkling with delight. "If the young couple is in agreement, it would be my esteemed pleasure to give the bride away."

"I would be honored, sir, as will Elisabeth. I am most anxious to be reunited with her and I hope our wedding could be as soon thereafter as practicable."

"Ah, yes, Will. I am mindful of your sense of urgency. Lucy and I were once as eager as you are." He paused, a slight smile on his face, recalling some intimate incident. "But now we are constrained by our noble struggle for independence." He smoothed his eyebrows with his fingers and pushed his chair away from the desk. "This war, as you know, has kept me from my beloved Lucy on many occasions. Such separations have been extremely painful for both of us. Now, unfortunately, you and Elisabeth must bear such tender agony for a while longer."

Will felt as if he had been struck in his chest by a musket ball. His jaw dropped, his throat was dry and his right hand clenched the facing of his jacket. The General, noting his distress, hastened to reassure him. "Elisabeth will be safe with our troops in control. I assure you. They will enter the city to maintain law and order as soon as the British depart."

Knox hoisted his heavy frame from the chair and motioned Will to approach a map spread out on the adjacent table.

"From the intelligence we have obtained, we believe their army will march overland with their equipment and baggage and not depart by sea. They will be encumbered on their trek through New Jersey to New York by their baggage train. And it will not be the 'Noble Train of Artillery' you and I escorted through the snowy Berkshires in the winter of '75." He gave Will a friendly nudge in the ribs. Bending over the map, Knox traced a route from the Jersey shore of the Delaware River northeast until his thick finger stopped at Amboy across from Staten Island. "It is General Washington's intention to pursue them and when the opportunity arises, to strike at their army and achieve a decisive victory."

Will stood hunched over the table, his eyes following the lines on the thick parchment, seeing only that all roads led away from Philadelphia.

"We will not leave Valley Forge until the Redcoats leave Philadelphia." He chuckled. "We should designate it properly - a British retreat, an exodus of Biblical proportions of all their Loyalist followers, and abandonment of our capital city." He traced the short distance from Valley Forge to Philadelphia. "A small body, perhaps two regiments will quick march to Philadelphia and fill the vacuum created by General Clinton's departure. The bulk of our army, including our artillery, will break camp and cross the river into New Jersey and chase the Redcoats like hounds on a fox, as they were so fond of saying when we were forced to retreat before them. Hopefully, they will turn and give battle before they reach New York."

Will knew he could ride to Philadelphia, find Elisabeth and bring her back to Valley Forge. She would be safe in Pennsylvania while he joined the army in pursuit of the retreating British.

"Sir. With all the confusion of the Redcoats' leaving, I could sneak into. . ."

Knox held up his meaty palm, revealing his ink-stained thumb and index finger. "My boy. After General Lafayette's reconnaissance in force at Barren Hill, the lobsterbacks are more alert than ever. Their patrols have increased and their pickets strengthened. I cannot sanction it and you will not engage in any such individual action."

The General did not specifically state it was an order, Will thought, as he heard the words. But his meaning was clear. Still, if he left at dark he could be back at Valley Forge with Elisabeth by the morning. It was less than twenty-four miles, and Big Red could easily carry two on the return.

"Will. Be of good cheer. I assure you, within the month, two at the most, you and Elisabeth will be wed in Philadelphia, and Lucy and I could not be more pleased to be present at such a joyous event." He grabbed Will's shoulders and with one arm around him escorted him toward the door. Given the General's height and two hundred and sixty pounds, Will felt himself swept from the room. He was unable to plead his case for dashing to Philadelphia and rescuing Elisabeth. "Be of good spirit, lad. Our forces will win a significant victory. Then the time will come for you to be reunited with your courageous and beautiful Elisabeth."

"Thank you, Sir," Will replied quietly. He did not share the General's optimistic view of his future. Instead, the closure of the door seemed to him the seal of doom and despair for his future happiness. How could the General be certain he and Elisabeth would ever marry? The thought that something could happen to Elisabeth was frightening enough. With a battle imminent, he could be killed. He thought of Elisabeth alone, unprotected by him after they had declared their love for each other. He choked down a cry of hopelessness.

There was a way to fulfill his overwhelming love for her. The decision was his, he thought, as he walked into the pasture and whistled for Big Red. The horse lifted his head, his ears perked forward and, sensing his master's indecision, walked slowly forward with his head drooping toward the ground. Will tightened the saddle cinch, put his foot in the stirrup and once seated, remained in the pasture, feeling the sun on his shoulders as he let Big Red nibble the new sprouts of spring grass. All it would take was a click of his tongue and the pressure of his knees for Big Red and he to be on the road out of camp. Then, wait until dark to stealthily enter the city.

He pulled gently on the reins and Big Red stopped. Rider and horse stood undecided and immobile where the road from General Knox's quarters led either back to camp or to the Gulph Road and beyond to Philadelphia. The consent of Elisabeth's father seemed worthless to him. If they never were able to marry, the consent mattered not a whit. If he balanced his love for Elisabeth and his fear for her safety against his newly taken oath and more importantly General Knox's trust and friendship, how did the scales tip? Sadly, he gave one long despairing look in the direction of Philadelphia, turned Big Red's head and reluctantly took the road that threaded between Mount Misery and Mount Joy back toward the rows of huts of the Artillery Regiment.

Elisabeth left the stalls on Market Street just before midafternoon. Prices for food had risen even further, once Superintendent Galloway ended all efforts to enforce the limits his administration had set. She pulled a lace handkerchief from her sleeve to cover her nose and mouth from the ripe stench of rotting garbage and human waste that emanated from the odoriferous piles present on every side street and made worse by the June heat. The smell was particularly horrendous around the State House. There, the British soldiers had deliberately used the building as a latrine and behind it dug a large square pit and dumped dead horses, other filth and even, it was rumored, bodies of unidentified men. Flies buzzed and swarmed everywhere, and the air was so filled with them that swatting them away was futile. /[7] She felt filthy simply by being outside and hoped she would not come down with some bilious fever that was transmitted by the foul air which had sickened many others.

The wharves were teeming with people and carts piled high with household furniture and goods. Once it had been announced that Loyalists and their families would be evacuated by ship, there was a frantic rush to move all manner of possessions down to the river. The panic was compounded by General Clinton's order to purchase or requisition horses to pull the wagons with the army's munitions and supplies overland through New Jersey to New York City.

She had seen with her own eyes, not only servants but young men of wealthy families manually pulling goat carts or staggering over the cobblestones with wobbly wheelbarrows loaded with furniture, trunks of clothing, pots, pans and other household items, through the streets to the waiting ships. Loyalist merchants, without their own vessels, loaded their drays with the goods from their stores and brought them to the piers. If they were to be evacuated by a Navy ship, the sailors as often as not, to the dismay of the Loyalists, dumped much of their property in the river. Those fleeing fared better with private schooners and sloops whose captains demanded exorbitant fees to cram their vessels with panicked Tories and their possessions. It was rumored that some Royal Navy transports, carrying American prisoners and sick and wounded British soldiers, had already left for New York.

The market was a frenzy of activity as people purchased as much food as possible, hoarding against the day the British abandoned the city and the Pennsylvania Supreme Executive Council and the American army returned. Elisabeth and Mary Lewis had divided their shopping. Mary had headed to the piers to purchase salted fish, which would stand them in good stead if meat subsequently became scarce or so expensive as to be unattainable. Elisabeth had purchased two five pound sacks of cheap flour for a price which, a month ago, she would have paid for the highest quality. She ignored a stall selling fruit. Under the circumstances these were an unnecessary luxury.

Instead, she bought early summer squash and carrots, good for soup ingredients that could be stretched into several meals. With her heavy basket under her arm, she walked up Market Street toward the Quaker Quarter thinking it was only a matter of days before the British abandoned the city.

Already, the streets were dangerous at night, the lamps unlit, alleys dark and foreboding. Deserters and unsavory rough men from the warren of cheap bars and brothels down near the river, prowled the better neighborhoods looking for newly abandoned homes to loot. The Lewises kept their front door barred and candles burning through the night. She passed the Quaker Meeting House at Fourth and Arch which, unlike the Presbyterian and Congregational Churches, had been left mostly undamaged. There were rumors that the dragoons, who had used the Old Pine Street Church as a stable, had chopped holes in the floor and shoveled their horses' manure into the basement, and even used the openings for their latrines. Although she normally discounted rumors, the stench in the city corroborated some of the malice being inflicted by the departing British.

Elisabeth thought fondly of her final meeting with Captain Montresor. She had called him John for the first time and told him she could not accept his offer. She pretended that, while she may have some difficulties with the Rebel authorities, she did not expect them to treat her harshly because of her friendship with him. He replied he understood and if she changed her mind, to write him in New York and he would provide the means for her transport. She had let him kiss her gently on the cheek. She wondered whether her fondness for him was due to his courtly and gentlemanly behavior or that the constant attention by this worldly, experienced man appealed to her vanity.

She forced such thoughts from her mind and instead envisioned her joyous reunion with Will. She had not seen him since September when he had taught her the codes for her secret messages and they had professed their love for each other. In her imagination she saw him, with his Regiment, in his faded blue uniform, his brown hair partially hidden by a tri-corn, riding Big Red pulling a polished brass cannon, past the crowds of cheering people lining the streets. She smiled thinking of their first moments alone together, his smell of leather, horse and gunpowder, her head upon his shoulder, the relief from the long and dangerous months apart.

Elisabeth reached into her cloth sack, removed the heavy iron key and fitted it into the lock. It turned easily. She pushed open the door before realizing there was someone behind her. Before she could turn she felt two hands on her back and she was thrust so violently into the hallway, she stumbled and fell against the side table, knocking the night lantern to the floor and shattering the glass. Righting herself on the floor, she stared up at John Stoner. He glared at her, a look of triumph on his fleshy face, his small eyes as intense with hatred as when she had seen him gambling at the faro table less than a month ago.

He bent down, seized the fabric of her dress in one hand, yanked her forward and slapped her hard twice, the backhand blow hitting her on her right cheekbone. "You Rebel slut. I will beat a confession out of you." He raised his hand again to strike her. Elisabeth felt a shard of lantern glass beneath her hand. She seized it and before he could hit her, she stabbed him in the forearm below the elbow. John stared at the triangular spike of glass protruding from the red sleeve of his uniform, now stained with the darker crimson of his own blood. With an angry shout of rage, he struck her hard on her temple with his closed fist. Elisabeth's head snapped back from the blow and her shoulders hit the floor as Stoner released his grip on her dress to attend to his wound.

Groggily, she crawled on her knees down the hall toward the kitchen. She had just managed to pull herself up, her hands on the wooden table, when she heard him stomping after her. He came into the kitchen enraged, his jacket off, his arm bound with a handkerchief below the elbow, the white shirt stained with a dark circle of blood. She screamed as he pushed the table roughly against her, trapping her between it and the coarse stone wall. Angrily, he pulled the table away and made to grab her. Elisabeth slid toward the fireplace feeling for the iron poker. She grasped at anything and ended up holding the short ashes shovel in front of her. Stoner laughed. She had never heard a more malevolent sound as he advanced toward her. He swatted the implement away with his wounded arm and with his good hand squeezed her throat. His thumb and fingers clenched tighter around her neck, as he pushed her against the wall, his other hand fondling her breast. "Now, you bitch. Tell me how you sent messages to those Rebel scum," he hissed in her ear. She felt his hips pressing against her, smelled his breath, saw the pockmarks on his cheeks. She knew she was losing consciousness. She must be, for behind Stoner, in the kitchen doorway, she imagined she saw Edward Lewis.

John heard a noise behind him but reluctant to release his hold on Elisabeth, only turned his head. Lewis immediately locked his arm around Stoner's neck, tore him away from Elisabeth and forced John's other arm up high behind his back. He was a tall, robust man and with one large hand on the back of John's neck, the other bending his arm painfully upward, he marched him back down the hall.

"Let me go. I am a representative of the British authorities," he sputtered. "That woman is a Rebel spy. I am arresting her."

"You will do no such thing," Lewis growled. He pushed Stoner out the open door and down the two steps, turned and threw his jacket uniform after him and remained menacingly in the doorway, fists clenched at his side. Stoner stood and raised his wounded arm, bleeding anew from the rough handling he had received from the Quaker.

"I will be back and you will regret this," he shouted waving his fist at Lewis.

"Come back when the Americans are here and see how you fare," he retorted. "And I already regret using force against you," Lewis said more softly.

When Mary arrived home shortly thereafter, she had to pound on the barred door to be let in. Her husband opened the door and she immediately saw from his face he was distraught. He led her to the kitchen where Elisabeth sat, a basin of hot water stained with blood on the table in front of her. Her face was swollen and beneath one eye which was almost closed, a large purple bruise spread down her cheek.

"Oh, you poor dear," Mary said, hastily putting down her basket and taking the cloth compress from her husband.

"She has a jagged cut on her hand," he said pointing to Elisabeth's palm. Mary cleaned it with warm water and vinegar and Elisabeth moaned slightly in response. Gently, she examined Elisabeth's face.

"There are no broken bones. These bruises will heal in time, my dear." She noted the red marks on her throat and washed them as well, uttering comforting sounds as she did so.

"Edward, I think Elisabeth should rest now. Perhaps, after I help her upstairs and settle her in bed you could bring the little bit of claret we still have."

Lying under the quilt, Elisabeth gazed up at Mary's kindly face. "It was your husband who saved me," she said quietly. "Remember that Independence Day when you questioned whether he would ever use violence to protect those he cared about." Mary nodded, recalling the conversation. Elisabeth had phrased it felicitously. Mary had urged her husband to declare whether or not he would fight to protect her from the patriotic thugs who were then threatening their home.

"He defended me," Elisabeth said softly. "As he would you. I believe he is tormented by having physically attacked," she hesitated before saying "John Stoner. Edward may want to talk to you about the turmoil inside him."

"And you? Is there anything you want to talk to me about?" She looked at Elisabeth shrewdly.

"Mary. You are more than a dear friend." Elisabeth's eyes welled with tears. "A confidant. Someone I can tell everything to. And have." She reached for the glass of claret and Mary held her head up as she sipped. "Please, neither you nor Edward must say anything about this to Will. I must be the one to decide to tell him." Mary nodded. "Do not worry. We will keep this our secret."

Elisabeth sighed. "I believe that one brother can be good and one evil. After all, the Bible teaches us that lesson. I love Will and my love for him is not in anyway diminished by his brother's assault on me. When I am with Will, and I pray it will be soon, but after I have healed so he will not look upon me as ugly, I see nothing but his goodness. If there are any other reservations from this today, our love will overcome them. It will have to. There is nothing else that matters."

Mary patted Elisabeth's hand. "Sleep now and when you awake it will be one day closer to the Americans returning to Philadelphia and your being reunited with him."

Elisabeth nodded. "Mary. When the men who imprisoned Edward return to power in this city, please know that I will do everything possible to ensure that no further retribution is visited upon him."

"I know that. It is something our community is concerned about. The men of the Council, however, are of a vengeful spirit."

As Elisabeth drifted off to sleep, she no longer thought of Will riding proudly into the city on Big Red. Instead, she saw him entering her bedroom, shocked by the bruises on her face, incensed by her account of his brother's assault, and consumed by a blind rage for revenge. She envisioned him on a battlefield, stalking John purposefully, unmindful of the trooper bearing down on him, sabre raised. She awoke with a scream before the sabre descended and lay shivering under the quilt even though it was a warm June evening, until she drifted off and slept fitfully.

Chapter 9 - Bloody Fighting in the Cauldron of Summer

The dust from the road caught in Private Christoph Weber's throat. It coated his tongue, clogged his nostrils and scratched his already irritated eyes. By his estimate, since crossing the Delaware River below Philadelphia, they had marched less than forty miles in six days.

The progress of the entire British army was slowed by the long caravan of wagons carrying their tents, munitions, and supplies that seemed to stretch for miles in front of them. The von Knyphausen Regiment and two Regiments of Grenadiers were part of the rear guard, protecting the Army and the cumbersome baggage train from attack.

Christoph was welcomed back when he crossed the lines into the city, starved, ragged and weak from fatigue. Once he regained his strength, he was given a new uniform, musket and kit and assigned to the remnants of his old Regiment. It was much reduced from its original full strength of eight hundred men, down now to three hundred and seventy due to casualties, soldiers captured, and a few desertions. Those too ill and unfit for duty had been sent by naval transport to New York.

And now, as they staggered through the sweltering late June heat and heavy blanket of humid air, Christoph struggled to put one foot in front of another. As a gesture to ease their suffering, Lieutenant Justus Brumhard ordered them to remove their brass helmets and stow them in their haversacks. It was indicative of how many officers they had lost at Trenton, to have a Lieutenant in charge of their company. Captain Seckendorf never would have allowed this, but the good Captain lay buried in a common grave behind the Anglican Church in Trenton. Christoph thought of how he, Andreas and Georg had complained about the bitter winds whipping through their winter barracks. Well, Robert Langley had taught him the meaning of being constantly cold, forcing him to labor outside in sleet and snow in his threadbare uniform and at night, huddling in the pig sty, against a slatted wall that barely kept out the bitter winds. Whether it was the thought of that terrible winter or his anger at the mistreatment by Langley, his legs felt less leaden. Nothing, however, could ease his discomfort from the constant dust that was kicked up by the horses' hooves and wagon wheels they were forced to follow. We are protecting them from the local Rebel militias and are repaid by having to eat their dust in this choking heat, he thought angrily.

Their slow progress had been further impeded by sabotage of their route by local militias: bridges burned or dismantled over small creeks, causeways dug up or collapsed into adjacent swamps, trees felled across the road, and worst of all, wells destroyed or filled with offal. For the thirsty Hessians, this was the foulest interference to be endured. Compelled to drink from muddy puddles left from the occasional violent summer rainstorms, or from slime- filled creeks and runoffs, many succumbed to crippling stomach cramps. Soldiers curled up on the side of the road, vomiting or soiling their breeches with brown watery excretions. The entire evacuation route was marked by roadside graves and troops lying helplessly in the blistering heat. There were rumors of desertions but no one from his Regiment.

Occasionally, the rear guard came under fire, but these were generally musket volleys, rendered ineffective by the distance. The Grenadiers, marching in their high fur hats, were more frequently felled by heat than musket balls. Two Grenadiers would pass through the Hessian ranks, dragging their prostrate companion between them, toss him on to the back of a wagon, and then return to their unit. As they did so, they would point to the bare-headed Hessians and snarl something in English, which Christoph knew was an insult. He was too thirsty and tired to let it bother him and was thankful his brains were not being boiled inside his brass cap.

That night, they camped in a flat field outside some small town, whose church spires they could see in the distance. The heat did not abate with the darkness and their tents did not keep out the swarms of mosquitos that rose from the remnants of marshes and swamps at dusk to feast on their bare flesh. Shortly before dawn, when the drums signalled to break camp, Christoph was covered with red welts and bloody bites he had unconsciously scratched open while he had slept fitfully. Any marching done before the rising of the blazing sun was to their benefit, Christoph thought, rousing himself from his cot.

He had not counted on the time it took for the wagoneers to hitch their teams, nor how slowly the train would form and get on the road again. While the front part of the Army, unburdened by the baggage train, made substantial progress, by noon the rearguard was merely approaching the little hamlet they had seen the night before. He expectantly waited for the order to remove their brass hats now that the sun was high above them.

Suddenly, a drum signaled them to halt and about face. Together with the Grenadiers they formed a line against a large advancing force of Rebels, attempting to strike them from the left of the road. In the shimmering heat of the late morning, Christoph thought he recognized them by their uniforms as regular troops rather than militias. Despite the heat, it felt good to quick march again, after that slow plodding pace. There was no dust in front of them now. Just the brownish, baked flat fields and the Rebels coming on. Once within musket range, the Hessians fired several volleys before being joined by dragoons and other infantry regiments who rushed back from the town. The Rebel troops began an orderly retreat in face of the reinforced British line.

On command, Christoph's company fixed bayonets and advanced rapidly through a wheat field, across a road and over a small stream that trickled into a swampy area. The Rebels' discipline collapsed, their ranks broke and the troops scattered, emerging from the dark black muck in small groups, forming to hold ground and then turning and sprinting across another flat open field. They always run like rabbits, Christoph thought, as his company charged forward. They flee before they feel the shock of our bayonets. Eager and now unmindful of the heat, he raced forward, a shout coming from his dry throat, whether of revenge for his captivity or because his blood was up, he did not know. [1]

Private Henry Gillet and the other men of the 2nd Rhode Island Regiment, gratefully reached the shade of the broad-trunked, forty foot swamp oaks, which lined the far side of the oven-hot ploughed field. Crossing through the sandy soil, many of the soldiers stripped off their jackets and shirts and stuffed them in their haversacks. They lay resting on the dank earth, covered in places by pine needles from the occasional conifers.

Their route for the past few days from Princeton southeast through New Jersey had followed the path of devastation and senseless destruction left in the wake of the retreating British Army: dead cattle lying in the fields and pastures where they had been shot, some with fly-infested bloody hind quarters marking where meat had been carved off their carcasses; farm tools of all kinds with their long handles broken in two; household furniture hacked apart; trees in orchards, heavy with cherries, chopped down waist high; barns, sheds and homes smouldering, their stone chimneys the sole survivor and silent witness to the wanton arson that had been committed.

They had been marching since sunup having left their baggage in the rear under guard, taking only their blankets, cartridges and provisions. Ahead of them, they heard the report from a light field cannon, a three pounder Gillet guessed, followed by an occasional musket volley.

"Hey, Henry," Oliver Whipple called to him, lying prone under a low branch. "Pass me your canteen. Mine is empty." Gillet tossed his, now less than half filled, to his friend. The last two wells they had passed had been filled with rubble.

"Remember the casks of hard cider the good people of Princeton shared with us as we marched through," Oliver said wistfully. Henry thought of their march at dusk through Princeton. He had been on the side of their platoon closest to the homes and in the early evening light he had seen the women, some with their children, cheering and waving as the soldiers went by. It had stirred within him a deep sense of loneliness and longing for his wife Judith and their daughter. He opened his cartridge box and rubbed the light blue fabric of the ribbon Judith had sent him. [2] Earlier this morning, before setting out, they had been issued forty cartridges each, a clear indication there would be a battle soon. He held the ribbon between his thumb and forefinger, thinking of it as a talisman to protect him.

Oliver sat down next to him and returned his canteen. "I have never been more eager for battle," Gillet said, looking at his friend. "I want to defeat the Redcoats, end this brutal war that desolates the countryside, and return to Judith and my daughter."

"Your two wishes have been granted," Oliver replied with a grin, revealing several teeth, blackened from repeated musket practice. "With all that incessant drilling, we marched rapidly and this day have arrived in good order to catch the Redcoats before they reach the protection of New York. I am of the opinion . . ." He was interrupted by a shouted order and drum signal first to form up and then retreat.

"What the devil," Oliver said, his lips curled in unconcealed disgust.

They quickly assembled, with many of the men reluctantly grumbling about retreating before contact with the enemy had even been made. The Regiment, instead of retracing their steps through the hot sandy field, turned slightly west and marched on a road through a ravine along a muddy, shallow brook. Rumors ran down the line as they sat by the side of the road to permit the retreating artillery to pass. The word was part of the army was in full flight and the Rhode Islanders' advanced position had become untenable. Why was the army retreating? No one had the answer to that question.

"The Generals seem as perplexed as we are," Oliver said pointing to General Washington riding forward, surrounded by a cluster of senior officers and aides. The men spontaneously stood and cheered as the entire entourage passed them. The group halted ahead on a road to confer with a General and his staff coming toward them from the front. [3] Oliver, standing on a tree stump to get a better view, reported, "I cannot hear what they are saying but from here it appears General

Washington is giving the other General a dressing down." In keeping with that impression, Washington galloped off to the front, followed by all but the General he had addressed. The sounds of cannon fire increased before an aide returned on his horse, stopped briefly to give Lt. Colonel Olney his orders, and was then off again, whipping his horse to a lather.

"By Company forward march," Olney shouted. The ensign carrying the colors proceeded to lead Gillet's company in a quick march out of the defile and toward level clear ground. They took up their positions behind a fence with thick brush intertwined among the slats and waited. Major Thayer rode behind the men shouting for them to hold the line, as the rest of the Army was coming up quickly in support. Their position was reinforced by the arrival of the rest of the Regiment, including some colored soldiers under the command of Captain Arnold.

"What do you think of them?" Oliver said, gesturing with his head toward the colored soldiers taking positions behind the hedgerow.

Henry looked their way and smiled. "To me, they seem as able as we to kill Redcoats." He knew his regiment was understrength. The addition of some sixty odd soldiers from the Black Regiment filled that need. [4] "For my money, they are brother soldiers."

"I fear they will cut and run," Private Fish said contemptuously. "Many were only slaves a few months ago."

"It appears that some of our troops retreated in a hurry or else why would General Washington be in such a fury?" Gillet asked. "Those were white troops. I believe the blacks will prove you wrong, Fish."

"Let us hope the rest of the army arrives soon," Oliver said. "There are more than enough Redcoats approaching for all." Henry peered through the greenery and saw a mass of soldiers, rapidly advancing in good order across the field. He heard the crisp orders of their platoon sergeant - "Cock Firelock! Take Aim! Fire!" Their musket volley tore into the advancing Redcoats. He sensed rather than heard the order for the second rank to move half a foot to the right and fire. The noise of their musket fire deafened him as he was already reloading. The drill orders echoed in his head: Prime! Shut Pan! Charge Cartridge! Draw Rammer (two motions)! Ram Down Cartridge (one motion) ! Return

Rammer! Cock Firelock! Take Aim! Fire! In front of them, the dead and wounded lay in the field, left behind by the retreating Redcoats.

Henry lost count of how many times the enemy reformed their ranks and charged through the field, and how many times he fired his musket. In the still air of the oppressive heat, a low white cloud of spent gunpowder wafted over their position. At some point they were ordered to pull back. He felt a sense of pride as his Company and the Regiment marched in good order away from the fence where they had held up the British advance. They slogged through a swampy lowland and clambered up a hill. Their new positions were beneath a battery of four six-pounders overlooking a level valley between them and another height in the distance. The slope was steep enough so that the cannons could fire over their heads. Below, on both sides of the one road on which they had rested, the bulk of the Army had taken up positions blocking the British who had marched in strength back from the little town. The Redcoats were aligned in two battle lines of three Regiments each, with one Regiment in reserve in the center. Henry could make out the high fur caps of the Grenadiers. The sun was high in the sky, just past noon.

"There will be plenty of hot action today," Oliver said, kneeling in position next to him surveying the scene below. "Fairly soon those troops down there will attempt to outflank our lines by coming this way."

Henry looked back over his shoulder at the four cannons. "Our artillery will help us stop them," he said. He was confident and resolute. All of that drilling had made his Company, nay his Regiment, capable of standing up to the hated Redcoats. He touched the ribbon in his cartridge box and wound it around his finger. It will not be long now dear Judith, he thought, until we shall be reunited. And then I will never leave you.

Bant knelt uncomfortably on the stubble of grass. Ahead was a roughly plowed field, with occasional stems of weeds and shrubs poking up here and there. He was accustomed to hiding in the woods, behind fallen logs, screened by bushes or crouching behind fences and stone walls. Being out in the open made him uneasy. He had volunteered again to join Morgan's Rifles, thinking they would harass and ambush the British as they retreated from Philadelphia. He had not anticipated being part of the front line, the troops that absorbed the impact of an assault by disciplined ranks of Redcoats.

Along with McNeil and some others from Colonel Hand's Regiment, they had marched forward to support the attack on the baggage train and rearguard. Before they had even caught up with their own troops, they were ordered to retreat, which he admitted had been done in good order but still made no sense. Instead of taking to the woods and picking off the British from a distance, they were assigned to General Alexander's brigade. Morgan's men told them Alexander was called Lord something or other. Bant thought it peculiar to be fighting against the Crown under the command of this Lord, not that it mattered to him. He had fought under "Scotch Willy," picking off tall Scots in kilts and hunting them down in the snowy hills of New Jersey.

Morgan's men also had taught him a phrase he took to heart. They called their sharpshooting "killing off the king birds," which meant aiming for the highest ranking officers in the field. He liked that idea and had listened carefully as to how to recognize such officers. Corporals and Sergeants shouted commands and led from the end of a file. An officer carried a sword and often rode a horse into battle, but not always. And they led from the front.

The men of Morgan's Rifle Corps were in two lines. Bant in the front line, along with McNeil, would fire first and reload while the standing second line fired over their heads. The four hundred or so men were spaced about two arms lengths apart, close enough to deliver a concentrated deadly fire, but with enough room to maneuver with their long rifles. None of them had bayonets, although many of Morgan's men, as well as McNeil, carried hatchets. Bant had his big-bladed hunting knife, strapped to his belt. His position was close to the adjacent Continental Regiment. He had heard they were from Connecticut. They had regular muskets and most had bayonets affixed to the end of the barrels.

Bant saw the British infantry steadily approaching in well-ordered ranks, as if on parade. Then he heard the high-pitched screech of bagpipes. A Scottish regiment, clad in dark and light green tartans with red and white checkered head bands, maneuvered smartly in position between the two infantry regiments. Together the entire line advanced with precision, the Scots almost directly opposite Bant. He ignored the color bearer, a tall man with a clean white strap across his chest, part of the harness for the flagstaff. Everyone would sight in on him. Instead, he picked out a smaller fellow in the front line, leading with his short sword pointing forward. He wore a bright brass badge on his cap. Bant assumed that was an indication of rank and settled on him as his target.

The British were less than thirty yards away when they halted and fired. Musket balls whistled through the air, followed by two more volleys from the second and third lines. Out of the corner of his eye, he saw men struck by the Redcoats' fire and collapse to the ground. The Continentals discharged a volley. Then a second one. Bant heard the order - "Front Rank, Make Ready." He lowered his rifle to his shoulder and sighted down the barrel. "Take Aim! Fire!" The smoke from the British muskets obscured his target but Bant thought he saw the man waving his sword and urging the Scots forward. He fired and saw the officer drop his sword but remain standing. Had he missed the man's head? Surely his aim could not have been that far off. Quickly, he reloaded as the men in the rear rank fired into the advancing troops. They were less than twenty yards away now. There were gaps in their lines but they were still coming on. Bant could hear their battle cries and above it all the piercing squeal of their bagpipes. He was seized by a fear of being hacked to pieces by a broadsword or speared on the point of a bayonet. He could clearly make out the fierce expressions on their faces as they rapidly advanced on the American lines. He fired his rifle and barely had time to see the soldier grasp at his throat and fall. He had no time to reload. They would be on him before he could do so.

"Company. Charge Bayonets!" With a roar, which almost drowned out the long drum roll, the Connecticut soldiers charged forward as a unit into the advancing Scots. All Bant could see was a mass of bodies, a tangle of feet, muskets raised in the air, men lying bleeding on the ground. Without thinking he reloaded and waited. When he looked again, the colors of the Scottish troops, held aloft in the center, waved and dipped, rose again and then were hidden from Bant's view. The bagpipes wailed a different tune, the Scots turned and, led by their color bearer, hurriedly retreated, leaving their dead and wounded behind. [5]

Bant heard the order to advance, saw McNeil raise his hand in solemn greeting, and moved forward with the rest of Morgan's Rifles in quick step. They soon caught up with the Connecticut soldiers. Together with the infantry, in the good order learned on the drilling fields at Valley Forge, they streamed after the retreating British. At some point, Bant heard the shouted orders and the recognizable drum signal. He halted and the company formed new lines. It was in the same kind of open grassy terrain and furrows that made him uncomfortable. He reached for his cartridge box and brushed against his empty sheath. Then he recalled he had drawn his hunting knife and stuck it in the ground in front of him when the Scots charged with their bayonets. A lot of good the knife would have done him against a more than foot long bayonet. He would have to go back and find it.

Out in the open, he felt exposed to both infantry assaults and shelling by the rows of cannons arrayed ahead of them and off to their right. Bant hoped they would not be ordered to attack the cannons. For the moment, it seemed unlikely. There were horses in their traces. It meant the cannons would move in support of some attack, probably not on their front. The retreating Scots and infantry had passed through their lines to regroup in the rear and there were no troops massing in front of Bant's newly formed line.

He waited in the hot sun, dissatisfied he had not picked off an officer and troubled that his aim had been off. If this were to be the experience with Morgan's Rifles, maybe next time he would not volunteer and stay with Colonel Hand's Regiment.

Will was pleased both Adam and Titus were with him, Adam, stocky and strong serving as powder handler and one-eyed Titus as runner and additional man if there were casualties. Both were Marblehead Mariners attached to his battery. He was confident he could rely upon them under fire, having fought together during the race riot at General Washington's headquarters in Cambridge.

There were three four-gun batteries, all brass six and nine-pounders interspersed to support General Wayne's Brigade. Their long days training in the fields outside of York had proven beneficial. After receiving orders, hurriedly issued by General Knox, they had ridden forward, pulling the cannons behind them, quickly unhitching the horses, manhandled the guns into position and off-loaded the side boxes with powder and shot.

They were in the center of the line spread on both sides of the road that sloped up toward them from a broad sandy plain. Captain Hadley commanded all twelve guns and rode the length of their position, shouting orders to protect the powder boxes, relocate the balls and grape shot, move a gun to take advantage of some natural protection. No such commands were needed for Will's four cannons. The crews were ready. At the nine-pounder where he was gun commander, he had Chandler, Baldwin, Davenport and Tyler, all veterans of prior battles. With the cannons in place and a brief lull before the advancing British troops were within range, Will assessed their position.

To his right, American troops occupied a low, round-topped hill, together with some artillery. It was the highest point of the terrain. From there, they would be firing on the left wing of the advancing British. Big Red and the other horses were in the woods behind Will's battery, where even an errant British cannon shot would not endanger them.

What his battery lacked was a nearby water supply. They would need water to swab the guns. The only water they had with them was in their canteens. If it came down to being thirsty or being certain there were no residual burning flakes of linen in the barrel to prematurely ignite the next powder charge, the men would have to go without. He remembered they had passed a church and parsonage. He hoped there was a working well there. When the time came, he would send Titus back to the church to scout for water. [6]

A somber thought occurred that he did not want to dwell on. In the event Captain Hadley was wounded or killed, Will would become the batteries' commander. He did not think himself capable of managing twelve guns. His grim assessment of his shortcomings was interrupted by Hadley's orders to load their guns and await his command. Swiftly, Levi Tyler took the charge from Adam and slid it down the barrel. Chandler rammed the charge home with a grunt and stepped aside as Levi rolled the nine-pound shot into the muzzle. Baldwin reached into his leather pouch, pricked the powder charge with a wire and inserted a quill filled with powder in the touchhole and shouted "Primed!" Will turned toward Hadley who had his sword raised in his hand. All he could think of was that he made an easy target for the British, sitting exposed on his horse in the midst of the cannons. His order to fire was overwhelmed by the crash of the musket volleys of the Americans. Will had seen Hadley's sword arm fall. "Give Fire!" he shouted. Davenport placed the slow match in the quill. The nine-pounder boomed and a cloud of white smoke rose and merged with the puffs from the muskets of the infantry.

The crew moved methodically and with calm efficiency: Tyler wormed the barrel, Chandler swabbed it, took the new charge from Adam and rammed it home. With the ball down the barrel the cannon was again primed. Hadley instructed the gun commanders that after the first round, they were to fire as soon as they loaded. "Give fire!" Will ordered. He was proud that his crew was the first to reload and let loose the second shot. During the endless drills, he had discovered that Davenport was a quick learner and steady at his post. He kept Chandler manning the sponge. A good man, calm and deliberate, but perhaps a little too old for the rigors of fighting. Their lives depended on him. One forgetful moment, one instance of carelessness and a burning ember could explode the new powder charge in the barrel, burst the cannon and slaughter them all with hot metal shrapnel.

The still air and oppressive heat kept the cloud of smoke from the gun powder overhead. He could see the decimated British infantry ranks retreating and reforming anew. On they came for another frontal assault and once again, they were met with concentrated cannon and musket fire that drove them back. The third time, Hadley ordered the battery to load with grape shot. Will lowered the gun's elevation. The small iron balls tore into the advancing soldiers, maiming them, taking their legs from under them like a scythe cutting wheat. They retreated leaving their dead to bloat and swell and their wounded to bake and suffer in the blistering heat.

Hadley rode up to their battery. "They will move up their artillery. Aim for their horses before they are out of harness."

Will readjusted the wedge under the breech. Adam, who had the keenest of eyes, balanced himself on the spokes of the carriage wheel and looked out on the battlefield. "Cannons coming," he shouted, pointing toward the left. Will saw the horses first and waved to the three other gun commanders in his battery. He motioned to Baldwin, and the two of them lifted the tiller and re-aimed the cannon. "Tyler. Worm the piece." Once again his cannon was the first to fire, followed quickly by the three other guns of his battery. The smoke from their muzzles obscured their targets. He fired another round, guessing the British had either not yet unlimbered their guns, or if so, were in the same place. He saw Chandler mouthing words but Will was too deafened by the cannon fire and could not hear him. Chandler ran up to him and cupped his hand over Will's ear.

"We are almost out of water."

Will unslung his canteen and handed it to Isaiah and directed him to collect the canteens from the rest of the crew. Chandler emptied them into the artillery bucket, filling it almost to the rim. Will waved to Titus and handed him the empty canteens.

"Run back to the parsonage. Fill the canteens at their well and find anything else that will hold water and bring it here." Titus nodded, wove his way past the ranks of troops and dashed toward the rear. If they ran out before he returned, Will intended to find an infantry officer and ask for his men's canteens. The heat was so intense, many of the troops, including his gun crew, had long since removed their jackets and were fighting in their shirt- sleeves.

The British artillery now was in position and opened fire. To Will, it seemed like every one of their guns was concentrated on his battery. Ball after ball tore into the soft earth around them and plowed into the troops. Musket balls whizzed menacingly overhead.

He ordered Davenport to fire at will and ran first to one cannon on his left and then to the other two guns in the battery. All were running low on powder and shot. At the furthermost cannon, he was kneeling when a cannon ball whistled overhead. He heard a scream and the gun commander fell, writhing on the soft earth holding his left eye, blinded by the force of the nearby passage of the ball.

Will sprinted behind the gun and accosted a Lieutenant of one of the regular infantry companies. "We need more shot and charges. Send one of your men to the wagons in the tree line with that message." The Lieutenant nodded. Will turned just in time to see a ball strike near the six-pounder adjacent to his gun and richochet into the carriage wheel, smashing the spokes. The cannon tilted down at an angle.

"We cannot right the gun," Sergeant Otis yelled at Will, pointing to the damaged wheel. Will directed two of Otis's crew to lift the cannon. Then he and Otis turned the wheel until the iron rim was propped up by the solid oak wedges normally used to elevate the breech. If it did not hold, he would disperse Otis's gun crew among the three remaining cannons.

The battery was engaged in a ferocious duel with the British guns, more intense than at Brandywine or any other battle he could remember. Titus returned with filled canteens and Will let each man take a long swallow before indicating the water was to be held in reserve. The British guns let up their fire. Through the smoke Will could see their Regiments massing for another attack, their muskets held high, the sun glinting off their bayonets. Each of the four cannons was loaded with grape shot. He ran from gun to gun telling them to hold their fire and wait for his signal. He knew they were as deaf as he was. Grabbing the rammer and holding it high, he waited until the Redcoats were well within range. Then with a shout of "Fire!" he lowered the rammer. The steady disciplined volleys by the Continentals, the withering blasts of grapeshot and the cannons firing down on the advancing British from the hill enfilading their left flank, broke their attack.

Their retreat provided no relief for Will's battery. The British artillery resumed their barrage. [7] The artillery duel continued unabated through the afternoon heat, intensifying before each renewed infantry assault. A ball struck near Otis's cannon, cut off the thigh of one of the crew just above the knee and the foot of another standing behind him. Both men lay on the ground screaming in agony, dark red blood pouring from their wounds and saturating the dry, sandy soil. The next shot hit the carriage a glancing blow, taking the six-pounder out of commission. Adam lifted the heavy powder box where it lay behind the disabled cannon and staggered with it a short distance before Titus rushed to help him. Together they brought it back to their nine-pounder just as a musket volley tore through the air around them.

"I looked in the side box," Adam said, panting from exertion and squatting low to the ground. "No more grape shot in there." Will knew they were out of the rounded small balls and another assault was imminent. Only one wagonload of powder had reached his four cannons. Whether the grape shot had been diverted to other guns, Will did not know and there was no time to find out.

"There are barrels of nails at the parsonage. I saw them in the shed next to the well," Titus said. Will shook his head. He could not hear him. Titus leaned forward, cupped both hands over his mouth and shouted his information. Will nodded he understood. "You and Adam bring those barrels here, quickly." Adam looked over at the two wounded men from the crew of the six-pounder. He motioned to Titus and each one hoisted a man on their backs and trotted off toward the rear.

Will took over Adam's role of powder handler. He handed the charge to Tyler who took it and slid it down the muzzle. Will looked for Chandler who stood, swaying on his feet. He stumbled toward the cannon, his knees buckled and he collapsed to the ground. His eyes rolled in their sockets, the whites contrasting with his face smeared with powder and flushed from the heat. Will grabbed a canteen, lifted Isaiah's head and helped him drink. Chandler groaned, his head lolled over and he passed out.

Will grabbed the wooden staff of the rammer and thrust it down the barrel. Davenport assumed the task of bringing the ball which he slid down the muzzle. Will rammed it home. Davenport raced from the muzzle to the touchhole, pricked the canvas bag and inserted the quill. "Give fire!" Will shouted as he took up a position behind the breech. They continued firing with Will swabbing the cannon, hearing

Chandler's calming words in his head about the importance of taking time to be certain rather than being hasty, making sure Baldwin blocked the touchhole with his thumb cover. "Four more balls left," he shouted, raising his hand to indicate the number.

They were down to the last one when Adam and Titus returned, each man staggering under the weight of a barrel of nails on their shoulders. Both men's lower backs and breeches were drenched with blood. At first, Will thought they had been shot but then recalled it was blood from the two wounded gunners.

Judging by the size of the nails, Will estimated half a barrel would fill the cannon to the muzzle. Adam brought him a powder charge, the usual size with enough gun powder to fire a nine-pound ball. It would send the nails flying through the air at great speed. Will swabbed the cannon, rammed the charge home and then stepped back as Adam and Titus poured the nails down the barrel until it was filled to just below the muzzle ring.

Captain Hadley rode up to the battery and raised his sword as a signal to fire at his command. A hail of musket balls whistled through the air and Hadley leaped off his horse as it was shot out from under him. The poor beast thrashed around on the ground before the Captain pulled out his pistol and shot the animal through its eye. Hadley stood on the horse's corpse with his sword held high. They let the tall-hatted Grenadiers approach closer this time, forcing them to step over their own dead and wounded. It slowed their progress before they could reach clear ground. Their long, lethal bayonets, lowered for the charge, reflected sharp blinding bursts of light, as their compact, orderly ranks, three deep, steadied once past their fallen comrades and began the quick march.

"Fire!" Hadley ordered, pointing his lowered sword at the advancing Grenadiers and infantry. The hail of nails hurtled toward the enemy and tore into their flesh, creating ragged irregular wounds more horrible than rounded grape shot. [8] Though he was partially deaf, Will heard the agonizing collective high-pitched scream of pain from hundreds of throats as their line staggered. Still they came on, although fewer in number. The second round of nails ripped into their already decimated ranks and forced them to retreat from the horrendous hail of the iron shrapnel and the concentrated volleys of disciplined musket fire.

The British cannons fell silent. The artillery duel was over. In the still air, two large clouds of smoke hung over the battlefield, each obscuring one side from the other. In between lay the dead and dying Redcoats. Once it was clear the British were retreating, the American Regiments around Will's battery marched to their left and down a road in pursuit. Will, exhausted by the heat but exhilarated by the battle, knelt next to Chandler, propping the Corporal's head in his hand. His skin was hot to the touch. Gently, he poured some water on Chandler's face and wiped it with his shirt sleeve. He thought of Chandler attending to him as he recovered from his brutal beating at the hands of patriotic thugs, those many months ago in Boston. Chandler moaned and his tongue licked his now moist lips. Will tilted his canteen and made him take small sips. Baldwin knelt next to Chandler, idly fingering several holes in his shirt where musket balls had missed the flesh but torn the fabric. He took a short swig and then slowly poured the remaining water from his canteen on Chandler's head.

"That is good," Chandler admitted softly. "How did the battle go?" he asked, as he sat up groggily.

"We are in possession of the field and the British are in retreat. Are you fit enough to ride in the wagon with the crew?"

Chandler nodded. Baldwin and Tyler helped him to stand. Behind them, the Regiment's drivers were coming with the wagons and horses. Will took Big Red's reins and the horse calmly waited for the traces to be attached to the nine-pounder's carriage. With the crews sitting on the rough boards, the artillery and wagons proceeded to the nearby road and followed the army.

Will patted Big Red's neck affectionately. He did not know whether it was over or not. It was late in the afternoon. If the British were as fatigued and debilitated by the heat as he was, the fighting would not resume before tomorrow morning. He had survived today and he would survive tomorrow. Then General Knox would surely permit him to ride to Philadelphia to be with Elisabeth. That thought gave him a surge of energy. He clicked his tongue and nudged Big Red lightly with his heels. The horse trotted down the road easily pulling the six hundred pound cannon behind them. [9]

Chapter 10 – Life in Liberated Philadelphia

Every time Elisabeth heard horses' hooves on the cobblestoned streets she expected them to stop and Will to appear at the Lewis's door. The British had requisitioned almost all of the horses in the city so she knew the sounds belonged to American troopers. [1] She waited in vain for five days, refusing to leave the house. She had to be there if Will arrived. That was her excuse to the Lewises but she did not want to be seen in public. Her face was still bruised, the deep purple mark where John Stoner had hit her on her temple having turned more blue. The swelling of her cheekbone had subsided enough so that her eye was not as puffy.

Mary Lewis became her eyes and ears. The Americans, a regiment of light cavalry, had spent most of the first few days galloping around the city, causing a tumult and accomplishing nothing except to frighten citizens, children and stray dogs. Their commander, General Benedict Arnold, had arrived in a coach. He walked with crutches, it was said due to a musket ball that had shattered his thighbone. His headquarters was on Fifth and Market Streets, the very same three-story brick mansion that General Howe had appropriated for his residence.

When Mary returned from her most recent outing she reported it was impossible to find anything to purchase in the markets. Broadsheets had been posted up and down Market Street, signed by General Arnold, prohibiting "the removal, transfer or sale of any goods, wares or merchandize, in possession of the inhabitants of the city." [2]

"This foolish administration intends to starve us all," Mary said angrily. "If it is their intention to make it a crime to sell flour, produce, meat and fish, how do they expect us to live?" She looked around the kitchen mentally making an inventory of the foodstuffs they still had. Her eyes lingered on the jar of hyson tea with its diminishing amount of precious tasty leaves.

"What about artillery? Did you see any cannons at all," Elisabeth asked.

"I am sorry my dear. Of course, you are anxious for news of your Will. I saw more newly arrived troops but they are infantry. Still, no one has called at the house?"

Elisabeth shook her head. "I had hoped there would at least be a letter."

"He will write or arrive in person," Mary replied, attempting to overcome Elisabeth's disappointment. "There are so few of their troops in the city, the bulk of their army must be somewhere else. Perhaps even marching on Philadelphia at this moment."

Elisabeth did not credit that thought. More likely they were pursuing the retreating British. It meant Will would probably be in the thick of battle. He could not be taken from her, not now in some hot distant field by a musket shot or cannon ball when, after months of occupation, they could at last be together. She could tolerate another separation but only after she had expressed her love for him again and felt his arms around her.

She was startled from these intimate thoughts by a knock on the door. Mary jumped up from her chair with her hand covering her mouth in alarm. Elisabeth hurriedly ran down the hall. Mr. Lewis, an envelope in his hand, was already replacing the heavy oak beam when Elisabeth cried out. She ran to the window and saw the back of servant walking away.

"It is for you," Edward said, his tense posture relaxing with relief. "I feared it was the military authorities or the new civil government come to take me away to prison again. They seem to suspect all of us as Loyalists."

Mary took her husband's arm. "Even those on the Executive Council cannot be so blinded by hatred as to conclude you aided the British occupation of Philadelphia. You were imprisoned in Winchester, Virginia, on their own order for all those long months."

Edward handed Elisabeth the envelope and smiled at his wife. "Your righteous indignation against those who unjustly detained me pleases my heart but troubles my mind. Our fear of the unknown should not cause us to spout angry words. Even against those who wish us harm. We are to remain neutral in these mean times." Mary uttered a dismissive "tsk, tsk" and patted his hand.

"Is it a letter from Will?" Mary asked, wondering whether it would ever be appropriate to tell Edward she had carried vital information through the lines and that Elisabeth had been a spy.

Elisabeth had eagerly torn open the envelope and quickly read the brief words inside. "No," she said, shaking her head. "It is an invitation from Peggy Shippen to tea tomorrow. I am resolved to go," she said. "It is time for me to be out and about. Perhaps I may learn when the artillery are coming to the city."

The following afternoon, somewhat self-consciously for the bruise on her temple and her swollen cheek were still evident, she walked slowly in the early afternoon heat up Fourth Street to the Shippen's townhouse. She covered her nose and mouth with a handkerchief to ward off the persistent foul stench and was grateful that it partially hid her face from passersby. She would have to tell Peggy and the others at the tea what had happened, or some version of the truth. It was obvious they would ask.

The servant who opened the door had the good manners not to stare or reveal surprise at her looks and led her to the upstairs drawing room where Peggy usually entertained. He knocked, opened the door and formally announced her presence. Peggy Shippen, her sisters and three others were seated on a banquette and chaise lounge in front of the high glass window overlooking the home's entrance, engaged in some discussion. Peggy Shippen was the first to turn. Her hands flew to her mouth in shock.

"Surely, I do not look so awful as to elicit such alarm," Elisabeth said laughing. The young women flocked around her, all asking the same question and touching her face gently.

"Perhaps, if you all continue to pat and stroke my bruises, your evident concern for my wellbeing will heal these marks. Now, enough. I was invited for tea and your company. I will tell you everything, just once, and then let us enjoy the afternoon," she said with mock sternness.

Elisabeth found herself the center of attention, something she knew would happen when she accepted the invitation. She had her story prepared. On the day the British evacuated the city, an officer had knocked on the door, demanded entry and began ransacking the house. When Elisabeth, who was home alone, had tried to stop him, he had hit her and made off with some of the Lewis's silver and pewter. That was all there was to it. It was plausible. Everywhere, one could see the depredations committed by the British in their final frenzy of looting. Empty homes with the doors torn asunder, windows smashed, pieces of broken furniture visible inside as well as household debris in the corridors.

Fortunately, John Stoner's finger marks on her throat were no longer visible so no further explanation was needed. The young ladies, enthralled by the danger Elisabeth had been in, and impressed by her brave resistance, chattered away how lucky she was the officer had not hurt her more grieviously.

"Was he good looking?" one of them asked. Elisabeth was shocked by the question. "I fail to see how that would make any difference," she replied icily. "The answer, however, is no." She saw John Stoner's face before her. "He was pock-marked, with bad teeth and had a dissipated look to him." The description of her assailant was accurate.

There was a knock on the door, the manservant announced the arrival of Peggy Chew and Elisabeth had to tell the story all over again. This was followed by tea and petite cookies, and as Elisabeth had hoped, the conversation turned from her to matters more urgent to the young ladies.

"Do you think there will still be balls, concerts and plays now that the Council is in authority?" one of the girls asked, her anxiety evident in her tone.

"If it is to be their decision to make, I would say most assuredly not," Peggy Shippen responded. "However, there are many handsome young officers who will come to the city and surely some will organize dances."

"Let us hope the Whig women have no influence on them," one of her sisters added. "They are so drab in their homespun clothes. And their shoes. Have you ever seen such crudely made footwear? One can barely walk in them, let alone dance." [3]

"I do not recall these patriotic officers as being as cultured as our recently departed British friends," one said wistfully.

"Major Andre cut a silhouette of me before he departed," Peggy Chew revealed.

"Show us, show us," they demanded in unison.

Slowly, basking in their attention, she opened her beaded bag and withdrew a small book. Inside, protected by the stiff cover, framed by a white rectangle, was a black cut-out of her profile. [4]

"That is exquisite. It is such a good likeness."

"Yes," Peggy Chew said. "I doubt we will find amongst the patriotic officers, ones who can draw, paint, sing and write verse, as did Major Andre."

Elisabeth could constrain herself no longer. "I myself am betrothed to a brave patriotic officer," she blurted out. "I care not a whit whether he paints or sings. In every fiber of his being he believes in our cause. That counts far more toward achieving our independence than rhyming verses." She felt her face flush with anger but did not care.

Peggy Shippen broke the silence that followed Elisabeth's outburst.

"Betrothed? To your strikingly good looking Lieutenant? The one with the magnificent horse? Why that is wonderful news." She smiled at Elisabeth. "Perhaps when he comes to Philadelphia you will invite us all to your wedding ball, that is if you hold one. And you can show your Lieutenant some of the latest dances you performed with Captain Montresor."

Elisabeth heard the condescending tone and noted the barbed assumption that without the means herself, nor her family present, there would be no ball. Peggy had even remembered that Will could not dance and implied she was unfaithful to her betrothed by being escorted by John Montresor. She had been spying for the Americans, she wanted to shout. She let it all pass.

"I sincerely hope that Lieutenant Stoner and General Knox's regiment will soon arrive in Philadelphia and all of you will find suitable beaus amongst his fellow officers," she responded quietly.

The clatter of iron-rimmed wheels on the cobblestones halted their conversation and drew them to the window. A military carriage stopped outside the Shippen residence, two aides jumped out and assisted an officer to alight.

"Why that is General Arnold," Peggy Chew said. "He must be calling on your father."

Elisabeth thought it peculiar that Edward Shippen, who, for the past eight months had regally entertained General Howe and his senior officers at dinners in this very home, was now receiving the military commander of the city. Unseen, the young ladies watched Arnold hobble past the gate and up the entrance steps before disappearing from their sight.

"He was wounded at the Battle of Saratoga," Peggy Shippen said authoritatively.

"A glorious victory for our side, resulting in the surrender of an entire British army," Elisabeth added, unable to resist the opportunity to poke back at the obvious preference of the young ladies for their recently departed gallants who had evacuated the city.

Toward the end of the tea, a servant knocked and stated that Judge Shippen would like to present his daughters and the other young women to General Arnold. They flocked into the downstairs parlor chattering and preening themselves as they went, fully aware of their collective charms.

Elisabeth was the last to enter the room. General Arnold sat in a large upholstered wing chair, his bad left leg propped up on a stool, his crutch leaning next to him at the ready. He was flanked by two uniformed officers. When the young ladies entered, Arnold grabbed the crutch and, unaided, gallantly rose to his feet.

"Not even my wound should preclude my duty to stand in the company of such abundance of beauty." His grey eyes twinkled with pleasure and Elisabeth noted that even the hobbling gesture of arising was performed with an athletic grace. The gold epaulets on his shoulders emphasized his solid build. He was of medium height with a few thin strands of gray mixed with his long black hair, all drawn tightly back and neatly tied with a dark blue ribbon well below his neck. Elisabeth concluded the most striking feature about him was his aquiline nose, long, narrow and well-formed above a slightly downturned mouth and square chin. He was definitely a handsome man, she thought, and well aware of the impression he made and the authority he exuded.

When Judge Shippen introduced each of his daughters, Elisabeth noted that, while the General was solicitous of all, he seemed most attracted to Peggy, bowing the deepest when he kissed her hand. She was so petite and doll-like next to his robust figure, it seemed he might almost lift her up on a pedestal to admire her better.

When it was Elisabeth's turn, Arnold looked at her with a piercing gaze, unabashedly staring at her bruised temple and cheek.

"Whoever dared to attempt to damage such beauty not only failed but is to be despised by all men of honor. Tell me, Miss Elisabeth, the name of this dastardly person. I will have it published for all of Philadelphia to know. Just approbation shall rain down on his dishonorable head and gallant patriotic officers will compete for the honor of challenging this scalawag to a duel."

Elisabeth was afraid she would not succeed in successfully lying, so strong and intense was his scrutiny. Fortunately, Peggy Shippen diverted the General's attention by retelling Elisabeth's story with some embellishment as to her struggle with the British officer.

"I wish all of my soldiers had the courage of this young lady in standing up to the British," he said to his two aides, who nodded appreciatively. "So this anonymous miscreant absconds with his loot and the rest of the Redcoats. Well, I will not be satisfied until he, and all of his hated compatriots, have been driven from our shores." Elisabeth curtsied slightly in acknowledgement.

"Please, sir. I am anxious for news of my fiancé, a Lieutenant in General Knox's artillery."

"Ah, Henry Knox. A fine man, a very capable commander and one who I am privileged to call my friend. I left him at Valley Forge not a week ago." Arnold leaned slightly against the wing chair, his left foot barely touching the wooden floor. "He and our army are pursuing the British as they flee for their lives to New York harbor. If Providence wills it, we will catch them and prevail."

"Thank you, sir, for this information," Elisabeth replied curtseying again.

"I promise you, once I receive dispatches informing me of the outcome of our pursuit, I will, with your permission sir," he nodded toward Judge Shippen, "communicate to Miss Peggy Shippen who will so inform you." He turned to Peggy and took her hand in his again. "Only of course if you consent to be my messenger, and I can assure you, I have never had, nor ever will have a more beautiful one."

Elisabeth was surprised to see her friend, the sophisticated socially experienced attendee of plays, concerts, and balls, not to mention the recent Mischienza, blush in accepting the compliment. "It would be an honor, General, to serve you in any capacity." Arnold chuckled and Elisabeth caught a quick mischievous glance between Peggy and him, before her friend lowered her eyes.

The following Sunday, the Lewises returned late in the afternoon from the Quaker Meeting House in a somber mood.

"They are only rumors, my dear," Edward said, settling his tall lanky frame uncomfortably in the wood-backed chair in the kitchen. Mary busied herself cutting vegetables intended for the pot hanging in the fireplace. It was clear to Elisabeth they had been in heated discussion on their walk home.

"Rumors with a kernel of truth," she replied, "in keeping with the mean- spirited character of the men of the Executive Council."

"What have you heard at the Meeting House?" Elisabeth asked, disturbed by their conversation.

"Nothing of substance to worry about," Edward said. His expression suggested that he hoped his wife would acquiesce in his desire to end the conversation. Mary was having none of it.

"A clerk to the Council reportedly has bragged that there will be up to one hundred arrests of Loyalists who offered substantial assistance to the British army."

"Yes, Mary, that is what we heard. But look at the source. A simple clerk, impressed with his own self-importance and fortified by alcohol. It is an exaggeration," he waved his hand as if shooing a fly in front of him. "Indeed, if the Council is seeking revenge they will pursue the rich among us, since the prosecutor receives a fee based on the value of the Loyalist property that is confiscated."

"Do not think for a moment, dear husband, that we will avoid the attention of the prosecutor's office. He will be spurred on by personal greed and the animosity members of the Council harbor toward we Quakers for our professed neutrality." She threw the vegetables into the pot and pointed her cutting knife at Edward. "I do not intend to meekly await their miscarriage of justice and be thrown out of our home and lose the businesses you have grown and I protected while you were imprisoned."

"What can you do, Mary? You are only a woman and a Quaker as well."

"I was a Quaker woman when I journeyed to Valley Forge, met with General Washington and his wife, and pled the case for release of you and our friends," she snapped. "In those same capacities, I will persevere against this Council and its prosecutor."

"I am again invited for tea at the Shippen's this coming Tuesday," Elisabeth said. "Perhaps, I may learn more of the rumors you have heard."

"That would be helpful," Edward murmured, deeming the conversation over.

After saying grace they ate their simple dinner of vegetable soup, salted shad, bread and cheese. The talk remained melancholy and turned to the sad situation of Mrs. Galloway, a Quaker and wife of the former Superintendent.

"I understand her husband leaving with the British, but to take her only child with him is more than a mother can bear," Mary said. "They will seize her property even though she brought her inheritance to the marriage and it is rightfully hers." [5]

"So you say, Mary but upon marriage her property became her husband's and it is as his they will confiscate it."

"What do you think, Elisabeth? If you inherited great wealth from your father, is it right it should by marriage be under Will's control? To dissipate, gamble away, or do with as he may with nary a contrary word from you?"

"Knowing Elisabeth and Will, you paint an unreal portrait of them as husband and wife," Edward said smiling.

"I have received nary a letter from Will for many weeks. The thought of how we will decide to manage property I have not yet inherited, with a man who is not yet my husband, seems particularly strange. However," she went on, "as well as I know him, I do believe we will be much like you, sharing opinions and decisions, though the law does not recognize a woman's right to the property she brings to the marriage. It should but does not." She looked at Mary and then directed her remarks to Edward seated at the head of the small wooden table.

"You are both dear friends, not only to me but also to Will. I assure you, he and I will do everything in our power to defend you from any injustice attempted by vindictive authorities." Edward raised his eyebrows questioningly. "Do not ask how. Just know there are those in power who will listen to us."

"I appreciate your sentiments, but the power is with the Almighty and it is in Him we must place our trust," Edward said and it was clear the matter was finally closed.

Elisabeth's bruises were barely discernible when she left the Lewis home for tea that Tuesday. She was no longer self-conscious walking in the street and since the young ladies invited to the Shippens had already seen her near her worst, she entered the sitting room without any trepidation. She gathered she was the last invited guest to arrive. It was immediately clear to her that Peggy Shippen was bursting to tell everyone something but was waiting until all were present.

"Father invited General Arnold to dinner, not once but twice. Imagine, the "Eagle of Saratoga" in our home. And I sat across from him on both occasions. Of course he must sit at a corner of the table in order to prop up his wounded leg," she added with offhand familiarity. As tea was served, she regaled the young ladies with a description of how noble he looked in his general's uniform, how gallant and courtly he was, how nonchalantly he had described his friendship with General Washington, the carriage ride with Mrs. Lucy Knox from Connecticut to Valley Forge, how he admitted his French was only passable but enough to engage in discourse with the Marquis de Lafayette.

"He is so modest in demeanor it only serves to complement his character as a gentleman," she added, unaware of the irony of her statement. "Why, when father asked him about his role in our army's victory at Saratoga, he spoke first of his men's bravery before recounting charging on his horse toward the British and being wounded. The aftermath was horrible. He was terribly injured and in great pain. Although bleeding profusely, he had to use all of his strength to persuade the surgeons not to amputate his leg."

"Will he walk again?" one of the young women asked.

"He hopes to do so with a cane in a month's time, and to wear a special shoe on his left leg. The bone was set so badly, it is now two inches shorter than his right, the poor man." Peggy's face reflected wistful sympathy.

"You seem smitten with him," Peggy Chew observed. "Attending balls with him may not be as gay an affair, given his shorter leg."

"I am not smitten. We are becoming acquainted. Only time will tell. For now, I know I am in the presence of a great man and would gladly sit out any number of dances to be the woman he chose to escort to a ball." She patted her freshly coiffed hair and tucked a wisp back away from her temple. "Besides, good manners require that a lady only commit to two dances with a gentleman, so after sitting for two, I can dance the rest of the night away." [6]

Elisabeth sat listening to Peggy chatter on. Her friend, she thought, had definitely set her sights on General Arnold. Perhaps her friendship with Peggy may prove useful if the civil administration caused trouble for the Lewises.

"There are rumors the Council will seek to arrest known Loyalists, or those who aided the British and confiscate their property."

"Oh, tish tosh," Peggy Chew said dismissively. " Really, Elisabeth. The ones they seek have left for New York and those of us who remained, like my father and Judge Shippen, merely entertained British officers as dinner guests. Surely, you must know it is all just idle talk, instigated by radical Whigs seeking to disrupt the order of things."

"Yes, I suppose you are correct," Elisabeth responded. She knew this was the reality after liberation. The rich and influential, the Shippens and the Chews, no matter how obvious their Loyalist preferences and what the Whigs deemed the scandalous fraternization of their daughters with British officers, had nothing to fear from the Council. It was the Lewises, already suspect as Quakers, and those without powerful friends, who were in danger.

Elisabeth hesitated to draw more attention to herself but was compelled by her anxiousness to know of Will's whereabouts.

"Is there any news of our army?"

"Oh," Peggy Shippen responded. "I have been so involved with the guest lists for the dinners father is arranging for General Arnold, I almost forgot. He received dispatches from General Washington," she said importantly. "General Arnold, as he promised, asked me to convey to you the news. A few days ago our army engaged the British and drove them from the field, somewhere in New Jersey. He expects his friend General Knox and others to visit Philadelphia shortly." She smiled sweetly at Elisabeth as if to say this General, who is infatuated with me, is so noble as to remember the minor matter of your Lieutenant.

Elisabeth had become accustomed to Peggy's condescension. I tolerated it, she thought, because she was useful to my efforts to spy on the British, to invite me to balls where I could meet British officers and become close to Captain Montresor. I do not belong to their circle. They care not a whit for our cause, know nothing of the suffering of our soldiers and devote not a moment to helping the sick and injured in our hospitals.

She left the Shippen home mid-afternoon, both elated at the thought of General Knox arriving in the city with Will and filled with trepidation that the General would be the one to tell her terrible news about him. As she walked the familiar street to the Lewis's home, she saw Mary standing on the front step looking out the door. She waved to Elisabeth, beckoning her to hurry.

She began to run, not knowing why or what she was running to, one hand to her throat, the other clutching at the folds of her dress. She was sobbing, forcing her to breathe in short gasps, knowing that in a moment she would learn her future, whether it was to be with Will or be without him.

Suddenly, there he was, leaping down the two steps, bareheaded and joyously shouting her name, grabbing her by the hand, one arm around her waist, almost carrying her into the Lewis home. Better to get off the street. Not that she cared anymore about appearances but it would reflect badly on the Lewis's reputation if they openly embraced in public.

Once inside the door, her feet well off the floor, her arms locked around his shoulders, she buried her face in his hair, smelling the salt from his sweat and the acrid residue of gun powder. He was here, unharmed. She felt the muscles of his arms, ran her hands over his uniform, as if to reassure herself he was whole and unwounded. And then she began to sob, unrestrained cries of relief from the anxiety of being revealed as a spy, the stress of pretending to be someone she was not in the presence of Captain Montresor, of being stalked by John Stoner.

Will lowered her and kept his arms wrapped around her, letting her cry, pressing her tightly against him and whispering into her hair that it was all right, they would be married, she was safe, he would protect her.

"Oh, Will. I am truly happy to see you and here I am crying and making myself more ugly in your sight."

"You will always be beautiful to me. Never ugly. Never," he said, brushing her cheek with his fingers. He noticed the slight discoloration on her temple, a faint blemish but still a mark and carefully examined her face. He touched the faded spot on her cheek, gently tracing it with his first two fingers.

"What happened? Were you hurt?" The concerned look in his eyes, the alarm in his voice made her hesitate.

She nodded. "I was, but not seriously. I will tell you what happened later. Now is not the time." She put her finger on his lips to shush him and felt his gentle kiss. "When Mary returned from Valley Forge with the other Quaker ladies without seeing you, I was so disappointed. I wanted her to be able to describe you, so in my mind I could once again see you and keep that image close to my heart. Eight months is a terribly long time to be apart."

"It will not be so again. I promise. General Knox has received a favorable response from your father. He has given his permission."

They ended their embrace at Mary's discreet cough from the hallway. Their fingers remained entwined when Mary appeared and suggested they join her in the kitchen. They preferred to sit next to each other on the bench at the table instead of in separate chairs.

"I want to be married as soon as possible," Elisabeth said. "I most certainly do, too," he responded squeezing her hand in his.

Mary beamed at the two of them. "It pleases me that you mention your plans before me and yet are so locked in each other's gaze you are barely aware I am sitting across from you." She laughed as they both stammered an apology. She went to the cupboard and brought out a bottle of claret.

"This definitely requires a celebratory glass."

Two days later, they were married by the Artillery Regimental Chaplain in the Lewis's home. The Dutch Reformed Church, Elisabeth's first choice, had been transformed during the occupation into a stable by British Cavalry in punishment for its pastor preaching to the Hessians of the justice of the Patriots' cause.

General and Lucy Knox, Will's friends, Samuel and Mercy Hadley, Nat Holmes, and the Lewises crowded into the small front parlor. It had rained earlier and the air had cooled, making the cramped room more bearable. Will and Elisabeth did not notice. Their marriage was duly recorded in the Regimental Bible and the Chaplain's Record of Activities with the explicit notation, General Knox was witness to the ceremony and vouched that Elisabeth's father had consented to the match.

The Knoxes were staying as guests at the Powel House on South Third Street, a magnificent three story brick home in the Georgian style. It was they who arranged a dinner for the newlyweds.

Will and Elisabeth arrived with Mary and Edward Lewis. Elisabeth knew Mrs. Powel was related to the Shippens and she had attended dinners and dances there before.

She had chosen for its relative modesty the emerald green dress she had worn to a theater performance. Mary Lewis's homespun dress and simple white cap emphasized her plain appearance and Elisabeth was afraid her friend would feel out of place at what she knew would be an elegant dinner party. Lucy Knox, although noticeably pregnant, had her hair done up in the current fashion, a towering construction adding a foot to her height. In her ostentatious patriotic manner, she had festooned her hairdo with red, white and blue ribbons.

"I am preparing for tomorrow's Independence Day festivities," Lucy announced to one and all, as she made her grand entrance into the dining room escorted by General Knox. She lowered her large bulk into one of four chairs at the head of the table and fanned herself vigorously.

Dinner at the long table set for twenty was a sumptuous affair. As befitting the Powels' wealth, each place setting of plates with a delicate floral design had matched silverware and table knives with ivory handles and cut crystal glasses. Will and Elisabeth were seated at the main table immediately adjacent to General Knox and Lucy, who were flanked by the Powels. Colonel Sargent of the Regiment and of course Nat Holmes and Samuel Hadley and his wife Mercy were also there. Besides the Lewises, Will knew none of the others. Elisabeth said many were prominent merchants and landowners, some accompanied by their wives. "A room filled with Loyalist sentiments," she whispered in his ear. "Most likely acquaintances of the Powels."

After the first course of savory veal pies, planked shad and roast chicken, served with dressed carrots and pickled cabbage, General Knox pushed his chair away from the table and stood up. The room became quiet.

"Today is a day ending a long and dangerous journey of two young people, resulting in the joyous occasion of bonding together this couple in matrimony. I bear no less affection for Lieutenant Stoner than I would if he were my own . . ." he paused and placed a hand on his wife's shoulder, "I should say our own son, for I know my beloved Lucy harbors the same sentiments as I express. I wish to relate the steadfastness of mind and spirit that has brought Will to this happy moment."

Self-consciously, Will listened to Knox recount the obstacles of hauling the cannons from Fort Ticonderoga to Cambridge, through the Berkshires in the bitter winter of '75; the holding action at the Battle of Brooklyn with Smallwood's Marylanders, the fog-shrouded escape across the East River and the long retreat down the length of New Jersey from the pursuing British Army. In stentorian tones he recounted the hellish crossing of the Delaware in the teeth of a nor'easter, lowering cannons by ropes down gorges and dragging them up the other side to blow the Hessians away in Trenton; the second battle of Trenton when the Americans, with their backs to the ice floe-choked Delaware and no boats to effectuate a retreat, had fought the British Army to a standstill until dark, and then marched twelve miles at night and won the battle of Princeton. From there, he took the guests to the bloody slaughter at Brandywine and the victory they almost won at Germantown.

"In every instance, on every battlefield, the coolness, bravery and good conduct of the lad I first knew as a teamster's son in upstate New York has exemplified the spirit of our army." Will blushed but realized that Knox was speaking of all the soldiers, using Will's personal history as a lesson to show how close to defeat and annihilation they had been.

"This past winter," he said in a stern tone, "we together endured the harshest test of our mettle, when our ill-clad soldiers starved and froze at Valley Forge, while those of means failed to provide sustenance and support for the Army charged with defending them."

There was an uncomfortable shifting of bodies in chairs and embarrassed quick looks around the table. The guests attending for the prestige of dining with the well-known General Knox had not expected a lecture at their expense. They were there for the opportunity to discuss mutually beneficial arrangements for the General to consider, which of course would make these gentlemen even richer. [7]

"We emerged stronger for the experience, a well-trained army prepared by our Prussian drill master, General Von Steuben. The proof was in the field against the best of General Clinton's forces. The effects of this latest battle at Monmouth will be great and lasting. It will convince the British that nothing is wanting to render our army equal to any in the world."[8]

Lucy tugged at her husband's sleeve to remind him that he had risen to propose a toast. He nodded and smiled down at her affectionately.

"So, first, a toast to General Washington and our brave soldiers!" This was greeted by cries, perhaps motivated by shame and embarrassment, of "To General Washington! To the Army!"

"Then to the Congress of these United States," followed by raised glasses and cheers of "To Congress!"

"And finally to Lieutenant Will Stoner and his bride, Elisabeth. I am constrained by discretion to say no more other than this courageous and brave young woman has acted in significant ways to benefit our cause."

Will and Elisabeth remained seated as all around them rose and cheered the newlyweds. Elisabeth noted Edward leaned down and whispered in his wife's ear and Mary shook her head. Mary would keep her secret, especially from her husband who still professed absolute neutrality in the war.

After the guests had settled themselves, Will rose hesitantly. General Knox signaled for quiet. Will looked at the faces at the table, focusing on his friends Hadley and Holmes to steady himself.

"I, too, must," he paused and started over. "On behalf of myself and Elisabeth, I thank General and Mrs. Knox for their steadfast friendship and generosity and their evident concern for our well-being." He extended his arm toward the Lewises, uncertain whether the social elite around the table knew them. "Mr. and Mrs. Edward Lewis have by their kind hospitality, protected Elisabeth during the late occupation and I am, I mean we are, deeply grateful to them." He took a deep breath, wanting to choose his words carefully.

"Tomorrow is Independence Day. It is the first we will celebrate together as man and wife," he said lowering his voice. "That will make it doubly joyous for us. However," he said continuing more confidently, "I propose a toast that tomorrow shall be the last Independence Day we celebrate with British troops on our soil. Let next July mark us as a free people in a land free of foreign armies." He raised his own glass to cheers of "Here! Here!"

As they walked home arm in arm, Elisabeth leaned her head contentedly on Will's shoulder. Inside the hallway after Edward had bolted the door, there was an initial awkwardness as the four of them stood in the hallway. Mary lit a candle and handed the holder to Elisabeth. "You two go upstairs to your room. It is late. We will follow shortly," she said simply and watched Will and Elisabeth climb the steps.

—∞—

The following morning, Will and Elisabeth stayed abed and came down by mid-morning, blushing and grinning at the same time. They washed separately at the pump behind the kitchen as Mary fixed them a breakfast of toast and cheese. "I have made hyson tea, I do not know why. The occasion seems to warrant it. It is so silly of me. Would you prefer cider?"

"No, Mary," Elisabeth said. "Will and I need nothing else at the moment," she said placing her hand on his and rubbing the backs of his fingers. "The weather is clear. We plan on walking about and enjoying the city's festivities."

The Independence Day celebrations were more muted and subdued than the previous year, whether due to lack of preparation following so quickly upon the British evacuation of the city, or a desire to conserve gunpowder, it was difficult to determine.

Will and Elisabeth wandered happily through the streets in the late afternoon, absorbed in each other. As it became dark they reached an area near the wharves where they had last been together in Philadelphia. Together with the crowd, they watched the skyrockets soar upward, saw the flashes of cannons from the batteries by the Delaware and heard, but did not see, the thirteen musket volleys honoring the Congress.

As content as they obviously were to be together, Elisabeth sensed a reticence in Will, as if he were unsure when and how to speak. She leaned against him and affectionately rubbed his arm. "We are husband and wife now," she said. "There should be no secrets between us."

Will sighed. "I am indeed fortunate to have such a wise and beautiful wife and one so perceptive of my mind."

He put his arm around her shoulder.

"General Knox came to Philadelphia to better regulate the ordnance for the artillery."

Elisabeth waited for further explanation, knowing the conclusion as if Will had blurted it out first. "He has held meetings with those who will cast the cannons and the balls and made arrangements for their payment. Some of the works are near these very wharves," he said pointing vaguely around them. "I will be leaving with the General, Captain Hadley and the others in a few days, three at the most. But you will still have Mercy and Mrs. Knox and of course Mary for company." He said it so quickly to reassure her, she had to laugh.

"You are silly my dear Will. Women's company cannot substitute for you my love."

"I promise I will send for you as soon as the army establishes a permanent camp. And I will write you often." The words tumbled out as he sought a way to soften his leaving. "You know how much Mrs. Knox hates to be apart from her husband. I am certain she will prevail upon him and you will come, too."

They walked with their arms linked back toward the commons. The celebratory throngs on the wharves had begun to depart, the fireworks at an end. "Even if the army is on the move, we will surely go into winter quarters by December, perhaps even as early as November," Will said hopefully.

Yes, she thought. And I will be anxious every day until you are safely in camp. "If we are to be apart for possibly several months, and together a maximum of only three days, then we should spend every minute of every day and night together," she said fervently. She felt him squeeze her hand.

"Now it is my turn to unburden myself and reveal my secret." She told him the entire story, from his brother accusing her of being a Rebel spy at Major Andre's ball, which Will knew of from her coded letter, to her sense of being followed everywhere, to the malevolent looks he gave her in public and finally, the assault a few days before the British left.

She felt him tense as she spoke, as he took her in his arms and held her tightly, and then his muscles relaxed and he stroked the back of her neck gently.

"I will thank Edward Lewis for saving you from my brother. John will never threaten you again. That I promise." Will's voice was calm but the steeliness and clipped tone frightened her. "I will not pursue him to New York nor hunt him down like the despicable wretch that he is." He pulled away from her and placed his hands firmly on her shoulders. "However, if Providence permits and I encounter him anywhere, I will kill him."

Elisabeth shuddered. She saw the animosity and vengeance in his eyes and wondered whether she had been wise to tell him. She was new at being a wife. Perhaps sometimes it is best to keep secrets from each other.

Part Three
A Deadly Game of Cat and Mouse

Chapter 11- Providence and Privateering

Camp White Plains
27th July, 1778

My Dearest Elisabeth,

I find it most difficult to reduce to paper my thoughts, although why it was easier to write before we were wed is something I am unable to explain. Since leaving Philadelphia you are always in my thoughts. Our brief time together has shown me what true happiness means - my Love and Passion for you knows no bounds. Were paper not so precious, I would tear this up and begin anew for I am not satisfied that the words I have written accurately convey the depth of my love for you, nor the terrible hurt I feel each day we are apart.

We promised each other to write frequently, even about events that seem ordinary and of no significance. I hereby fulfill that promise as follows:

Since departing in the company of General K. and the other officers, we followed the depredations of the British Army through the ruined State of New Jersey, first briefly resting at Brunswick. We crossed the Hudson River at King's Ferry, proceeded to Tarrytown, marched South and now are camped at White Plains. The British unfortunately retreated to Sandy Point without any further significant losses and thence were taken by their Transports to the safety of Staten Island and New York. I hope they will either emerge from their havens and chance a battle or we will enter their lair and root them out. General K. believes the Enemy has no dangerous designs and observes that after two years of war, both Armies are back at the very point they set out from. [1] *You must know it is my fervent wish that we win this War before another two years pass. Captain H informs me his wife has returned to her home in Morristown, which fortunately for him is closer to our Camp than Philadelphia. I live at present with Nat Holmes who has received a letter from his wife that she is well and their son continues to thrive although there is no news about the birth of their second child. He is most anxious to know. We dined with General K last night, along with several other Officers.*

I will write you of one Day as an indication of the rest. I arise with the Sun and water and feed Big Red. We begin training others new to the Artillery at 6 oClock which lasts till 8 - then we breakfast upon tea or coffee, some bread and cheese. After, I am assigned to either inspect our Emplacements or haul cannons to specified sites. Then, my time is my own and I ride, read and write you, before dinner which is soup, good beef or fish and bread and occasionally an apple pie. At 5 oClock we begin training again and leave off with the setting Sun. I have a cot and one blanket for the nights are chilly. I am comfortable enough but yearn for your warmth beside me. Some of the men suffer due to a great deficiency of blankets that we hope to remedy shortly. The Day I have described is typical and as much as it is filled with activities, they do nothing to assuage the pain of our Separation.

I know in my heart that you have already written and I curse the distance that delays your letter. I will treasure whatever words you write, read and reread them, until your next letter. Your words and the memories we share of our brief time together will sustain me as does the thought that this Separation we must endure will end and we will be entwined again as one.

Your loving husband

Will

The men of the 2nd Regiment of Colonel Angell's Rhode Islanders marched eagerly along the pike. They had passed Hartford two days ago and were near the border between Connecticut and Rhode Island. They needed no encouragement and covered eighteen to twenty miles a day, easily outdistancing their wagons loaded with their tents, cots and baggage. Each day ended with their camping just before sunset, waiting for the train, setting up their tents, lighting cooking fires, eating and sleeping. The next morning before daybreak, they struck their tents, ate a cold breakfast, filled their canteens if there was water nearby, and set off. They were part of General Varnum's Brigade being sent to reinforce the Continental Army in Rhode Island. The men needed no incentive to proceed with the utmost speed, although they had been promised by Colonel Angell they would have a week's leave, depending upon the military circumstances when they arrived.

Two nights after they crossed into Rhode Island some of the men swore they could smell the ocean, although they were more than twenty miles from the coast.

"'Tis your imagination, " Private Oliver Whipple stated. "Look," he said holding up a green leaf. The wind is blowing from the northwest." They were sitting around the cooking fires having unloaded their pots and pans from the wagon, leaving the tents lying on the ground until later. Hunger took precedence over comfort for the moment.

"I know which way the wind blows but I smell it for certain," Abraham Fish insisted with conviction in his voice.

"I smell roasting beef," one of the soldiers around the fire said. The others laughed agreeably. Their morale was high because they were going home, regardless of whatever military actions lay ahead. That night, Henry and Oliver and some of the others ambled around the camp, past the tents of the Rhode Island militias, beyond the Massachusetts and New Hampshire State Regiments and up a hilltop.

"From here, one can indeed smell the sea," Oliver said, looking toward the east. Henry found the north star and turned his face northeast toward where he knew Providence lay. "We will be home soon, Oliver. I fear with all these troops marching the Generals have plans for battle, where I cannot say."

Oliver turned around and surveyed the sparks of yellow flames dotting the darkness. "'Tis a pretty sight, like giant fireflies, but for knowing that around each light, there sits men armed who will soon be in the thick of it and many will not emerge unharmed."

Henry thought of the men from Providence, with whom he had signed up, who were no more. Killed at Fort Mercer, Brandywine and Germantown, dead of disease at Valley Forge, or wounded and invalided and sent home. After all they had been through, and to be this close and not to see his wife Judith and his little Sally, would be more than he could bear.

In the first week of August, under a clear blue sky, the men of the 2nd Rhode Island Regiment marched into Providence, every one of them grinning, and occasionally, in a breach of military discipline, waving to the crowds lining the streets. They assembled on the Common to hear their orders for the day read to them - four days leave, with those from Providence required to report for Regimental Roll Call each morning at 8 a.m. [2] The men roared their approval and upon being dismissed raced down the familiar stone streets to their homes. Others headed for the waterfront to habituate the bars and brothels eager for their patronage.

Early on August 6th, under overcast skies to match their glum mood, they left Providence and by nightfall set up camp at Tiverton on the mainland across from British-held Aquidneck Island, with Newport at its southern tip. They could hear cannon fire to the southwest.

"'Tis the Frenchies giving the Brits a pounding," Fish said. "Too close to be from the river," he said authoritatively. "Their ships are more likely near Newport in the bay channel."

"Maybe the Redcoats will surrender and we can all return to our homes again," a soldier's voice said hopefully from the darkness. "For me, there are a few more girls to try at Mrs. Humphrey's," another added to ribald laughter, whistles and hoots.

Henry smiled and nudged Oliver. "You have not said much since leaving Providence."

"My little girls have grown. The youngest did not recognize me but warmed after a day. They almost starved while I was away. Now,

I am off again." He waved his arms helplessly. "Worse for me, my brother-in-law was part of a prize crew and narrowly escaped capture when a British sloop intercepted them off the Maine coast. It took him the better part of a fortnight to return home, poorer than when he first left. I cannot look to him to support my family."

Henry had no words of consolation. He had been overjoyed to be with Judith and Sally again and they to see him. He too had noticed his wife had seemed thinner, her face pinched and more harried looking. Food and necessities were expensive and his pay was worth less each month. The good patriotic merchants of Providence were reluctant to extend credit, lower prices or even offer a little charity. He and Oliver and the rest of his regiment who had signed up for the duration were fighting to defend these people who were getting richer because of the war. Damn them, he cursed. Filthy war profiteers. Then he dampened his anger. No good would come of it.

"At least Oliver, we are close to our loved ones. After this business is over, I am certain we will be given leave again. And with the French fleet in the Bay, surely Providence will favor our efforts." Whipple shrugged in reply. "Perhaps," was all he said.

The following day, the Regiment was ferried across the Sakonnet River and together with the rest of the Brigade marched down the eastern side of the island. For a week they left their muskets in their tents and dug entrenchments within cannon shot of the British batteries in Newport. The first few days were easier. Then steady rains came, filling their trenches with pools of water, the newly shoveled soil slick under foot and the earth turned to heavy muck. All work halted during a storm of hurricane force that blew for two days. When it ended, heavy cannon were brought up and positioned in the newly dug emplacements. The bombardment of the British positions was continuous. In response, their cannons lobbed the occasional ball at the Americans at night to disturb them.

The early morning began with the usual artillery answered by a substantial barrage from the British battery. The men of Captain Ward's company occupied the trenches and were relieved around midafternoon. In the waning light, when they returned to their tents after gathering wood for cooking fires, they noticed dust rising from the East Road.

"Reinforcements," Fish said, shielding his eyes with his hand. "No," he concluded quickly, "they are troops and wagons heading toward Howland's Ferry and Tiverton."

"Maybe the Generals think we have enough men already to storm the British in Newport," one soldier said sarcastically. Henry was puzzled but remained silent. He noticed Lieutenant Tew moving from place to place speaking quietly to the small groups of men. When he reached their platoon, he squatted down on his haunches and talked in a low voice. Henry liked the Lieutenant. He had brought a letter from Judith to Valley Forge, a kindly gesture.

"Men," Tew said. "The French fleet, battered by the hurricane and bloodied by the British Navy, have left their position off Newport and sailed to Boston for repairs and refitting."

There was a chorus of groans. "And the French troops?" a voice inquired from the gathering darkness, barely masking the owner's contempt. "The ones they landed with all that musick and such?"

"They are on board their ships and will disembark in Boston as well."

"We can still take the Redcoats, Sir," Fish said. "Drive them out of Newport." Others joined in agreeing with his sentiment.

Tew nodded his accord. "Your steadfastness is admirable and I know the Colonel will be proud. Unfortunately, when the news spread among the militias, entire regiments deserted en masse and at this very moment are leaving the Island. [3]

There were various cries of dismay at the abandonment of the Army by both the French and the militias.

"Damn Frenchies. I knew we could not trust them."

"To hell with them. What about our own militias? Ill-trained farmers who run at the first sign of battle. Damn them all."

Lieutenant Tew waited for the men to finish venting their frustrations. After the insults and complaints had died down, he addressed them again. "Tonight, we must maintain the appearance of full strength. You will return to the trenches. Sentries will be assigned between the lines.

We do not want these Redcoats to become emboldened too soon." [4]

Henry's sentry duty was from midnight to four o'clock. The parole was "Saratoga," the countersign was "Victory." There were ten of them in a copse of trees and shrubs, chilled in the dark, without a fire to warm them. By common understanding, no one spoke in louder than a whisper. They were on the extreme right of the American trenches and could hear the guttural German of the Hessians behind their fortifications. Their talk died down in the early morning hours and all was quiet.

Oliver heard the noise first, a foot stepping on a branch, then a sucking sound of a boot being pulled from the mud. More sounds of movement, quietly creeping toward them. He touched Henry's arm who nodded and alerted the man next to him. They all knelt and raised their muskets. Oliver shouted the password and dropped to the ground as the reply of musket balls whistled in his direction. Henry sighted on the muzzle flash, fired and hurriedly reloaded. He hid behind a tree and waited. Another volley from the advancing enemy raked the shrubs and branches. He fired again, this time below the flash of a musket held by a standing soldier. There were several screams for help in German, followed by groans and retreating noises of bodies being hauled away as they cried out in pain. Henry did not fire where he thought the enemy was. They were withdrawing and that was enough. At dawn, they discovered the bulk of the American Army had retreated up the Island. [5] Colonel Angell's Regiment was now part of the rearguard.

After marching for no more than half an hour, Henry and his company took up positions behind a stone wall on both sides of the road leading up the west side of the island. Through the chinks in the stone he could see the Hessians advancing toward them, led by some light infantry in hunting green uniforms. Their first disciplined volley decimated the Hessians' well-ordered lines. The next volley, fired by their second line forced the enemy to hesitate and then retreat. The platoon was ordered to reload and hold their positions.

Again the Hessians came on and once again the Rhode Islanders fired two volleys. This time, instead of remaining, his company retreated in good order. Henry lost count of how many times, in the valley between gentle sloping hills, they crouched behind stone walls, fences or hedgerows marking the farmers' fields. Each time, they let the Hessians closer before firing devastating volleys, took fire in return and then, after delaying the enemy's advance, withdrew.

They took cover behind yet another stone wall and waited for the oncoming enemy. After taking two concentrated volleys, the Hessians continued their advance and, for the first time that morning, made it to the American lines. Henry, with the stone wall in front of him, raised his musket at an angle, planted his feet firmly and impaled a tall mustached soldier attempting to leap over the rocks. He sidestepped the Hessian who toppled over, his chest bloody and then on the order of "Charge Bayonets," clambered over the wall. Surprised at the intensity and fury of the attack, the Hessians retreated but formed up quickly. Henry heard an officer call for them to "Halt!" and "By Company! Ready! Take Aim! Fire!" The Hessians were arrayed no more than fifty feet away, their front rank kneeling. The first and second ranks' volleys struck the Hessians before their first line had fired. Their thinning line did manage a round and several men in the Company fell.

As the Rhode Islanders retreated in good order through an orchard, the Hessians brought up their field pieces, the range being too great for muskets. Henry saw a ball land close behind Oliver, spewing up a column of soft earth and knocking Oliver to the ground. Henry and two others rushed over. Oliver lay on his face, blood oozing from his ears, his arms hidden underneath him so it was difficult for Henry to know if they had been blown off. To his joy, Oliver groggily raised himself to his knees and with Henry's help scrambled to his feet and rejoined their ranks.

The orchard ended at the top of a slight incline, marked by another stone wall. There their Company again took up positions and rested. Henry felt a wetness on his side. Fearing the worst, he pulled back his jacket. He saw to his relief, his shirt above his breeches was soaked but not bloody. He reached for his canteen and discovered it had been holed by musket balls in two places and the water had leaked on to him. Sheepishly, he looked at Oliver and grinned. Oliver smiled back and then gestured with his chin. The Hessians were advancing once again.

This time, Lieutenant Tew instructed them to fire two volleys and then retreat at quick step to a redoubt, a U-shaped fortification of earth and stone on a small hill to their rear. They took their positions behind the earthen works of stone and soil alongside other units that had been part of the rolling retreat. To his right were the blacks of the First Rhode Island Regiment, their white hunting frocks and breeches begrimed with dirt and gunpowder. On Henry's left was a light infantry regiment he did not recognize.

The Hessians, their ranks three deep and drums beating, gave a loud yell that carried above the noise of battle and charged up the hill.

"Aim low," Lieutenant Tew shouted to his company of soldiers to the right of the battery. "They wear a strap across their chests which ends at the hip. Aim to the right of the hip."

Henry found it easy from their height on the slope to depress his musket barrel. He sighted on the white strap, followed it down to the soldier's hip, moved his barrel slightly to the right, and at the order, fired. Their volley was effective as the front line buckled, with many falling, and then the momentum of the second two ranks propelled the remnants of the first rank forward. The second volley tore into the oncoming Hessians and Henry, having reloaded, fired again. The Hessians regrouped, charged yet again and once more they were met with a hail of musket fire as well as three pound balls from the field pieces, which bounced down the hill and through the forward ranks into soldiers coming up behind.

Henry heard the Lieutenant shouting to retreat by Company. Along with the rest of the Regiment they made a hasty descent on the open, northern side exposed to musket fire from the redoubt they had abandoned, and up the slope to a much higher hill that was held in force by their own troops. They passed through the lines to cheers of the soldiers manning the fortifications. Captain Ward's Company was positioned along gaps in the line and awaited a new assault. It seemed to Henry as if much of the army held this hill in force, having benefitted from the rearguard action his Regiment had fought in delaying the enemy. He took comfort in the numbers and the numerous cannons that were interspersed amongst the troops.

The Hessians, with additional reinforcements of their own, formed up in the valley below and waited. The sun beat down on Henry's bare head. He had lost his tri-corn and wished he still had his canteen. He reached into his cartridge box and fingered the blue ribbon from Sally's dress. Beat the enemy back here and then he could go home to Providence.

The high-pitched sound of the hautboys wafted up from the valley below, accompanied by the steady drum beat as the Hessians began their assault. The three gun battery of six-pounders to Henry's right, which he judged by the lack of uniforms to be militia and not a Continental Artillery Regiment, opened fire as the Hessians passed through the cornfields below and reached the beginning of the slope. The sun, now lower in the sky, must be in the Hessians' eyes he thought, feeling its warmth on the back of his neck. Still, on they came, their ranks thinning from the cannon barrage, not yet within musket range.

Out of the corner of his eye, Henry saw a militia officer step to the side of his six-pounder to observe where his ball had landed. In doing so, he moved in front of the muzzle of the adjacent cannon, set too near to his own, just as that gun commander shouted "Give Fire!" The ball went through his body and blew him to pieces. His frame was held together only by the skin of his belly, with his right arm totally severed from his torso. Blood spattered everywhere. Henry felt his stomach contract, bent over and dry heaved. He had nothing to eat since the prior night. [6]

"By Company! Make Ready!" Henry knelt behind the low wall made of stone and freshly dug earth. He heard the second rank behind him shift one step to the side. "Take aim! Fire." Almost three hundred muskets fired simultaneously. Henry focused on loading, following the routine that they had practiced on the parade ground of Valley Forge for days at a time. Volley after concentrated volley of musket balls hailed down on the advancing Hessians, devastating their ranks. The massed disciplined firepower of the Americans was too much for any body of troops to withstand. The Hessians retreated down the slope and with the arrival of dusk, the battle was over.

Henry was one of a small party of men sent back down into the valley to search for wounded. With no wheelbarrows available they used sections of canvas cut from tents and muskets for carrying poles to make stretchers. They looked only for blue clad wounded, not having enough men or stretchers to take care of the Hessians. Accompanied by the usual night noises of crickets and cicadas, they moved toward the sound of groans and cries of pain, stooping down to identify the soldiers on the ground, before rolling them as gently as they could on to the canvas and carrying them back toward their lines.

It was Oliver who stumbled across Fish. He lay there, his eyes blinking as his head moved from side to side, his hands wet with his own blood, clutching a wide gash below his ribs. Softly, he repeated the word "no," drawn out into a long moan as if he could not believe he had been wounded. He cried out as they stumbled back up the hill and loaded him on to a waiting wagon.

The remainder of the night was spent marching to Howland's Ferry and being rowed across the narrow strait to Tiverton. Once there, they camped for a day and on the last day of August again marched through the streets of Providence. [7]

In early September, Henry reluctantly left Providence and with the rest of his regiment marched to Bristol. He consoled himself that now he was closer to Judith and Sally. On the first Sunday, the Regimental Chaplain read a list of those who had died in the battle. Private Abraham Fish's name was among them, having succumbed to his wound at the hospital in Providence. There were eighteen killed from the 2nd Regiment. Eighteen families that would likely become destitute, living off a reduced amount of worthless paper money, Henry thought bitterly. His Judith and Sally were not much better off. He did not hold much hope the French would return and drive the British from Newport. No, he thought. We will have to help our families ourselves and end the war on our own. In the meantime, he would talk to Colonel Angell himself. Their Colonel was an influential and respected member of the community. Perhaps he would be able to persuade the good merchants of Providence to assist the soldiers' families.

Captain Holmes and Privates Adam Cooper and Titus Fuller, after days of a bone-jarring wagon ride over ice-rutted roads, welcomed the chance to leave the horses and wagon with a patriot militia in New Brunswick. They enthusiastically took to the water in a small square-rigged trading sloop. The river boat men were wary of roving New Jersey Loyalist militias, rumored to be extremely active in the area, and welcomed the addition of three armed soldiers. They stood guard, scanning the shoreline as the crew vigorously manned the poles to move the vessel, laden with barrels of flour, butter and salted pork down the shoal-obstructed Raritan. In South Amboy, the former Marblehead Mariners found a tavern with a room for the night. The owner looked askance at Adam and Titus, even though they were in uniform.

"I suppose there is no harm, since 'tis only the three of you sleeping in the same bed," he scowled as he swept the coins Nat had laid on the counter into the pocket of his dirty leather apron.

"Ah, but think of the risk to you of having your fat throat slit in the middle of the night by this Continental, offended by your remarks," Adam said, removing his short knife from its sheath and testing the blade with his thumb. The innkeeper stepped back from the table, rubbing the unshaven stubble on his neck, and looked quickly over his shoulder as if seeking reassurance someone was there to help him.

"Come along, Adam," Holmes said calmly. "We have our room. No need to scare the man unnecessarily."

"I trust you as an officer to keep them under control," the owner shouted after Nat, as the three of them went up the creaky stairs to the loft. [8]

The next morning, Nat prowled the wharves, the collar of his short blue wool jacket turned up against the brisk October wind blowing from the northeast. It would be colder in Salem this time of year, he thought. In years past, he would be returning from the fishing grounds by no later than the third week of the month ahead of the oncoming northeasters. He prayed his wife Anna would keep their second son warm. Benjamin Warren, born the week after Independence Day, whom she described in her last letter to him as having a ruddy complexion like his father, also had Nathaniel's set of lungs. Nat had been tempted to take leave and make the journey to Massachusetts. The army was in place, watching the British in New

York, waiting for any sally in force and harassing their foraging parties up and down the Hudson. No action seemed imminent.

Instead, Holmes had agreed when General Knox proposed to utilize Nat's knowledge of ships and cannons to make a reconnaissance trip to assess the numerous harbors and anchorages being used by American privateers. He was to recommend which ones should be fortified against British raids from Staten Island and in what manner. South Amboy harbor, like Hoboken, Paulus Hook and others he had seen further north, lacked any defenses - no redoubts, emplacements, batteries, and no militias based nearby. True, an alarm could be raised and the militias called up, but by then it would be too late. The ships and yards would all have been burned to the ground and the supplies in the warehouses, including foodstuffs to supply the American army this coming winter, would either have been destroyed or carried off by the British raiding parties.

His professional eye took note of the number of quays and the variety of ships tied up. There were flat-bottomed rafts, several unarmed shallow-draft river sloops, and a larger deep water sloop with a mounted three-pounder and two swivel guns. Obviously a privateer, he thought, and responsible for the two captured merchantmen, riding high in the water, their cargoes having already been unloaded. His eyes were drawn to three whale boats, lashed together and tied to the pier with stout ropes. They bobbed silently in the light waves without a creak or groan from the planking. They were about thirty feet long, one with a removable mast, stored with its sail below the gunwales, and another with a swivel in the bow. The eight sets of oarlocks on each were covered with leather, dark and stained from usage. There is only one reason to cover oarlocks, Nat thought. For silence.

That afternoon, when he met up with Adam and Titus, the wind of the morning had brought a darkening sky and the promise of a cold rainy night. Adam recounted their day spent around the shipyards and warehouses, and in fish houses and taverns, listening and talking to sailors, most of whom were part-time privateers and wharf rats, spending their prize money on women and rum. The slave laborers had stared at them in their uniforms, as if they were strange creatures of another species. The white sailors, at first reticent, found common ground with them once the talk turned to sailing, treacherous weather, shoals and privateering.

"There is talk of a Captain Gradon who is recruiting men for a special raid. He intends to recapture a Rhode Islander brig, a privateer captured by the British along with two sloops, the Islanders' original prizes, all of which lie at anchor at Sandy Hook."

"When is this attack to take place?" Holmes asked.

"That is the difficulty," Adam replied. "This Captain Gradon is short of men. They are brave enough for the privateering part, because there is money in it. The task of capturing an armed brig, and two sloops, all manned by British Navy prize crews, is not to their liking."

"If these ships were taken by the British, there must be American prisoners still on board," Nat reasoned. "Do we know how many Americans the British might be holding?"

"The men we talked to could not tell a shoal of herring from a school of cod," Adam said contemptuously. "Some say a dozen, others more than thirty. From our experience at privateering, I would say five or six were on board for each sloop and maybe ten for the brig."

"That would be my estimate as well," Nat replied. "Twenty to twenty-two American sailors captured and destined for the prison ships in New York harbor." They had reached the end of the stone breakwater and Nat turned back into the wind.

"It is our duty to rescue them," he said. "Let us find this Captain Gradon and offer our services."

When they entered the Riversnake Tavern, the third one they had searched, they discovered the Captain seated in a snug room off of the boisterous main bar room. "Yankees from the sound of you," he said looking up at them from under his arched black eyebrows after Nat, Adam and Titus had introduced themselves. If he were a ship, Nat thought, he would be a frigate named the Resolute. He was of a stout physique, with a thin line of a mouth, a firm, almost pointed chin and locks of greying curled hair that tumbled down over his ears. He fixed his eyes on each of them and then on Nat. "What is a sailor like you doing in the Continental Army as a Captain?" he asked.

Nat explained the three of them were Marblehead Mariners from General Glover's Regiment and had enlisted to serve on General

Knox's staff. "Artillery is artillery on land or sea," he added.

"'Tis harder to hit a target from a floating platform. Otherwise, I take your point," Gradon replied, biting the words off as if they hurt his mouth to speak them.

Nat offered their services, mentioning the raid being planned on Sandy Hook. "When do you propose to carry out this . . ."

"Tonight." Gradon said brusquely, then added by way of explanation, "The weather may change tomorrow and our prey will no longer need the shelter of Sandy Hook cove." He looked them over, noting the well-maintained muskets and Nat's sheathed sword. "With you three, we will be twenty-one in all, enough to man three whale boats." He challenged Nat with a harsh stare. "I am the Captain of the flotilla and you will take orders from me. Is that understood?" Nat nodded his agreement. "We meet at the shed next to the salt works at eight o'clock."

The rain had abated to a drizzle when the three whale boats left the pier and rowed through the gentle surf into the pitch blackness of the night. Nat stood in the stern with his hand on the tiller. Immediately in front of him seated across from each other, Adam and Titus were the lead pair of rowers, setting the rhythm for the five pairs of privateers behind them. Gradon was in the lead whaleboat, with the mast up and sail unfurled, towing the second whale boat with the swivel gun and some shot and powder. The Captain had eight men with him, enough to row silently after they dropped the sail, as they closed with the ships sheltered in the cove. The plan was to approach from the Jersey side of the sheltering arm of the Hook, coast silently down on the favorable current, send one whale boat closer to scout and then attack quickly and silently. The men were armed with cutlasses and pikes. Nat carried his pistol in a leather pouch slung over his shoulder.

Holmes could barely discern the outline of the cove and Gradon's whaleboat ahead. The men in the second whaleboat had cast off and were rowing silently into the cove. Nat's boat bobbed quietly in the water, keeping its distance from Gradon and waited for the scouting boat to return. When it did, Gradon jumped lightly over the side, huddled with the man he had placed in charge and had them row him close to Nat's boat.

"There are no lights on the brig," Gradon said. "Of the other two, one is a cutter, the other a sloop. There is one sailor on watch on each. I will take the brig. You take the cutter closest to the brig, this crew will take the sloop." Having given those orders, he returned to his whaleboat and clambered aboard. Nat saw the mast being lowered and then with Gradon in the lead, the little convey silently ghosted ahead into the sheltering cove.

Nat whispered instructions to cease rowing. Only Adam and Titus continued until the whaleboat glided alongside, edging toward the cutter's stern. It was definitely a cutter, its mast further aft and longer than a sloop with more room for cargo in the holds below. He wondered if all of the American prisoners were held on board.

As they bumped gently along side, Nat raised his hand and three sets of grappling hooks arched up and set into the wooden bulwarks above. Quickly, the armed men swarmed up and onto the deck. The one sentry on watch returning from the bow saw the shadows flitting about the deck, shouted the alarm and was immediately cut down by two sailors. The patter of feet on the deck aroused the crew below. Light from lanterns filtered up from the hold. Nat stood at the hatchway, pistol and cutlass in hand as the first of them attempted to reach the deck.

"Try it and I will blow your head off."

"Damn you if you do," the officer shouted advancing up the stairs, brandishing his sword.

Nat aimed his pistol at the man. It misfired. Quickly, he slashed down with his cutlass and the man fell back spouting blood from the gash in his neck. Behind him, a group of blue-coated men from the prize crew massed in the corridor but the narrow stairway made it difficult for more than one man at a time to mount an attack. Nat sent Adam and two others to guard the entrance of the after cabin, while Titus and others dragged the hatch cover into position. Titus bent down to adjust the cover, unaware of a British sailor with a pistol creeping up the ladder. He came at Titus from his right side, the one where he wore a patch over his gouged-out eye. Nat shouted a warning at the same time the sailor fired, the ball striking Titus in his head, blowing him back onto the deck.

Adam, at the other end of the cutter, saw Titus fall. With an angry scream, he charged down the steps leading to the after cabin, pike in hand, followed by two other privateers.

Nat ordered two more to reinforce Adam, and then with the remaining Americans pulled back the hatch cover and led them down the stairwell. The British sailors were caught between a vengeful, beserk Adam and Nat's men. They threw down their swords and cried out in surrender. Adam would have none of it. He gutted the sailor in front of him on his pike, put his foot on the dying man's chest, removed his weapon and would have killed another if Nat had not stopped him.

The remaining British sailors from the prize crew were herded below and locked in the same filthy pen that had held the freed Americans. There were only seven of them, all simple sailors and not an officer among them. [9]

"Where are the others?" Nat asked one of Americans.

"We were taken by a frigate and our Captain and the Lieutenant were forced on board. Said to be hung from the frigate's yardarm when they reached New York." He was obviously a Rhode Islander by his accent and when the rescued Americans discovered that Nat and Adam were Marblehead Mariners, they became more talkative.

"We were twenty men plus our Captain and Lieutenant when we sailed from Providence. We captured four merchant ships in the first two weeks, left them in New London and resumed our cruise."

"Then, we hit a squall and saw no action for a while," another added. "Until we picked up this cutter and that little sloop. We were heading for somewhere on the Jersey coast when we were overtaken by the Fox, with its twenty-eight guns. We could not outrun her, nor could we stand and fight."

"That was a black day indeed," another said.

Nat went up on deck as Captain Gradon approached in the brig, his whaleboat tied to and trailing from the stern. The night was still black as ink, but the brig was showing lights below through the gun ports.

"Can you sail the cutter to South Amboy?" he shouted through cupped hands.

"We will follow your course," Nat yelled. "We have freed seven

American sailors. Any prisoners on the brig?"

"Eight for us. None on the sloop," Gradon shouted back.

Well, Nat thought, at least we have rescued fifteen good men bound for prison ships or hanging.

With the addition of the recently freed Rhode Islanders and the whaleboat crew, the cutter's sails were quickly raised. Nat took the wheel, feeling the salt spray in his face as the wind swiftly whipped the ship toward the Jersey shore. She was trim and fast and would have overtaken the brig, but for the skill of the crew and the ship's responsiveness. The little sloop trailed behind and the fleet made South Amboy shortly after dawn.

Word had spread at the sight of the three sails making for the harbor and a crowd of men greeted their arrival. Slaves, directed by their masters, ran up and down the piers unloading the cargo of cordage, sails, muskets and powder, mostly from the Rhode Island brig, The Revenge; barrels of salt and butter from the little sloop Mayflower; and rum, madeira, wine and brandy, as well as tea, coffee and bales of cloth from the cutter, Hope. All was taken to one of the warehouses on the wharf, to be counted and assessed in determining the prize money to be awarded.

Adam kept a piece of the sailcloth from the cutter and wrapped Titus's body in it. Nat hired a wagon and together with the driver they rode through the muddy streets to the church graveyard. It was not much of a church to look at, with boarded up windows, no fencing around the graveyard and many inscribed grey slate stones, broken and lying shattered on the graves they were supposed to mark.

"What church is this?" Nat asked the driver.

"'Tis St. Peter's Episcopal Church." He spat on the ground. "Ravaged by the Redcoats and Hessians when they passed through in '77. They used the gravestones to make their ovens. Baked their bread on the names of the deceased," and, thinking he had said enough, fell silent.

Nat and Adam labored through the morning digging the grave until they were satisfied it was deep enough and unlikely that the site would be desecrated. They lowered Titus's canvas-shrouded body into the ground and filled in the site. Their work done, they donned their jackets, and with their tri-corns in their hands, bowed their bare heads. Nat recited a brief prayer and somberly they rode back into South Amboy.

"If he had a good right eye, he would still be alive," Adam said gruffly.

"It is my fault for not keeping a better watch on the hatchway."

"No, Captain," Adam insisted. "It was the loss of his right eye, gouged out by some backwoodsman at General Washington's headquarters in Cambridge."

"That was a brutal melee," Nat recalled. "Many of us Mariners suffered injuries. Poor Caesar died."

The injuries you suffered, Adam thought, were because we stood and fought together. But the backwoods bastards went after the Mariners of color. That is why Caesar died and now Titus is no more. He decided not to give voice to his anger. Captain Holmes was a good man but he would not understand.

In the early afternoon, Nat and Adam, their uniforms and boots encrusted with the dirt from the graveyard, found Captain Gradon seated at a long table in the warehouse with a large ledger in front of him, a quill and ink to the side. The cargo unloaded from the holds of the three ships was stacked according to their nature in neat rows of barrels and bales, alongside piles of sails, ropes and guns. Gradon noticed them, standing against the wall near the large double doors and strode over to meet them.

"Your man was the only fatality. We had two pretty badly cut up on the brig. They are being sewn together somewhere in town." He waved his hand at the cargo stacked up in the warehouse. "The calculation of prize money will require some time," he said. "There are no prize courts in South Amboy and the records must be submitted to Perth Amboy for determination." He was much more talkative now that the raid was successfully completed.

"You will have to wait for your share. Will you claim a share for your dead man's family?" Gradon asked, knowing that the rest of his crew would receive more if the prize money were divided among fewer officers and sailors.

Nat looked surprised. It had never even occurred to him to claim any prize money. He drew himself erect. "Captain Gradon. We went on this raid in the uniforms of the 14th Continental Regiment, formerly the Marblehead Mariners. Had we been captured, we would have asserted our right to be treated as prisoners of war, not as privateers whom the British consider pirates. Not having run the risk as privateers, we decline to receive shares of the prize."

Gradon arched his eyebrows. When he saw that Nat was serious, he clapped him on both shoulders. "Very well said, Captain Holmes. You are an honorable man." He looked at Adam's somber face and attributed his demeanor to the death of his friend.

What have you done? Adam wanted to shout. Holmes had just given away the prize money he needed to purchase Sarah's freedom. Adam had done some rough calculations, having an appreciation of the value of ships from their year privateering off the Massachusetts coast. With the cordage, cannons and guns, he estimated his share would be close to one thousand dollars in hard coinage, not to mention whatever price the cargo would bring. And it was all gone. In the time it had taken for Holmes to make his fine speech. True, they would have claimed the privilege of uniform and the right to be treated as prisoners of war. But they had not been captured. They had returned safely to port with three ships and a valuable cargo. He was entitled to his share. It meant Sarah's freedom.

"All we need," Adam heard Holmes saying, "is a transport to take us up the Raritan as far as New Brunswick. "From there, we will find our way back to the army we left north of White Plains."

Will Sarah be at Camp? Adam wondered. Has she been returned to Reverend Penrose? What was he doing fighting in this war when the woman he loved was no more than a barrel of rum, a horse or cordage from a ship, all property to be disposed of by its owner. Adam thought the return trip without the hope of purchasing her freedom would be the longest and most miserable journey of his life.

Chapter 12 - Ambush and Betrayal

Philadelphia
21st October, 1778 (Letter No. 11)

My Dearest Will ,

My Love, my Husband - The four months we have been apart now represent One Month for each of the Four Precious Days we were together. I long for the Luxury of being with you day after day, instead of this endless and uncertain separation.

In your latest Letter you wrote about the dinner with General Knox and his Officers. Or I assume it was your last letter. My Love, Please copy my habit of Numbering your Letters. It would pain me so much to miss any one of them. How I wish I could be there to enjoy the Friendship and good cheer evident from your description. Venison stew is not our usual fare here although the Shad run has been plentiful and the fish fresh and succulent.

We agreed when we parted to be Honest in our letters. I cannot write of Inconsequential Things when I am overwhelmed by Despair due to recent events. The Civil Administration here is vindictive and mean spirited against those who, before this War, lived in peaceful civility with their neighbors. [1] *Our Friends the Ls have suffered grievously from the harm to their Community. Their neighbors, John R and Abraham C were taken to jail in August, accused of treason, tryed in October and found guilty. They were hang'd on the Commons two days ago. Together with the Ls I visited the widows who are wonderfully supported by the Quaker Community while they and their little ones suffer with their Grief.*[2] *The unjust verdict and their punishment is particularly Evil when well-connected Loyalists like the wealthy merchant, Mr. T.C., merely take the Oath of Allegiance to the Government of Pennsylvania, after profiting from their business with General Howe, and are Acquitted. The stench from this miscarriage of justice pollutes the Air of our City, although General A's Administration has Finally Cleansed it of the carcasses, offal and waste the British left us as their departing gift.*

General A's courting of Peggy S. continues undiminished. If anything, his Ardent Pursuit has increased in intensity. The wags assert that since the General has Successfully Stormed every Fort he has assailed, he will conquer the heart of his desires and overcome any reservations of her Father. The principal one appears to be the General's lack of substantial means to Support the Judge's Daughter. There are accusations from the Civil Government, as yet unproven, that Monthly the General becomes more wealthy through private dealings.

As I have previously written, many of my hours are taken with care of Little Lucy, who lovingly calls me Lisbet. She is a most active child, very Inquisitive and continually asks many questions. Mrs. K and baby Julia are thriving as well, receiving many Visitors and Well-Wishers. I will not bore you with the many sweet words Little Lucy has to help quiet baby Julia when she is fitful. Children are so lovely in their Kindness and Innocence.

As we approach the end of October, I am Hopeful the Army will soon seek winter quarters in either Pennsylvania or New Jersey and you and I, my Love, will be together again. I am assured by Mrs. K that she will not spend one day more than necessary away from her Dear Harry and I intend to travel with her. I only Pray that you will remain with General K and not at some distant encampment in northern New York.

I conclude this in haste as Mrs. K has penned a letter in time for a Courier leaving Philadelphia and it is my fervent wish my letter accompanies hers, which travels with the utmost speed and is more certain to reach you.

My Dearest Husband, I hope this letter finds you in good Health and as eager as I am to be reunited. It gives me great Pleasure to sign this letter as always.

Your loving wife,

Elisabeth

Bant considered himself lucky to have left the winter quarters at Middlebrook. The huts, this time constructed with wooden floors, hinged doors and proper windows, as well as hewn slabs of wood to cover the roof timbers, were completed by mid-January. The seven-foot high walls pleased McNeil, who was tall. It mattered not to Bant. He felt confined by the wood framed beds, one on top of another along the walls, twelve men to a cabin.

Had he been in a more accepting frame of mind and not fearful of another long winter of confinement as at Valley Forge, Bant should have been content. It was an area he was generally familiar with. The camp was near Bound Brook. Unlike Valley Forge, the Middlebrook encampment gave the impression of dense orderliness, the straight lines of huts, with the officers' cabins, according to their rank, situated in front of those of the soldiers, the company kitchens in the rear, all snuggled up against the base of the Watchung Mountains. Roll-call and sometimes drills and parades were held in the open ground in front of each Regiment's line of huts, the ground being swept clean every morning. Food, while not plentiful, was adequate. The men received their allotted rations on time and the local population welcomed the Army as protection against Loyalist militias and raiding parties, and contributed their harvests of fruit, vegetables and flour, for a price of course.

Yet, Bant would have none of it. He did not see himself engaged in senseless exercises or menial duties day after day for six months, until the campaign resumed. No sweeping of the parade grounds one day for him and filling in the offal pits another. The close confinement of the mess and sleeping intimidated him. He still had his nightmares and his seemingly irrational rages that caused the men to avoid or taunt him, depending on their mood. Only McNeil stood by him.

The local militias were fighting Loyalist bands and conducting their own punishing raids on Tory farms and towns. Further north, closer to the coast, there were said to be large British and Hessian foraging parties, confiscating food, flour, and hay for the Army in its winter quarters in New York and Staten Island.

When the call came for a company of Continental riflemen to volunteer to support the Somerset County militia, Bant had been the first to step forward. They were once again under the command of Colonel Hand. After a few weeks alongside the militia, scouring the countryside for signs of the enemy without any action, Bant was beginning to think he had made a mistake. He had not fired his rifle in weeks, except to kill a wild turkey several days ago. Still, he acknowledged to McNeil, it was better to be camping in the woods or sleeping in the barns of sympathetic farmers, than to be back at Middlebrook.

"Best hope this mild weather holds. You will be singing a different tune when there is snow above your knees and your stomach growls in protest for lack of food," McNeil said, arching his back against the tree trunk and flexing his shoulders. "Of course, you being so short, the snow would only be up to my ankles and no bother for me." He laughed at his own joke and Bant granted him a smile. They had been together since Trenton and McNeil was the only person Bant could call friend in the entire army.

Early next morning, Lieutenant Stringfellow led twenty of the riflemen northeast on a quick march. The weather was crisp, perhaps a bit warmer than one could expect for early February. At sunset, Bant estimated they had covered almost twenty miles. The next morning dawned colder with an overcast grey sky. Approaching a bend in the road in the late afternoon, they were challenged by dismounted pickets of Continental Light Dragoons, who were camped in the farmhouse and barns beyond. Once inside the split rail fences, they lounged about until the Lieutenant directed them to one of the barns, a weathered shingled low A-frame, with a sharply pitched roof and barely enough space to stand up, except in the center. The fresh hay in the loft smelled pleasant enough but Bant preferred to sleep outside. He scouted around behind the barn and found a small overhang, sheltering a stack of firewood from the elements. When night came, he could move some of the logs and curl up there, he thought. He ambled along the split rail fence around the yard, poked his head into the other barns where the troopers had stabled their horses, and then simply settled himself against the stone wall that surrounded the well and waited, which is where McNeil found him.

"The talk is there are British troops in the vicinity," McNeil said, not expecting a response. "Maybe cavalry. Our dragoons have been out scouting but have not found them yet." Bant grunted. "I guess when they do locate them you will have your opportunity to bag a cavalry officer."

"It has been a long time," Bant said, rubbing the stock of his rifle. McNeil knew his friend would say no more.

That evening, before the men bedded down, Bant was seized with stomach cramps. Grasping his rifle in one hand, he rushed into the bushes. His shit came out in liquid bursts, leaving him feeling weak. He returned to the fire, laid his rifle across his knees and bent over feeling the gas moving within him. As the men ambled toward the barn, Bant found the shelter for the firewood, moved enough of the logs away to make a niche for himself, pulled his blanket over his shoulders and shivering, curled up in a ball. He left his rifle leaning against the remaining stack of split wood, stock within easy reach.

Sometime in the night he awoke with a sudden urge to relieve himself, so strong he feared he would not make it to the bushes. He grabbed his rifle and ran in a crouch as if that would delay his shitting, slipped through the split rail fence and managed to drop his breeches in time. Groaning softly, he pulled up his breeches and squatted with his back to a tree. It helped ease the cramps coursing through his lower stomach.

Suddenly, he heard shouts of alarm followed by two musket shots, screams of distress and then quiet. Dark shapes appeared on the road, ranks of troops moving quickly toward the stone farm house and barns. Light from lanterns shone through the windows and doors as some of the men hastily awoke and came outside, frantically trying to load their weapons. It was too late. The British infantry were upon them, bayonets at the ready, stabbing all who resisted.

Bant watched in horror as six or seven dragoons stood half-dressed in front of a barn, their swords at their feet and called for quarter.

"God damn you Rebels. Here is your quarter," a Sergeant responded, plunging his bayonet into a dragoon's chest. His men quickly cut down the others, herded more dragoons out of the barn and dispatched them in the same manner.

Bant looked over at the A-frame where McNeil and the riflemen had been sleeping. He saw one or two dark shapes creep around the side and run the twenty or so yards to the split rail fence and disappear into the brush. The British rushed into the barn and brought out more than a dozen of the riflemen. In the light of a lantern, held high by an officer, Bant watched as they were slaughtered, one man pinned to the wooden shingles by a bayonet through his stomach. Even after the riflemen lay bleeding on the ground, the British continued to stab them until blood oozed from multiple wounds. An eerie silence followed the butchery, broken only by the coarse comments of the soldiers as they stripped the dead bodies of boots, swords, jackets and knives.

From where he hid, Bant could make out a group of British officers on the porch of the farm house, one was giving orders to others and directing the few prisoners to be taken toward the road. Bant exhaled quietly and sighted on the officer's forehead. Once he fired, he would have to run for they would see the muzzle flash and be quick to follow. The officer who appeared to be in charge obliged by turning more toward Bant, surveying his troops looting the bodies of the dead Americans. As he pointed toward his men, Bant fired. He saw, with satisfaction, the officer fall backward, his tri-corn dropping off his head. [3]

Bant sprinted to his left and up hill, away from the fenced corner of the yard, through an orchard, the bare branches grabbing at him as he passed by. He was startled to hear another rifle shot, a sharp bark rather than the deeper bang of a musket and then all was quiet again. He topped the hill, almost rolled down the other side, found himself alongside a shallow creek and walked in the ice cold water for thirty or forty yards, before clambering through dense shrubbery growing on the far bank. The moon broke through the clouds, illuminating a farmhouse on a distant hill. Bant determined to avoid any habitation and struck off further up the creek, keeping the brush between him and any possible pursuers. He finally stopped to reload. In the predawn quiet of the woodland, the noise of the ramrod sliding down the long barrel seemed exceedingly loud. He crept into the bushes and rested on his haunches, surrounded and hidden by the low dense brush, and listened, his breath condensing in short puffs in front of his face. Nothing. Good, he reasoned. If they were after him, there would be several of them and they would make noise.

He took off his slouch hat and felt the gentle breeze on the back of his head. Bant was about to move when he heard the sound of branches being slowly parted. He froze, moving his rifle imperceptibly in the direction of the noise. A buck, with an eight point rack, edged down to the creek and lowered its head to drink. Bant remained motionless. The deer raised its head toward the hill between them and the orchard, its nose twitching. Then, seemingly unconcerned, and oblivious to the man with the rifle, so close but upwind, the buck melted silently into the shadows.

At dawn, it took all of Bant's courage to retrace his nighttime flight and return to the farm and barns. He waited in the grey light at the top of the orchard. A low mist clung to the yard, like a thin blanket covering the white, half naked bodies lying stiff in the morning cold. A thin wisp of smoke came from the chimney of the house, the only sign of life, until a man in shirtsleeves came out, drew a bucket of water from the well and retreated inside. Bant noticed there were no bodies on the porch. The British must have taken their dead officer with them.

Cautiously, he descended through the orchard, pausing frequently to hide behind a gnarled apple tree trunk. Satisfied no British troops remained he continued on, his stomach knotted and tight, this time from fear. He crouched behind the split rail fence, steeling himself to examine the bodies, before slipping under the middle rail and treading quietly into the yard. Some of the dead Americans were lying on their backs. Stripped of their jackets, shirts and breeches, their skin was pale white, their torsos and thighs, slashed with numerous cuts, the blood caked and dried crimson on their wounds. The multiple lacerations bespoke the savagery of the slaughter. Bant examined each of them, looking for McNeil. He found the Lieutenant whose body was particularly gashed with perforations in his arms, chest, and abdomen, as if his rank warranted the excessive viciousness.

Some of the men had died with fearful wide-eyed expressions. The faces of others were frozen in pain, or contorted in shock. Only a few seemed to be asleep, having succumbed to their wounds in peace. He could not bring himself to touch them, to close their eyes and mouths. They were stiff already, he reasoned. Looking at their faces, he saw again the faces of those militiamen hung by the British, the faces of those who still, two years later, populated his nightmares. He clasped his arms tightly around his shoulders to stop himself from shaking.

He was obligated to look for McNeil. Their friendship compelled him to do so. Slowly he walked to the low barn, gagged, hesitated at the open door and entered. Four stripped bodies lay inside, three face down. Gingerly, Bant grabbed the hair and lifted the head of one and saw it was not McNeil. He did the same with the other two and then, his throat constricted, he dashed outside, gulping for breath. When he looked up, he saw the figure of McNeil, leaning against the split rail fence, waving to him.

"No. No." Bant screamed at the hallucination. "Leave me alone. There was nothing I could do. I could not help you," he cried out between frantic sobs.

McNeil walked toward him. "Bant. It is me. I am alive. I escaped." Bant stood frozen as the apparition came closer. He felt McNeil's callused hands grab his short curled ears and shake him. He smelled the real odor of gunpowder and sweat and saw the unshaven stubble on his chin. Bant collapsed at his friend's feet. He clung tightly to McNeil's legs, feeling his muscled calves and crying out over and over his friend's name, relieved McNeil was real and not another horrific burden on Bant's sanity.

Together, they walked up to the farmhouse. "After the alarm, ours were the only two shots fired," McNeil said. "I killed the other officer on the porch." There were two dark patches of dried blood on the wooden floorboards and bits of bone and brain embedded in one of the supporting beams. "These Redcoats came with intent to bayonet the dragoons. Some local militia men must have guided them to this place."

The farmer opened the door, having heard their footsteps on the porch.

"Please, I do not want any trouble," he said holding up his arms palms toward them. "I did nothing more than host the dragoons. Please do not kill me." By his accent, Bant guessed he was Dutch, a portly man in breeches too tight for his meaty thighs and torn stockings gone grey with use and washing.

"We do not intend you any harm," McNeil said. "We wish to wash and eat, bury our dead and leave," he said as they brushed past the man. "Get us some food. Then shovels and help us move the dead to an appropriate place."

Once inside the kitchen, the man tapped his heel on the floor. A trap door opened and his wife and three children emerged from their hiding place. The oldest boy, who looked to be about ten, led Bant and McNeil to the well and pulled up a bucket of water. Back in the kitchen they sat silently, eating bread and cheese and drinking apple cider from a jug, while the children stood in the far corner open-mouthed, staring at them.

"There is a vale near the tannery, under a tree where the earth is soft and easy to dig. You can bury your . . ." the man began to say 'friends' but after the first sound quickly blurted out "dead," a little too loudly.

"Get three shovels. You will help us," McNeil said pushing his chair back. He put his tri-corn on, touched it as a gesture of respect to the man's wife and thanked her for the food. He nudged Bant who muttered something, already dreading touching the dead bodies. "If you would," McNeil said, turning in the doorway, "please give us some more bread, cheese and a few hunks of cured pork before we leave."

They dug a long trench, about two feet wide, fifteen feet in length and six feet deep. McNeil, to make it easier for Bant, always took the shoulders and left it for Bant to lift the feet, so he would not have to look directly at the faces of the dead soldiers, particularly the riflemen. It took them until the early afternoon to complete the mass grave, tamping down the newly turned soil and raking dead leaves, twigs and branches over the site. McNeil quietly uttered a prayer he had heard the Regimental Chaplain recite far too often during the bleak days at Valley Forge.

"It would be thoughtful of you," McNeil said to the man as they were leaving with the food in their haversacks, "to mark the graves when it is safe to do so."

"And when will that be," the man replied angrily. "I am a farmer and must deal with all sorts of regulars and militias, each demanding something and threatening all manner of injury to me, my wife and little ones if I do not comply."

"We have just buried more than a score of our brother soldiers," McNeil responded, "and have been fighting for more than two years. Do not talk to us of hardships. You will know when the time is ready to mark the graves. Do so when your conscience tells you." He beckoned to Bant and the two of them proceeded down the road in the direction where the main body of militia and riflemen had been only two days ago.

The Pluckemin Artillery Cantonment, several miles northwest of the Army's main winter camp in Middlebrook, was constructed in the shape of a capital E, tipped on its side, with the spine of the letter huddled below a ridge line of the Wachung Mountains. The Officers' barracks and repair shops for gunsmiths, wheelwrights, blacksmiths and carpenters were located on the spine. The barracks for the soldiers were the bottom line of the E. The top comprised a long line of sheds for wagons and storage.

The shorter center line contained more barracks and the newly completed "Academy" - fifty feet long and thirty feet wide with its plastered arched ceiling topped by a cupola. There, the officers attended courses in mathematics and tactics. [4]

Adam paced back and forth outside the entrance hall to the Academy.

The distance from Middlebrook was a severe hinderance for him. He rode poorly and did not own a horse. While wagons frequently went back and forth between the Cantonment and the winter camp, he was not at liberty to simply take leave. He was miserable and alone. Captain Holmes had been granted permission by General Knox to go to Boston. Ostensibly, it was to present a list of ordinance, powder, ball and shot that were needed. Adam knew it was a favor to allow Holmes to visit his wife, who had written their newborn son was sickly and she was beside herself with worry.

The General had then left Pluckemin for Philadelphia to plead with Congress for funding to purchase more cannon and powder. He had taken Will with him as an aide-de-camp. Another favor, Adam thought, to enable Will and Elisabeth to be together. He had learned his lesson. These officers took care of themselves and left the enlisted men to suffer. With a sense of shame, he admitted his was an uncharitable thought. Will had always been his friend and he could rely on him. He was only absent now, at a most inopportune time.

Adam needed to get to the winter camp and more specifically to see Sarah. After several weeks, General Washington and his wife had recently returned from Philadelphia. It seemed logical to him that with the General once again at Middlebrook, Sarah would be needed in the winter camp to cook for his official family. Unless Reverend Penrose had not lent her to the General, or sent someone else in her stead, or offered her to one of the Generals in New York, keeping watch on the British in New York City, or even sold her. His head was filled with these troubling anxious notions so when Captain Hadley emerged from the officers' class, Adam had worked himself up into a frenzy of desperation.

"Captain," he called out and rushed up to Hadley as he came out of the hallway into the brisk February wind. "A word with you, please," he said, angry with himself for using a begging tone. Hadley held his tri-corn on his head to prevent it blowing off and put his other arm around Adam's shoulder.

"What is it, Private Cooper? You seem distraught. Not bad news I hope."

Adam intended only to ask the Captain for some reason to send him to Middlebrook and stay there for a few days. Instead, his worries caused him to pour out his concerns about Sarah and his desperation to learn of her whereabouts. They emerged from the building and stood exposed to the wind, looking out over the artillery parked in neat rows, the muzzles of the light three, six and nine pounders and siege guns pointing out over the dusty fields below, the mortars and large brass howitzers' stubby tubes directed skyward.

"It took several days to assemble all these cannons at Pluckemin," Hadley observed. "Teams of oxen and horses pulling them over rutted roads, stopping every few miles to grease the axles." He clapped Adam on the back. "This very morning I mentioned to Colonel Sargent there was a scarcity of animal fat and if the weather holds and we begin maneuvers, the axles will lock up." Adam waited expectantly. "The slaughterhouse is on the south side of the army's camp. I will remind Colonel Sargent of our discussion this morning. For all eighteen companies of field artillery, I estimate our needs for animal fat will be great. It would take several wagons to haul the barrels to Pluckemin and a few days to render enough to meet our requirements. I assume you have no other duties that would prevent you from leaving once the orders and requisitions are issued?"

"None, Captain. None at all," Adam reassured him.

"Well, then it is done. It will have to go through the Commissary of Military Stores for the proper authorizations. I anticipate no difficulties. Colonel Sargent and Frothingham, the Deputy Commissioner, know each other from Boston." Hadley broke into a broad honest grin. "And that is where you and I first met, is it not? When we rescued Will Stoner from that mob ready to tar and feather him."

"That is true, Captain. I thank you for remembering and your help now."

"I expect a full report when you return. How your courtship has proceeded with the young lady."

"Yes, sir," Adam replied, holding his thought that one is not allowed to court a slave.

Two days later Adam rode one of four ox-drawn wagons into the Middlebrook encampment. Having presented their requisition at the slaughterhouse and been informed that butchering and feeding the army came first and rendering of the carcasses later, the men were released by the Sergeant in charge of the detail.

Adam did not mind the light rain that was falling in the late afternoon. From the vantage point of the wagon, he had seen several of Washington's Lifeguards, easily recognizable in their smart blue and buff uniforms with the distinctive white-plumed blue helmets instead of the traditional tri-corns. They were encamped at the entrance to a narrow road leading to a red brick Georgian house. There were newly constructed huts on the opposite side of the road, along with temporary open-sided shelters serving as makeshift stables for their horses.

The Lifeguards welcomed Adam's offer to help in their construction of more permanent stables, especially since he was skilled with a broad axe. He willingly fell to splitting the trunks of freshly cut oaks into slabs for the stable walls. He kept an eye out for people coming and going from the house, but by the end of the first day had not seen Sarah.

The next day, he helped load a sled with firewood and offered to deliver it to the Wallace House which he had learned was the name of General Washington's headquarters. Adjusting the leather straps across his chest, he dragged the load sled around the side of the brick building to a newly constructed one-story kitchen and shed. Adam unloaded the logs, stacking them in rows, alternating between width and length, washed his hands in a bucket beside the well and opened the wooden door leading to the kitchen. It was almost mid-afternoon and he thought if Sarah were in the camp, she would be busy preparing the dinner meal.

He saw her immediately. She was at the fireplace turning a large slab of beef on a spit, her hair spilling out from under her prim white cap, her apron begrimed with grease and charcoal. She stopped in mid-turn and cried out his name. He saw the surprised delight in her green eyes and the amusement of the other women preparing dinner for the General's official family. Adam took the cloth from her hand and turned the iron spit handle, smelling the aroma of the roasting meat overpowering a faint hint of the soap she used for herself.

"I am not able to see you until later, after the main meal is prepared, served and our other duties are completed," she said loudly over the bustle of the small hot room.

"If you permit me to turn the spit and thus be in your presence for even a little while, I can wait until the late evening if that is when it will be."

She rewarded him with a smile and set about her other duties. The male cook, whom Adam recalled was named Isaac, gruffly acknowledged Adam, who briefly stopped turning the spit to remove his wool jacket.

"An additional hand is welcome as long as you do not interfere with our preparations," Isaac said. Adam merely nodded in response and kept his eyes on Sarah.

It was dark and cool when Sarah finally emerged from the kitchen, a shawl over her head spreading down on to the shoulders of her cloak. Adam liked the way it framed her face, accentuating her high cheekbones.

"May we walk together," Adam asked, inviting her to amble with him toward the main road.

"I am very pleased to see you again Adam. I was with Reverend Pence and his family in Hackensack until the General sent word he would be at his winter camp here and required my services."

He sensed she was distraught and there was more to tell. "Were you mistreated by the Reverend?" Adam inquired, the concern evident in his voice.

"No. Not that. The Reverend is a gentleman. I was welcome at their home and well provided for." She sighed. "Oh, Adam. I see no end to my miserable situation."

He tried to reassure her. "I promised to help you purchase your freedom and I will. Some of my friends are officers who may be willing to lend me some sums which they know I will repay." Adam regretted blurting out the thought. His officer friends, even if inclined to do so, had no money for their own families and certainly no excess funds to lend him.

Sarah's shoulders sagged and she began to sob. He tried to console her, putting his arm around her and was pleased when she leaned her head against him. He let her cry, thinking of where else he could obtain the money. Fifty-three pounds was not an exorbitant sum.

"Adam," she said. "You are most kind and generous and I know you would do your utmost for me. It is that," she paused dabbing at her eyes, "it is no longer possible."

"What is not possible?" he demanded angrily.

"Reverend Pence. He has taken note that I serve as cook to General Washington and have even worked for the Marquis de Lafayette." Adam smiled as the title rolled easily from her lips. "I have learned more French and am adept enough to converse, which I did with Mrs. Pence. The Reverend overheard."

"I do not understand," Adam said.

"Reverend Pence believes I am now more valuable. I heard him say to his wife that after we win the war, many people in New Jersey and even New York, would pay top dollar to have as their cook a woman who prepared meals for General Washington or could teach their children French." She started to cry again. "He is proud of my accomplishments. By my own efforts, I have increased my worth as his property. He now states he will not grant me my freedom for less than two hundred pounds and believes he could sell me to some fine gentle family for at least that amount."

Adam clenched his fists. "That greedy sanctimonious scoundrel. I would grab him by the throat and shake him until he begged for his life."

"No, Adam. Violence is not the answer. I will continue to work for General Washington. We must trust somehow my situation will improve."

"Improve?" he shouted. "How may it improve? Your good Reverend most likely will raise the price of your freedom again. And then again. You are his property Sarah. No matter how kindly he treats you." Adam saw a few of the Lifeguards on sentry duty turn and stare at them.

"There is a way," Adam said, lowering his voice. "There has to be. I will find it and you will be free forever. I promise you that upon my life."

They walked back toward the Wallace House, the building looming ahead in the dark, the windows cheerily lit with candles.

"Sarah," he said taking her hands in his. "Remember my promise. And promise me in return your trust in me will endure and you will wait for me."

"Adam. What will you do? What will happen to you?"

"Promise me Sarah. Please promise me."

"I promise you." And the look of concern in her green eyes and what he took as love was enough to assure him she meant it.

Will, mounted on Big Red, felt a surge of elation as he came upon the familiar road to Pluckemin. The horse seemed as exhilarated as his rider, this clear cold February afternoon, splashing across the shallows of the Raritan River. Ahead of them, twenty dragoons trotted along in pairs, assigned by General Knox to escort his family from Philadelphia. Will recognized the terrain and knew they were close. Behind him in the first carriage were Elisabeth, Mrs. Knox and her two children, newly born Julia and little Lucy. The second carriage contained Catherine Greene, wife of General Nathaniel Greene, now Quartermaster General of the Army, and two of her lady friends. And bringing up the rear were three wagons, piled with trunks containing clothes, household goods, dishes, glasses and silver, foodstuffs, casks of ale and bottles of wine for the General's table.

The Knox family was staying at the Vanderveer House, Mr. Vanderveer having graciously agreed to rent most of his home to the Knoxes for the General's Headquarters and residence. Captain Samuel Hadley and Mercy had leased a nearby stone building from Vanderveer. It had one fireplace in the kitchen for warmth and cooking and two bedrooms upstairs. Will and Elisabeth were sharing the house with the Hadleys. They were compatible with each other, an important matter in close quarters. Since joining the Army in April of '76, with few exceptions, Will had never lived anywhere other than a barracks filled with soldiers or out in the open, or if he was lucky, in a white canvas tent. And certainly never with women. He permitted himself a smile that turned into a broad grin. Sharing meals with Elisabeth at his side, seeing her when he returned to the Lewises, and lying together in bed at night no longer seemed strange but a source of constant pleasure and even wonder. He could not imagine himself being any happier than he was now. And this being February, they would remain together at least through May or even June before the Army took to the field again.

The location of their snug quarters was within the fences of the Vandeveer property and adjacent to the Dutch Reformed Church. Hadley mirthfully had named it the Hadley-Stoner Mansion. Its proximity to the Knoxes allowed Elisabeth to easily assist Mrs. Knox with the children at any time of day or night. The General had ridden on ahead of his family to consult with General Washington at Middlebrook on some matter involving the Congress.

However, Mercy was there to greet them, and while she showed Elisabeth to their new home, Will together with the wagon drivers unloaded the trunks of clothing and necessaries, transporting them up the central wood stairway and depositing them as directed by Mrs. Knox. The barrels were stored in the cellar and two filled with wine were driven off to General Washington's headquarters at Middlebrook, a gift from General Knox to his Commander. Samuel Hadley joined them after his session at the Academy, and together they enjoyed a late but plain dinner with Mrs. Knox in the Vanderveer dining room.

The following morning, despite the drizzle, Will commanded a three gun battery in the standard drills for maneuvering field artillery. Inside the Academy's classroom, with the odor of the officers' uniforms smelling like wet sheep, he tried to follow the Preceptor's lecture on geometric concepts of gunnery and gun quadrants. The dry New England accent of Mr. Colles reminded Will of Sergeant Merriam. His mind wandered to the promontory below Dorchester Heights where Merriam had fired a ball from The Albany that had disabled a floating British battery. As he left the Academy in a crowd of officers he was lost in his memories of the good Sergeant and his frequent quoting of bible verses. We went through much together, Will thought, smiling at the image of his old Sergeant lecturing him after he had attacked that foppish Captain for insulting Elisabeth. And now, Elisabeth was his wife. He smiled. What a joy for him every day.

The sentry outside the Vanderveer House saw Will heading to his quarters and hailed him. "Sir. General Knox has given orders for you to attend to him the moment you return."

Puzzled by the need for urgency, Will scraped the mud off his boots on the iron wedge and waited in the alcove off the center hall, together with others seeking a meeting. He gazed out of the window at the Hadley-Stoner Mansion and thought how pleasant it was to know that Elisabeth was inside, or perhaps in this same building, upstairs with Mrs. Knox, and, they would share their meal together.

When he entered the General's office, Knox did not greet him jovially as he usually did and Hadley stood leaning grimly against the mantle.

"Captain Hadley has conveyed to me most distressing news, so painful as to cause me to question my judgment of men. One who was attached to my Regiment and performed all tasks assigned to him in good soldierly fashion." He nodded to Samuel who straightened his back as if to deliver a death sentence to a condemned man.

"Private Cooper has deserted."

"Adam?" Will said incredulously. "It is not possible."

"Two nights ago, he was arrested by the General's Lifeguards for causing a disturbance outside of Headquarters. At first the Guard thought he was only drunk," Hadley added. "Adam persisted in calling on His Excellency to free the slaves in his employ, and when he refused to be silent, he was placed in the prison hut."

Will turned pale, recalling Adam's confession to him that one day he would run away with Sarah and kill anyone who tried to stop them, even General Washington himself.

"Yesterday," Hadley continued, "he was no better, refusing an offer of release for his promise to cease these unseemly disturbances before Wallace House."

"Even worse, " Knox continued in his deep voice, for once low in tone in light of the gravity of the matter. "Last night, he overpowered the two guards when they brought him his food. I am told he broke the arm of one, took a musket and knife, eluded the sentries' challenge and has disappeared."

"It cannot be," Will stammered. "Adam has endured as much as I, we have fought alongside each other. He saved my life in Boston," Will's voice trailed off with incomprehension.

"A mounted patrol is in pursuit and if he is captured, he may very well be executed as an example to deter others who may be tempted to desert," Knox said. "I will do my best to appeal for a lighter punishment but General Washington has expressed strong concern before about the rate of desertions and promised the severest penalties."

"Sir. I do not believe that Adam deserted our cause to join the Loyalists. Until I hear his explanation from his own lips, I have faith there is another reason for his conduct."

Knox scowled and then his expression softened. "It is an admirable human trait to remain loyally steadfast to one's friends. One day we may learn his reasons. I hope they dispel the appearances of his desertion. However, for the moment we must assume he will relate to the British his knowledge of our camp, the guard and routine at the Wallace House, and the recent mission I assigned him with Captain Holmes to the ports in Southern New Jersey."

Will shook his head vehemently. "He will not for a moment give up that information." No, Will realized with dread, but he might accept payment for it from the British, money with which to buy Sarah's freedom. He was no longer so certain of his friend's motivations. Still, he secretly wished Adam well and hoped he escaped unharmed.

Chapter 13- Confidences in New York and Secrets at Pluckemin

During his first few weeks in New York City, John Stoner shared quarters on lower Broadway with Lieutenant Chatsworth and four other dragoon officers. Chatsworth, with the aid of Colonel Harcourt, had reasserted their claim on the merchant McDougall's home, their previous quarters when the 16th Dragoons were in New York. In doing so, they made enemies of a few of the officers of the 42nd Highlanders, a Grenadier Regiment they displaced. John, along with Chatsworth and the dragoon officers, ignored the angry scowls of the grenadiers, when the two groups found themselves dining in the same long room at Fraunces Tavern.

With the influx of the British Army and the desperate Loyalists who had fled Philadelphia, New York City's population had increased overnight by more than half. Over thirty thousand souls crowded its streets, the higher-ranking officers and their staff, the wealthy merchants, bankers and ship owners living in luxury at the tip of Manhattan Island in fine red brick Georgian mansions.

The less fortunate, newly arrived mechanics and tradesmen, the poorer sort of Loyalists, and former slaves attracted by the promise of freedom, were crammed into shanties and shacks on the City's west side, shoddily rebuilt after the great fire of '76, ignited, as everyone knew, by the retreating Americans. These poor masses provided a cheap workforce for the wharves and shipyards on the East River, where the tall masts of frigates and ships of the line swayed above the smaller merchant vessels filled with all manner of cargo from the

Caribbean and the latest luxury items from England. Coastal traders brought foodstuffs and live animals from the farms of southern New Jersey and Pennsylvania, preferring the hard currency of the British to feed its army in New York, to the worthless Continentals offered in Philadelphia.

With no specific duties or assignments, John spent time reacquainting himself with the city, prowling the streets, noting the ease with which people came across the East River from Brooklyn and beyond, the common laborers and tradesmen with unfettered access to lower Broadway and thus General Clinton's own headquarters at No.1, and the nearby home of Mayor David Matthews. His instincts told him, while he was observing and gathering his own intelligence, this dross could be parlayed into the gold of a prominent inside position.

He cajoled Joseph Galloway to provide an entrée to the civilian authorities. That avenue seemed closed due to the ossified nature of the existing administration. John believed better opportunities lay with the military. Despite Galloway's constant complaints about the injustice of the seizure of his home and personal property by the Pennsylvania Government, John coddled his injured ego and squeezed every favorable recommendation and introduction from his former superior. Finally, these efforts led to a meeting with Major Pritchard on General Clinton's staff, who had expressed an interest in John's experience in ferreting out spies and sympathizers in Philadelphia.

John, through Chatsworth, hired a tailor who let out a seam here and there, fitted his newly cleaned red jacket and polished the buttons that still indicated he was attached to General Ruggles's Loyalist Associators. He would have preferred brass buttons with a more prestigious insignia but these would have to do.

He and the Major met in a building on lower Broadway, not far from Clinton's headquarters. Dust from the streets rose in clouds, churned up by marching patrols and carriages carrying well-turned-out ladies to their morning social engagements. John hastily brushed the front of his uniform with his palms and readjusted his jacket. He licked his lips nervously, thinking in a panic that if he were not retained in some capacity, he had no other attractive possibilities. After being announced by Pritchard's orderly, he forced himself to calmly enter the room and took the seat the Major indicated. The desk between them was neat, with a stack of folders to one side, and a quill and inkwell, full John noted, in the middle. The Major was balding with his grey hair cut short on the top and curled over his ears. He had full almost feminine lips, a double chin and dark eyes, which, while not piercing, gazed at John intently. John wondered if the Major had obtained his position through family influence or merit. If I am to be assigned to his staff, he thought, he would find out more about him.

"Tell me of your achievements in Philadelphia, Lieutenant. I have heard reports from others but wish to hear from you directly." Before John could utter a word, Pritchard added, "And no bragadaccio. Only fools engage in trumpeting their successes. My time is important and I do not wish to waste it on fools."

John noted the accent of the British upper class and the patronizing tone. He smiled what he hoped was a relaxed grin and hoped his own accent had changed enough by mimicking Chatsworth and others to dispel any impression he was one of those uneducated Yankee Colonials.

"Yes sir. My initial activities when His Majesty's troops occupied the Rebel capital were to improve the security around General Howe's headquarters." John described how he had created files on all who owned or lived in houses near the Commander, the Generals and their senior staff, created a network of informers to report any suspicious behavior and closely monitored those whose loyalties were suspect.

"I recognize the Army's senior command has only recently arrived in the city. Without being critical of the efforts around His Excellency's Headquarters and the other buildings on lower Broadway, permit me to say I personally have observed a certain laxness during the day, but especially at night, with all manner of ordinary people in the vicinity."

Pritchard shifted his portly figure in his chair, which creaked slightly. "Go on."

"There have been whaleboats crossing the sound from Connecticut, seeking to capture prominent Loyalists. It would be an easy matter for some of these Rebel looters to disguise themselves as farmers, and on wagons come by ferry across the East River and attempt to kidnap, or worse, assassinate, the Army's leaders." John saw he had the Major's attention.

"There are draymen, waggoners, carpenters and workmen of all sorts about day and night, unloading goods, doing this or that in the very buildings that house senior staff. They could be spies or sympathizers. Why yesterday, I even saw several Continental Officers on parole strolling up and down Broadway."

"They have given their word they will neither attempt to escape nor engage in hostile acts."

"Yes sir, but they have eyes and ears. Surely, when they are exchanged, they could report the routines of the guards outside General Clinton's Headquarters, the entrances and exits to the building, vital information for raiders on a mission of kidnapping. Or assassination," he added ominously.

"Gentlemen would not convey such information," Pritchard said smugly. "Our own paroled officers when exchanged do no such thing. That is why we have spies."

John sensed he had offended the Major's sense of upper class superiority and quickly moved on.

"I have also employed spies to venture into the Rebel camp, then at Valley Forge, and used the intelligence I gathered for an attempted kidnapping of prominent Rebels at Princeton." Both had ended in failure, but John was reasonably certain Pritchard would not know that.

"My charge is the security of General Clinton and others. External operations, as you have mentioned, are Major Drummond's concern," he said haughtily, inclining his head toward an adjacent office. Ah, John thought. That is a useful tidbit of information.

"I will ask General Ruggles to reassign you to my office," Pritchard continued. "You will continue to draw your pay from his Regiment. Additional funds will be provided to you, as needed from this office. Present me with your plans with specificity both as to restricting access and this census, you mentioned, of owners and residents in the vicinity of the various headquarters. In four days time. I tolerate neither indolence nor excuses. Is that understood, Lieutenant Stoner?"

"Yes sir."

Well, John thought, very pleased with himself as he sauntered east on Beaver Street. I have worked for pompous pricks before and this Major Pritchard is not the worst of them. I will make myself extremely useful so as to come to the attention of the Major's superiors. And I will pad my expense accounts, starting small to begin with and gradually create a regiment of paid ghost informers. Oh yes, he chuckled. I will turn a pretty shilling in this endeavor.

—∞—

The carriages began arriving in Pluckemin from Philadelphia two days before the festive celebration planned for the first anniversary of the alliance with France. None created as much of a stir as that of General Arnold's ornate carriage, with Peggy Shippen and the General seated within. Escorted by twenty-four cavalry, twelve in front and twelve behind, in spotless uniforms, mounted on well-groomed horses, the leather saddles and bridles buffed to a deep lustrous brown sheen, the carriage halted on the road to the entrance to Vanderveer House. The way was too narrow and short to accommodate the entire procession. After some initial confusion, the driver proceeded without the troopers to the house where General Arnold alighted with assistance from one of the uniformed soldiers riding postilion. Using his crutch, and with an elegantly attired Peggy Shippen gracefully adorning his arm, he struggled up the few steps to be greeted by General Knox himself at the doorway. [1]

Elisabeth observed their arrival from the window of her bedroom and rushed over to offer her assistance to Mrs. Knox. She did not look forward to idle conversation with Peggy, whom she had not seen since marrying Will. Elisabeth had declined her invitations to teas and dinners, claiming the duties of a newly married woman. She had no desire to hear more of their Loyalist sentiments and condescending ridicule of Whig women. Perhaps, with General Arnold's persistent courtship, Peggy had changed her view, Elisabeth thought.

She left her cloak with one of the servants and, following the noise and commotion, entered the sitting room unannounced. Arnold was seated in the upholstered wide wing-backed chair, usually favored by General Knox, with his bad leg propped up on an ottoman.

"Ah, the courageous lady who resisted an incorrigible Redcoat rascal," he said, waving to her. "If we but knew that scoundrel's name, we could someday have him brought to justice." Will, standing off to the side of General Knox, looked at her puzzled. "Forgive me, but my injured leg has stiffened from the carriage ride and I am, for the present, unable to rise in your presence."

"Why, Elisabeth," Peggy said moving quickly from alongside the General's chair. "How fulfilled you look. Married life certainly becomes you." Elisabeth blushed deeply, which drew an uncharitable guffaw from Arnold. "It is my intention, my dear, once your father accepts my representations and entreaties, to have you look as fulfilled. However, I daresay your present beauty cannot be improved upon by the mere formality of marital status." Arnold beamed up at Peggy who giggled and curtsied in mock honor.

"It is good to see you again, Sir," Elisabeth said. "Please excuse me. I must see if Mrs. Knox requires any assistance."

"Elisabeth," Knox said. "If you would be so kind as to stay with Little Lucy and the babe upstairs, I know Mrs. Knox would be most eager to renew her acquaintance with the General who did us the honor of escorting her from Connecticut to Valley Forge."

Elisabeth was playing with Lucy while Julia slept in her cradle when there was a gentle knock and Will appeared. She saw the troubled look on his face and knew the question he would ask. Lucy looked up and ran to Will, grabbing him around his knees, and hugged him. "Are you" she said with a serious expression, "and Lisbet going to the dance? Momma said she will dance with Genr'l Washington."

"Of course we are," Will replied. "And I will dance only with Elisabeth."

"And Momma will dance with Poppa," she answered with the certainty of a three and a half year old who knows the proper order of the world. "Can I show you my dolls."

"Arrange them for me," Will said. "I will be over to see them."

With Lucy distracted in the corner, Elisabeth said softly, "I do not keep secrets from you, my love, but from others. I could not tell Peggy nor General Arnold, even though he asked directly, that I had been assaulted by your brother." She was seated on a low stool, gently rocking the baby's cradle with one hand. How beautiful she is, Will thought, gazing at her blue eyes, staring back at him with utmost honesty.

"I related a British officer had attempted to loot the Lewis home and I had fought him off." She shrugged. "They accepted that version and your brother never entered into it."

Lucy looked up from her cloth dolls. "Will," she called. "You promised to see my dolls." He kissed Elisabeth on her forehead and squatted down next to the little girl.

"If your brother comes to visit you and Lisbet, he may play with my dolls, too." Will laughed heartily and hugged her, smiling over her head at Elisabeth, who mouthed the words, "Little ones have big ears."

Peggy Shippen insisted that Elisabeth ride in the carriage to Middlebrook where she would be staying at the Wallace House. Propriety demanded that she not sleep under the same roof as her ardent suitor, General Arnold.

"This carriage affords us absolute privacy," she assured Elisabeth, who raised an eyebrow. "Oh Elisabeth. How could you even think that of the General. You know he is such an honorable gentleman. He would never attempt to take advantage of my person on the ride from Philadelphia."

Not take advantage, Elisabeth thought, but if offered encouragement, Arnold was amorous enough to engage in any games Peggy would like to play. And you are enough of a flirt, she thought, to arouse and hasten him to prevail upon your father.

"It is a snug and private place, however. That is why I requested you ride with me. I have no one else I may be frank and open with about the dear General and the state of our courtship."

Elisabeth nodded. "I am flattered by your trust in me."

"Well. You are a newly married woman and now know the passions that consume those in love." She giggled and waited for Elisabeth to recount her amorous experiences. When she remained silent, Peggy began to cry. The suddenness of her tears surprised Elisabeth, who was unsure whether they were sincere or a ploy to gain her sympathy.

"Father insists that Benedict, that is General Arnold, acquire substantial wealth to be able to support me in a proper fashion." She dabbed at her eyes with a lace handkerchief. "I want that, I confess, but not at the expense of this prolonged delay of our marriage. He has proposed in secret and I have accepted. I have never met a man with a more commanding presence, one with a kind and gentle side to complement his steely hardness of purpose. We wait only for father's permission."

"I am certain you will be able to persuade your father, if General Arnold cannot," Elisabeth said sweetly. Before the lavish Mischienza, there had been rumors that Judge Shippen had prohibited his daughters from participating. He said the nature of the party and the costumes designed for his daughters to wear were scandalous and undermined the dignity of the Shippen name. Servants gossiped that Peggy refused food for three days, screamed at her father constantly, threw tantrums that could be heard by passersbys on Fourth Street, and ultimately Judge Shippen had given his permission.

"Oh, father will come around. You are right," Peggy said dismissively, stuffing her handkerchief in her sleeve. Elisabeth marveled at how rapidly her friend had gone from tears of woe to sterness of purpose. "Our difficulty now is these horrid accusations by the evil Mr. Reed. He is no longer the prosecutor you know. He has risen, as filth floats to the top of an offal pit, to become President of the Supreme Executive Council." [2]

Elisabeth wondered whether Peggy had ever been near an offal pit. It was well expressed but the salty reference probably originated with her ardent General.

"That unpleasant man most certainly has paid for the most scandalous accusations to be published in the Pennsylvania Gazette and broadsheets against our heroic General. Why Benedict has even been accused of selling confiscated Tory goods for his own benefit," she sniffed as if to state the allegation was to prove its preposterousness. "And this business of his involvement with the Charming Nancy," she went on, waving her hand as if it was too much of a burden to even tell Elisabeth. [3]

"What are we to do? Under his military administration, Benedict has brought order to the city, civil society has flourished, and he protects the rights and liberties of all, including, yes, those accused by these nasty radicals as having been staunch Tories. And his reward is constant harassment from them, threats of legal action and anonymous attacks on his reputation." Peggy's voice rose in anger. "Reed and his verbal assassins, who have never risked their lives in battle in which my dear General has suffered a most grievous wound, are not fit to be in the same room with him. After all his sacrifices, Benedict is entitled to make a profit as much as those merchants who now claim to be steadfast patriots but in reality ship their goods to New York City to obtain a better price."

"You defend him with such vigor," Elisabeth said quietly. "'Tis a sign of your deep devotion and love. Together, I am sure you will persevere against any adversary."

Peggy reached over and patted Elisabeth's hand. "I was so certain I could unburden myself to you. Yes, Benedict and I will prevail. His intelligence, sense of honor and duty, the wealth he is deservedly accumulating, despite the false accusations, will see us through."

She leaned forward conspiratorially. "When we return to Philadelphia, Benedict will formally ask father for my hand. He has told me he has purchased a fine estate along the Schuylkill. [4] That will satisfy father's condition that Benedict bestow upon me a substantial settlement prior to our marriage." She laughed, a high-pitched sound, betraying her nervousness.

"You, my dear Elisabeth, and your handsome husband will of course be invited. I anticipate it to be an April wedding. When the apple trees and dogwoods are in bloom and the air is filled with the fragrant scent of their blossoms."

If the Army is still in camp, Elisabeth thought. She and Will had married as soon as possible because the future course of the war could not be predicted. How conceited of Peggy not to permit the thought of the war disrupting her plans for party and pleasure.

Two days later the grand ball at Pluckemin, to celebrate the one year anniversary of the alliance with the French, was held in the Academy. It began with the discharge of thirteen cannon, which occupied Will as one of the officers responsible for returning the guns to the artillery park.

When he arrived at the Academy, the festive hall was crowded with far fewer women than men. Accordingly, following an elaborate dinner, with numerous toasts to liberty, independence and the certainty of the war's outcome, Elisabeth and Mercy, abiding by the customs of a formal ball, danced with officers other than their husbands. The only exception was General Washington. After the first required dance with Mrs. Knox as the hostess, who although overweight was surprisingly light and graceful on her feet, their Commander monopolized Catherine Greene for the entire evening. [5] Peggy, while the center of attention with all eyes upon her during a minuet, would occasionally retreat from the floor to adoringly seat herself on the arm of General Arnold's chair. And then, she would rejoin the merriment, escorted by some fortunate officer who had the courage to ask for her as a partner and brave the General's initial glare of disapproval.

Will stood before one of the thirteen painted arches, this one next to the center arch, depicting Louis the XVI as America's friend and ally. He preferred the ones of battles, the confrontation at Lexington, and the victory at Saratoga. The artist had painted a reasonable likeness of General Arnold, astride a white horse, urging the troops onward. He wondered if the General or Peggy had seen it. [6]

Turning to the dance floor, he admired Elisabeth's gracefulness as she effortlessly floated across the highly polished wood. Her partner, a Captain on General Washington's staff, his back straight and his chin held high, looked more like he was posing for a portrait than a gentleman enjoying himself. He did seem to think he presented a noble countenance for those who were watching, but did not realize that their eyes were not on him but on Elisabeth. Will thought, to hell with propriety. He would assert himself and partner with Elisabeth for the next minuet. That would be only his second dance with her this evening. No, he thought, only the second time they have danced together as husband and wife.

He intercepted her as she came off the dance floor, her face flushed with excitement and escorted her to the punch table. "It would be a great pleasure, Mrs. Stoner, if you would favor me with the next minuet. I will do my best not to step on your toes, as I did before."

She laughed. "I feared you would never ask. I would much rather enjoy your stumbling around than the far smoother steps of another officer of higher rank."

He enjoyed her teasing him. "I take that as a compliment. Shall we?" he asked, extending his arm as the musicians began to play.

She beamed at Will as they honored each other, he bending slightly at the waist in a bow, she holding her skirt between her thumb and four fingers. They were at the end of two lines, because of Will's rank, but it mattered not. Elisabeth lost herself in the simple pleasure of partnering with her husband, the very thought of their dancing together giving her a rush of enjoyment.

When the fireworks display was announced, the crowd moved outside to view the spectacle in the gathering darkness. Will affectionately wrapped his arms around Elisabeth to warm her. She nestled within them and swayed slightly, humming a refrain from a minuet. Her mind went to the last time she had seen fireworks, at the Mischienza when Captain Montresor had presented her with a pearl necklace and she had felt his breath on the nape of her neck as he closed the clasp. Thinking back on that evening, she convinced herself she had thought it was Will with her at that moment. But if that were so, why had she not worn the necklace this evening. It remained in the bottom of her trunk, wrapped in a cloth and buried under her petticoats and blouses. She had not thought of Montresor since he left Philadelphia. Why had he intruded on her enjoyment this evening? Nothing had passed between them. She had merely done her duty as required and obtained information from him. While he may have preferred to make her his mistress, she had maintained the boundary.

She squeezed Will's forearms more tightly around her and decided she would have to tell him more about that celebration, and even the necklace. Will would understand. There could be no secrets between them.

Chapter 14 - Freedom for All

He had been fortunate so far in the nine days since he deserted. Using the familiar constellations in the sky that were second nature to him as a fisherman, Adam set his course northeast from Middlebrook. He moved only at night, stopping when the early dawn provided just enough light for him to find a secure hiding place in thick underbrush or beneath rocky outcroppings. He was surprised at how many men were on the country roads at night, some legitimately and others up to no good. He avoided contact with all of them, the farmers, doctors, ministers and waggoners. He was especially wary of armed groups. The danger came from militias patrolling the roads as well as others out for plundering and looting of Loyalist or Rebel homes, or simply armed thieves caring not for the cause supported by their victims, as long as they had something worth stealing.

Because of his caution progress had been slow, but he was reasonably certain he had eluded any patrols sent out to capture him. He was as yet undecided whether to make for the coast or continue inland by foot. He hoped, if he came to a navigable river, he could find work on some shallow draft transport and work his way further north.

He awoke in the late afternoon, opened his eyes and remained motionless, listening for any sounds. He heard shouts from far off and warily raised himself from the bed of leaves he had fashioned to cushion him from the cold, rocky ground.

From the vantage point of the craggy overlook, he saw a militia in their ill-disciplined manner, proceeding down a dusty road which curved around his hill and disappeared into the pinewoods where he had slept the night before. By their lack of uniforms and ragged lines, he guessed they were local Rebels rather than Loyalists. Ahead of him, in the distance, a grey haze of smoke rose into a cloudy sky and hovered over a tree-lined field. Beyond that was a cluster of shacks and, further, a stout stone farmhouse. If they had burned and looted the farm, he could safely assume the inhabitants were Tories. If they had left it untouched, it probably meant Rebel sympathizers lived there. Either way, he ran the risk of being captured and given over to one side or the other - as a Rebel to the Loyalist militias roaming the area, or to the county's Rebels who would return him as a deserter to the Army.

Although he knew it was more dangerous, Adam decided to move, while there was still light, toward the hazy smoke and the open fields. Crouching low he descended the rocky escarpment, pausing behind large boulders and scouring the terrain ahead before proceeding further. He threaded his way through the pine and maple trees until he was close enough to hear voices. At the edge of the woods seven blacks clustered around a large tree stump, which they were attempting to dislodge with pry bars. A team of two oxen stood docilely by, worn leather straps dangling from their haunches and wound around the massive roots of the remains of the felled tree. Smoke rose from the burning stumps that had already been pulled out.

Adam guessed they were slaves clearing new ground for early spring planting. If they were all owned by the farmer, this must be a wealthy man, and thus more likely to be a Tory than a Rebel sympathizer. Yet the militia had left the farm untouched. If he were still in Monmouth County, camp gossip was the people of the countryside supported the Rebel cause, the proof being that they willingly sold their cattle, pigs, food, cider and even ale to the Quartermaster's agents. Then again, according to that same camp gossip, there were roving bands of Loyalist militias about, eager to punish Patriot farmers for their support. And there were farmers who trimmed their sails to accommodate whoever was in their neighborhood, Rebel or Loyalist, and when they could, sold their goods in the so-called "London Trade" to New York City, receiving gold and silver in return. Hard to know the loyalties of this farm from a distance and the slaves may be able to help him.

Adam decided to chance it. He needed solid information about this farm and others in the area. He stepped from behind a tree, carrying his musket with the fixed bayonet loosely in his hand.

One slave, deep in the hole created by the partially torn-out tree, looked up in the act of tossing a shovel full of soil, saw him and shouted in fear. The others, seeing him walking out of the woods, retreated several steps from the fellow in the hole, looking as if they would bolt across the plowed field.

"Good evening," Adam said. "What is the name of this place?"

They peered at him, bending forward slightly to get a better look, the more timid preferring to remain partially hidden behind the others, peeking around the shoulders of the ones in front.

Adam laughed. "Am I so strange that you are dumbstruck?" He took his tri-corn off and scratched his head in puzzlement. They were barefoot, clothed in ragged breeches and an assortment of dirt-stained shirts, some with holes, some too long, others too short.

"Where you cum frum?" one of the bolder ones asked. "You be talkin' funny."

Adam doubted any of them had heard of Boston. "I am from far north of here where everyone has my accent." They looked at him uncomprehendingly. "Who owns that farm?" he said gesturing with his musket to the building in the distance. His movement startled them and caused them to retreat further. "The building back there and these fields?" using his free hand to wave to the upturned clods of earth.

"Massa DeGraw," the bold one said. "He own us'ns too." The others nodded in agreement. "We be goin' back," he said pointing to the gathering darkness. "Massa miss us, cum lookin'." He pointed at Adam's musket. "With dat."

Good to know the farmer was armed but he anticipated that anyway.

"How many men at the house?" They looked bewildered by his question. "Who lives there?" he asked, gesturing in the direction the slaves had.

The bold one took a step forward ahead of the group but still wary. "Massa DeGraw, heavy son, mean son, small son. Massa's wife and liddle girls gawn away."

At least two other able-bodied men, maybe three if small meant fully grown but short. Probably all had muskets as well.

"I need food - bread, potatoes, corn, oats. Can you get some for me?"

"We's got corn," another slave said. "Tatoes too," the bold one added.

"Back dhere," he said pointing toward their huts. Adam weighed going with them. He could not watch all of them. One of them could alert their master at the house. He would take whatever food they could spare, put it in his haversack and be gone quickly.

The slaves undid the leather straps from the massive stump, flicked them on the oxen's haunches and the entire party, with their shovels and pry bars on their shoulders, plodded through the plowed field, with Adam staying close to the group. He would be hidden from anyone who might venture out onto the broad porch which he could clearly see overlooked the fields. He heard the slaves muttering amongst themselves but could not distinguish their words. He was not even certain they were speaking English. Every once in a while one would look furtively over his shoulder to see if Adam was really still there or had vanished like some strange apparition.

When they reached their shacks two of the slaves continued up the hill to bring the oxen into the barn. The house was a little further beyond. Adam warily watched them go, apprehensive but unable to control the situation. It was getting dark, and the bold one squatted down and restarted a fire in front of a windowless shack with a tattered old sack for a door. The others gathered around the fire, skewering ears of dried corn and potatoes on sticks and holding them over the flames. Adam surveyed his surroundings, thinking if he had to run, he would make for the gap between the two shacks and sprint for the distant trees. It was time for the other two slaves to return. He was nervous, but the corn and potatoes were almost done and he was hungry. The bold one offered him a piece of the Indian meal he had cooked on a flat stone. Adam put down his musket and stuffed it into his haversack as four dark figures surrounded the little group.

"Leave your musket where it is and stand up" a gruff voice commanded. Adam did as he was told and a small man darted forward and took the musket in hand.

"Light the lantern, Jacobus, and let us see what we have here. Never know whether our Negroes are telling the truth or jabbering nonsense." Adam stood with his hands in the air and stared at a large, stout man who he immediately knew to be the father of the other three.

"I mean no harm," Adam said stretching his arms out. "I have been discharged from the Army in Middlebrook and am making my way home to Boston. My regiment, the Marblehead Mariners, was disbanded," he added, keeping as close to the truth as possible.

The father grunted and lowered his musket. Adam noticed the other one kept his at the ready, and the son behind him used Adam's own bayonet to prod him forward away from the fire and toward the light. The one called Jacobus, built stocky and thick like his father, raised the lantern to illuminate the way. They trudged up the slope and turned into the barn.

"You have any papers to show you were discharged?"

"I lost them when I slipped on a rock in a river I was crossing. They were signed by Colonel John Glover," Adam replied with authority.

The father grunted and motioned to Jacobus. The young man took down a coil of rope from a peg and bound it tightly around Adam's arms, tying him up like a pig bound for market. With a quick motion he kicked Adam's legs out from under him and continued wrapping the thick rope around an upright beam.

"Cannot be too careful with armed Negroes," the father said to his sons, studying Adam's worn boots and uniform in the glow from the lantern. "You may be what you say and you may not."

"I am a private in the Marblehead Mariners. I have fought at Trenton and most recently when the Redcoats retreated from Philadelphia. If you are Patriots, untie me and let me continue on my way.

"What are you planning to do with him?" the shorter son asked.

DeGraw wagged his head from side to side as if contemplating how much a calf would bring at market. He replied in the guttural words of low Dutch.

"There are bounties offered for deserters. We will wait until a Continental unit comes through and turn him over to them for the price. Let them decide on the truth of what he says. In the meantime, keep an eye on our slaves. No telling what ideas have gotten inside their thick heads, seeing a colored man armed and in uniform."

Jacobus who seemed to be the oldest, took the lantern and held it high. The light shone brightly in Adam's eyes and he lowered his head.

"Maybe he is a scout for Colonel Tye's raiders. The Militia Captain warned us they had been burning farms near Brunswick. I say we beat the truth from him."

Adam kept his eyes down, staring at his knees. It was to his advantage he understood Dutch and the DeGraws did not know that.

"He is not escaping this night. The militia that passed through scoured the woods and roads to our north and found nothing. I will decide tomorrow morning if we need to break a few of his bones to learn if he is who he says."

DeGraw turned and, followed by his sons, left Adam in the barn in total darkness. He should not have trusted the slaves. He should have followed them, taken their uncooked corn and potatoes and left immediately. Well, he thought, now he knew there were Loyalist raiding parties inland, if he ever escaped and made it that far. He fell asleep with his chin dropped down to his chest, his spine grating against a protruding knot in the wooden beam and his arms tingling from the ropes that tightly bound him. He awoke in the complete darkness that had enveloped him when the DeGraws had left, chilled by the night air. One of the oxen snuffled and the horses in their stalls stamped and moved about. Restless are you, he thought. I wish I was free to move around as you. Off in the distance, he heard an owl hoot, answered shortly by another from a different direction.

He dozed off only to be awakened by a sharp whinny. He snapped his head back, banging it against the post he was tied to, still drowsy, wondering whether he had heard musket fire or dreamed it. Several more shots, followed by shattered glass, screams of men fighting, fearful shrieks and then silence. Adam heard the sound of feet running toward the barn before he saw the triangle of light approaching. Two Indians in buckskin shirts and breeches came through the open barn door, the candlelight glinting off the hatchets in their hands. They stopped short at the sight of Adam, tied to the upright. One approached him carefully, placed the lantern on the floor and squatted off to his side, studying him, while the other ran back out. If this was a band of Rebels, why had they attacked the DeGraws? Adam's confusion was compounded by the arrival of a black man, lean and well over six feet, his face partially hidden by a broad slouch hat. He wore an evergreen uniform jacket with buff facing and on his hip, a leather holster from which protruded a brass-handled pistol.

"And what do we have here?" he said in a nasal sharp accent, looking down at Adam.

"I am Private Adam Cooper of the Marblehead Mariners." Adam gambled that the raiders were Tories. "I deserted from the Army at Middlebrook and am making my way home," he answered in a firm voice.

"Are you an enlisted slave?" the man asked with an edge to his question. "I have heard the Rebel ranks are filled with them, sent by their masters who are fraid to serve."

"I was born free," Adam said slowly for emphasis and with pride. "I have no master."

Your accent tells me you are from Boston."

"Marblehead is north of Boston."

The man was pleased with himself. "Some of the Loyalist Associators I have fought alongside are from that city." He turned as several of his men came into the barn. To Adam's surprise, they were all colored. "Put those saddles and bridles on the wagons, and anythin' else worth takin', hitch up the oxen and drive them up to the house. There are barrels from the cellar to be loaded. Be quick about it. We must be gone before light."

"Are you not going to release me?"

"Tell me first how you came to be tied up."

"I followed the DeGraws'slaves to their huts for food and the old man and his sons captured me." Adam decided not to reveal he understood Dutch. Save that for later. "And you are?" he said gesturing with his chin toward the man.

"Why I am Colonel Tye, the man wealthy Rebel farmers fear all across Monmouth County." He leaned back on his heels, his hand on his chin, contemplating whether Adam was worth bothering with. "You will come with us. I will decide what to do with you later." He motioned to one of the Indians who hacked at the knot with his tomahawk, uncoiled the rope and tossed it into one of the wagons. "Do I have your word you will not try to escape?"

"You have my word," Adam said, standing and flexing his arms and rolling his shoulders to get the blood flowing.

"Good. 'Cause if you attempt it, you will see I am not a man who allows anyone second chances."

The scene at the house was one of quiet efficiency. The DeGraws' seven slaves were in a line passing barrels of foodstuffs from the cellar to the wagons. One of Tye's raiders was saddling the horses. A few men emerged from the house carrying packs made of blankets and linens bulging with loot. Adam, standing to the side on the porch, counted two of DeGraw's sons lying in pools of their own blood at the far end beneath the window. He wondered whether DeGraw and the other son had escaped. Pigs squealed and sheep bleated as they were thrown trussed, none too gently, into the second wagon among the bushels of potatoes, cabbages, oats and sheaves of hay.

On command from Tye, one of his men raised the glass on a lantern and lit a torch of straw. Methodically he used it to set fire first to the curtains and then a pile of cloth on the floor. Another ran with a flaming bundle of sticks to the barn and ignited the loose hay and straw within. With the flames beginning to lick at the wooden structures, sending eye-burning clouds of smoke into the night sky, Tye on horseback led the raiders down a narrow cattle track, through a field and into the woods. Adam rode on the wagon seat next to a thick-set dark-skinned black man, with heavy-lidded eyes that gave him a perpetual angry, surly look. His round face was topped by a slouch hat that would have better fit a man with a larger head. DeGraw's slaves were in the back, holding on to the sideboards, looking back at the fiery destruction of their deceased master's farm, moaning and uttering soft sounds of distress.

These poor dumb souls do not even realize they are now free, Adam thought, although he had no idea what Tye intended to do with them. Probably turn them over to the British to be part of work brigades, repairing roads and redoubts. Hard work but certainly no harder than being slave field hands for the Dutchman.

The sky was beginning to lighten when Adam saw the circular shape of a Dutch Reformed Church looming ahead. The little tower on the top was tilted at an angle, some of the shutters were hanging askew and the windows on the front were devoid of glass. Clearly, it had been abandoned. As they got closer, the two Indians emerged from the shadow of the building and signaled to them, before disappearing in the damp morning mist beyond the stone structure. The raiders, who had been bringing up the rear trotted up, dismounted and without any order fanned out as pickets.

"Have any thoughts of jumpin' off during the night?" Tye asked walking up to the wagon.

"I gave you my word."

"That you did. Good thing you abided by it. Nero here is very good with a knife. Cut up his former master nice and slow. It gave the bastard time to think of his sins before dyin'." He nodded at the round-faced driver who hopped to the ground, in the process revealing a bone handled hunting knife stuck in his waistband.

"Come with me," Tye ordered. Adam followed him into the circular Church. There were no pews, the altar was missing and the interior was empty except for a long table in the center and a few simple wooden chairs. "We will wait here," Tye said, pulling up a chair and gesturing for Adam to do the same. Although it promised to be a sunny spring day, the stone walls still retained the damp night coldness. Adam raised his collar to ward off the chill.

Tye removed his slouch hat, openly appraising him. Adam held his stare. The Colonel, if that was his official rank, which he doubted, was light skinned, his face clean-shaven with pock marks here and there but not so many as to be disfiguring. His nose was narrower than Adam's, although too broad when matched to his sharp cheekbones and thin lips. His black curly hair was neatly cropped. In the daylight, Adam could see that Tye's uniform was neat, well cared-for but worn. Tye's grey eyes flickered with amusement as if he enjoyed Adam being bold enough to judge him back.

"Why did you desert?" he asked bluntly. Adam decided to tell the truth, or as much of it as he could safely relate. He told of his first meeting with Sarah Pence, his anger over her mother serving like a brood mare for their master on the plantation, Sarah's service as a slave cook and the Reverend raising her purchase price, after promising to let her buy her freedom for much less.

"You must have created a scene," Tye said throwing his head back and laughing deeply. "You, a Negro Private in front of Gen'ral Washington's headquarters, demandin' that His Excellency, the plantation slave owner, free his cook, who you say is owned by a Reveren'." He studied Adam again, more closely, as if he seeing him in a new light.

"Last night, we freed that Dutchman's slaves. I am bringin' this war to every Rebel slave-holder in Monmouth County and beyond."

"And what will become of DeGraw's slaves?" Adam asked.

Tye was about to answer when Nero entered the Church, and pointed over his shoulder.

"Later," he said, pushing his chair back. "My guests have arrived."

Adam followed him outside and made himself unobtrusive by remaining in the shadow of the angular wall on the west side. A troop of about twenty cavalry, smartly attired in bright redcoats with dark horsehair helmets, had dismounted in the cleared area before the church. They were accompanied by a band of foot soldiers, Loyalist militia armed with Brown Bess muskets, most likely provided by the British, Adam thought. From the look of some of them who could be brothers, he guessed many were the sons of farmers from the area.

Tye whistled softly and his men drove the wagons from behind the church. Without hesitating, Tye led two cavalry officers over to the wagons and stood aside as they counted the barrels and bushels of food and the pigs and sheep. DeGraw's seven slaves stood in a pathetic group, with no possessions but the clothes on their backs, thin and shivering in the morning chill. The two officers barely looked at them and took more interest in DeGraw's horses, examining their teeth and remarking on their age, before following the Colonel into the Church. Adam peered through the slats of a broken shutter. One officer pulled a pouch from his jacket, counted out gold coins and placed them on the table. Tye talked quietly with both of them. Outside, the mounted troopers, followed by the two wagons with the liberated slaves perched on the sideboards, and the foot militia bringing up the rear, led the way down an overgrown path and toward a road that ran north before it disappeared into a wooded area.

Tye's band remained at the abandoned church until mid-morning. When they left, Adam rode in front of Nero seated in a saddle too small for the two of them. He held on to the horse's mane as they threaded their way on deer trails and narrow pathways, surrounded by a forest so dense in places he could barely see the sky. Colonel Tye was in the lead but Adam suspected the two Indians preceded him as scouts, although he never caught a glimpse of them until they arrived at a snug clearing.

A small stone house, its shingled roof green with moss, nestled among a copse of tall pines. Several low wooden shacks, barely visible amongst the thick shrubbery, were spaced around the perimeter of the clearing. Far enough apart to prevent an attack from overwhelming all of the raiders at once, Adam thought, unless the force was very large. But then the chance of so many getting so close, undetected, was unlikely.

Adam was surprised as more men emerged from the woods, all colored, decently clothed and well armed from the quick look he got of them. A few stared at him curiously but most paid him no attention, being more interested in greeting their brethren and hearing about the raid. Tye motioned for Adam to follow him. The inside of the stone house was surprisingly well appointed with a stout oak table and chairs of various styles and design, obviously looted from different homes. A wide jambless fireplace in the Dutch style dominated the rear wall, with pots and chains, black with soot, hanging from an overhead stone lintel and a long spit pushed back against the fire wall. There were some blankets laid out in the corner and a ladder to the left led to a loft.

Adam realized that having been brought to their secret camp, Tye could never permit him to leave alive. He would either be killed or what? He did not see any alternative. To attempt escape seemed futile. He sat tensely and waited.

"No need to worry yet. I have not decided what to do with you," Tye said, as if he had read Adam's thoughts. "I believe you have been honest with me and I am a good judge of character. I caution you not to lie. It will mean your death." Adam grunted and thought it better to say nothing. Instead, he pretended to be interested in examining his interior surroundings, a gate leg table against one interior wall, side tables, a travelling desk resting unceremoniously on the floor alongside several trunks of different sizes, some with brass bands and locks, others rougher with iron finishings, an assortment of chairs, and even a spinning wheel.

"What will happen to DeGraw's slaves" he asked, "now the British have taken them?"

Tye seemed surprised by the question. "The British will employ them. They will receive decent rations, new clothes and then their freedom. Free in a Crown colony where formerly they were slaves of those who claim to fight for freedom," he snapped.

Adam let the silence between them last for a time. "I saw how those cavalry officers looked at the slaves. They were not seen as human beings but more as property looted from the farmhouse. Like pigs and sheep, the oxen or even the wagons and bushels therein."

Tye studied Adam, startled by his vehemence. "Ah, I understand your point of view. You are offended because they saw the Dutchman's slaves as Gen'ral Washington and this Reveren see your Sarah. Property to be owned, sold at will or taken in a raid."

Adam angrily clenched one hand into a fist and struck the palm of his other several times, making a sharp smacking sound. "I would kill that Reverend if I could. Damn that pious bastard for owning her."

"She cannot be courted but may be bought." Tye waved his hand casually, his fingers making a small circle in the air "And then this Reveren' raises the price to make it impossible for you, a simple Private, to obtain the goods for sale. Tell me Private Cooper, do you not also feel anger against the Rebel Gen'rals and Officers who used you in battle but do not recognize you as a human bein when you are courtin'?"

"The same anger I feel when I see Loyalist Officers treating colored men as looted property. Tell me Colonel Tye, does it not bother you that the slaves you liberate are not recognized as human beings?"

Tye stared at Adam and then began to laugh. "By God, I have missed havin' a decent conversation with an intelligent man for months. It is a rare pleasure for me." He held up his hands in mock protest. "Do not misinterpret my words. My men are loyal, brave and excellent fighters. However, none of them speak the King's English. And Pompey, Samson and Blue Jacket, those three from Virginia, slur their words so I have a devil of a time understandin' them. Like all officers, I wish to be surrounded by intelligent men at my dinner table, to engage in stimulatin' discussion on issues, such as who is really fightin' for freedom, the Rebels or the Loyalist militias, and freedom for whom?"

"Why freedom for every one," Adam said, matter of factly. "I note that you have not answered my question."

Tye leaned back in his chair and studied Adam, as two of his men carried in armloads of split wood and started a blaze in the hearth.

"I will tell you about myself so you will better understand my answer. I do not know to this day who were my mother or father. At a young age, I was a slave to an evil man, a Quaker named John Corlies, here in Monmouth County. In my youth, Quakers who owned slaves educated and freed them on their twenty-first birthday. Corlies fulfilled only the lesser of part of that bargain. I was educated, which did me little good as I labored in his fields and was whipped when the mood seized him." [1]

He continued, relating at the age of twenty-two or twenty-three he ran away, joined the British, changed his name from Titus Cornelius to Tye and became a Captain in the Ethiopian Regiment, a black unit raised by Lord Dunmore from among Virginian slaves. He had been at the Battle of Monmouth.

Adam tensed his jaw and tried to maintain a calm interest in Tye's story. If Tye had seen Adam on the battlefield, then . . . He did not finish the thought.

"I captured an American Capt'n. He was from a Virginia Regiment and was so shamed by being seized by a colored soldier, he would not look me in the face."

"This is the respect I mean," Adam asked, relieved that Tye had not fought against Will's artillery unit. "We are not animals."

Tye was silent recalling the scene. "I humiliated him, this proud Virginian slave-holder. Made him take off his boots, hat and jacket, and marched him barefoot behind the lines. I kept his sword." He laughed, a deep hearty chuckle, enjoying himself.

"This Capt'n, when he is exchanged, will be unable to give an honest account of his capture. To his mind, his honor has been stained."

"'Tis more stained from owning and trading in human beings," Adam added firmly.

Tye nodded in agreement. "True. True. Since Monmouth, I have commanded these men and raided plantations of slave-holding Patriots, includin' that of my former master. Unfortunately, he escaped before I could force him to watch our destroyin' everything he owned - his grand granite stone house with the wide porch, his barns smellin' more clean and fresh than our slave shacks, the well and root cellar, and of course the slave quarters where I spent my youth. All built by me and his other slaves who were whipped, starved, and frozen at his whim." He patted the seat of the chair. "This chair was his. Now it is mine. It gives me pleasure to sit in it, but I would derive more if I could, with my own hands, hang him on a well-traveled county road for all to see. Then, after the crows had picked at his sightless eyes, I would give him a proper burial and a tall gravestone - "Here Lies John Corlies-A Slaveowner-May He Burn in the Eternal Fires of Hell."

He seemed lost in the reverie of his description of his former master's demise. Suddenly, Tye jerked his head up and stared at Adam.

"My answer to your question is I will liberate every slave it is in my power to do so. I have earned the respect of British and Loyalist Officers alike for my deeds. The slaves I free can also make a way for themselves. They have no such opportunity if they remain slaves. Is that not so, Adam."

"I agree," he replied, noting that Tye had used his first name.

"Better to be a common laborer able to earn respect, than an enslaved field hand never entitled to it."

"Do you know how to write?" Tye asked, as if the question had suddenly occurred to him.

"I do."

"And basic mathematicks?"

"Yes."

"Excellent. Inside that chest is a ledger, quill and ink. Make ready. The men will be here soon for their payment. Each time when I receive coins from the Loyalists for sellin' them the livestock, foodstuffs and whatever from a raid, I distribute the proceeds among them. They also have first pick of the household goods and clothin' before we pass it on to the militias." He looked Adam up and down. "You could use a new shirt and maybe even breeches. In return for your clerical services, I will permit you to select those items. After my men have had their turn, of course."

Adam acknowledged the offer. "'Tis fair enough," he said as he took the key from the Colonel and opened the brass lock on the oak chest. "May I ask what happened to old man DeGraw and his other son?"

"Blew the father's head off myself with this pistol," he replied patting the holster on his hip. One of my men bayoneted the other. For such a strappin' big fellow he squealed as a stuck pig. Ah, speakin' of pig, here is our dinner ready for the spit," he said as the men filed in, one carrying the skinned animal while another inserted the iron spit through the haunches and out the fat animal's throat.

When the gold guineas had been distributed, dinner finished, and Adam was ready to leave, carrying a clean linen shirt, an almost new pair of work trousers, and most importantly for him, a wool blanket, Tye beckoned him back. The room still smelled of roasted pork, potatoes and ale, the two barrels the men had filled their mugs from lying empty on their sides in the corner.

Adam apprehensively sat down opposite Tye, knowing that his fate had not yet been decided. The Colonel opened a bottle and poured rum into two unmatched cut glasses. "Our Dutchman had some fine madeira stored in his cellar. I gave it to the British officers. It is more to their taste. This rum is more to mine." Adam held the liquid in his throat before letting it slide smoothly down. The warmth would help ward off the night chill.

"You are the first free-born colored I have met," Titus said. "All the others, Nero, Pompey, Samson, Felix, all bear their master's names." He belched loudly. "Some do not even have proper names - Blue Jacket, Sam the Traitor and Poor Taylor. But you, you were born free. The sound of that pleases me." He downed the rum and poured himself another glass. "My children will be born free. That I swear, by God."

Adam thought of being married to Sarah and having a family. He saw himself taking his sons out in the dory, riding the waves and teaching them to fish. As he had taught Will before they had marched from Cambridge to New York.

"You are more like me than you may care to admit," Tye said pointing an index finger at Adam's chest. "I wish to hang John Corlies - you to strangle the Reveren'. We are moved by the same reason - we are fightin' for dignity and respect. To free our colored bretheren."

He stared directly at Adam, who held his intense gaze before sensing it prudent to avoid the challenge. He looked down at his glass.

"Do you see yourself as a liberator of slaves?"

Adam hesitated before answering. "Are you asking if I would join with you?"

"I am."

"I will be honest with you. I would willingly participate in raids against anyone, Loyalist or Rebel, to free their slaves," Adam said, speaking slowly and deliberately. "I am not a thief or some conniving rascal who preys on defenseless women. I am a man of honor and, if necessary, I will go to my grave as one."

Tye smiled at him and leaned across the table to clap him on the shoulder. "Well said, Mr. Freeborn. We do not prey on the helpless and there are no Loyalist slaveholders in Monmouth County. Only bloody Rebels who claim to fight for freedom. Or those who support them."

Adam thought it better to ignore Tye's last remark. "I would willingly enlist in your band on two conditions."

"State them."

"My name is Adam Cooper. You may not bestow on me a name of your choosing. I am free born and thus neither you, nor any other man, have that right. Second, I expect a share of the gold, equal to that your men receive."

"Ah. To purchase your Sarah. Perhaps someday we will liberate her instead. Think of tha,t Adam. There is a raid to contemplate." Grandiose foolishness, Adam thought but said nothing.

Tye grinned at Adam, pleased with their exchange. "I accept both conditions. However, an intelligent man as you, with responsibilities for maintainin' the ledgers, cannot be a mere Private. I hereby promote you to Sergeant. You are now Sergeant Adam Cooper of Colonel Tye's Black Brigade."

Tye pulled out a long thin bladed knife from inside his sleeve. Adam had never seen one like it. It was lethally elegant. The straight blade glittered in the lamplight. The Colonel sliced a thin line with the point on his palm, drawing blood. He then turned the amber colored handle toward Adam and gestured for him to do the same. Adam ran the razor sharp blade lightly along the palm of his right hand and laid the knife down. Tye reached across and they clasped bloody hand to bloody hand.

"Now it is done," Tye said. "You are one of us."

Chapter 15 - Raids on Paulus Hook and Long Island

The Knox baby died the week after the artillery companies left Pluckemin and moved north with the Army. [1]

Elisabeth and Mercy were with Mrs. Knox when Julia, her emaciated body wasted by her losing struggle against consumption, breathed her last. Mrs. Knox held her second daughter in her fleshy arms and sobbed quietly. Mercy consoled her as Elisabeth sat in a chair, her eyes filling with tears, gently rocking little Lucy. They heard the General's heavy slow footfall on the steps. He opened the door, saw his wife holding their frail infant and let out a long soft moan of despair. He motioned to Elisabeth. She lifted little Lucy, unable to comprehend the grief around her but wailing in bewilderment, and carefully descended the stairs.

Outside, in the warm morning sun of early July, with the orchard in bloom and the air fragrant with the flowers that grew in profusion where the forests of oak and maple had been cut to make the soldiers' winter quarters, it seemed that all was right with the world. She sat on a bench in front of the happy home Will and she had shared with Samuel and Mercy Hadley for several months and stroked Lucy's curls. Elisabeth distracted her by pointing out the robins and sparrows, and an occasional bluebird flitting about from fence posts to shrubs, twittering away. Tree swallows, deprived of their natural habitat, swooped low over the grass, darting from the eaves of the barn to the nearby church and back again.

Will, who had stayed behind as part of the General's official family, walked toward them from the meadow holding a bouquet of wild flowers in his hand. Her expression told him that the dreaded event had occurred. He knelt down before them, divided the flowers and presented the bunches to Elisabeth and Lucy. The little girl giggled, her tears forgotten.

"Tomorrow is the one year anniversary of our marriage," he said softly to Elisabeth, without a smile.

"I know, my love. I wish today were not one of such sorrow." She took a few of the daisies and entwined them in little Lucy's hair.

"Save some for my baby sister. She can wear them too."

Elisabeth lowered her lips to Lucy's head and kissed her hair gently.

"Where has baby Julia gone?" she asked Will.

He shook his head, unsure how to explain death to a three year old. Lucy twisted her chubby little body on Elisabeth's lap and looked up expectantly.

"She has gone to Heaven," Elisabeth replied. "She is with God and his angels in Heaven."

"Can I go, too?"

"Yes," Elisabeth sighed. "But not right now."

"Why not? I want to go and play with my baby sister."

"Because we all must stay here on earth with your mother and father."

General Knox composed himself in the doorway before joining them. He picked up Lucy, covering her with kisses. She giggled at the attention and buried her face in his neck, something she always liked to do.

"Lisbet says we cannot go to Heaven to see baby Julia. I want to see her."

He handed his daughter back to Elisabeth. "We will see her again in due course, my sweetness. I must meet with Mr. Vanderveer and the Minister to make arrangements," he said by way of explanation to Will and Elisabeth. He looked up at the drawn curtains of the bedroom window. "Mercy is there giving comfort to my Lucy," he said to no one in particular. He lumbered off slowly as if by delaying a talk about grave-digging he was avoiding the finality of the death of his infant daughter.

He returned shortly, striding purposefully, his face flushed with anger, trailed by an anxious Cornelius Vanderveer.

"You must accept the decision of the Minister as I had to upon the death of my dearest daughter," Vanderveer said hurrying to keep up. "It is heartless, I admit, especially for one so young. Nevertheless, . . ."

Will jumped to his feet. "General. What is it?"

Knox shook his head in disbelief. "They refuse permission to bury our Julia in the Church graveyard. Their reason - We are Congregationalists and they are Dutch Reformed." He spread his arms expansively and gestured toward the mountains to the north. "Are we to exhume the bodies of all our heroic fallen soldiers, buried in church graveyards throughout New Jersey and Pennsylvania, if they are of different denominations?" His voice boomed out over the yard. "This is preposterous foolishness," he said, speaking more softly and glancing nervously again at the second story bedroom window. "It will cause much anxiety to my dearest Lucy, who as a grieving mother is already suffering the unbearable, nay unspeakable burden of having to bury an infant child. They will not even consent to ring the church bell."

Vanderveer, alarmed at the General's fury, presumptuously hooked his arm in Knox's and walked him toward the mansion. "My own daughter is buried behind the house. She was only twenty-two when I placed her there in the shade of the hazelnut trees. The Minister denied her burial in the graveyard for she had fits and seizures all her life. The elders thought she was possessed of the Devil." He choked at the memory. "It would be an honor to offer you the ground next to my own dearly departed Phebe." [2]

One of Vanderveer's farm hands dug a deep, short and narrow grave, while another, out of sight in the barn, made the little coffin. When the sounds of the shoveling and hammering ceased, it was time. Will carried the empty coffin on his shoulder into the house and returned bearing it the same way, the weight of the dead child inside barely making a difference. Outside, he and Samuel carried it between them behind the mansion and lowered it gently into the ground. General Knox and his wife stood at the head of the tiny grave, Elisabeth holding little Lucy somewhat behind them, swaying back and forth to calm her.

The officers of the General's staff, the closest of his official family, whom he had asked to remain behind with him, were arrayed around the freshly dug earth. One of them, who occasionally served at Chaplain, read Psalm 23 from a worn and stained bible. The mourners recited the familiar words together - "The LORD is my Shepherd. I shall not want." As they concluded "And I will dwell in the house of the LORD forever," the Church bell began to solemnly toll. It rang for a full minute and Knox looked surprised but pleased. The sorrowful sound ended and a peaceful silence enveloped the mourners as Captain Hadley and Mercy rejoined the group. The General and his wife stood slightly away from the gravesite, holding hands and receiving condolences. When Samuel and Mercy approached, the General held the Captain to him and then bowed slightly and kissed Mercy's hand. "Thank you for the Church bells for our dear little girl," he said, his eyes filling with tears and his voice breaking. He beckoned Vanderveer to him.

"I do not blame you for the obstinacy of your Church. I feel some peace knowing my little treasure lies next to your daughter and I entrust you to care for Julia's gravesite as you do for hers." [3]

The next morning they left before noon to rejoin the Army. A small contingent of troopers would escort the ladies, Mrs. Knox, Elisabeth, Mercy and little Lucy, to Morristown where they would stay with the Van Buskirks. In the bright sunlight of another fine July day, Will and Elisabeth barely had time to say their goodbyes. "You leave on our anniversary," she said, trying to hold back her tears. "I will write you, my love," Elisabeth whispered into his ear as they embraced.

"As I will write to you. As soon as we establish a permanent camp, I will send for you, as the General will send for his wife and daughter," Will replied. "It will not be long before we are together again."

Unless, he thought, we attempt a major assault on the British in New York City. They would have the British navy to contend with. It would not be easy.

"Perhaps so," she sighed. "Even if it is of short duration, I will miss you."

She bit her lip. The months of safety were over and Will was returning to the war. How many more years of the cycle of winter camps and spring campaigns must they endure?

"And I you," he said, gazing into her blue eyes and gently wiping the tears from her cheeks. They held hands for a few minutes and then Will turned and mounted Big Red. The horsemen formed up outside the entrance to the mansion. The General and his escort trotted through the little hamlet of Pluckemin and, once they reached the main road, the order came to proceed at a gallop. Will pressed his knees to his horse and Big Red responded, his powerful muscles rippling beneath his shiny coat. It was as if the General had decided to outrun the gloom and misery of the last few days. For Will, the joy of riding at full gallop assuaged his melancholy at leaving Elisabeth. Tonight, he knew with certainty each of them would sleep alone, comforted only by the memories of being together for the past several months.

The mosquitos from the surrounding marsh buzzed annoyingly around Christoph's ears. He swatted them away. There was no relief. They found the bare skin of his neck and hands and stung him incessantly. He vigorously scratched his hands, his neck, his face, providing only momentary relief from the intense itching.

It was his third straight night of sentry duty after being ferried across from Staten Island to Paulus Hook. There were two companies of soldiers from the Von Knyphausen Regiment to reinforce New Jersey Loyalists and some British Regulars. Why do they not take their turn at sentry duty, he thought, but then recalled more than one hundred and fifty of the Jersey volunteers had marched out of the fort at dusk. He leaned over the forward edge of the redoubt adjacent to the fort's gates and listened to the incessant scraping sounds of the cicadas, punctuated occasionally by the rustling of the reeds in the swampy water.

He estimated it was somewhere between two and three in the morning, a bit too early for the summer dawn and the end of his sentry duty. He peered into the darkness and thought he discerned figures approaching. The New Jersey men returning from their raid. Shots rang out from the blockhouse above the gate. Christoph fired into the darkness. He heard the drums signal the alarm and the footsteps of troops running behind him toward the gate. And then, a mass of men swarmed over the embankment. He caught the flash of light on their bayonets and, with his musket unloaded, he threw it down and raised his arms in surrender. More shots were fired and then it was quiet. He stood with more than one hundred prisoners in the fort's center, surrounded by uniformed Rebels, their breeches stained with mud and grime from fording the canals and swamps that surrounded the fort. Sporadic fire came from the inner redoubt where some of the British and Hessians had retreated.

The Rebels herded their prisoners out of the line of fire, while others raced through the barracks lining the quadrangle. Christoph heard the metallic hammering from the embankments. They are spiking our cannons, he thought, which meant they do not mean to hold the fort. He was terrified at the thought of being a prisoner once again, being starved, beaten and mistreated by some cruel farmer until the end of the war. Perhaps, they would keep him imprisoned because he had escaped once and rejoined his Regiment. By gestures, the Rebels indicated the prisoners were to leave their hats and brass caps, their swords, knives, and cartridge boxes, and line up in columns of two. [4]

They marched out of the open gate and immediately forded a canal where, due to the rising tide, the water came up to Christoph's chest. The Rebel guards splashed alongside them, their muskets held over their heads. Once across, they slogged through a foul marsh, the boots of those in front stirring up the mud and vapors and making the going slippery underfoot. Upon reaching high ground they moved through a dense forest before coming to a road, a wagon's width across. The prisoners in front of Christoph were whispering a message down the line. When it reached him, he understood enough of the English - the Rebels could not use their muskets- their powder was wet. He turned and passed the information to the two Hessians in column behind him. One of them grinned and nodded.

Escape, Christoph thought. If one of the officers gave the command, they could all run and scatter, and the Rebels would not be able to snag them all. He would vanish in the dark woods, circle back and find a British or Loyalist militia patrol. He would take any risk to avoid being imprisoned again.

A light ahead revealed a tavern at a crossroads. Christoph and the others were herded tightly together and forbidden to sit or speak. He watched in despair as Rebel troops emerged from the barns and outbuildings. As the column resumed its march, they took up positions as flankers and the rear guard.

Christoph damned their bad luck. The opportunity to bolt had been lost. These new soldiers had dry powder and their muskets and rifles primed and ready. He marched as if in a daze, every step taking him closer to the horror of a dank prison, crowded together with diseased and starving men in the stifling summer heat, or if he lasted long enough, freezing to death in an icy cell. An hour after dawn, the column was joined by more Rebel troops who marched quick time to the rear.

Now, Christoph thought, there is hope. If the Rebels fear an attack, then the rest of the troops at Paulus Hook are in pursuit. Maybe, when the alarm was sounded, soldiers were ferried from Staten Island and are at this very moment trailing the Rebels and waiting for a favorable opportunity to fall upon them. He kept these thoughts foremost to ward off his desperation. A prisoner again. He was certain it was an ordeal he would not survive. Better to take his chances by attempting to escape.

The morning sun rose and with it Christoph's spirits. He imagined the Redcoats and Hessians, his messmates closing rapidly with the rearguard, coming to his rescue. By mid-morning, as they were marched further and further away from Paulus Hook, he became despondent again.

He would have to act, before they reached a larger town and all chance of escape was gone. Christoph became more alert, surveying the countryside ahead, looking for cover close to the road, noticing where the flankers and guards were. He was certain the latter's muskets would not fire, but the flankers were the danger.

The lane curved through a gap in the trees. With one of the guards walking alongside the column of prisoners six men ahead, he could slip out of line. He would not know where the skirmishers were but he would take that chance. He uttered a silent prayer and, running in a crouch with his eyes on the Rebel guard ahead, he left the road, sprinting through the waist-high rye grass, heading toward the tree line, less than twenty yards away.

He was almost there, when he heard a shout behind him -"Stop. Halt." He tensed for the sound of a musket shot but there was none. He almost laughed in relief. Wet powder like our Regiment had at Trenton, where I was first captured. Now it is their muskets that cannot fire. Ten yards to the tree line. He would race through the forest. They could not send men after him. It would leave fewer to guard the remaining prisoners.

The rifleman stepped out from behind a large oak, pointing the muzzle at Christoph's chest. Christoph did not hesitate. Death is better than prison he muttered and charged on. He screamed words of defiance. The Rebel raised his rifle and fired. The sound reached him as he saw the smoke from the discharge. Did he see the muzzle flash? He felt the hammer blow strike his chest. He knew he was falling backwards. And then he knew no more.

Damn that stupid assbag Pritchard, John cursed silently. My job is to provide information from agents, not sally forth in the field where I could be killed. Go with the dragoons, Major Pritchard had ordered. Make sure some of the prisoners are brought back alive. The information they provide to save their miserable lives may be useful. Easy for him to say, John fumed.

There was no way out, and thus, he found himself riding alongside Captain Chatsworth, now of the 17th Light Dragoons. More damn rotten luck, he thought. The 16th had been disbanded, the officers had sold their commissions and were returning to Britain, all except Captain Lieutenant Richard Chatsworth. [5] No, Chatsworth could not return to the comforts of the foxhunts on his family estates and the theater and other pleasures of London. Not him. He said he had to avenge the deaths of his troopers at Princeton and would not rest until the informer or spy had been uncovered and the wretched traitor hung from the highest gallows. Involuntarily, Stoner felt his neck, swallowed hard and looked surreptitiously at Chatsworth sitting easily in his saddle, eyes straight ahead and fuzee strapped behind his back. The two columns of forty troopers trotted past the rolling farms of Flatbush, the summer wheat and rye being harvested by slaves under the hot autumn sun.

The thought of vengeance obsessed Chatsworth, an arm's length away, and brought to mind more bad luck, as if unknown forces were colluding against him. Less than a week past, John had been leaving Major Pritchard's office. He was surprised to see Ann Bates in the hall, waiting for Major Drummond. [6] The brazen trollop had the audacity to wink at him, as if they were close friends. John had hurried past her without any indication of the slightest recognition. If Mrs. Bates were to tell Chatsworth what she knew about the Princeton raid, John was a dead man. Chatsworth would challenge him to a duel and kill him outright, using the pistols John had given him as a gift. If he could eliminate Mrs. Bates, he would rest easier. But how? More immediately, how to avoid getting shot by these Rebel raiders. He cursed the pompous Pritchard for the prick he was and tried to plot how best to protect himself in the skirmish certain to occur.

John's informant, a pock-marked scummy rascal, who fished the waters of Long Island Sound and frequented the disreputable shore line taverns, had told him, in return for two gold guineas, of a plan to kidnap some high level personages on the Island. Whaleboat raiders, numbering about thirty men, had crossed the Sound four days ago. Instead of conducting a lightning strike, plundering and returning the same night, as they regularly did, they had gone into hiding, place unknown. Fortunately, David Matthews, the Mayor of New York, was at his residence on Lower Broadway instead of enjoying the cool breezes and fresh air of his Long Island home. The Hessian General Friedrich Riesdel, commander of the few British troops on the island, had his own headquarters guard, sufficient to repel any ragtag band of pirates and militia. That left, as the most likely targets, the wealthy Jacob Suydam, living on his large plantation, the well-known Judge

Thomas Jones, despised by the Rebels for the sentences he meted out for their treason, and Brigadier General Cortlandt Skinner, formerly the Crown- appointed Attorney General of New Jersey and now the commander of the New Jersey Volunteers. [7]

With only forty men, Chatsworth decided Skinner was on his own, probably well protected by his own experienced militiamen. He left a Lieutenant in command of a dozen troopers to guard Suydam and, taking John with him, rode through the early evening to the Judge's mansion.

"Thomas is a far more attractive hostage than a mere landowner. Do you not think so, John?"

"I believe you are correct," John replied, swallowing hard and thinking that it would have been better for him to be at the location the whaleboaters would not attack. As they approached the Judge's estate, Chatsworth slowed the pace and sent two troopers ahead as scouts.

"We are more than fifty miles inland from the Sound," he said. "If they seek Judge Thomas, they would have marched at night to avoid detection, slept one day to rest up and tonight will be their time to attack." John fidgeted nervously in his saddle, pretending he was stiff from the ride.

When the scouts returned, Chatsworth dismounted and they conferred in the darkness and out of earshot. John sat on his horse wondering how he could find safety toward the rear of the troop without losing face. He removed his pistol from his saddlebag, placed it in the large pocket of his jacket and rested his hand on his sword hilt, more for reassurance than anything else. Lost in his fear of an encounter with well-armed Rebels, John did not notice Chatsworth approaching. He motioned for Stoner to lean down.

"It appears Judge Thomas is hosting a gay dinner party with musical accompaniment." He patted John's horse on the neck. "You are to ride forward alone and present your compliments to the Judge. Tell only him we anticipate a raid by a sizeable number of Rebel scum. If they come, he is to barricade the house and engage in a stiff resistance. With the Rebels concentrating on their attack, we will take them from behind."

Chatsworth held the bridle firmly. "John. Take care not to alarm the guests. No shuttering of open windows and barring of the doors. We do not want to give the Rebels any warning they are walking into a trap. Now, off you go."

He rode down the dark, tree-lined entrance toward the house, his horse's hooves loudly pounding the compacted earth. He grasped his pistol handle tightly, terrified a Rebel raider lurked behind every thick tree trunk or hid in the shrubbery surrounding the house, ready to pounce on him before he could cry out. He was more certain than ever that the Rebels would come here, attracted toward the light as a moth to the flame. John found the bright candle lights in the open windows and the sound of someone playing the harpsichord so foolish as to be beyond belief.

He dismounted, tied the reins of his horse to the post and, with his knees shaking, lifted the brass knocker in the shape of a lion's head and rapped on the door. A bewigged, liveried black servant asked him politely to wait and went to find his master. Judge Thomas himself came to the alcove, a glass of sherry in his hand and a welcoming smile on his pudgy face. He was shorter than John, older by at least ten years, though not as heavy and more well preserved. There was a stern elegance about him, from his grey hair and long sideburns to tailored rich brown jacket.

John, suppressing the tremor in his voice, explained Chatsworth's plan and, almost as an afterthought, added that they were not to give any indication of awareness of the impending attack.

"My dear fellow," the Judge replied in a hushed voice. "We must at least ready ourselves by gathering our muskets and pistols. I will inform my son, who fortunately is attending this dinner, and he will see to it that it is all done discreetly." John was about to object but then realized he was safer inside a mansion turned into a fortress than outside with Chatsworth engaging in confused hand-to-hand combat in the darkness. He briefed Thomas's son, a Lieutenant, wearing the uniform of some Loyalist Regiment John did not recognize. He did not like the young man's brash attitude and the gleam of excitement in his eye at the coming encounter. John proposed they close most of the windows on the first floor in the back, a necessary precaution but not one that would alert the Rebels. The son acquiesced but insisted that all of the windows in the front be left open, especially in the sitting room. "Let the scum climb over the sills and we will give them what for," he said as the Judge acknowledged the wisdom of his son's tactics.

With the rear of the house relatively secure, and the front door closed but not barred, John sat with the other guests in the front sitting room, listening to the harpsichord played by the Judge's wife. They sipped sherry and applauded her performance, all of them now in on the plan, contrary to Chatsworth's wishes. Damn him, John thought. Now I am an obvious target in a room of fools, mostly wealthy landowners and elderly acquaintances who have never seen military service. He glanced nervously at the muskets hidden behind curtains, chaise lounges and on the floor beneath the harpsichord, and fingered the smooth handle of the pistol in his pocket. He could get off one shot and then, retreat to the back of the room pretending to get a musket and wait until, hopefully, the troopers attacked and cut the Rebels down from behind.

Mrs. Thomas was playing softly when there was the sound of running, followed by the splintering of wood as the front door was slammed by the Rebels' battering ram. At the same instant, several burly men clambered through the window, armed with pistols, pikes and swords, and shouting for all to surrender. John pulled his pistol from his pocket and fired, bringing down the man closest to him. Several other shots rang out but whether they were from the Rebels or the Judge's guests, he was not certain. Someone shouted to bar the door. Too late for that, John thought, as he retreated behind the couch and reached for a fowling piece. Praying it was properly loaded, he fired at two of the Rebels whose backs were turned as they ran toward the entrance hall to open the front door. The blast blew them forward onto the floor as the buckshot tore into them. Three of the guests struggled to close the heavy wooden interior shutters of the front sitting room. One of them threw up his hands, his waistcoat rapidly soaking with his own blood, and emitted an agonizing scream of pain as the Rebel outside yanked the pike out of the man's chest.

John searched frantically for another musket. The sounds of the battering ram on the front door were echoed by the same sound on the less sturdy door to the kitchen in the rear. Unable to find another musket, he desperately unsheathed his sword.

"I will go to the back," the Judge's son shouted. "You stay here and defend the front door." He rushed out of the sitting room, followed by two or three others. John terrified, crouched in the room adjacent to the front door which had already splintered. One more charge with the battering ram and they would break through. The ugly iron-encased snout of the ram brutally shattered what remained of the door, ripping it off its hinges. In that instant, four men swarmed through the opening. Their leader, sword in one hand and pistol in the other, spotted John and aimed his pistol. John froze and uttered a shriek of fear. There was a flash in the pan but it failed to ignite the powder in the chamber. John bellowed, more from abject fear than rage, and slashed at his would-be assailant, cutting him deeply on his thigh. As the Rebel's leg buckled, John stabbed him in the side and scurried further down the hallway away from the demolished door and three advancing raiders. One of them, half-turned behind him as the savage strike of Chatsworth's sword severed his arm at the shoulder.

Troopers rushed in behind their Captain, ordering the Rebels to surrender. Distracted by the appearance of Redcoats, the two Rebels closest to John hesitated. John saw his chance and lunged forward, piercing the chest of the nearest one, a large muscular brute of a sailor wielding a long evil-looking pike. The remaining Rebel lowered his arm, preparing to drop his sword. John struck down at the man's neck. There was a sharp metallic clang as Chatsworth intercepted the stroke with his own saber.

"Now, now, John. Control your blood lust," he said calmly. "We must leave a few of them alive to question. That is your province, is it not?" The Rebel fell to his knees, shaking with fear.

"Not so bold anymore," John snorted derisively, pricking him with the point of the blooded sword, none too gently on his exposed neck. He felt the pounding in his temples as he willed himself to calm down. He had survived and, better still, acquitted himself well enough. He almost laughed aloud from relief. To mask his giddiness he hurriedly went toward the sitting room, muttering to Chatsworth that he must see to Mrs. Thomas.

The Judge was comforting his wife, who seemed to have borne all the violence around her better than many of the guests. "You were extremely brave my dear. You did your part by continuing to play until these scoundrels invaded our home. Well done."

"We must thank Lieutenant Stoner for risking his life by staying here with us. Why, he shot one of the Rebels, that one lying there," she said, pointing at the lifeless body whose blood was staining the patterned rug under the harpsichord. "I was certain he was intent on attacking me where I sat."

John thought the dead Rebel had been coming straight for him, with his lethal looking pike, before he had fired his pistol. He merely shrugged with what he hoped was a gesture of humility and effected a slight bow to Mrs. Thomas.

"I am deeply in your debt, Lieutenant," the Judge said. And I will call that debt due someday, John thought.

Chatsworth came in just in time to hear the exchange and John puffed up even more.

"How many did we capture?" John asked, in his mind reasonably including himself as one of the dragoons.

"Fifteen. We killed nine outside and there are the four in here." Chatsworth watched as the Judge's field slaves lifted the body of one dead Rebel and carried him outside. "Unless your informant was mistaken in the number, they may have left two men to guard their whale boats."

The troopers stayed the night, liberally imbibing the Judge's sherry and port. The next morning, with the surviving rebels tightly bound and seated none too comfortably in a wagon borrowed from Judge Thomas, and driven by two of his slaves, they left in high spirits. Before they reached the ferry at Brooklyn, John became drowsy from the hot August sun and the effects of their drinking the night before. To his chagrin, Chatsworth showed no ill effects and even chided John to sit up straight in the saddle to promote respect from those they passed on the road.

"We are dragoons," he admonished. "Not scruffy, ill-trained colonial cavalry."

The bitter dry taste in John's mouth came more from Chatsworth's condescending tone than the heat of the day.

Once on the ferry, John looked the prisoners over and marked the man Chatsworth had saved from the stroke of his sword. They would all go to the prison at the old Sugar House. And all would know that, not being a uniformed militia, they would be treated as common criminals - robbers and brigands - and would be lucky if they were not hanged within a week. That will loosen their tongues, John thought.

Two days later, rested and refreshed and enjoying tea in the sitting room of his quarters, with his role in fighting the Rebel marauders inflated in his own mind to heroic proportions, John Stoner took stock. Major Pritchard had been very pleased with the outcome, taking credit with his superiors for discovering the plot to kidnap Judge Thomas but praising John for gathering the intelligence. He had engaged in combat, risked his life, emerged with an enhanced reputation and a powerful and influential man indebted to him.

And now there was more good news. Captain Montresor had not been appointed General Clinton's Chief Engineer and would be returning to England. [8] John had always resented him, thinking he was either a gullible fool for being taken in by Elisabeth, or turned a blind eye to her machinations for the privilege of escorting her to all those dinners, balls and plays. If only Montresor had been able to entice Elisabeth to come to New York where, John fantasized, he would entrap her, expose her as a Rebel spy and then, then what? When he had grabbed her by her creamy white neck and felt her firm young breast in his hand, he recognized the terror in her eyes. How he had enjoyed that moment.

Before the raid, he deemed events conspiring against him. Now, the wheel had turned and favored him. Once General Clinton defeated the ragtag Rebel army spread thin on the other side of the Hudson, they would reoccupy Philadelphia. Then, he would find Elisabeth van Hooten, and this time, she would not elude him.

Chapter 16 - With the Black Brigade

The Black Brigade of more than thirty, all colored except for the two Indians, left the pine barrens hideout and moved to their main camp at Refugeetown on Sandy Hook. There they remained for the better part of three weeks. Adam was surprised at the snugness of their quarters, stout plank wooden cabins, with pine-shingled roofs, built on stone rubble foundations. It was on the bay side of the peninsula, approximately five hundred feet from the octagonal lighthouse that Adam estimated was at least one hundred feet high. Taller than the one that had stood on Little Brewster Island in the outer Boston Harbor, before the British Navy blew it up with a timed charge of gunpowder. The presence of the lighthouse, the salty taste of the early morning air and the sound of the sea gave Adam some comfort, although he chaffed at the Brigade's inactivity.

Two companies of British Regulars were camped near the lighthouse within a compound formed by a series of redoubts, with four eighteen-pounders pointing seaward. A large barn-shaped structure housed their officers and the men were quartered in adjacent outbuildings. Other Redcoats manned a U- shaped stockade at the neck of the peninsula and guarded the holding pens for cattle, the makeshift shelters containing forage, and the storehouses of barrels of foodstuffs, blankets, linens and clothing, all plundered from Rebel farms and awaiting transport on vessels to Staten Island or New York City.

During those weeks, Adam had relieved his frustrations by

taking to the sea in a dory, rowing until he felt the welcome ache in his shoulders, enjoying the feel of the swells and the satisfaction of catching rockfish and sea bass on a line. He thought of Sarah, trying to recall her face, seeing her seated in the stern as he dipped the oars deep into the waves. He talked to her about fishing, the sea and his plans to teach their children the skills he knew. But after the fishing was done, with the bow pointed toward the sandy shore, he became melancholy, despairing of ever seeing her again.

The fish were a welcome change to their diet of salted beef, potatoes, corn and squash, along with the occasional ducks the Indians, Cocquetak and Aquadonk, had ensnared in the marshes bordering the sandy beaches. Within the Brigade, the two Indians stayed apart, except for sharing the main daily meal. Adam did not know the names of all the men, and had to admit he had not become close to those of the band who had been with Colonel Tye at the DeGraw's farm.

He avoided Nero who was as disagreeable as he was uncommunicative. Pompey, Samson and Blue Jacket were from Virginia. Tye had recruited them from Lord Dunmore's Ethiopian Regiment. Of the three, Adam had taken a liking to Blue Jacket. Tye told him the slave had arrived wearing an expensive whelk blue frock coat that was too long in the sleeves and too wide in the rear. His master must have been a larger man. He had refused to give the British or later even Colonel Tye, his name, saying it had been a slave name and he no longer had any need for it now that he was free. His former master's coat had since been replaced by a more serviceable hunting shirt that he wore under a faded red wool soldier's uniform, but the name Blue Jacket had stuck. He had a ready grin, a broad nose and was dark as the night. According to Tye, Blue Jacket was quick as a cat with a pike.

Sam the Traitor had gotten his name from his New Jersey master who had screamed it at his house servant as Sam showed Tye's raiders where the family's gold coins, silver and jewelry were buried in the vegetable garden behind their house. Tye informed Sam's master his slave had done him a favor and saved him from Nero carving him up until he revealed the hiding place. As Tye's men carried the valuables away, bundled up in the mistress's best bed linen, Sam confronted his master and spat in his face. He then rode off on one of his former master's horses. The Brigade used him as a spy for he was an observant and intelligent fellow. Dressed for the role, he would enter a town, driving a wagon as if on an errand for his master or mistress, purchase a few goods, and once back, report to the Colonel directly.

Returning from half a day of fishing in the early afternoon, with the skies rapidly becoming an angry grey, Adam carried the bushel of fish up to their encampment and, using a flat plank, began to gut and clean them. Blue Jacket joined him and silently worked alongside until the task was done. Inside, at the makeshift table, the men were seated on rough-hewn benches, Colonel Tye in his chair at the end closest to the fireplace, dividing up the roasted potatoes and ears of corn and cold meat. He supervised the distribution of the cider, limiting each man to one mug. Adam showed Blue Jacket how to lean the green wood skewers against the iron spit and make certain the skin crisped but did not burn on the outside while the white flesh was cooked and juicy underneath. He squatted in front of the fire and turned the skewers every few minutes, barely feeling the heat from the red hot coals on his tough callused hands.

"Hey, Fisherman," Tye called. "Are they ready yet?"

Adam motioned for Blue Jacket to pull several skewers from the fire and distribute them around the table.

"What say you now? They must be done. We are all hungry for your fresh catch." Adam thought the Colonel may have drunk more than he allowed the others. His face was flushed and he seemed edgy.

Adam and Blue Jacket walked around the table. Adam left it to Blue Jacket to serve Tye, and sat himself down at the far end opposite the Colonel.

"Fisherman. Come sit by me. I want a word with you."

Adam deliberately finished munching the hot fish off the skewer, wiped his hands on his trousers and stood up.

"Colonel Tye," he said calmly, and the quietness of his tone brought silence around the table. "Are you a man of your word," he paused letting the question hang in the smoky, close room, "or are you one who dishonors himself by breaking promises accepted in good faith by others?"

Tye rose from his end of the table and glared at Adam as several of the men pushed back, ready to clear a path between the two of them at a moment's notice.

"Are you challengin' me?" he said, reaching in his sleeve. Adam knew the long narrow-bladed knife rested in a sheath sown inside. He waited, calming himself.

"I remind you before these men that when I joined your band as a free man, you promised to call me by my name and agreed you had no right to bestow upon me one of your choosing. I am Sergeant Adam Cooper of the Black Brigade. You went back on your word and have called me Fisherman, twice tonight and once before. I let the first time pass but no longer." Adam saw Blue Jacket nodding in agreement. "If that is your intent, I resign from the Brigade and will take my leave." He did not move, his palms on the table, ready to vault to one side if Tye hurled his knife. Adam hoped he would be fast enough.

Tye threw back his head and laughed. Several of the men nervously snickered with him. "By God, Adam. You are a bold one." He waved his arm toward the entire group. "Mark what dignity a free man has. We liberate the slaves of Monmouth County to provide them an opportunity for such dignity."

He motioned to Samson and Pompey to roll the cider barrel forward. "Another ration for everyone. Now, Adam," he waved him forward. "Come sit by me."

Adam strode, as resolutely as he could, controlling the shaking in his knees, to the other end of the table. The noise rose in the room as the men resumed their talk, further lubricated by the additional mug of cider. He thought Tye was capable of sticking the knife in his ribs, catching him unawares, but he had to chance it.

"I should've known a man who bellowed for Gen'rl Washington to free his domestics and then deserted, would dare me when I called him Fisherman." He put his arm around Adam's shoulder. "Wait until winter. I have plans in my mind that will please you. In the meantime, we will seek revenge against the Rebel slaveholders of Monmouth County for what their Retaliators have done to loyal citizens." [1] Adam smiled in agreement. He did not know whether Tye had been testing him to see if he could make Adam more compliant or whether it had been done out of pure malice. Either way, Adam thought, he had won Tye's respect and that of some of the men as well.

In the final week of October, with the weather turning starkly colder, as the mallards, pintails, coots and wild geese formed up in the grey skies, Tye dispatched a third of his men, Sam included, off the Hook. Adam and the others followed a few days later. Tye said nothing about their plans and Adam knew enough not to ask. They did not have enough horses for all the men and Adam, who still disliked riding, was satisfied mounted double, although he would have preferred not to be paired with Nero.

At night Adam knew from the stars and the receding sounds of the ocean behind them, that they were traveling south by southwest. They camped one night beside a river. The two Indians left before the others had settled down. When they returned they conferred with Colonel Tye, drawing lines in the dirt at his feet. At daybreak, they moved away from the river and rested deep in a forest of mixed gnarled thick hardwoods and straight pines. When it was dark, they retraced their way to the river, where the two Indians guarded one wide flat-bottomed skiff tied to a thick weathered grey tree trunk sticking out from the muddy bank. With all of them crowded on to the one vessel, they moved out into the slow current. Colonel Tye stood at Adam's shoulder in the square bow, quietly whispering directions. Nero and Poor Taylor, both strong but inexperienced on the water, propelled the boat forward from the rear. The rest of the Black Brigade knelt motionless and quiet on the boat's planks, their muskets resting on their laps.

"Over there," Colonel Tye murmured to Adam. He nimbly switched sides and turned them sharply to the right. Tye signaled to Nero and Poor Taylor to desist. The tall cat-tails rustled against the wooden sides as they glided forward until they bottomed on the muddy flats. Adam held the boat sideways and steady with his pole deep in the muck, as Cocquetak and Aquadonk jumped into the shallow water and disappeared in the darkness. Tye followed and led the Black Brigade up the gently sloping embankment until they reached a field bordered by brambles and berry bushes entwined in a split-rail fence. They trotted down a narrow path, no wider than their shoulders, until Tye halted and hooted once softly like an owl. There was an answering hoot to their left, followed by another. Tye waited and then called twice more. The Indians came out of the darkness and the Colonel squatted down with them on his haunches and listened to their few words and signals. He rose smiling and motioned for his men to gather round.

"There are twelve local Militia in Shrewsbury. At the Tavern. They have not set out sentries," he whispered, "and some are in the yard without arms. We will use bayonets. Softly now. Follow me." Creeping forward, they instinctively crouched down below the top of the thick hedges although there was no need shrouded as they were by the blackness of the cloudy night. They paused at the corner of a church, no more than one hundred feet from the tavern. "Take no prisoners," Tye commanded. Adam was uncomfortable with that merciless order. He resolved to do what he could to avoid it.

On Tye's hand signal, the fifteen men of the Black Brigade ran forward, the two Indians in the lead. They covered half the ground before any of the militia was even aware of their onslaught. There were shouts of alarm and several of them rushed toward the tavern door to grab their muskets. One was felled with Aquadonk's tomahawk in his back, a few made it inside and the ones who turned and raised their arms in surrender were bayonetted by Samson, Pompey and Blue Jacket who were in the lead.

Adam dashed into the building, turned left toward a smaller room and found three of the militia hastily snatching their muskets from an upright floor rack on the far wall. One managed to get a gun in his hands and as he was turning, Adam hit him on the back of his head with the butt of his musket. He clipped another one under the chin, snapping his head back, before Sam and Nero, close on his heels, plunged their bayonets into the two prostrate militiamen. The third soldier, a farm boy with blond hair and a chubby, innocent face, fell to his knees, blubbering repeatedly, "Please. Please. Do not kill me." Nero, without hesitation, ran him through with such force his bayonet came out the poor boy's back. Adam turned away in disgust. By knocking the two soldiers out instead of bayonetting them, he was as responsible for their deaths as if he had killed them himself.

A search of the other rooms of the tavern found only terrified travelers and merchants quaking in their beds and protesting they were not militia but only honest and poor folk. The sight of armed Negroes with fresh blood on their bayonets only intensified their fright, so much that they voluntarily gave up their purses, and in some cases, their cloaks, coats and even their boots.

Tye directed his men to search the tavern's barn and take all the horses and wagons. He sent Sam the Traitor with his wagon and those of the Black Brigade, who had been guarding the road from Shrewsbury in case any of the militia escaped, to ransack all homes for barrels of flour, butter, cheese and smoked meat or fish, cloth and clothing and anything else they deemed useful.

Without much prodding, the awakened and terrified guests, many shivering in their nightshirts, assembled in the tavern's main room. The innkeeper, wearing a long smock-like shirt stained with food and charcoal, pleaded with Tye not to torch his building.

"Why would I do that?" the Colonel said sharply, quickly tiring of the man's whining. "I am Colonel Tye and I choose to leave it standin' so that when I return I will find many of these fat rich Whig chickens to pluck, their fine horses to take and sturdy wagons to use." He moved from warming himself before the dying fire to stand up close to the innkeeper.

The man hastily took two steps back, treading on the bare feet of one his guests standing behind him. The traveler squealed in pain causing Tye to laugh out loud.

"I know you Josiah Halstead. Do you know who I am?" Tye asked.

"I believe you were that Titus fellow who was raised in our county."

Tye hit him hard with his open hand and a trickle of blood appeared at the corner of the innkeeper's mouth, accompanied by a stifled whimper.

"Raised in our county? Raised did you say? I was enslaved in your county. By John Corlies, well known to you, I believe. Is that not true?" Tye leaned forward, towering over him.

"Yes," Halstead replied. "I know him."

Tye slapped him again. "Know him. Bollocks. You dined with him and his wife, you little shit. Am I correct? "

"Yes. Yes. You are right. Absolutely correct, Colonel Tye." The innkeeper raised his hands to protect his face from the slap he anticipated.

"Remember this, Halstead. Tonight me and my men visited you. We will be back once Shrewsbury has restocked its supplies and there is somethin' worth carrying away." He poked Halstead in the center of his chest with his finger.

"Take care until we return not to do anythin' that may anger me. No coddlin' up to Retaliators and hostin' county militias." He ran his finger down the middle of Halstead's stomach and stopped at his navel. "Or else I will gut you myself and burn down this building as a warning to all slave-ownin' Whigs." Halstead, pale with all color drained from his face, could only mutter repeatedly, "yes sir, yes sir," and rock back and forth on his feet.

As they left Shrewsbury, Adam found himself seated besides Nero on one of the wagons filled with the dead militia's jackets and coats, muskets and cartridge boxes, and saddles, bridles and forage looted from the town's barns. "Dis be sum ting," Nero grinned, speaking the first words to Adam since they had left Sandy Hook. Adam grunted in reply. [2]

In the wagon ahead, the only three slaves they had found and liberated, huddled together wide-eyed and shivering from the cold October night air, surrounded by odd pieces of furniture, barrels stacked precariously, trunks and nondescript bundles. Behind Nero and Adam, several of the Black Brigade served both as a rear guard and drove the herds of cattle and horses they had seized. Adam signaled for Nero to slow their wagon. Wordlessly, he clambered in the back, selected two or three heavy coats taken from the dead militia, jumped off the wagon and trotted forward. He handed them to the three slaves, whose tattered shabby shirts and trousers indicated they were field hands, not house servants. It was their good fortune to have been brought by their masters to Shrewsbury, although they did not seem to appreciate it, as they sat spiritlessly in the wagon bearing them to freedom.

"Col'nl not gonna like dat," Nero said menacingly as Adam climbed up next to him. Adam shrugged. A lot of blood had been shed to free only three slaves. He preferred that they raided farms where there were slaves to be freed rather than attacking small towns for plunder and forage to give to the British.

By dawn they found refuge at a Loyalist farm, although Adam sensed the owner was nervous surrounded by armed Negroes returning from their bloody raid. Tye was the only one invited inside the owner's brick home and he returned to his men's campfires in the early evening. He picked out several of them, Adam, Nero, Pompey and Samson along with a few others and they followed Tye into the barn, now crowded with the stolen horses.

"Our host has informed me the notorious Elihu Cook I wanted to capture in Shrewsbury is rumored to be hidin' with relatives several miles north of here. I know the place." He waved at the group of horses. "Nero. Pick a calm one for Adam and help him saddle it. We will make a rider out of him yet."

Adam felt relieved he would not have to ride double with Nero but apprehensive about being on his own. He had ridden some, usually slowly in daylight. A night raid would tax his limited abilities. The Colonel could have chosen someone else. It was Tye's way of paying him back for openly challenging him at their Sandy Hook refuge. They rode single file. Adam was in the middle of the group, awkwardly trying to hold on to his unloaded musket and the reins with both hands, while the mare trotted along obediently, following the ones in front and sensing those behind it.

Tye unerringly led their band on cow paths that cut through fields, up narrow creek beds where the overhanging limbs forced the riders to crouch low in their saddles, and through deer trails in woods so dense as to obscure the starry sky. When they rode uphill, Adam leaned as far forward as he could over his horse's neck, fearful of sliding backwards. When they went downhill, he did the opposite, gripping the reins and the mane with both hands, while stretching as far back as possible in the saddle.

After about two hours, they emerged at the top of a long sloping field, the corn stalks broken and cut close to the ground after harvest.

Nestled at the bottom, clear in the light of a half moon, about one hundred yards away was a long, low house, with two gables and a columned front porch. The dark shape of a barn loomed to the right.

They left the horses at the edge of the woods, loaded their muskets and stealthily crept through the field, spread out between the rows of broken stalks until they were close to the house. Tye motioned three of the men to circle behind and sent two others to guard against escape through the side door, now visible that they were closer. Satisfied that no one seemed to be astir in the house, Tye led Adam, Nero and the others on to the porch and pointed they should stand guard at each of the large windows. Then he pounded on the door with his fist and shouted loudly.

"Elihu Cook. Surrender and no one else will be harmed. Resist and I will burn this house and kill all those inside." Tye pounded again but there was no response. Adam heard sounds of someone running inside. Suddenly, the glass of the window he was standing next to was smashed and a musket barrel emerged pointing toward Tye still hammering on the door. Adam knocked the muzzle downward with his musket, and as it discharged, grabbed the barrel with his free hand and yanked it forward hard. The person holding the stock let go and cried out in pain as the jagged edges of broken glass cut into flesh. Tye and two of his men battered down the door were already inside.

Adam smashed the remaining shards of glass and climbed through. In the dim light, he made out the shape of a young boy, cowering in the corner of the room, the left arm of his nightshirt stained red. He looked like he was no more than twelve and he bit his lower lip as he tried to stanch the blood.

Nero, running down the hallway to the main staircase, saw the boy in the door frame and turned to bayonet him.

"No, Nero." Adam shouted and jumped forward to protect the youth.

"You kill em, den," Nero snarled and bounded up the stairs. Adam bent down, ripped a piece of the boy's nightshirt and bound a tourniquet below his elbow.

High-pitched screams of a woman came from upstairs, followed by boots clumping down the stairwell. Nero and Samson roughly pushed a disheveled white-haired man, his nightshirt hanging over his breeches, through the hall and out the door, now hanging askew on one hinge. Tye followed them, saw Adam kneeling and peered into the room. He snorted at the boy's slight frame on the floor. "He almost shot me. Probably related to Cook, the scummy brat. Finish him off and be quick."

Adam put his finger on the boy's lips. He drew his bayonet and covered it in the blood already sopping the shirt and then signaled for him to scream. Adam left the house and joined the Colonel and others who were standing on the porch. He wiped his bayonet on his trousers, making sure Tye saw him.

Elihu Cook, his hands tied tightly behind his back, turned and glowered at Adam. "That was my nephew you murdered in there. I will see you hanged for that."

"Hardly, you Rebel bastard," Tye replied, kicking the old man in the butt and forcing him down the stairs. "You will rot on a prison ship in New York harbor until you pray for your death to come."

Adam waited nervously for the horses to be brought down from the tree line. He threw his musket across the pommel, and with his left foot in the stirrup, awkwardly succeeded in hoisting himself up. His ungainly manner drew a laugh from Tye, who brought his horse along side.

"I owe you my life, Adam. Even a boy can kill a Colonel. A good night's work and the British will reward us well for it."

Tonight he had saved a life. The night before, Adam thought as they rode back through the cornfield, he wished he had been able to spare the three militia from Nero's bayonet.

—xx—

"I can understand hanging for desertion," Whipple muttered softly to Henry. "But for plundering? In one case 'tis abandoning your brother soldiers and causing them grievous harm. In the other, 'tis the mere taking of property." He shifted uncomfortably in the freezing ankle-deep slush and wiggled his toes in his shoes.

"You heard the verdict of the court martial. He took money and silver plate. In defiance of General Washington's orders. He is to be made an example. Do you think I like standing here in the cold to watch the poor bastard swing?" Gillet replied. [3]

The two friends stood in rigid lines on the Danbury Common, part of a large rectangle of men encompassing a makeshift scaffold. They were among the fifty soldiers ordered to represent the Second Rhode Island Regiment, together with fifty from every other Regiment of Stark's Brigade. They had been marching south from Providence through Connecticut to join the main army somewhere across the Hudson.

The condemned man, a private from a Connecticut unit, escorted by an armed guard of Light Infantry, was led on to grounds accompanied by the solemn throbbing beat of the drums.

"If he had deserted, it would be the Rogue's March for him," Whipple said. "A much better tune that and it would not stretch his neck."

Gillet nodded and lowered his eyes, not wishing to see the actual hanging. His thoughts were of his last day with Judith and their daughter, one of three days' leave in Providence, granted after the British abandoned Newport at the end of October. His final glimpse of his wife was of her waving seemingly proud and resolute, amongst the crowd on the streets as the Second Rhode Islanders, led by their Colonel, paraded out of town. Henry took some solace in the knowledge the town council, free from the threat of British attack, had generously established a fund to provide food, fuel and clothing for the families of soldiers. As further proof of their new-found generosity, in his baggage were a new wool tunic and trousers, socks and a blanket, all provided by the good citizens of Providence for their brave sons marching south.

The warm clothing was welcome and put to good use almost immediately, with the first snow occurring so early in November as to cause the soldiers to dispute whether there was a year when it had happened sooner. Their usual pace was fifteen to twenty miles per day and in good weather they could accomplish it. On those occasions, they would sleep in barns or out in the open, having outdistanced their baggage wagons. When the weather was bad, as it had been on the slog through rain and hail down to Danbury, they had made only nine miles at best, and had rested uncomfortably, cold and wet for most of the day until the wagons had arrived with their cots and tents.

Henry was aware of the silence and shifting of feet. He looked up and the convicted soldier was swinging from the gallows, his head hanging down at an unnatural angle. They were dismissed after the a Regimental Surgeon officially declared him dead.

Two days later they crossed the Hudson by ferry, it taking the better part of the day and night to get all the troops over. Colonel Angell had insisted the Regiment's baggage train immediately follow his men so that, once on the New York shore, and ten miles inland from the river, they camped in relative comfort inside tents with their blankets to ward off the frigid December cold. From there, it was a long miserable plodding march. Some days they covered sixteen miles on roads where the churned-up mud came over their shoes, other days they trudged through ankle-deep snow. Henry was grateful for the respite from marching when it stormed, and they remained inside their tents. On the Colonel's orders they would not break camp that day. He did not know whether they were in New York or had yet reached New Jersey. It mattered not. They were cold, tired, barely dry, unable to keep a fire going for cooking, subsisting on salted pork, stale bread and a gill of cider or rum.

The next day, with the drums signaling to strike the tents and prepare to march, they were up at six and the entire Brigade was on the move by seven. It was another frigid day where the sky was low and heavy with the promise of snow, and the wind mercilessly in front of them. By mid-morning they began encountering couriers. The riders came from the southwest and with their presence came rumors of what was up ahead.

"You are daft to believe we are heading to the lines to do battle with the Redcoats," Henry said to Whipple as they plodded along, casting an apprehensive eye at the sky. "'Tis winter camp where we are going and a damn cold time of it if there is no shelter when we get there. Our tents will give us little comfort if this storm is as fierce as it looks."

"I am telling you," Whipple insisted, "when we last stopped, one of the sutlers said we are less than thirty miles from New York City and the Redcoats have sallied forth in force to block our advance."

"Ah, now that I know it was a sutler who gave you this rumor, I am even less inclined to believe it," Henry replied, waving his hand dismissively.

"You will whistle a different tune when Lieutenant Tew shouts, "Company! Forward!" and you double-time it hoping that your powder is dry." Whipple patted his hip where his cartridge box lay snug under his jacket flap. "My stockings are under the lid," he said with conviction.

Henry let it pass. Oliver's worn stockings would no more protect his cartridges than a fish net. He continued on, preferring the silence, thinking of Judith sitting before the warm fire, darning his own stockings and smiling at him occasionally. He gritted his teeth. Another winter apart and from the start of it, it would be a brutal one.

That afternoon, when Lieutenant Tew ordered them to "Carry-Arms!" followed by "Close Ranks," Henry nudged Oliver who grinned back. They marched through the outskirts of a small town, past the snow-covered common and a three-story brick tavern, toward heavily wooded hills and mountains beyond. Once in the hills, they passed two Connecticut Regiments, who had pitched their tents and were warming themselves around their cooking fires. As the Rhode Islanders unloaded their tents from their baggage wagons, it began to snow. Large flakes fell fast and quickly covered the men's shoulders as they hurriedly tried to clear the ground before erecting their tents.

"This foretells a long cold winter," Oliver said as he pounded in an iron tent peg.

"If we do not want to freeze to death in our tents, we had better be quick about building our huts," Henry said, looking enviously at the rows of log cabins of the Regiments that had arrived earlier. Plumes of smoke drifted aloft from their chimneys and he imagined the soldiers clustered snug around the fireplace. Tonight, all they had for warmth were their blankets. He hoped the snowfall would not be so heavy as to collapse the tent.

Tomorrow, he was certain the entire Brigade, regardless of the weather, would be in the woods, cutting and trimming trees, notching logs, splaying shingles, and gathering stones for the chimneys. He hoped the ground was not too frozen yet to dig for clay. They would need it to close the chinks between the logs and the gaps between the stones. [4]

—∞—

Will drove the sled away from General Knox's farmhouse, down the road covered by freshly fallen snow, away toward Morristown. Elisabeth, heavily pregnant, sat beside him, her head, partially hidden by the cowl of her cloak, affectionately resting on his shoulder her bare hand on his. He smiled down at her, recalling crossing the Hudson at Albany, with a much younger Elisabeth sitting next to him, flirting and fluttering her blue eyes at him, while the family cook fussed at her forwardness. It had been a winter day then, too. How much had happened to both of them since. And now, he was filled with worry and concern for her and their baby. This constant anxiety was a new emotion for him. He felt her shift on the hard seat and sigh softly.

"Are you uncomfortable? Is there anything I can do?"

She shook her head. "Our child is stirring within. It will pass when I am able to lie down."

Big Red lifted his hooves high, trotting along through the powder, easily pulling the sled behind him. Will, mindful of Elisabeth's condition, pulled back on the reins a bit to slow the horse's pace. All was quiet except for the well-worn ash runners of the sled whispering through the snow. They passed the newly erected tents of the recently arrived soldiers. In the distance on the snowy slopes, men feverishly chopped down trees, while others trimmed and hauled them downhill to the construction sites for their huts. The construction would be faster, he thought, if they used thin trees horizontally for the roofs instead of slat shingles. Not his business.

He and Elisabeth had been living in the farmhouse General Knox had rented, a familiar salt-box construction with the rafters running continuously to the low, lean-to shaped rear of the building. The General, Lucy, and little Lucy occupied one front room, his clerk lived in the other that also served as the General's office. Will and Elisabeth shared one of the two small quarters in the back, their bed abutting against the kitchen chimney for added warmth. The Hadleys were on the opposite side of the kitchen in identical quarters with a sharply slanted low ceiling. [5]

Will would have been more reassured if Mercy had remained at the farmhouse. But Theodosia, her mother, had asked Mercy to move to the Ford Mansion, to help with her medical duties nursing the sick soldiers at Dr. Tilton's hospital. With Mercy gone, the remoteness of the Knox farmhouse increased the risks for Elisabeth and their baby. One heavy snowfall could make the roads impassable. General Knox's headquarters, near the artillery cantonment would be completely isolated. It was not possible or appropriate to ask Lucy Knox, as the only other woman in the house, beside the cook, to act as midwife.

Mercy Hadley was the experienced one. She and Elisabeth would be sharing the same bed. Mercy would be right there when Elisabeth went into labor, he thought, trying to reassure himself. And he would sleep alone for the first time since his return to Philadelphia after the battle in Monmouth. It would be strange and lonely.

The Mansion itself was already full with people as the headquarters for General Washington and his staff. In addition, Mrs. Washington and their servants were housed there and Mercy had reported there was barely enough space for the servants of the Fords and the General to perform their duties in the same kitchen. And now, he was leaving his beloved Elisabeth, close to her giving birth to their first child at this crowded place. [6]

They passed the huts of the General's Life Guard, about seventy-five yards from the Mansion. Will clicked his tongue and Big Red slowed and turned onto the path to the General's Headquarters. He gently brought the sled to a halt, nodded at the four sentries, jumped down and reached for Elisabeth. He took her easily in his arms and carried her up the few steps.

"How would it appear if a young Lieutenant carried his bride across his Commander in Chief's threshold?" she asked giggling at him. "Put me down, Will. It is more dignified if I enter on my own two feet."

Once inside, Will ignored the bustle of officers coming and going and carried his wife's trunk through two rooms and into a wing to the right of the main entrance. A double bed, too large for the small room, filled the cramped space. Will put the trunk at the foot, helped

Elisabeth off with her cloak and eased her feet on to the bed. She lay there, smiling at him, breathing softly, her hands on her extended belly.

"I will be alright here, my dear. Mercy shall be with me. Just think, my love. I will have a child and need to send a messenger to you to announce its arrival."

"And I will fly to you on the back of Big Red and you will introduce our newborn babe to its father."

He sat on the edge of the bed and held her hand in his. "You are cold," he said with concern.

"Only from the ride. It will be warm enough in here." She squeezed his hand. "I will miss you tonight my love."

"And I you," Will replied and then sat up suddenly at a knock on the door.

"Ah, you are here. I was afraid the snow would delay you," Mercy said. She removed a knitted quilt from the chair and gently placed it over Elisabeth's stocking feet.

"Do not trouble yourself, Will. Elisabeth is not the first woman to give birth, nor you the first man to worry." Will blushed, embarrassed that Mercy had seen the concern on his face. He hoped it was not as obvious to the sentries out front.

"I am comforted by the thought of you and your mother, with Dr. Tilton nearby, tending to her," he said with more reassurance than he felt.

"Oh, tosh and be gone with you. Dr. Tilton is as unnecessary as a fifth leg on a table. We women know all about this business of birthing."

Will left with the warmth of Elisabeth's kiss on his lips, feeling more hopeful that all would be for the best. The sled ride back to his quarters was faster and he caught some of Big Red's enthusiasm for a brisk journey in the cold clear air. It was only as he got closer that he realized, in passing through part of the General's headquarters, he had seen a glimpse of a slender Negro girl carrying plates into a room. He wondered if she was the one Adam had spoken of. And then his thoughts turned dark as he thought of his friend. Adam, he said out loud into the wind. I pray that you are safe.

Only Cocquetak and Aquadonk were allowed to hunt. The Indians brought down game with bows and arrows. The Colonel did not want to attract any unwarranted attention by the sound of muskets. The two would slip away from the Black Brigade's woodland camp, be gone a few days and return with one or two deer, strapped to triangle-shaped stick frames, gutted and cleaned. The rest of the men maintained a strict routine of picket and sentry duty in four hour shifts, without fires to warm them, hiding in clever pine bough blinds the two Indians had constructed around the perimeter of the camp.

When Adam was not on sentry duty, he and the others soaked split ash strips in pots of hot water and bent them into teardrop shapes as Aquadonk had taught them. They drilled holes at even lengths along the strips and fastened the two ends together with a thick wooden peg. The real work began when the two Indians returned. First, they taught the men how to scrape any remnants of skin and flesh from the bloody, tough deer hides before cutting them into uniform narrow strips. Next, the men were tasked with inserting two cross bars about the length of a man's foot apart, fastened by wooden pegs to the ash frame. When it came to weaving the uncured rawhide strips from one side of the tear drop shape to the other, the two Indians would converse and then break out in uncontrolled laughter. Aquadonk was the serious one and it was Cocquetak who would utter guttural words to his friend, pointing at one or another of the men, until both were convulsed with laughter. Adam sensed this must be women's work and the Indians were amused by the men's clumsy efforts. It was all done good-naturedly and since the weather was bitter cold and it frequently snowed, these inside tasks were preferred by far to sentry duty.

By the end of two weeks, they had made not only forty-five pairs of serviceable snowshoes but two sturdy triangle frames, laced with rawhide. On the first day the men practiced walking with their snowshoes strapped on to their boots. Adam was amazed at how fast he could move over the packed snow. Colonel Tye led half of them on five and ten mile marches through fields and woodlands, and then to demonstrate his stamina, led the other half himself the following day.

The triangular frames puzzled Adam. There was no need for the Brigade to be so equipped simply to hunt game, even if they were after elk or bear. The answer came the following day. The frames were lashed together with straps extended from the point of the triangle and the Colonel ordered Sam the Traitor and Nero to each lie down on one of them. Nero protested but the Colonel's baleful glare disabused him of any further objection. The group set off on their usual route, easily pulling their comrades over the packed snow for several miles, taking turns riding on the frames as the others did the pulling.

Now it was obvious to Adam that the Colonel intended to conduct a winter raid and capture some prominent leader of the Rebel militia or perhaps even the Governor of New Jersey, whose brutal acts against Tory militias were well known. That night, after dinner in the large cabin, when the men were busy playing cards or mending their clothes, Adam moved down the bench and sat next to Tye who was staring into the fire.

"Colonel," Adam said. "If it is a winter raid you plan, I have a suggestion."

Tye looked at him with amusement. "A winter raid you say? You are a smart man and a bold one. None of the others have even asked, although I believe our two Indians know of my purpose."

"Look around the room. Many of the men have taken off their jackets or coats of dark green, blue, red and black, and wear white linen shirts underneath. If they wore the white over their jackets they would be less visible from afar on a snowy field."

The Colonel clasped his hands together under his chin and thought for a moment. "We have enough linen shirts taken from Rebel homes for the men to wear one under and one over," Adam continued. Tye was silent and Adam thought their conversation was done.

"It is a good idea and useful until we arrive at the site. Then, I intend to attack during a snowstorm. The Rebels' guard will be down, their sentries huddled inside their huts, perhaps snow-bound and numbed by the cold."

"Sentries, Colonel? Who would have sentries outside his home?"

Colonel Tye laughed, his eyes sparkling with anticipation at revealing his surprise to Adam. "Why Gen'rl Washington, of course. The British may try to kidnap him by sending a large force across the frozen Hudson. They will not succeed, the snows will be too much for their men and horses." He beckoned Adam to lean closer. "You have seen how fast we can travel over snow. It will be the Black Brigade that kidnaps the Rebel Gen'rl and brings him back to be turned over to the British. [7] The slave holding commander captured by free Negroes." He glanced at Adam and smiled. "Including one freeman as well."

Adam shook his head in disbelief. "How can we accomplish this under the noses of their entire army?"

"Gen'rl Washington is not guarded by his entire army. His headquarters are more than three miles away from their encampment. It is only his headquarters troops we have to contend with. What did you call them, his Life Guards?" Adam nodded in astonishment at the audacity of Tye's plan.

"We are camped, this very moment, less than twenty miles from Washington's headquarters. I am only waiting for the weather to turn as foul as it can. A drivin', blindin' snowstorm that makes the roads impassable. Then we will strike, quickly coverin' the distance on snowshoes."

Tye reached over and grabbed Adam by both shoulders. "Think of freein' your Sarah. Carry an extra pair of snowshoes for her. She will have to keep up on the return. "

"I will carry her on my back if necessary, no matter how far we travel. Even to Paulus Hook."

"Oh, 'twill not be that far," Tye said airly. "The British will send a battalion of troops and cav'lry to meet us. Of that you can be certain."

That night, for the first time in many days, Adam thought of Sarah, as she had been in the Headquarters kitchen in Middlebrook. He saw her in a different kitchen now, rushing to him, her arms outstretched, her green eyes sparkling with love. He, too, now wished for heavy weather- a massive snowstorm that would mask their advance and reunite him with Sarah.

End Notes

Part One- The Winter of Despair and Merriment

Chapter 1- Starving Together at Valley Forge

1) After the British occupied Philadelphia, they used the city as a base for kidnapping prominent Whigs and other Rebel leaders. Reverend Henry Muhlenberg wrote "We hear . . . light cavalry and Tories are sweeping through the country to capture, dead or alive, any inhabitants who have held offices or posts under the independent government, such as officers of the militia, etc., as a high price has been placed on their heads." (McGuire, Thomas J., The Philadelphia Campaign- Germantown and the Roads to Valley Forge, Vol. II, p. 327, Note 47.)

The capture of Colonel John Hannum, an officer in a battalion of Chester County militia, is an actual event. He was taken from his home in East Bradfordship Township, around thirty miles west of Philadelphia. In his own words,

"I was Taken Prisoner the Night of the seventh of October 1777 by a Detacmt. of the 16thj Ridgm. of British Dragoons, was Conveyed to the City and was Lodged in the state house with A number of American officers." (McGuire, pp. 135-136.) McGuire cites the Hannum family history as stating the Colonel "was captured one night in his bed by a party of British light-horse, who had been piloted hither by a Tory neighbor, and he was carried a prisoner to

Philadelphia. . . [T]he party robbed Mrs. Hannum of her gold watch, and took everything of value in the house that they could carry away." (McGuire, p. 136.)

The use of a frozen body as a warning is based on an incident in New Jersey involving the Loyalist spy, Thomas Long. He was hung in early November 1777. His corpse was exhumed and his body was propped up with a pail over the head against the door of another Tory sympathizer. During the night, Long's body froze and when the Tory opened his front door in the morning, the corpse fell into the house. (Nagy, John A., Spies in the Continental Capital, p. 43.)

2) On November 22, 1777, several large mansions on the outskirts of Philadelphia were burned to prevent the Americans from using them as observation posts. That same day, an unusual earthquake was felt in Philadelphia and sixty miles away in Lancaster. (McGuire, p. 237.)

3) In mid-December, 1776, General Charles Lee was captured at the White Horse Tavern, near Basking Ridge, New Jersey, by British cavalry led by Colonel Harcourt. The General had unwisely established his quarters several miles away from the main body of the American army. He was taken by an advance patrol led by Coronet Banastre Tarelton and brought back to Brunswick. (Hackett Fischer, David, Washington's Crossing, p. 149.) He was held prisoner until exchanged in 1778. During the Battle of Monmouth on June 28, 1778 Lee led an assault on the British forces and then retreated, contrary to orders. He was reprimanded on the field by General Washington, and subsequently court-martialed and left military service. He died of a fever in Philadelphia in 1782. Banastre Tarelton was promoted to Brigade Major of the cavalry by the end of 1776. He was twenty-two years old.

4) Due to a lack of soap to wash with, the soldiers at Valley Forge became infected with scabies, which they called "the itch." First, small sacs developed between the fingers. When they broke from scratching, the ooze spread to the rest of the person's body. A soldier was tormented

by continuous itching and fits of feverish scratching, rendering him unfit for service. In early January, General Washington ordered those infected with scabies to be isolated. Doctors treated them with sulfur in hog's lard. (Fleming, Thomas, Washington's Secret War- The Hidden History of Valley Forge, p. 135.)

Private Joseph Plumb Martin believed he became infected with scabies when he was inoculated against small pox. At Valley Forge he described the itch as so intense, "I could scarcely lift my hands to my head." Through soldiers they knew in the artillery, they acquired sulphur, mixed it with tallow for grease, which they applied to their infected skin while lying around the hearth. They also imbibed generously of "hot whisky sling[s]" and "we killed the itch and we were satisfied, for it had almost killed us. This was a decisive victory, (over the scabies) the only one we had achieved lately." (Martin, Joseph Plumb, Private Yankee Doodle- Being a Narrative of Some of the Adventures, Dangers and Sufferings of a Revolutionary Soldier, George Scheer, editor, p. 111.)

5) Dr. Albigence Waldo, a surgeon at Valley Forge in an entry in his diary in mid-December described the scarcity of food:

"Heartily wish myself at home, my Skin and eyes are almost spoil'd with continual smoke. A general cry thro' the Camp this Evening among the Soldiers, "No Meat! No Meat!" - the Distant vales Echo'd back the melancholy sound - "No Meat! No Meat!" Imitating the noise of Crows and Owls, also, made a part of confused Musick.

What have you for your dinner boys? "Nothing but Fire Cake and Water, Sir." At night, "Gentlemen the Supper is ready." What is your Supper Lads? "Fire Cake and Water, Sir." Very poor beef has been drawn in our Camp the greater part of this season. A Butcher bringing a Quarter of this kind of Beef into Camp one day who had white Buttons on the knees of his breeches, a Soldier cries out - "There, there Tom is some more of your fat Beef, by my soul I can see the Butcher's breeches buttons through it." (Allen, Thomas, B., Remember Valley Forge- Patriots, Tories and Redcoats Tell Their Stories, p. 32; Waldo, Albigence, Dr., Diary of a Surgeon at Valley Forge, 1777.)

6) Washington's General Order issued on December 18, 1777, required the building of huts and specified their size and construction. Washington himself lived in his field tent up until Christmas, when many of the soldiers were already occupying the newly built wooden huts. (Allen, p. 25) He then moved into a modest, compact two story stone house, with two chimneys at one end built by Isaac Potts who owned the forge, and made it his headquarters. Instead of seizing the Potts house, he rented it as his quarters. (Chernow, Ron, Washington - A Life, p. 324.)

7) The character of Sarah Penrose is based upon the life of Hannah Mason, a fifty–six year old slave who worked as a cook for General Washington at Valley Forge. Her master was Reverend John Mason of New York who assigned her to Washington and was paid most of her wages. When she was set free upon the total payment of fifty-three pounds to Reverend Mason, she remained in Washington's service as Hannah Till, taking the name of her husband, Isaac Till, instead of that of her master. She worked as a cook for seven years during the American Revolution, serving both Washington and Lafayette. After the war, she lived in Philadelphia and died in 1824 at the age of 104. (Loane, Nancy K., Following the Drum- Women at the Valley Forge Encampment, pp. 106-107.)

8) In January 1778, Washington approved the recruitment of black troops by Rhode Island General James Varnum. The state promised to free any slaves willing to join an all-black battalion and compensated their masters with their fair market value. In May 1778, Rhode Island's General Assembly repealed the slave purchase act that allowed the State to purchase slaves from their masters for military service. Free men of color could continue to enlist in the "Black Regiment." The First Rhode Island Regiment was all black with white officers, a total of 242 men of whom 197 were colored soldiers. (Popek, Daniel M., "They . . . fought bravely but were unfortunate: The True Story of Rhode Island's 'Black Regiment' and the Failure of Segregation in Rhode Island's Continental Line, 1777-1783," p. 195.

Connecticut permitted slave owners to avoid military service if they sent their slaves in their stead. An August 1778 census of troops listed 755 colored, almost five percent of the total number in the Continental Army. (Chernow, pp. 333-334.)

According to Thomas Allen, more than five hundred freed negroes were among the soldiers at Valley Forge. (Allen, p. 25.)

9) Galloway actually wrote to General Washington asking permission for his wife to join him in Philadelphia and bring with her their furniture and household effects, presumably silverware, dishes, glasses and the like. Washington responded that while he would immediately prepare a pass for Mrs. Galloway to travel between the lines, she could not bring anything with her because the Pennsylvania Assembly had decreed that all Loyalists forfeited their property. (Fleming, p. 17)

10) Ann Bates worked as a school teacher in Philadelphia where she came to the attention of someone in British General Sir Henry Clinton's espionage network. When the British evacuated Philadelphia in June 1778, she went with her husband, a soldier and gunsmith, to New York City and was an operative for one of General Clinton's spy handlers. She traveled and mingled among American soldiers and camp followers, posing as Mrs. Barnes, a "peddler of thread, needles, combs, knives and some medicines." As she sold these goods, Mrs. Barnes, who once even penetrated General Washington's headquarters, noted the number of troops and weapons in American's camp at White Plains, New York. (McBurney, Christian M., "Ann Bates: British Spy Extraordinaire," Journal of the American Revolution, Annual Volume 2016, pp.221-226; Berkin, Carol, Revolutionary Mothers- Women in the Struggle for America's Independence, pp. 141-142; Braisted, Todd W. Grand Forage 1778-The Battleground Around New York City, pp. 36-40; Nagy, pp. 111-112.) Her role as a British spy in Philadelphia, recruited by John Stoner, is purely fictitious.

Chapter 2 – Setting a Trap

1) Colonel Harcourt of the 16th Queens Dragoons was indeed one of General Howe's harshest critics, blaming him for the disastrous surrender of Burgoyne's army. He shared his opinion with his father, Earl Harcourt in London. (Fleming, p. 50.)

2) Fitzpatrick's words are a combination of a direct quote from his writings to his brother, the Earl of Upper Ossory, and Lieutenant Loftus Cliffe of the Forty-Sixth Infantry Regiment in his letters to his family. (Fleming, pp. 50-52.)

3) The prologue or poem was written by Loyalist Jonathan Odell who mocked the naïve American audiences and their pretensions. New Englanders were frequently referred to as "Brother Jonathans," ridiculing their pious attitudes, what we today would consider being "holier than thou." (Fleming, p. 66-67.)

4) Quakers were vociferous in their opposition to plays and actors in Philadelphia. They and other religious leaders railed against them in sermons and articles, condemning plays as "a source of all worldy corruption." (Fleming, p.64.) In 1766, the Southwark Theatre was built just outside the city limits to avoid the jurisdiction of Philadelphia's anti- theatre legislation. The original location was at what is now South and Fourth Streets. The motto over the stage was "The whole world acts the player." (The Philadelphia Stage and Beyond, York County Heritage Trust.)

The play, "The Liar," together with a farce, "A Trip to Scotland," was performed on May 1, 1778 most likely by Howe's Strolling Players. Seats in the gallery and pit cost one dollar.

5) The Quakers' natural compassion for the suffering was at odds with the position Quaker leaders had taken against what they saw as "an attempt by Presbyterians and other radicals to establish 'tyranny' in America." At the yearly meeting in January 1775, Quakers were warned they faced discipline if they supported the Revolution.

Quakers were banned from holding any office, paying taxes or taking oaths of allegiance to the Rebel cause. (Fleming, pp. 63-64.)

6) Reverend John Witherspoon was President of the Presbyterian College in Princeton, which later became Princeton University. He signed the Declaration of Independence and was a member of Congress from June 1776 until November 1782. His oldest son, James, was killed at the Battle of Germantown on October 4, 1777. I have imagined that after Witherspoon fled Philadelphia with the other members of Congress, he chose to return to his home in Princeton to bury his son.

Dr. Benjamin Rush, an ardent Whig and prominent Philadelphia physician, was also a signer of the Declaration of Independence and a member of Congress. He was the Director of the hospital at Princeton.

I have assumed he would take up residence with Reverend Witherspoon in the latter's mansion. The idea of the two of them living under one roof may be a stretch, because Witherspoon once said, "Rush's addiction to 'strong and superlative expressions' made him uneasy." (Fleming, p. 93.)

Chapter 3 – For the Love of a Slave

1) In 1775, pay was in dollars, divided into 90ths and not the modern 100ths. One pound sterling equaled two and 2/3 dollars. A private in the regular infantry was paid six and 2/3 dollars per month; a lieutenant, 13 and 1/3 dollars; a captain, 20 dollars, a major, 33 and 1/3 dollars and a lieutenant colonel, 40 dollars. Congress, in October 1776, approved increases for commissioned officers but not enlisted men and that disparity remained for the duration of the war. By 1781, due to inflation, 167 and ½ Continental paper dollars equaling one dollar in specie, meaning in coin, making the paper virtually worthless and "giving rise to the phrase,'not worth a Continental.'" (Barbieri, Michael "The Worth of a Continental," pp. 98-101, Journal of the American Revolution, Annual Volume 2015.)

2) In addition to widespread desertions by enlisted men, officers resigned their commissions in droves, giving a variety of reasons for

abandoning the patriotic cause. Officers were expected to pay for rations, clothing and equipment out of their own pockets, while enlisted men, in theory, were provided with these necessities at public expense. Letters from home by wives complained about living on gruel as the buying power of the officers' salaries diminished due to depreciation of the Continental dollar. (Fleming, pp. 161-162.)

Congress, at the time dominated by ideological Whigs, assumed that "patriots in a wife's hometown would . . . step forward to make sure she was not in want while her husband risked his life in defense of American liberty." (Fleming, p. 162.) This proved to be an "idealistic fantasy." Indeed, one officer at Valley Forge asked the question, "Why should an officer have empty pockets and watch his family suffer while everyone else was making money from the booming wartime economy, especially when the officer was called upon to risk his life on the battlefield?" (Fleming, p. 162.)

3) Over two thousand men, nearly one-sixth of the entire army, died at Valley Forge, mostly from disease. While typhus, typhoid fever, pneumonia, dysentery and scurvy were common and killed many during the winter months when malnutrition and exposure to cold were prevalent, many also died in the warmer spring. (Chernow, p. 327; Chadwick, Bruce, The First American Army, p. 223.) The dozens of hospitals at Valley Forge, and in the nearby towns of Reading, Bethlehem, Yellow Springs, Easton and elsewhere in Pennsylvania, were notoriously over-crowded, understaffed and unsanitary. Dr. Benjamin Rush wrote Patrick Henry, "Our hospitals crowded with six thousand sick but [only] half provided with necessaries or accomodations, and more dying in them in one month than perished in the field during the whole of the last campaign." (Chadwick, p. 224.)

4) Fevers were thought to be caused by "effluvia," that is the airs or vapors arising from stagnant and contaminated water. Vinegar, in appropriate doses, was prescribed as a cure. An ague fit was one of chills and shaking. "[A]s much exercise between the fits as he can bear" was thought to be helpful because "Nothing tends more to prolong an intermitting fever than indulging in a lazy and indolent disposition."

(Burdick, Kim, Fever, Journal of the American Revolution, Online Magazine, November 12, 2015.)

Today, we know that fevers are caused by ticks, mosquitos, fleas, and contaminated food, putrid water, bacteria and spread by crowded conditions. The men brought to the hospitals wore shirts and brought blankets they had used in the field. These were infested with lice, the carriers of typhus.

5) Rush complained to General Washington about the lack of guards and officers to maintain order at military hospitals. There was no discipline imposed on the patients. Those who were ambulatory went out and sold their muskets, blankets and even clothing to buy rum and food. Fights among the patients broke out and frustrated the doctors' efforts to restore their health. (Fleming, p. 145.)

6) In late December 1777, Rush, then the director of the hospital at Princeton, sent a letter to Washington, detailing the overcrowding and dismal conditions at Princeton and in the army's hospitals in general. He recommended that the sick soldiers be placed in local farmhouses "where 'the air and diet' would speed their recovery." (Fleming, p.145.) Washington responded by letter dated January 12, 1778 that he had forwarded the letter and Rush's recommendations to Congress.

Rush was part of a cabal of Whig ideologues, seeking to replace Washington with a General of their choice. In an unsigned letter to Patrick Henry, then Governor of Virginia, Rush complained about the state of the Army, the conditions of the hospitals, the "idleness and ignorance and peculation" of the commissary and quartermaster departments, and suggested that Washington be replaced. Despite Rush's request that Henry burn the letter after he read it, the Governor forwarded it to Washington. (Fleming, pp.147-148.)

7) Many women served as Continental Army nurses in hospitals. One such remarkable person was Abigail Hartman Rice who was a nurse at the Yellow Springs hospital, about ten miles from Valley Forge and about a mile from her family's farm. She participated, together

with other nurses in a protest over lack of pay and an ultimatum that unless they were paid, they would refuse to serve. The Yellow Springs Hospital Director, Dr. Otto Bodo, in May of 1780 wrote to Congress complaining about the deplorable lack of medical supplies, blankets, soap and food, as well as the failure to pay the hospital's nurses. Congress took note and the nurses received their pay.

Abigail Hartman Rice, during her service at Yellow Springs, contracted typhoid fever, which permanently weakened her. She died in 1789. There is a memorial plaque, honoring her dedicated service, in the Washington Memorial Chapel at Valley Forge National Historical Park. (McGready,Blake, Abigail Hartman Rice, Revolutionary War Nurse, Journal of the American Revolution, November 28, 2016.)

8) In the winter of 1777, as the British and Hessian troops withdrew to garrison towns, Monmouth County was the scene of brutal skirmishes between Loyalist and Whig militias. "Many a score was settled with all the rage and cruelty of a civil war." (Hackett-Fischer, p. 349.) Tory militias served together with British cavalry in raids in the Pennsylvania countryside. There was an ongoing operation to capture prominent Rebel figures and militia leaders. (See End Note 1 to Chapter 1.) However, the raid on the Princeton Hospital to capture Dr. Rush and Reverend Witherspoon, while plausible, is fictitious.

Chapter 4- The Hospital at Princeton

1) Martha Washington arrived at Valley Forge the first week of February 1777. At the time, it was the fourth largest city in the independent colonies. (Chadwick, p. 210.) She was later joined by Caty Greene (General Nathaniel Greene's wife), Lucy Knox, and General Stirling's wife, Lady Sarah Livingston Stirling and their beautiful daughter, Kitty. (Chernow, p. 330; Berkin, pp. 77-78.)

By late February, General Knox, who had been given leave by General Washington to visit his family, was in Boston and only returned to Valley Forge in the early spring. On May 2nd he was in charge of the artillery that fired a thirteen round salute to celebrate the treaty of alliance with France. (Brooks, Noah, Henry Knox- A Soldier of the Revolution, pp. 114, 116-117.) I have placed him at Valley Forge when Will returns from the Princeton hospital for purposes of the plot.

Twenty-two year old Lucy Knox arrived in late May 1778, long after the brutal winter was over. (Drake, Francis S., Life and Correspondence of Henry Knox, p. 56.) She brought with her little Lucy, the Knox's two year old daughter, and was accompanied by General Benedict Arnold, who had joined them at New Haven. He "provided the horses for the trip, 'no small service,' General Knox acknowledged." (Drake, p. 56; Loane, pp. 81-82.)

2) About 1,500 horses died of starvation at Valley Forge. (Allen, p. 33.) "Dead horses and their entrails lay decomposing everywhere, emitting a putrid stench into the winter air." (Chernow, p. 325.) The idea of sending the horses and artillery away from Valley Forge and further into Pennsylvania, while logical and even likely, at least during the winter months, is a guess on my part. It is an historical fact that the horses and artillery units were in Valley Forge in late March and early April 1778.

Chapter 5 – The Madness of Anger

1) Washington was fond of Lafayette and "embraced him as his most intimate protégé." (Chernow, pp.331-332.) Hannah Till, who together with her husband was Washington's cook at Valley Forge, was "lent" by Washington to Lafayette, most likely during the winter before Lafayette left to lead the abortive effort to strike at the British in Canada. (Loane, pp. 106-108.)

2) In January 1778, Washington approved a proposal made by Brigadier General James Varnum of Rhode Island to recruit black troops for the regiments from that state. Rhode Island, to induce Negroes to join, promised to free any slaves who signed up. Two other states, Massachusetts and Connecticut followed suit, with Connecticut exempting white masters from military service if they sent their slaves instead. (Chernow, pp. 333-334.)

According to Thomas Allen, there were more than 500 free Negroes at Valley Forge. (Allen, p.25.) Chernow records that an August 1778 census "listed 755 blacks as part of the Continental Army, or nearly five percent of the total force," although there is no breakdown between free men and slaves sent by their masters. (Chernow, p. 334.)

Part Two - The Army Awakens

Chapter 6 – Drills and Dinner

1) Gillet's confinement in the hospital at Princeton, for purposes of the plot, occurs before Varnum and other officers of the Rhode Island regiment departed for Providence to raise a Negro regiment, and his return to Valley Forge occurs before the new black regiment joined the Army.

2) On January 6, 1778, twenty-four year old Catherine "Caty" Littlefield Greene arrived at Valley Forge to join her husband, General Nathaniel Greene, who was twelve years older than she. Their two children remained behind in Providence. She was fluent in French, vivacious, flirtatious and "one of the most brilliant and entertaining of women." (Loane, pp 58-59.) She also became pregnant while at Valley Forge and was bed-ridden at the end of February and beginning of March.

3) Fort Mercer, along with Fort Mifflin, was one of two forts, four miles below British occupied Philadelphia, blocking the British fleet from coming up the Delaware River to supply their army in the newly captured city. Fort Mercer was on the Jersey side of the river, supporting Fort Mifflin on Mud Island. A Hessian assault on Fort Mercer, on October 22nd, failed with heavy casualties and the loss of two British warships. After a heavy bombardment of Fort Mifflin, the Americans were driven to take refuge at Fort Mercer which was attacked by 5,000 British troops. They succeeded where the Hessians had failed and the Americans were forced to abandon Fort Mercer on November 20th. (Savas, Theodore P., and Dameron, David J., A Guide to the Battles of the American Revolution, pp. 151-155.)

Colonel Angell and the Rhode Island Infantry, Second Regiment were among the besieged Americans at Fort Mercer. Angell wrote the following about the unsuccessful attack by the Hessians:

"22nd this day we Continued Dilligent on our works until the after Noon about one oclock, when the Enemy Arrived within musket Shoot of our fort. We fired a Cannon or two at them on which they Retired, and kept Sculking in the woods until half After four oClock, when they Sent in a flagg Demanding the fort but was answered that the fort was not to be Given up on any terms, in Reply to this, they answered that if we Still remain'd obstinate, our blood might be upon our own heads, for we should have no Mercy Shone us. Our Answer was we asked none and Expect none. So granted and in about ten minuts after then begun as Smart a fire as Ever I heard from Eight field pieces. . . they had placed against us, at the Same time advanced in two Colems to attack our fort by Storm, when there begun an incesant fire Musketry which Continued forty minuts, when the hessians Retreated In the most Pescipited manner leaving 200 kill'd and wounded in the field, we Spent the greatest part of the Night bringing in the wounded."

Private Joseph Martin, in his usual acerbic and macabre humorous manner, wrote about the battle for Fort Mercer:

"I was at the siege [of Yorktown], and the hardships of that were no more to be compared to this [the siege of Fort Mercer] than the sting of a bee to the bite of a rattlesnake. But there has been little notice taken of it, the reason of which is, there was no Washington, Putnam or Wayne there. Had there been, the affair would have been extolled to the skies. Great men get great praise; little men, nothing. But it was always so and always will be." (Martin, p. 95.)

4) Despite the punishment of five lashes across the back, many men relieved themselves inside their huts instead of at the outside latrines. To alleviate the stench, Washington ordered the men to cut windows in their huts and remove the mud in the chinks to allow the breezes to air them out. (Allen, p. 41.)

5) Baron Friedrich Wilhelm August von Steuben, a Prussian born military officer who had served in the army of Frederick the Great,

arrived at Valley Forge on February 23, 1778. He was accompanied by his private secretary, three French adjutants and his dog, Azor, alternately described as an Italian greyhound or a Russian wolfhound.

Initially, he trained a model company of one hundred soldiers, drilling them personally twice a day. Although he spoke no English, he communicated by acting out the manual of arms, or through French speaking officers or by a few memorized commands in English. The soldiers from his model company in turn proceeded to teach the drills to other units. (Bergen County Historical Society, Friedrich Wilhelm von Steuben; Allen, p. 39.) Von Steuben turned "the drills into contests between regiments, and the men, sometimes as angry with each other as they were with the British, welcomed the competition." (Chadwick, p. 240.)

6) When Baron von Steuben first arrived at Valley Forge and began drilling a select group of soldiers, Captain Benjamin Walker, who spoke French, volunteered to assist him. Von Steuben was delighted, stating that "If I had seen an angel from heaven . . .I could not have been more rejoiced." Walker became his aide-de-camp. (Fleming, p. 221.)

Von Steuben peppered his pupils with oaths in French and German, interspersed with the occasional "Goddamn." One typical outburst, with Walker at his side was: "Viens, Walker, mon ami! Sacre! Goddamn de gaucheries of dese badauts. Je ne plus. I can curse dem no more." (Allen, p. 222.)

7) Baron von Steuben's record of drill instructions developed at Valley Forge became the "Regulations for the Order and Discipline of the Troops of the United States," and was the basic manual for military training and discipline until 1812. A facsimile reprint of the 1794 edition of von Steuben's Revolutionary War Drill Manual contains instructions on everything from simple commands such as Attention, Rest, Left and Right Face, as well as instructions for accomplishing more complicated maneuvers such as opening of the ranks, to the right and left wheel, the oblique march and the march by files. (Baron von Steuben's Revolutionary War Drill Manual, pp.

32-36.) Besides maneuvers, the soldiers had to learn drum signals, one a "flam" or two note drumbeat, with different signals for "turn or face to the right," and "to the left." (Allen, p. 40.) This discipline and training was important because prior to von Steuben's drills, the American army deployed into battle in single file lines. Now they were able to maneuver in orderly units and bring disciplined firepower more quickly to the battlefield.

8) Baron von Steuben projected the image of a militarist with his soldierly bearing and his appearance in uniform, bedecked with various medals and the Star of Fidelity. His Prussian heritage and experience in the armies of Frederick the Great, who led Prussia to become the dominant and most feared military power in Europe, also enhanced his reputation as a warrior.

One soldier at Valley Forge wrote: "He seemed to me a perfect personification of Mars (the God of War). The trappings of his horse, the enormous holsters of his pistols, his large size and strikingly martial aspect, all seemed to favor the idea."

Randy Shilts in his book, "Conduct Unbecoming: Gays and Lesbians in the U.S. Military," writes that Frederick the Great's court was notoriously gay. In August 1777, a written accusation of homosexuality was made against von Steuben and he fled Europe to avoid dishonor. The scandal surrounding von Steuben did not reach America until several years after the Revolutionary War. Shilts speculates that Benjamin Franklin, who met with von Steuben in Paris and offered him the opportunity to assist the American Army, was also probably unaware of the accusations against the Prussian drill master. (Shilts, Randy, Conduct Unbecoming: Gays and Lesbians in the U.S. Military, pp. 7-10.)

Walter Benemann in his work, "Male-Male Intimacy in Early America," asserts that Captain Benjamin Walker, who became von Steuben's aide-de-camp at Valley Forge, was reputed to be the Baron's male companion. However, Benemann concludes that "Walker had no scruples about exploiting the Baron's sexual interest although he had no intention of reciprocating." (Benemann, Walter, "Male-Male Intimacy in Early America: Beyond Romantic Friendships,pp.102-103.)

It makes no difference today whether Baron von Steuben was homosexual or not. What matters is how history is taught and whether historical figures are accurately portrayed or behavior, thought to be reprehensible at the time our history books were written, is obliterated from the record.

9) The journey from Philadelphia to Valley Forge, began on April 5, 1778. Four Quaker women, Elizabeth Drinker, Susanna Jones, Phebe Pemberton and Mary Pleasants made the trip by coach, arriving on April 6th. The description of their coach, "complete with 4 horses and two Negros who rode Postilion," is from Elizabeth Drinker's diary entries. (North, Louise V., Wedge, Janet M., Freeman, Landa M., In the Words of Women-The Revolutionary War and the Birth of the Nation, 1765-1799, p. 115; Journal of the American Revolution, Annual Volume 2015, Loane, Nancy K, "An Elegant Dinner with General Washington at Valley Forge," p. 236.)

I have included the fictitional character of Mary Lewis as the fifth woman in the party. The conversations with Martha Washington, the General and various Staff Officers during the dinner which the Quaker ladies in fact attended, are also fictitious.

10) Elizabeth Drinker's diary entry recounting the meeting with General Washington stated: "he told us, he could do nothing in our busyness further than granting us a pass to Lancaster, which he did. . ." (North et al., p. 115.)

In fact, Washington wrote a letter dated the same day, addressed to the President of Pennsylvania's governing body, Thomas Wharton Jr., in favor of the release of their husbands:

"Sir: Mrs. Jones, Mrs. Pleasants and two other Ladies, connected with the Quakers confined at Winchester in Virginia, waited upon me this day for permission to pass to York Town, to endeavour to obtain the release of their Friends. . . You will judge the propriety of permitting them to proceed further than Lancaster; but from appearances, I imagine their request may be safely granted. As they seem much distressed, humanity pleads strongly in their behalf." (Loane, Journal of the American Revolution, 2015, p. 239, footnote 12.)

11) The menu for the dinner is based on the Household Expense Book, kept by Captain Caleb Gibbs, which listed the kinds of foods purchased and available. It was usual to serve two dining courses of three main dishes and several side dishes. Speculation on the actual dinner is based upon the suggestion of Clarissa F. Dillon, an expert on food of the Colonial and Revolutionary periods. (Loane, Journal of the American Revolution, 2015, pp.238-239.)

12) The Pennsylvania Council, without meeting with the women, ordered the release of the Quaker men held in Winchester, Virginia. Whether that was due to their own decision or General Washington's letter is unknown. The men arrived in Lancaster on April 25th, and the entire group returned to Philadelphia on April 30th. (North, et al., p. 116.)

13) The treaties with France, recognizing American independence, were completed on February 6, 1778. France agreed to a military alliance with America that meant the supply, not only of weapons, but the commitment of French troops and naval vessels. It took a few months for the news to reach the new United States. Washington staged a celebration on May 6th at Valley Forge. The text of the treaties was read aloud to the assembled troops, thirteen cannons were fired, soldiers performed a feu de joie, a running fire of muskets, and there were cheers of "Long Live the King of France." (Chernow, p. 335, Allen, p. 42.)

Chapter 7 – In Licentious Philadelphia

1) Using the conversion rate (adopted by Congress in 1775) of one pound equaled two and 2/3rd dollars, the fifty pounds John Stoner gambled was equivalent to around $133 in those days and more than $8,000 in U.S. dollars in 2016. To put the amounts being wagered in perspective, a Colonel in the Continental Army was paid $50 per month; a working man's wages for a year were twenty six pounds. (Journal of the American Revolution, 2015, Barbieri, p. 99, note 2.)

2) As bizarre as this festival may seem in the middle of a war and staged in the British occupied city of Philadelphia, the Mischienza actually took place. It was financed by private contributions from high ranking officers, an indication of how wealthy they were; it had a medieval theme, and the ladies chosen by their "knights," were dressed in "exotic Turkish costumes;" the four hundred guests were entertained at Walnut Grove, the mansion owned by the former Joseph Wharton; the ballroom, designed by Major John Andre, was decorated in "a light elegant style of painting," with eighty-five mirrors; there was a stupendous fireworks display at ten pm, followed by dancing. Dining took place in a newly constructed two hundred and ten foot long room with seats for four hundred and thirty people who were served "1,200 dishes, plus fifty pyramids of sweetmeats, jellies, and cakes." (Fleming, pp. 268-269.) Allen describes the young women as wearing "Turkish-style gowns and jeweled turbans," and the guests were served by "twenty-four black slaves in Oriental dresses, with silver collars and bracelets." (Allen, pp. 47-48.) For a description focusing on Peggy Shippen's attendance, see Stuart, Nancy Rubin, Defiant Brides-The Untold Story of Two Revolutionary-Era Women and the Radical Men They Married, pp. 9-10.) The dancing and revelry continued until dawn.

All was not merriment. There was a war on. Shortly after the fireworks ended American cavalry, who had snuck up to the wooden sharpened stake structures defending Philadelphia, ignited the timber barricades and set them afire. The guards in the redoubt towers fired muskets at the Americans and drums signaled an attack. The raid was led by Captain Allan McLane. The guests were told it was just another part of the festivities and they partied on. (Fleming, p. 270.)

Chapter 8 – The Campaign Resumes

1) Washington sent a reconnaissance force of 2,200 men, led by the Marquis de Lafayette, to block any offensive thrust by General Clinton with orders to engage only in a holding action until the rest of the American army could arrive. Lafayette chose a place about five

miles west of Philadelphia, called Barren Hill and now known as Lafayette Hill. (Fleming, p. 290; Allen, p. 49.)

2) Uneasy about the possibility of a surprise attack on Lafayette's troops, Washington included in the force two platoons of his own lifeguard, fifty of Morgan's riflemen, a troop of cavalry to serve as scouts, and forty-seven Oneida Indians.

During the French and Indian War, the Oneidas had been allied with the French. At a conference in upstate New York attended by Lafayette, the Oneida were told that Lafayette represented the French King. They adopted the young Marquis into their tribe and named him "Kaywela", after one of their great warriors. Lafayette referred to the Oneidas as "scalping gentlemen." When the Oneida warriors arrived at Valley Forge, Washington received them with courtesy and ceremony. (Fleming, p. 291; George Washington's Mount Vernon, Oneida; Sawyer, William, National Park Service, The Oneida Nation in the American Revolution.)

3) Private Joseph Martin describes the Indians, and an incident before the British attacked Lafayette's troops, with the prejudice of the time and his usual humor:

"The Indians were stout-looking fellows and remarkably neat for that race of mortals, but they were Indians.

. . . The Indians were amusing themselves and the soldiers by shooting with their bows, in and about the church. I observed something in the corner of the roof . . . and desired an Indian . . . to shoot an arrow at it. He did so and it proved to be a cluster of bats; I should think there were nearly a bushel of them, all hanging upon one another. The [church] was immediately alive with them, and it was likewise instantly full of Indians and soldiers. The poor bats fared hard; it was sport for all hands. . . . I never saw so many bats before nor since, nor indeed in my whole life put all together." (Martin, p. 118-119.)

4) Fleming writes the Oneidas "released a tremendous war whoop. Neither the British horses nor the men in the saddles had ever heard

anything like it. Horses bolted and dragoons leaped to the ground and ran for their lives." (Fleming, p. 295.)

5) The Oneidas did not receive the credit they deserved , both for holding up the main British advance in their initial encounter with the dragoons, and for their part (together with the riflemen) in the rear guard action that followed, allowing Lafayette and the rest of his force to escape General Howe's trap. (Fleming, p. 297.)

6) On May 27, the Congress, still sitting in York, approved a raise in officers' salaries, which turned out to be about half what a British officer of the same rank received. However, the American officers' pay was not too far above the monthly salaries paid Sergeants and Privates. This was in keeping with "the general idea of equality as stated in the Declaration of Independence. . ." (Fleming, p. 283.)

By a vote of six states to five, Congress approved the obligation of half pay for seven years for officers who took an oath of loyalty to the government of the United States. (Fleming, p. 283.) The actual oath provided that the named officer,

"do acknowledge the UNITED STATES of AMERICA to be Free, Independent and Sovereign States, and declare that the people thereof owe no allegiance or obedience to George the Third, King of Great Britain; and I renounce, refute and abjure any allegiance or obedience to him; and I do swear that I will, to the utmost of my power, support, maintain and defend the said United States against the said King George the Third, his heirs and successors, and his or their abettors, assistants and adherents, and will serve the said United States in the office of [rank], which I now hold, with fidelity, according to the best of my skill and understanding." (Allen, p. 43.)

The oath was then witnessed by another officer who also signed.

Ironically, the oath taken by Major General Benedict Arnold was witnessed on May 30th, 1778, at the Artillery Park, Valley Forge by Henry Knox, Brigadier General. (Allen, p. 43.)

7) For purposes of the plot, I have kept General Knox at Valley Forge and in the field. However, shortly after the British evacuated

Philadelphia on June 18th and before the battle of Monmouth Courthouse on June 28th, General Knox and Lucy left Valley Forge and entered the city. He commented that "it stunk so abominably that it was impossible to stay there, as was her first design." (Drake, p. 56; Fleming, pp. 330-331.)

When Dr. Benjamin Rush returned to Philadelphia, more than a month after the British had left, "he found dozens of frightened, feverish patients writhing in the summer heat. In September, he himself came down with a fever so severe, he thought he would die. (Fleming, p. 331.)

Chapter 9 – Bloody Fighting in the Cauldron of Summer

1) The Battle of Monmouth Courthouse took place in blistering heat on June 28th 1778. Temperatures reached over 100 degrees by noon. When the British left Philadelphia and crossed the Delaware at Cooper's Ferry, now Camden, New Jersey, they were slowed substantially by a baggage train of 1,500 wagons carrying the army's supplies. As they marched at a snail's pace northeast heading for Sandy Hook, Washington's faster moving American Army, which had crossed the Delaware north of Trenton at Coryell's Ferry, and marched down through Princeton and Englishtown, caught up with the retreating British at the small town of Monmouth Courthouse, today Freehold, New Jersey, on June 27th.

On the morning of June 28th, before daybreak, General von Knyphausen led approximately half of the 10,000 strong British army out of Monmouth. General Clinton and the remainder of the army left four hours later except for a rear guard of approximately 1,500 troops who remained in Monmouth to protect the baggage train. The von Knyphausen Regiment was not part of the rearguard and my placement of Christoph's company in this protective role is fictitious. (Savas, Theodore P., and Dameron, J. David, A Guide to the Battles of the American Revolution, pp. 171-172; Chernow, pp. 340-341.)

Washington had given General Lee orders to vigorously pursue and attack the rearguard separating that part of their army from the rest of General Clinton's men. Washington and the main bulk of the Americans would follow. Lee failed to make a coordinated attack. The British, under General Cornwallis, turned the tables and a strong British infantry force and the 16th Light Dragoons just north of Monmouth Courthouse turned to meet Lee's forces and crush them before the main body of the American army could arrive. The Americans broke before this assault and fled in disarray, hotly pursued by the British infantry and Dragoons. (Savas and Dameron, p. 174.)

2) This description is based on an account by Private Joseph Martin as the troops marched through Princeton.

"Some of the patriotic inhabitants of the town had brought out to the end of the street we passed through some casks of ready-made toddy. It was dealt out to the men as they passed by, which caused the detachment to move slowly at this place. The young ladies of the town, and perhaps of the vicinity, had collected and were sitting in the stoops and at the windows to see the noble exhibition of a thousand half-starved and three-quarters naked soldiers pass in review before them. I chanced to be on the wing of a platoon next to the houses. . . and had a good chance to notice the ladies, and I declare that I never before nor since saw more beauty, considering the numbers, than I saw at that time. They were all beautiful. New Jersey and Pennsylvania ladies are, in my opinion, collectively handsome, the most so of any in the United States. But I hope our Yankee ladies will not be jealous at hearing this." (Martin, p. 123.)

3) Historians agree that when Washington arrived and saw the Americans fleeing he was furious and confronted General Lee, who was trailed by his dogs he had brought with him. Chernow has Washington demanding, "What is the meaning of this, sir? I desire to know the meaning of this disorder and confusion." Lee, taken aback by Washington's wrath spluttered, "Sir? Sir?" and then responded, "The American troops would not stand the British bayonets." Washington, who normally did not use profane language then called Lee, "You damned poltroon, you never tried them," and then cursed Lee out "until the leaves shook on the trees." (Chernow, p. 342.)

Fleming relates the confrontation with Lee in much the same

way, with Lee first blaming Generals Scott and Wayne and then complaining that he had found himself on "'the most extensive plain in America' where British cavalry could have annihilated his troops." Lee than added, "Besides, the whole thing [meaning the plan to attack the British rearguard] was against my opinion" [in the war council Washington had held the day before]. Washington's response was "All this may be true, sir but you ought not to have undertaken it unless you intended to go through with it." (Fleming, p. 317.)

I leave it to Private Martin to have the last word. His company was sitting by the roadside when Washington and his aides rode by. Washington asked Martin's officers "'by whose orders the troops were retreating' and being answered by General Lee's, he said something but as he was moving forward all the time this was passing, he was too far off for me to hear it distinctly. Those that were nearer to him said his words were 'd___n him.' Whether he did thus express himself or not I do not know. It was certainly very unlike him; but he seemed at the instant to be in a great passion. . ." (Martin, p. 127)

Washington then observed the lay of the land and gave orders to establish defensive lines. I have placed Private Gillet and his Rhode Island Regiment first alongside the road to observe the confrontation of Washington and Lee, next in a defensive line to hold the advancing British at bay until more of the American army arrived, and then to Comb's Hill, overlooking the left flank of the British lines.

4) According to an exhaustive history of Rhode Island's Black Regiment, Colonel Angell's Second Regiment was under strength before the battle with only 349 officers and men. The detachment of fifty-seven officers (white) and men (black) from the First R.I. Regiment, the "Black Regiment," increased the number of officers and men to 406. (Popek, p. 206.)

5) I have placed Colonel Daniel Morgan's Rifle Corps on the Americans' left, commanded by General (Lord Stirling) Alexander. In the middle of the oppressively hot afternoon, the British light infantry and the 42nd ("Black Watch") Regiment of Foot attacked the Americans. They were driven back by the "steadfastness of the newly

trained American riflemen [who] blunted the assaults of some of the world's finest infantry." (Savas and Dameron, p. 176.)

6) The parsonage referred to was the Old Scots Church later called the Old Tennent Church in memory of Pastors John and William Tennent. It was a Presbyterian Church just off the Englishtown Road and behind the Americans' main lines. Wounded soldiers were said to have been treated there.(Gilman, Malcolm B, Col. M.D., Monmouth Road to Glory, p. 46.)

7) The artillery duel was most intense during the broiling mid-afternoon heat. It occurred at the center where General Anthony Wayne had positioned his brigade slightly in advance of the American line. (Savas and Dameron, p. 176)

8) Gilman is the only historian I have read to mention the artillery used nails against the British. He writes: "As the afternoon wore on, Knox's artillerymen found two kegs of hand-cut nails in a red barn nearby, back of the parsonage. They charged the guns to the muzzle with nails and created panic among the British troops." (Gilman, pp. 33-34.) Truth or fiction, it adds to the horror of the carnage inflicted on soldiers whether by cannon balls, grapeshot or nails.

9) The Battle of Monmouth Courthouse was the last major battle fought in the Northern colonies. It was also the longest battle of the war and the largest artillery duel. Washington congratulated the army for "the victory obtained over the arms of his Britannic Majesty yesterday and thanks most sincerely the gallant officers and men who distinguished themselves upon the occasion." (Chernow, p. 344.)

General Knox wrote Lucy on June 29th:

"I have had several officers killed and wounded. My brave lads behaved with their usual intrepidity, and the army gave the corps of artillery their full proportion of the glory of the day.

Indeed upon the whole, it is very splendid. The capital army of Britain defeated and obliged to retreat before the Americans, whom they despised so much! I cannot ascertain either our or the enemy's losses, but I really think they have lost three times the number we have. . . . The Britons confess they have never received so severe a check." (Drake, pp. 57-58.)

Chernow puts American casualties at 362 killed, wounded or missing with the British suffering losses of between 380 to 500. (Chernow, p. 344.) Savas and Dameron state that the Americans suffered 72 killed, 161 wounded and 137 missing, including 37 dying from heat stroke. However, they note that many authorities believe the British casualties were higher - 1,200 total with 400 German deserters who surrendered in Philadelphia one week later. (Savas and Dameron, p. 177.)

General Charles Lee's conduct at the Battle of Monmouth Courthouse led to his court-martial and the end of his military career. He was charged with: 1) disobedience of orders in not attacking the enemy on June 28th; 2) misbehavior before the enemy by making an unnecessary, disorderly, and shameful retreat, and 3) disrespect to the Commander-in-Chief by sending him two insulting letters. On August 11, 1778, he was found guilty of all three charges, although the Court modified the second charge to having made an unnecessary but not shameful retreat, and disorderly only in a few instances. He was sentenced to be suspended from the army for a year. (Fleming, pp. 329-330; Savas and Dameron, p. 177.)

Most historians cite Lee's lack of planning with his subordinate officers, failure to ascertain the terrain and a breakdown in command of the different segments under his control for the retreat from the battlefield. A contrary view is offered by Mark Edward Lender and Garry Wheeler Stone in Fatal Sunday - George Washington, the Monmouth Campaign and the Politics of Battle. The authors argue Charles Lee had a difficult assignment. "He had to lead a vanguard of some 3,500 to 4,000 men of mixed commands, led by officers he didn't know, into terrain he didn't know, against an enemy whose strength and intentions were unknown. He had to do this in the face of conflicting intelligence reports and without adequate cavalry or other scouting capabilities.

Nevertheless Lee executed a nearly perfect movement to contact, quickly assessed the enemy situation, and formulated a reasonable plan to cut off what he thought was a relatively small British rear guard. It would have been exactly the limited blow and victory [George] Washington had in mind. When faced with an overwhelming British counter-attack, and an unauthorized retreat by a sizable part of his command, Lee pulled back in fairly good order, looking for a place to make a stand until Washington brought up the main army." Their conclusion is that all in all, Lee fought a good battle at Monmouth.

The Battle of Monmouth Courthouse also gave rise to the legend of Molly Pitcher. The wife of one of the soldiers or gunners, most probably Mary Ludwig Hays (or Hayes) carried water either for the thirsty soldiers or for swabbing a cannon. "Molly" was an affectionate name used by soldiers for women and calling "Molly! Pitcher!" may have been a cry for water. Private Martin wrote he witnessed a woman manning a gun along with her husband, and nonchalantly continuing to do so, after a British cannon ball passed between her legs taking away the lower part of her petticoat. (Allen, p. 53; Savas and Dameron, pp. 177-178; Fleming, p. 321; Martin, pp. 132-133.) Gilman states she was received that evening by Washington himself and made an honorary Sergeant the following day. (Gilman, p. 35.) The Blog, Boston 1775 traces the evolution of the story with some versions having Washington himself giving her the rank of Lieutenant. (Boston 1775, August 27, 2016.) The same Blog also reports a Mary "Moll" Pitcher of Lynn, Massachusetts who was a fortune teller and rumored to be a "witch," although she was never accused and tried as such. (Boston, 1775, August 31, September 1, 2016.) Obviously, the "Molly Pitcher" of Lynn was not the same woman who participated in the Battle of Monmouth Courthouse. For an account of the evolution of the legend of Molly Pitcher, see "Molly Pitcher and Captain Molly," by Ray Raphael, Journal of the American Revolution, Volume 1, pp. 138-140.)

Chapter 10 – In Liberated Philadelphia

1) The last British troops left Philadelphia on June 18th. American light horse cavalry arrived in Philadelphia on June 19th, followed by a regiment of infantry. The Battle of Monmouth Courthouse, described

in Chapter 9 took place on June 28th. Elisabeth's attendance for tea at the Shippens occurs a few days before the battle. I have chosen to describe the battle in the preceding Chapter for purposes of momentum and action.

2) Washington gave Arnold direct orders to provide "'security to individuals of every class and description' regardless of loyalties." Arnold intended to do this by using martial law. Washington also gave Arnold the order to "prevent the removal, transfer or sale of any goods, wares or merchandize, in possession of the inhabitants of the city. (Wells, Cody, "Philadelphia and the Fate of General Benedict Arnold," Armstrong Undergraduate Journal of History, 4, no. 2 (Nov. 2014.) It was Washington's intention to prevent Loyalists or smugglers from moving supplies to New York City, critical for the newly arrived troops and hordes of displaced Loyalists from Philadelphia.

3) The comment about the drabness of the patriotic Whig ladies is attributable to Peggy Shippen's friend, Becky Franks, who referred to their "drab homespun dresses, crudely nailed leather shoes, and dull entertainments." (Stuart, p. 44.)

Rebecca (Becky) Franks was the daughter of a wealthy Jewish merchant, David Franks, and Margaret Evans who was Episcopalian. Her parents were Loyalists and entertained British officers at their home in Philadelphia. Rebecca herself was part of Peggy Shippen's group of friends and attended many of the dinners, balls, concerts and plays to which the young ladies were invited by British officers. (North, Wedge and Freeman, pp. 119-120.)

4) Major John Andre was not only an artist and produced silhouettes, he actually wrote Peggy Chew a farewell poem:

If at the close of war and strife
My destiny once more
Should in the varied paths of life
Conduct me to this shore:
Should British banners guard the land

And factions be restrained;
And Cliveden's mansion peaceful stand
No more with blood be stained—
Say! Wilt thou receive again
And welcome to thy sight,
The youth who bids with stifled pain
His sad farewell tonight?
(Fleming, p. 332.)

5) On July 21st, three days after the American troops came to Philadelphia, Grace Galloway was visited by five authorized agents of the new administration. They "took an inventory of everything even to broken China & empty bottles. . . they told Me they must advertise the house I told them they must do as they pleased but till it was decided by a Court, I wou'd not go out Unless by the force of a bayonet but when I knew who had a right to it I should know how to act. . ." (North, Wedge and Freeman, p. 124.)

Grace Galloway was forcibly evicted from her home on August 20th, and never regained her inheritance. She was helped by Quakers but to no avail. Her property was sold at auction and she died "three years later, impoverished, bitter and lonely." (North, Wedge and Freeman, p. 126.)

6) Betsy Franks referred to the convention of the times relating to a young lady's obligation at balls:

"No loss for partners, even I am engaged to seven different gentlemen for you must know 'tis a fix'd rule never to dance but two dances at a time with the same person." (North, Wedge and Freeman, p. 120.)

7) Unlike other military men of prominence, Knox maintained a high moral standard when it came to refraining from profiting from his position. In a letter to his brother, after explaining he had visited Philadelphia to better regulate the ordinance department, he commented:

"Besides the satisfaction of having the business of the public done better, the only advantage that will result to me will be some pay expressing for the management of the ordnance department in the field. I undoubtedly might have first stipulated for some pecuniary advantages for myself; but I know not how it is, I do not approve of money obtained in the public service; it does not appear to me, in a war like ours, to be right, and I cannot bring myself to think differently, although poverty may be the consequence." (Drake, p. 60.)

8) General Knox's comments are taken directly from his letter to his brother from Camp Brunswick, dated July 8, 1778. His exact words are:

"The effects of the Battle of Monmouth will be great and lasting. It will convince the enemy and the world that nothing but a good constitution is wanting to render our army equal to any in the world." (Drake, p. 59.)

Part Three- A Deadly Game of Cat and Mouse

Chapter 11 – Providence and Privateering

1) George Washington observed, "It is not a little pleasing, nor less wonderful to contemplate that, after two years Manoeuvring . . . both Armies are brought back to the very point they set out from." (Martin, p. 134)

Private Martin recounted the march from King's Ferry to Tarrytown and down to White Plains. Then, he and others who had been in the Battle of White Plains in 1776 visited the battlefield.

"We saw a number of the graves of those who fell in that battle. Some of the bodies had ben so slightly buried that the dogs or hogs, or both, had dug them out of the ground. The skulls and other bones and hair were scattered about the place. Here were Hessian skulls as thick as a bombshell. Poor fellows! They were left unburied in a foreign land. . . . But they should have kept at home; we should then never had gone after them to kill them in their own country. But the reader will say, they were forced to come and be killed here, forced by their rulers who have absolute power of life and death over their subjects. Well then, reader, bless a kind Providence that has made such a distinction between your condition and theirs. And be careful, too, that you do not allow yourself ever to be brought to such an abject, servile and debased condition." (Martin, pp. 134-135.)

2) General Varnum's Brigade, which included the 2nd Rhode Island Regiment, left White Plains around July 22nd and arrived between July 31 and August 2nd. (Popek, p. 212.) The plan was, together with the newly arrived French fleet and 4,000 French soldiers, to besiege the British in Newport. The neighboring states of Massachusetts and Connecticut sent infantry regiments for six weeks service. (Popek, p. 212.) There is no evidence that the Rhode Island troops paraded through Providence and were given home leave prior to taking up siege positions on Aquidneck Island.

3) It was the French navy commanders who persuaded Count d'Estaing to withdraw to Boston for refitting following damage from the storm and the encounter with the British Navy. D'Estaing's own flagship lost all three masts and was heavily damaged. Lafayette argued, to no avail, for the French to remain and coordinate the planned attack against the British in Newport. Once the French ships with the troops aboard left, many of the New England Militias deserted General Sullivan's army and went home. (Popek, p. 223.) So many of the milita left, Sullivan's army was reduced by almost half. (Savas and Dameron, p. 185.)

4) Colonel Angell wrote in his diary for August 27th that he lost one Ensign and "14 men taken prisoners by British troops as they was a Setting their sentries the Ensign was John Viol." (Field, Edward, Diary of Colonel Israel Angell Commanding the Second Rhode Island Continental Regiment During the American Revolution, 1778-1781, p. 6.; Popek, p. 223.)

5) General Sullivan gave the order for the Army to retreat to Butts Hill Fort on the night of August 28, 1778. When the British discovered the Americans had abandoned their siege lines on the morning of August 29th, they formed two detachments, one to go

up the East Road of the Island, and the other, composed of Hessians, to advance on the West Road. American light infantry impeded their progress by a "masterful fighting withdrawal, firing behind stone walls, where available." (Popek, p. 224.)

6) This description of an officer being blown to bloody pieces by stepping in front of a cannon as it fired is not gratuitous gore, invented by the author. Colonel Angell, with his unusual spelling, capitalization and punctuation, described such an incident that occurred on August 30th:

"Lt. Arnold of the artillery was killed accidentally as he had fired his Piece Stept off to see where the Shot Struck and Steping before the mussel of another Gun as the officer gave the word fire the ball went through his body blo'd him too peaces his Body hung togeather by only the Skin of his belly, one Arm was blown Clear off." (Field, Angell Diary, pp. 10-11.)

7) After the successful crossing of the straits of the Sakonnet River to Tiverton, the remaining militias were dismissed and the regular army regiments took up defensive positions. General Varnum's Brigade, of which the Second Rhode Island Regiment was a part, marched to Bristol and Warren. (Popek, p. 236.) I have given the Regiment home leave in Providence before taking up such positions. General Sullivan ultimately went into winter quarters in Providence, while the British maintained control of the strategic harbor of Newport and sent an additional 4,000 troops as reinforcements. (Savas and Dameron, p. 188.)

The casualty reports vary but generally the British lost 38 killed, 210 wounded and 12 missing; the Americans 30 killed, 137 wounded and 44 missing.

The main casualty of the battle was the loss of trust between the Americans and the newly arrived French forces. General Sullivan claimed the French had left his men stranded on the Island and he and General Greene wrote a letter to d'Estaing "accusing him of craven betrayal." (Chernow, p. 348.) To smooth the ruffled feathers of the alliance, John Hancock held a banquet at his Beacon Hill home in

Boston for the French Vice Admiral and presented him with a portrait of George Washington. "I never saw a man so glad at possessing his sweetheart's picture, as the admiral was to receive yours," was how Lafayette reported it. (Chernow, p. 349.)

American troops were not impressed by the French soldiers in their white uniforms and high-heeled shoes. The French returned the disdain, particularly toward the militias who one officer described as "a laughable spectacle, . . . mounted on bad nags and look[ing] like a flock of ducks in cross belts." (Chernow, p, 349.)

Most accounts of the battle report that black troops from Rhode Island (the First Regiment) played a prominent role in repulsing the Hessian attacks. (Samos and Dameron, p. 187.) A publication of the Rhode Island Historical Society states that the 202 men of the First Rhode Island Regiment were praised for their "desperate valor" in anchoring the right flank of the American army. (Rhode Island History, Volume 62, # 3, Fall, 2004, Conley, Patrick T., The Battle of Rhode Island, 29 August, 1778 - A Victory for the Patriots, p. 58.) Popek, on the other hand, based on eye witness accounts of the battle and an exhaustive review of Regimental Muster and Pay Rolls, pension records and casualty reports, concludes that the First Regiment (Black Regiment) was not in the thick of the battle. The "deeds of desperate valor," was a legend created by an abolitionist historian at Brown University." (Popek, pp. 235-236.)

Whatever the truth is of the First Regiment's role in the Battle of Rhode Island, it is ironic that the "only New England Continental Regiments at the Battle of Rhode Island that were not integrated were the First and Second Rhode Island Regiments. . . . [A] few of the veteran Massachusetts and Connecticut Continental Line soldiers . . . were men of color." (Popek, p. 235.)

8) According to the 1790 Census, New Jersey had 11,423 slaves or 6.2% of the State's total population. (Historical Census Browser, 1790 Census.) Bergen County was the largest slave-holding county in the State. Slaves were generally used in agriculture but also worked in shipyards and ports.

New Jersey was the last Northern State to abolish slavery, passing a law in 1804 that only provided for gradual abolition. Not until 1846 did New Jersey officially abolish slavery almost entirely, but qualified it by stating that slaves born before the law was passed were considered indentured servants apprenticed for life. It was only with the passage of the Thirteenth Amendment to the U.S. Constitution in 1865 that slavery was finally ended in New Jersey.

9) British ships frequently took shelter from the weather within the arm of Sandy Hook, before continuing on to Staten Island and New York harbor. Daring raids by American privateers on ships at Sandy Hook, as well as in the waters around New York ,were fairly common. This one by Captains Gradon and Holmes, while fictitious is based upon facts drawn from actual attacks, as described in "The Whaleboat Wars of the Revolution -The New Jersey whaleboat men who braved the might of the Royal Navy to carry the war to the enemy," from WHAT MANNER OF MEN, Cook, Fred J. pp. 278-288, and "The Whale-Boat Men of Long Island Sound," Kuhl, Jackson, Journal of the American Revolution, November 1, 2013.

Chapter 12 – Ambush and Betrayal

1) It was extremely difficult to be even politically moderate as many Pennsylvania Quakers were. The general perception among both Patriots and Tories was that Quakers were not to be trusted, although almost 1,000 Quakers in Pennsylvania were disowned for taking up arms to support the patriotic cause.

The Quaker poet, Hannah Griffitts characterized the disaster of the war as the "mean Distinctions times have made," and broke "each sacred Tye, each Social Band/and in affliction plunge the parent Land." (Wulf, Karen, "Despise the mean Distinctions [these] Times Have Made": The Complexity of Patriotism and Quaker Loyalism in One Pennsylvania Family."

2) Elizabeth Drinker, in her diary, recounted the arrest, trial and hanging of two of her Quaker neighbors, Abraham Carlisle and John Roberts, the former being tried and convicted of high treason on September 25, 1778, and the latter on October 2, 1778. Both were

hanged on the Philadelphia Commons on November 4th. Drinker visited the Carlisle family and noted the "poor afflicted widdows, are wonderfully upheld and supported, under their very great trial - they have many simpathizing Friends." (North, Wedge and Freeman, pp. 123-124.)

The historian Thomas Fleming renders a harsh judgment of the civil administration of Philadelphia. Of the eighty-seven indictments obtained by prosecutor Joseph Reed, acting on behalf of the radical State government, the city's judges dismissed fifty-seven of them. Of the remaining thirty cases of alleged high treason, Reed was able to obtain convictions of only Abraham Carlisle and John Roberts, both Quakers. In Roberts's case, the verdict was "more egregious." Roberts, a miller, "who had concealed the journals of the Continental Congress when they were given to him by panic-stricken Congressman James Lovell, . . . was sentenced to death for making 'verbal utterances' against the state government, something four-fifths of the citizens of Pennsylvania did regularly." (Fleming, pp. 333-334.)

Pleas for clemency to the Supreme Executive Council of Pennsylvania, including "forty state militia officers, and a thousand other Philadelphians, including the judge and jury that convicted Roberts," went unheeded. (Fleming, p. 334.) "Conspicuous by his absence among these pleaders for mercy was Congressman Lovell, who could have made a powerful statement on Roberts's behalf by testifying to the way he had protected the vital journals of Congress until they were recovered by General Washington. [He] chose to remain silent, rather than reveal his pusillanimous conduct. . .Roberts was hung before a crowd that included [his] weeping wife and nine children." (Fleming, p 334.)

3) This fictitious event of the British slaughter of American dragoons is based on an actual attack that occurred on September 27, 1778 at the farm of Cornelius Blauvelt, near Old Tappan, New Jersey, about six miles north of Paramus. The British Light Infantry, led by three Tory guides, surprised Colonel Baylor's 3rd Light Dragoons while they slept and slaughtered them with bayonets. The soldiers' flints and charges from the firelocks of their muskets had

been intentionally removed in order to prevent accidentally alerting the sleeping Americans, and to enable the British to identify any muzzle flash as that coming from the enemy. Numerous eye-witness accounts substantiate the claim that the British bayonetted dragoons who had surrendered and asked for quarter, as well as the execution of Americans being held prisoner after being captured. The British also stripped the bodies of the dead Americans. (Braisted, pp. 100-108.)

4) In addition to lectures in tactics and gunnery, there were "work huts for those employed in the laboratory." (Brooks, Noah, Henry Knox - A Soldier of the Revolution, p. 130.)

Chapter 13 – Confidences in New York and Secrets at Pluckemin

1) General Washington returned to Middlebrook in February 1779 after six weeks in Philadelphia and after the anniversary date of the French alliance. The celebration with Washington in attendance was held on February 18th and Knox wrote it "was a most genteel entertainment given by self and officers." (Drake, p. 60; Chernow, p. 353.)

Peggy Shippen, who married General Benedict Arnold later in April of that year, did not accompany him when he visited Middlebrook in early February, before the celebration. He was on his way to upstate New York where he had been offered a "vast estate at the southern tip of Lake Champlain." Instead, against the advice of senior officers at Middlebrook, he returned to Philadelphia to face the charges hastily filed against him by Joseph Reed, then President of the Pennsylvania Supreme Executive Council. (Philbrick, Nathaniel, Smithsonian Magazine, May 2016 - Why Benedict Arnold Turned Traitor Against the American Revolution.) He also probably returned because he was deeply in love with Peggy Shippen, writing her from Middlebrook, "Six days absence without hearing from my Dear Peggy is intolerable. Heavens! What must I have suffered had I continued on my journey- the loss of happiness for a few dirty acres [the estate offered in New York]. I can almost bless the villainous … men who oblige me to return." (Philbrick, Smithsonian, May 2016.)

2) Some of the eight charges Reed filed against Arnold were petty, such as "being ungracious to a militiaman and preferring loyalists to patriots," and some were more substantive such as "illegally purchasing goods upon his arrival in Philadelphia." (Philbrick, Smithsonian, May 2016.)

Knox wrote to his brother William on February 13, 1779, after Arnold's visit to Middlebrook:

". . .You will see in the papers some highly colored charges against General Arnold, by the State of Pennsylvania. I shall be exceedingly mistaken if one of them can be proven. He has returned to Philadelphia, and will, I hope, be able to vindicate himself from the aspersions of his enemies. (Drake, p. 60.)

3) Black markets for all manner of goods developed in Philadelphia, after the American Army returned. Arnold profited from selling goods confiscated from Loyalists and in the case of the Charming Nancy purchasing goods from the ship and issuing a pass to Robert Shewell, a Philadelphia merchant and owner, for the ship to leave Philadelphia and sell the goods elsewhere, that is, in New York City. Arnold stood to personally gain by issuing the pass and the scandal angered other Philadelphia merchants who were not allowed to transport their goods to be sold to Tories and the British Army. (Wells, "Philadelphia and the Fate of General Arnold.")

4) To satisfy Judge Shippen's condition that he had the financial means to take care of his daughter, in March 1779 Arnold took out a loan of 12,000 pounds and bought Mount Pleasant, a 96 acre estate with a mansion overlooking the Schuylkill. (Philbrick, Smithsonian, May 2016.) He and Peggy were married on April 8, 1779.

5) General Washington did indeed, after the socially obligatory dance with the hostess "the obese Lucy Knox. . . danced all evening with Caty Greene. Her husband wrote "His Excellency and Mrs. Greene danced upwards of three hours without once sitting down." (Chernow, p. 354.)

6) There is a detailed description of the Academy at Pluckemin and the celebration of the anniversary of the alliance with France in "The Great Anniversary in Pluckemin," by John W. Barber and Henry Howe, Historical Collections of the State of New Jersey, pp. 441-442.)

After noting that the event was attended by General Washington and other officers, Mrs. Washington, Mrs. Knox and Mrs. Greene as well as other ladies and gentlemen, they describe the thirteen gun salute, followed by an elegant dinner in the Academy. "The room was spacious, and the tables very prettily disposed both as to prospect and convenience. . . In the evening was exhibited a very fine set of fireworks." Afterwards, "the company returned to the academy, and concluded the celebration by a very splendid ball."

Of the Academy's thirteen arches, the ninth one depicted the battle of Saratoga. I have added to the painting a depiction of General Arnold engaged in that battle.

Knox described the event as "the first of the kind ever exhibited in this State at least. We had about seventy ladies, all of the first ton in the State and between three and four hundred gentlemen. We danced all night - an elegant room." (Drake, pp. 60-61.) Knox's use of the word "ton" is French for breeding or manners. (Chernow, p. 354.)

Chapter 14 – Freedom for All

1) Titus Cornelius or Colonel Tye was a feared Loyalist guerrilla leader in southern New Jersey, primarily in Monmouth County. He was born a slave and owned by a Quaker, John Corlies (or Corlis), who contrary to Quaker practice, did not free him when he became 21. He ran away and joined the British. Corlies advertised in newspapers, offering a reward of Three Pounds. In that advertisement, Titus was described as:

". . . about 21 years of age, not very black, near 6 feet high; had on a grey homespun coat, brown breeches, blue and white stockings."

Having been raised in Monmouth County, Colonel Tye not only knew the terrain and the numerous rivers and inlets, but also who were Rebel sympathizers. Tye's Black Brigade raided former masters and known slave-holding Rebels and their sympathizers.

Tye's background, as he describes it to Adam Cooper, is accurate. He did capture an American Captain at the Battle of Monmouth Courthouse but his prisoner was Captain Elisha Shepard of the Monmouth Militia and not a Captain from Virginia.

The guerrilla war in New Jersey was brutal on both sides. Loyalist farms and property were confiscated by Patriots, and known Tories were hung first as part of vigilante justice and then under martial law as declared by Governor William Livingston.

The Royal Governor of New Jersey, William Franklin, the Loyalist son of founding father Benjamin Franklin, authorized attacks on Patriot leaders. Tye's Black Brigade captured prominent Militia leaders, killed John Russell, a Rebel commander responsible for raids on British-held Staten Island, captured Major James Mott of the Monmouth Militia and raided the home of Captain Joshua Huddy, who was known for his swift execution of captured Loyalists. That raid took place on September 1, 1780 and Tye was shot in the wrist. He died, probably of tetanus and gangrene, a few weeks later. (Adelberg, Michael, S., The American Revolution in Monmouth County -The Theater of Spoil and Destruction, pp. 89-90.)

Chapter 15 – Raids on Paulus Hook and Long Island

1) Julia Knox, the second daughter of General and Lucy Knox, died on July 2, 1779 at Pluckemin. Two weeks after her death, General Greene wrote that Mrs. Knox "bore the loss of her daughter 'with a degree of fortitude that marks a phylosophick [philosophic] temper.'" (Loane, p. 83.)General Washington sent Lucy a note of condolence and "an anonymous friend sent her a copy of 'Elegiac Lines, Inscrib'd to Mrs. Knox, occasioned on the death of her Infant Daughter, who deceas'd near Pluckemin, N. Jersey, July 2d, 1779.'" (Brooks, p. 134.)

2) Two websites for the Jacobus Vanderveer House, located in Bedminster, New Jersey both state that the local Dutch Reformed Church refused to allow Julia Knox to be buried in their cemetery because the Knoxes were Congregationalists. Vanderveer's insane daughter (who I have fictitiously characterized as having seizures) had

previously been refused burial in the cemetery. This is supported by a reference in "New Jersey - A Guide to Its Present and the Past," on page 448, to the Vanderveer's own daughter being refused burial in the cemetery because "she was possessed by the devil."

Vanderveer's daughter and Julia Knox were buried on Vanderveer property, which later was acquired by the Church so that their gravestones came within the boundaries of what is now the Bedminster Reformed Church Cemetery.

3) One website reports that Jacobus Vanderveer took General Knox "by the hand and led him to the grave of his daughter saying, 'Gen'ral, this is my ground, bury your child here."

That same site reports that the gravestone reads: "Under this stone are deposited the remains of Julia Knox, an infant who died the second of July, 1779. She was the second daughter of Henry and Lucy Knox, of Boston, in New England." The inscription is confirmed in "Historic Houses of New Jersey," by Weymer, Jay Mills, p. 82.

4) On August 18, 1779 a force of Americans, led by Major "Light Horse" Harry Lee attacked Paulus Hook, now Jersey City. The fort was held by New Jersey Tory Volunteers led by Colonel Abraham Van Buskirk and two hundred or so British regulars. Lee's troops started at New Bridge, marched fourteen miles through dense forest and the final distance through marshes and a rising tide, to attack the fort around three a.m. Unknown to Lee, Van Buskirk had earlier led a force of about one hundred and thirty volunteers out from the fort to engage in raids in the surrounding countryside. The Americans' surprise attack enabled them to capture Paulus Hook, suffering two killed and three wounded. They took one hundred and fifty-nine prisoners and killed or wounded thirty British soldiers. The remainder of the garrison, including about twenty- six Hessians, retreated to a smaller inner redoubt and kept up a steady defensive fire. Lee, together with the prisoners, retreated back the way they had come. While his men's weapons were useless because their powder was wet, he was joined by part of his original column which had become lost, and whose powder was dry, and further on by two hundred or so fresh troops who acted

as his rear guard. Toward the end of the march, Van Buskirk and other Tories attacked the Americans but were beaten back. Lee arrived victorious in New Bridge around one p.m. August 19th.

Coincidentally, Paulus Hook was the last British military post in New Jersey at the time of the Treaty of Paris. It was evacuated on November 22,1783, two days before the British sailed out of New York harbor for good. (Petrocci, Charles A. "The Battle of Paulus Hook," Military History, August 2000.)

5) Sometime following the British evacuation of Philadelphia, the 16th Light Dragoons disbanded, its officers returned to England and the men and horses remaining were transferred to the 17th Light Dragoons. (McBurney, Christian, "Abductions in the American Revolution - Attempts to Kidnap George Washington, Benedict Arnold and Other Military and Civilian Leaders," p. 88.)

6) Ann Bates continued her remarkable career as a British spy. Together with her husband, an armorer in the Civil Branch of the Royal Artillery Regiment, she accompanied the army to New York City. She was introduced to Major Duncan Drummond, an aide-de-camp to General Clinton, responsible for gathering intelligence about the American army. She crossed the lines and frequently entered the American camp, selling ribbon, thread, needles, combs and like goods, while determining the number of soldiers and cannons, including the "weight of Ball of each Cannon" in the different Companies, Regiments and Brigades. (Braisted, pp. 36-40.)

7) In response to raids by the King's Militia Volunteers and other Loyalist units on prominent Rebel militia leaders in Connecticut, the Connecticut militia crossed the Long Island Sound in whaleboats, seeking to kidnap notorious Tories, either military or civilian. One such raid took place on November 4, 1779. About thirty men landed on Long Island, hid all day and marched almost fifty-two miles in two nights, to kidnap Judge Thomas Jones. The infamous Tory Judge was hosting a dinner party. The raiders broke in, grabbed the Judge and his nephew and escaped with their captives, crossing the Sound again in their whaleboats to Connecticut. Thomas was exchanged

for a Connecticut General, Gold Selleck Sillman, commander of the Connecticut Coastal Militia, on April 27, 1780. (McBurney pp. 80-82.)

8) Captain John Montresor resigned his commission in March 1779 and returned to England. The island he owned and now called Randall's Island was confiscated by the Americans after the British left New York City. Ironically, it was John Montresor who was responsible for stealing the head of King George's statue, torn down by a large crowd at Bowling Green on July 9, 1776. When the British defeated Washington's army in Brooklyn and occupied New York City, Montresor sent men to Moore's Tavern where it had been buried, resurrected the disfigured head of the King and "sent the Head by the Lady Gage to Lord Townshend in order to convince them at home [London] of the Infamous Disposition of the Ungrateful people of this distressed Country." It in fact had reached the Townshends. When the former Royal Governor of Massachusetts visited in November 1777, "Lady Townshend asked me if I had a mind to see an instance of American loyalty? And going to the sopha, uncovered a large gilt head. . .that of the King. . .The nose is wounded and defaced, but the gilding remains fair; and as it was, it was well executed, it retains a striking likeness."

(Ruppert, Bob, Journal of the American Revolution, September 8, 2014,"The Statue of George III".)

Chapter 16 – With the Black Brigade

1) From 1776 until the end of the war, Monmouth County itself was racked by communal violence. Local patriotic militias, aided by Continentals, clashed with local Tories and the Loyalist New Jersey Volunteers. Whigs confiscated Loyalist estates and sold them at auction. Raids into the County were conducted from the Loyalist and British base on Sandy Hook and Staten Island.

Retaliators were members of the Association for Retaliation, a Whig organization in Monmouth County, formed in the summer of 1780.

It took revenge on behalf of its members for any harm or plundering by Loyalist militias or raiders. (Adelberg, Michael pp. 16-22.)

2) This fictional account of the raid on Shrewsbury is a combination of two actual raids. The first, known as the Allen House Massacre, occurred in the summer of 1779. Allen House was a tavern in Shrewsbury and at the time about a dozen soldiers, either militia or Continentals, were stationed there to monitor the movements of Tories. They were attacked by a band of Loyalists (not Colonel Tye's Black Brigade) who came up a branch of the South Shrewsbury River, landed near the Episcopal Church and surprised the Americans by a bayonet attack. The Tories killed three, took nine soldiers prisoner and escaped.The second raid that occurred on July 20, 1779 was conducted by Colonel Tye on Joseph Halstead's Tavern, (the same Allen House). The New Jersey Gazette (a Whig newspaper) reported: "About fifty Negroes and refugees landed at Shrewsbury, and plundered the inhabitants of nearly eighty head of cattle, about 20 horses and a quantity of wearing apparel and household furniture. They also took William Brindley and Elihu Cook, two of the inhabitants." (Adelberg, p. 85.) The word "refugees" applies to Tories who had fled Rebel violence. They probably were white men.

3) Colonel Israel Angell's Diary records that on September 12, 1780, "a Soldier in Col. Stewarts Battalion was hanged this day on the Grand Parade for Plundering the Inhabitants agreable to the Sentence of a Gen. Court Martial." (Field, Angell Diary, p. 115-116.)

Edward Field, the Historian of the Rhode Island Society of the Sons of the American Revolution who transcribed the original diary and added notes, quotes General Washington's order as follows: "'The Gen'l again exhorts officers and soldiers of every rank to pay the closest attention to the conduct of their men and to use every precaution to prevent the soldiers from rambling and committing such outrages, the subject of daily complaint and representation to him. It is highly incumbent on them to do this, to prevent the consequences which will follow as he is determined to show no favor to soldiers who are convicted of these pernicious and disgraceful offenses.' – Rev. Order of Gen. Washington." (Field, Angell Diary, p. 116.)

4) According to the National Park Service, approximately 10,000 soldiers and officers were housed in 1,200 huts constructed at Jockey Hollow south of Morristown. They were laid out eight huts in a row, three or four deep, each hut approximately fourteen feet wide and sixteen feet long. There was a chimney at one end and a door at the other. Twelve soldiers per hut slept on wooden plank bunk beds. (Spending the Winter at Jockey Hollow, The History Girl.)

5) It is not clear where General and Mrs. Knox stayed during the winter of 1779-1780 at Morristown. In "Following the Drum," the location is described as a "farm near camp." Three of Knox's biographers, Mark Puls, Noah Brooks and North Callahan are all silent on the location of the place where the General and his family stayed. Drake does not quote any letter or entry by Knox in his diary detailing the Morristown location. The Morristown County Tourist Bureau, in describing "The Willows" which was the former mansion of Paul Revere's grandson, states that it is "locally believed to have been the home of General Henry Knox during the Continental Army's encampment of 1779-1780." I have described the Wick Home, a salt-box house where Major General Arthur St. Clair lived during the winter of 1779-1780, as a stand-in for the farmhouse occupied by General Knox and his family, Will and Elisabeth Stoner and Samuel and Mercy Hadley.

6) General Washington's headquarters, and where he resided with Martha, their eighteen servants and his staff of five (including Colonel Alexander Hamilton) was at the Ford Mansion just outside Morristown, about three miles away from the Army's main encampment at Jockey Hollow. Theodosia Ford, the widow of Colonel Jacob Ford, Jr. (and mother of my fictitious character, Mercy Hadley), her servants and four children lived in her mansion as well. The General had the use of "two rooms on the first floor, and all the upper floor, kitchen, cellar,

and stable, Mrs. Ford and her family occupying the few remaining rooms." (National Park Service, Morristown National Historical Park.)

7) In February 1780, General Knyphausen was the interim commander in chief of the British forces in New York City (while General Clinton was supervising the assault on Charleston, South Carolina). The bitter winter froze the Hudson and the waters of Newark Bay, enabling British cavalry and troops to cross the ice into New Jersey. Knyphausen authorized a raid to kidnap General Washington, and in a report to General Clinton stated: "General Washington having taken up his quarters at a distance from his army, under the protection of a small corps of infantry, it appeared practicable to surprise that body with cavalry and to penetrate the neighborhood of Morristown." (McBurney, p. 87.)

The overall plan was to stage a series of diversionary attacks at Elizabethtown, Woodbridge and Rahway while the raiding party of the 17th Light Dragoons, accompanied by cavalry from the Queen's Rangers, moved on Morristown. The mission to grab Washington was originally scheduled for February 8, 1780 but, due to a snowstorm, was delayed until February 11th. Leaving Paulus Hook, the cavalry passed through Hackensack and made it another five or six miles towards Morristown. However, the roads were impassable due to the heavy snow of a few days earlier and "an uncommon fall of rain, . . . encrusting the top of the snow, cut the fetlocks of [the] horses, and rendered it absolutely impossible for [Captain Beckworth] to succeed." (McBurney, p. 93; Huggins, Benjamin, L., "Raid Across the Ice: The British Operation to Capture Washington," Journal of the American Revolution, Annual Volume, 2015, pp. 274-279. Huggins attributes the horses' difficulties to "a recent fall of sleet [that] had created a layer of ice that cut the horses' fetlocks.")

Colonel Tye's attempt to kidnap Washington is fictitious but not far-fetched, given his audacity as a guerrilla commander and his intimate knowledge of the terrain. There is no historical evidence that Native Americans were part of the Black Brigade or that Tye attempted to kidnap General Washington by equipping his band with snowshoes and travois.

Author's Notes and Acknowledgements

"Spies and Deserters" continues exploring the theme of invisible diversity, a phrase, suggested by my wife, to describe the role of blacks, women, Native Americans and even homosexuals in the American Revolution. They were all present during our War for Independence. Their roles simply have not been taught in our schools or acknowledged in most history books. Historical accuracy and certainly not any sense of political correctness compels me to include their stories.

Adam Cooper, who, the reader first met in "Cannons for the Cause," is a black free man in the Marblehead Mariners, perhaps the first integrated unit of the Continental Army. As Adam frequently is compelled to explain, he was born free and is not a freed man, that is, a slave who has been freed. Approximately five hundred of the 9,000 to 10,000 soldiers who suffered through the deadly winter at Valley Forge were African American, either free men like Adam, or slaves who gained their freedom by enlisting, or slaves who were permitted to serve by their masters in their stead, and were promised their freedom at the end of the war. For purposes of comparison, the 1790 census reported New Jersey had approximately 11,400 slaves or 6.2 % of its total population.

The First Rhode Island Regiment, consisted of more than four hundred black soldiers with white officers. They were recruited from both free men and slaves and participated in the battles of Monmouth Courthouse and Rhode Island. Ironically, the only segregated units at the Battle of Rhode Island were the First and Second Rhode Islanders. Other States' Regiments were integrated to some degree.

Sarah Pence, General Washington's cook at Valley Forge, is based on the real character of Hannah Mason, a slave lent by her master, Reverend John Mason of New York to General Washington. Washington in turn lent her services temporarily to the Marquis de Lafayette. After returning to work for Washington, Hannah was able to purchase her freedom and married Isaac Till, another of Washington's Valley Forge servants. After the war, she lived in Philadelphia to the ripe old age of 104, dying in 1824.

By creating Sarah as a young woman to whom Adam is attracted, I am able to explore the contradiction of a soldier fighting for freedom while being unable to court a slave cook because she is simply property, like a farm animal or a piece of furniture. "Fighting for freedom for whom?" Colonel Tye asks Adam who replies, freedom for all. What did blacks in the army think when they passed by farms and towns where slaves labored under the watchful eye of their masters? I have given Adam an almost uncontrollable anger, over Sarah's childhood on a southern plantation and her current plight as a slave, as he and she struggle to purchase her freedom.

The name of her master, Reverend Pence, was chosen at random from a list of colonial families and officers, long before Governor Pence was nominated to be and elected Vice-President. There is absolutely no political significance to the use of the Pence name.

Colonel Tye is another real character- a masterful guerrilla commander of the Black Brigade that terrorized Whigs in Monmouth County, as those supporting the Revolution in turn terrorized Loyalists and suspected supporters. Not much is known about him, other than through reports of the raids he conducted, freeing slaves, punishing their masters, and looting for the purpose of providing supplies to the British.

What is known is that he was not freed by his Quaker master as was the custom when he attained age 21. I have therefore provided him with a degree of righteous anger against all slaveholders and a mission to free as many slaves as possible. However, he recognizes the attitude of the time - educated whites, and in particular his British, class-conscious allies, regarded blacks as almost sub-human beings, barely brushed with a thin veneer of civilization.

Native Americans were simply savages, meaning they were characterized by their apparent savagery, although the brutality of the guerrilla war in New Jersey and elsewhere would lead one to conclude there was enough savagery to go around. Even the Marquis de Lafayette, who was honored by the Oneida, called them "scalping gentlemen." Their crucial role in saving Lafayette from being encircled and captured by General Howe outside Philadelphia has never been adequately recognized. If Lafayette had been captured it could have been a turning point in the war or, at least, severely tested the new alliance between France and the United States.

I have created two Native American characters, as members of Colonel Tye's Black Brigade. Neither have major speaking roles but they teach Tye's men how to make snowshoes for a crucial winter raid.

The role of women during the Revolution has also long been ignored. Sure, there is the myth of Molly Pitcher at the Battle of Monmouth Courthouse, courageously manning the cannon as her wounded husband lies nearby, or Betsy Ross dutifully designing the American flag. Women were spies on both sides. Ann Bates, to whom I give a fictional role as being employed by John Stoner, was an accomplished agent for the British. She frequently crossed through the lines and entered the American camps. With her knowledge of cannons and guns, she accurately reported on armaments as well as the disposition of Regiments to her British controllers. On one occasion, she even penetrated Washington's own headquarters.

Elisabeth Van Hooten is a fictional stand in for the many American women who passed information by secret codes and invisible messages in common everyday letters. Her friends among the upper class young ladies of Philadelphia, among them, Peggy Shippen, who later married Benedict Arnold, are examples of the beautiful young women who fraternized with the charming British Officers, their love of entertainment far outweighing their commitment, if at all, to the rebel cause.

Many women served as nurses at Continental Army hospitals where they tended to the sick and wounded and probably assisted the surgeons in operations, the most common being amputations. They were exposed to the diseases prevalent among the soldiers - typhus, typhoid, dysentery, and pneumonia. Mercy Hadley typifies one such nurse.

We know from the correspondence between Abigail Adams and her husband and others, that women were involved in politics. They also ran their husbands' businesses when they were away for long periods of time serving in the army. When the Pennsylvania State Government imprisoned more than twenty prominent Philadelphia Quaker men on questionable evidence, their wives not only tended to the businesses, but managed the households, cared for the children and petitioned for their release. It is a historical fact that four Quaker women visited General Washington to plead their case and then went on to York, Pennsylvania to do the same before the State Government.

Finally, Randy Shillet in "Conduct Unbecoming: Gays and Lesbians in the U.S. Military," presents convincing evidence that Baron Friedrich Wilhelm August von Steuben, the epitome of Prussian militarism, the man described by an eyewitness as personifying the God of War himself, was homosexual. Yet, from all the history books we have been assigned throughout our studies of the American Revolution, there is not a hint of this.

Today, it does not matter whether or not he was homosexual. What does matter is that had we been taught the diversity of those who contributed to our war for independence - blacks, Native Americans, women, homosexuals- we might have been more readily accepting of the current diversity in our society. These people were there from the beginning of the Revolution and the successful conclusion of the war is attributable, at least in part, to their participation and sacrifice.

The more I read about the American Revolution, the more I realize we are prisoners of our myths. Valley Forge is embedded in our collective memory as a place of severe deprivation, ragged unpaid soldiers freezing to death, dying of a wide variety of diseases and suffering from starvation. Approximately 2,000 soldiers out of a total force of around 9 to 10,000 died at Valley Forge, more than had been killed in all the Revolutionary War battles to date. Over 1,500 horses died. Their deaths required that the soldiers assume the role of beasts of burden, hauling firewood and supplies on sleds in the bitter cold.

Much of this happened, yet the winter of 1777-1778 was much milder than that of 1779-1780 when approximately twenty-eight snowstorms battered the army in its camp at Morristown. Many of the senior Generals' wives lived at Valley Forge, including Martha Washington, Lucy Knox, and Caty Greene, and amidst the deprivation there were dinners and entertainment.

Most Americans have no knowledge that ordinary soldiers also had the company of their spouses. In addition, there were the usual camp followers, women who "followed the drum," did the laundry and other such chores and were deemed to be of loose morals. There were at least four hundred women at Valley Forge, some wives and others simply camp followers. Heaven forbid that we should teach students that there were immoral women at the sacred site of Valley Forge. Or that the soldiers gambled, cursed and avoided Sabbath services.

If we are to understand our history, we need to adhere to the truth as much as possible and not some mythical heroic story of absolute purity of character, steadfast morals and noble deeds.

As with the preceding three novels in the series, I am once again indebted to my friends and family who read different iterations of the manuscript. My beloved wife, despite her aversion to battles and violence, slogged through the draft and offered many insightful and helpful suggestions. I am amazed that her excellent writing skills in developing policy papers can be transferred to critical, constructive comments about my novel.

My son, Marc, once again performed wonders in preparing the striking cover and formatting the text. The clean appearance of the book is entirely due to his efforts.

I continue to be indebted to my editor, Ben West, who has meticulously read for character development and plot consistency.

One of the joys of writing is receiving feedback from respected and dear friends. My law school classmate, Curtis M. Caton, not only fulfilled that role but voluntarily assumed the tedious task of providing editorial assistance. His sharp eye for consistency in spelling, capitalization, punctuation and spacing have relieved others of the irritation of having their reading experience spoiled by such mistakes.

It was a necessary but not thankless task because he has my complete admiration for his thoroughness and obviously my thanks in making "Spies and Deserters" a much smoother read.

Big Red is a stand-in for a magnificent horse of the same name owned by my friend Glen Baquet. Glen has been a constant source of knowledge about horses – their diet, diseases, personalities and behavior. I am thankful to him for assisting me in creating the noble character of Will Stoner's companion.

All remaining errors of fact, grammar or spelling are of course my sole responsibility.

My oldest grandson continues to be a model for little Lucy Knox, now three plus years in "Spies and Deserters." His language skills and development have enabled me to more accurately portray the younger daughter of General and Lucy Knox.

Finally, without ascribing any supernatural influences to the process of writing, sometimes, the characters do "tell" me how they should develop. I rarely take them down a wayward path and then scrap that version because it does not seem right. Rather, because the characters live within me, I intuitively recognize how they would react or feel. Over the first four novels, John Stoner evolved as so totally evil I feared that he would become too much of a caricature. However, every story needs a great villain and his stalking of Elisabeth while not knowing she is his brother's fiancé seemed too good an opportunity to miss. It also seemed natural to give him some redeeming quality and I chose an accidental act of courage. Of course, being true to his selfish, scheming personality he then uses his bravery to enhance his own position.

I cannot say where my characters will end up in the next volume or the final one. I hope that those of you who began with "Cannons for the Cause," will continue to enjoy the saga as it plays out.

Martin R. Ganzglass
Washington, D.C.
March 2017

Bibliography

The following are books, blogs or websites I have read for historical background. The blog, Boston 1775 as well as the Journal of the American Revolution, and its blog, All Things Liberty, continue to offer numerous, and to me invaluable, articles on a wide variety of Revolutionary War subjects. Collectively, they are like discovering a gold mine, the only problem being which veins to mine in incorporating events into the novel.

Since it is easy enough to search a book or article on line by author and title, I have omitted the customary reference to publisher and date of publication.

Adelberg, Michael, S.,
The American Revolution in Monmouth County-The Theater of Spoil and Destruction

Allen, Thomas, B.,
Remember Valley Forge- Patriots, Tories and Redcoats Tell Their Stories

Angell, Israel Colonel,
Diary of Colonel Israel Angell Commanding the Second Rhode Island Continental Regiment During the American Revolution, 1778-1781, Edward Field, Editor

Barber, John W., and Howe, Henry,
"The Great Anniversary in Pluckemin," Historical Collections of the State of New Jersey

Barbieri, Michael,
"The Worth of a Continental," Journal of the American Revolution, Annual Volume 2015

Benemann, Walter,
Male-Male Intimacy in Early America: Beyond Romantic Friendships

Bergen County Historical Society,
Friedrich Wilhelm von Steuben

Berkin, Carol,
Revolutionary Mothers- Women in the Struggle for America's Independence

Braisted, Todd W.,
Grand Forage 1778-The Battleground Around New York City,

Brooks, Noah,
Henry Knox- A Soldier of the Revolution

Burdick, Kim,
Fever, Journal of the American Revolution, Online Magazine, November 12, 2015

Chadwick, Bruce,
The First American Army

Chernow, Ron,
Washington- A Life

Cook Fred J.,
What Manner of Men

Conley, Patrick T.,
The Battle of Rhode Island, 29 August 1778-A Victory for the Patriots, Rhode Island History, Volume 62, # 3, Fall, 2004

Drake, Francis S.,
Life and Correspondence of Henry Knox

Fleming, Thomas,
Washington's Secret War- The Hidden History of Valley Forge

Gilman, Malcolm B, Col. M.D.,
Monmouth Road to Glory

Hackett Fischer, David,
Washington's Crossing

Historical Census Browser, 1790 Census

The History Girl,
Spending the Winter at Jockey Hollow

Huggins, Benjamin, L.,
"Raid Across the Ice: The British Operation to Capture Washington," Journal of the American Revolution, Annual Volume, 2015

Kuhl, Jackson,
"The Whale-Boat Men of Long Island Sound," Journal of the American Revolution, Online Magazine, November 1, 2013.

Lender, Mark Edward and Stone, Gary Wheeler,
Fatal Sunday- George Washington, the Monmouth Campaign and the Politics of Battle.

Loane, Nancy K.,
Following the Drum- Women at the Valley Forge Encampment

Loane, Nancy K.,
"An Elegant Dinner with General Washington at Valley Forge,"Journal of the American Revolution, Annual Volume 2015

Martin, Joseph Plumb,
Private Yankee Doodle- Being a Narrative of Some of the Adventures, Dangers and Sufferings of a Revolutionary Soldier, George Scheer, editor,

McBurney, Christian M.,
"Ann Bates: British Spy Extraordinaire," Journal of the American Revolution, Annual Volume 2016

McBurney, Christian M.,
Abductions in the American Revolution- Attempts to Kidnap George Washington, Benedict Arnold and Other Military and Civilian Leaders

McGuire, Thomas J.,
The Philadelphia Campaign- Germantown and the Roads to Valley Forge, Vol. II

McGready,Blake,
Abigail Hartman Rice, Revolutionary War Nurse, Journal of the American Revolution, Online Magazine, November 28, 2016

National Park Service,
Morristown National Historical Park

Nagy, John A.,
Spies in the Continental Capital

North, Louise V., Wedge, Janet M., Freeman, Landa M.,
In the Words of Women-The Revolutionary War and the Birth of the Nation, 1765-1799

Petrocci, Charles A.,
"The Battle of Paulus Hook," Military History, August 2000

Philbrick, Nathaniel,
"Why Benedict Arnold Turned Traitor Against the American Revolution" Smithsonian Magazine, May 2016

Popek, Daniel M.,
"They . . . fought bravely but were unfortunate:" The True Story of Rhode Island's 'Black Regiment' and the Failure of Segregation in Rhode Island's Continental Line, 1777-1783,

Raphael, Ray,
"Molly Pitcher and Captain Molly,"Journal of the American Revolution, Annual Volume 1

Ruppert, Bob,
"The Statue of George III,"Journal of the American Revolution, Online Magazine, September 8, 2014

Savas, Theodore P., and Dameron, David J.,
A Guide to the Battles of the American Revolution

Sawyer, William,
"The Oneida Nation in the American Revolution," National Park Service

Shilts, Randy,
Conduct Unbecoming: Gays and Lesbians in the U.S. Military

Smith, Alejandra,
"Oneida," George Washington's Mount Vernon

Stuart, Nancy Rubin,
Defiant Brides-The Untold Story of Two Revolutionary-Era Women and the Radical Men They Married

von Steuben, Baron Frederick Wilhelm Augustus,
Baron von Steuben's Revolutionary War Drill Manual (A Facsimile Reprint of the 1794 Edition)

Waldo, Albigence, Dr.,
Diary of a Surgeon at Valley Forge, 1777

Wells, Cody,
"Philadelphia and the Fate of General Benedict Arnold," Armstrong Undergraduate Journal of History, 4, no. 2 (Nov. 2014.)

Weymer, Jay Mills,
Historic Houses of New Jersey

Wulf, Karen,
Despise the Mean Distinctions [these] Times Have Made: The Complexity of Patriotism and Quaker Loyalism in One Pennsylvania Family

York County Heritage Trust,
The Philadelphia Stage and Beyond

The thrilling saga of our War for Independence continues with . . .

Treason and Triumph

They left the west side of the city in the predawn darkness and crossed the frozen ice of the lower Hudson and Newark Bay. The horses were skittish on the unfamiliar surface and the troopers struggled to keep their mounts under control. A strong wind blew from behind, billowing their newly issued red wool capes around their shoulders. Ahead, Paulus Hook and the Jersey shore were barely discernible. The only sounds were the wind, the occasional nervous whinny of a frightened animal and the clop of the horses' hooves. Two thin shadowy ribbons of cavalry, almost three hundred in number, spread out in long lines, parallel to the shore, a precaution although the ice had been tested and was thick enough to bear the weight of a twenty-four pounder. The troopers converged as they neared Paulus Hook. Their horses nimbly picked their way through the jumbled slabs of ice, randomly scattered by wind and tide into a frozen white breakwater, constructed by the harsh forces of nature. Many of the local Loyalists claimed it was the coldest winter in memory.

The troopers of the 17th Light Dragoons regrouped on the snow covered common, hunched against the fierce winds still blowing behind them. Ahead, Lieutenant John Stoner could make out the other part of the strike force, the Hussars of the Queen's Rangers in their distinctive high fur hats. Those would keep my pate warm, John thought, pulling his tri-corn down more tightly. It would also make me a more distinctive target. He would have preferred to wear the leather helmet of the Dragoons, with a death's head on the facing and a stylish crest of dyed red horsehair. But he was not one of them and Chatsworth would never have proposed to make him so, even in appearance.

John was normally averse to the dangers of the battlefield. Judge Thomas had related, in his sober, dignified manner, to British officers of rank at the numerous New York City dinner parties the good Judge attended, of John's bravery in repelling the Rebel raiders and defending the Judge's wife, heedless of the threats to his own safety. His role in confronting the three menacing and heavily armed whale boatmen was enhanced with each telling. John, himself, was almost convinced of the exaggerated accounts of his coolness and courage under fire. Now, he had a reputation to live up to and that alone compelled him to join the dragoons in the raid.

There was another reason as well. John had been responsible for the mapmakers, those Loyalists who knew the back roads of Essex County, from Elizabethtown and Hackensack to Morristown and more importantly to the Ford Mansion, General Washington's headquarters. Stoner's agents had identified common mechanics, millers, farmers and ferryboat men, people driven from their homes in New Jersey by roving bands of Rebel militias. They now resided in exile in New York, barely eking out a living, grateful for the Crown's protection and harboring strong animosities toward their former neighbors. It was John who had brought them to the attention of Major Pritchard, milked them for information without ever revealing the ultimate purpose and produced the maps that now were in the saddlebags of Lt. Colonel Samuel Birch, the commander of their combined cavalry units.

As the troopers headed northwest toward Hackensack, instead of south toward Elisabethtown, John knew which plan of attack had been chosen. There was a road from Hackensack over the Acquakanunk Bridge that skirted the Cedar Swamp and led directly into Morristown. General Washington's headquarters was almost five miles east of the town and the main Rebel encampment. The cavalry would overwhelm the General's Life Guards, abduct their Commander and bring him to the Newark Mountain meeting house. There, they would be met by a regiment of light infantry to provide additional security in case of Rebel pursuit.

It was as if Nature itself had conspired against the Rebels, freezing the waters separating the British from New Jersey, and then sending one snowstorm after another to impede the roads and curtail Rebel patrols. The heavy snows of three days ago had postponed their mission. /3 It had also covered the roads with three feet of soft and powdery snow, and their passage was unmarked by other man or horse, sled or wagon. With the snows higher than the fence posts and stonewalls that demarked the fields, only one with a strong familiarity of the terrain could discern the edge of the road from the white, bland adjacent flat countryside. Their local guides conferred frequently and led them on until, under the ominous grey skies, they saw the spires of churches in the distance.

At the outskirts of Hackensack, they passed stoic sentries manning the checkpoints and enduring the frigid winter air, with nary a fire to warm them. The town was secured by two regiments of British infantry. No wagon, horse, carriage or foot traveler was permitted to leave under any circumstances.

John handed the reins of his horse to Chatsworth's batman, ignoring the fellow's scowl at being tasked with watering and feeding another mount. He floundered through the knee-high snow, following Chatsworth to the Sign of the Drum, one of the inns adjacent to the drift covered village green. Once inside, he removed his heavy damp cloak and joined the other officers around a roaring fire, warming his frozen fingers and turning his rear and shoulders toward the flames. Gradually, he felt the stiffness in his neck and back easing. From the degree of mulled cider, beer and wine being imbibed, he anticipated they planned to spend the night. Tomorrow, they would leave for Morristown, roughly twenty miles away.

That night, John was awakened by the sound of hail and sleet on the Tavern's roof. Asleep, in the upper loft, three to a bed, he was the first to react. Chatsworth and the other officer stirred. John pulled his boots on over his stocking feet, drew his cloak that had served as his blanket around his shoulders, and peered out the window. A lantern glowed from the barn and cast light on fast falling pellets of ice, bouncing off the snow. Perhaps, the mission would be postponed another day. He could tolerate holed up in this comfortable tavern instead of riding out in this miserable weather.

Two orderlies stomped along the well-beaten path to the barn. A bad sign, John thought. They would be readying the officers' mounts. Sounds of men being roused throughout the tavern confirmed that the raid would be today. Soon they were all assembled in the main room, spooning hot porridge from pewter bowls and drinking coffee laced with rum. Colonel Birch ordered the officers to have the men mounted and moving out by the hour of four. He intended to be half way to the Ford Mansion by daybreak and cover the other ten or so miles before midday.

"The weather favors us," he said loudly. "The Rebels will have gone to shelter from the snows of a few days ago, probably starving as well. This hailstorm is a God-send. It will keep them inside with their heads down."

The barn was crowded with troopers silently readying their mounts, cinching the saddles tightly and checking the bridles. The men buckled the straps holding their sheaths across their chests and drew and reset their sabers, the sound of the steel against the metal casing, echoing off the low oak beamed ceiling. They had no muskets or fuzees this time. Only pistols. John made sure his was loaded and carefully placed it in his saddleback under a canvas flap to protect it from getting wet.

The troopers lined up in twos, John paired with Chatsworth, only a few rows behind the Colonel. He thought his chances were better up front. The element of surprise would be in his favor. If any of the Rebel guards were aroused, they would be shooting at those behind him, if their powder was dry.

The crust of ice that had formed on the snowy surface crunched under their horses' hooves as they passed by the sentries. The snow on the road from Hackensack to the Acquackadonk had been somewhat compressed by horse patrols during the night. In less than a mile, they crossed the bridge over the narrow frozen river and entered a vast white countryside. Their progress was initially slowed by windblown snowdrifts, some as deep as their horses' chests.

Although it was still sleeting, as the road turned more west toward the mountains, the going became easier. The sloping foothills had shielded this part of the land from the brunt of the early snowstorms. The snow, covered with an icy sheet that shattered easily under their horses' hooves, barely came up to their mounts' fetlocks.

It was almost dawn of a day that was cold as hell with the hail and sleet continuing to fall, peppering them with icy pellets. John sensed a quickening of excitement from the officers' ahead. They had reached the half -way point. He would reap the glory from this mission. Oh yes he definitely would. Perhaps even parlay it into a field promotion and a permanent staff job in the warm confines of New York City. Another ten miles, then overwhelm the unsuspecting guards, a quick skirmish and they would carry off General Washington, the greatest prize possible and end this rebellion once and for all.

Made in the USA
Columbia, SC
01 June 2017